PANAMA FLAME

PANAMA FLAME

Mirna Pierce

A DELL BOOK

Published by
Dell Publishing Co., Inc.
1 Dag Hammarskjold Plaza
New York, New York 10017

Dell ® TM 681510, Dell Publishing Co., Inc.

ISBN 0-440-16822-8

Printed in the United States of America
First printing—March 1982

To Alex

Author's Note

During most of the nineteenth century the Isthmus of Panama formed part of the country in South America known today as Colombia.

PROLOGUE
1861

The Isthmian rain pounded and lashed the hard red-tiled rooftops and the more fragile ones made of palm leaves. It quickly filled the rain barrels left out for collecting drinking water, as well as the gutters that lined the streets, so that by now the ditches were torrents of dirty water racing and leaping toward the bay, carrying away the refuse of the city.

Inside the patio walls Carmen's boardinghouse, the Pensión Marisol, was smugly entrenched, secure against the assaults of wind and water. The house squatted against one side of the yard so that its own front entrance and the stone and mortar fence around the building formed an inside court where in prettier moments a variety of local plants blossomed. Now, however, the little twigs were either broken or wallowing sadly in great mud puddles. The thick, cool

7

walls of the house had been whitewashed with care, but were unavoidably spattered with mud.

In the kitchen two maids chattered excitedly until one carried away a medium-sized kettle filled with boiling water. The girl's blouse was flimsy enough for Panama's tropical climate, adorned by an embroidered ruffle that fell off one shoulder to reveal a smooth brown curve of flesh and bone. She hurried up the steps in the hall with her awkward cargo and paused to catch her breath at the landing before opening the door to Mariana's parlor, one of two rooms that formed her suite.

A sudden shrill scream of pain followed by the wail of a newborn creature pierced the thunderous blockade of the storm, but did not reach far beyond the sitting room of that simple suite where Burland Jones was nervously pacing the floor. His anguished marching halted as he lifted his head to make sure of what he had heard. Silence. Then, hesitantly, he resumed his somewhat erratic pacing, his hands behind his back in the classical posture of a man with weighty problems on his mind. He had long ago discarded his linen jacket, then had rolled up the long sleeves of his white cotton shirt, which had begun to pull out from the pale gray trousers he preferred. He barely acknowledged with a nod of his head and a wild-eyed look the presence of the maid who now was hurriedly crossing the parlor to disappear with the kettle of water into the adjacent room.

The drum rolls of the thunder became more insistent, exploding and cracking suddenly over the roof of

Carmen's pension. The sky opened to release a new downpour of water.

At the deafening noise Burland's spine tingled from some unfathomable and primeval apprehension. His instinctive fear was quickly mingled with pity for Mariana and for himself, and he suddenly felt a greater yearning than before to rush to her side, to embrace her tightly and protect her against the gods and man, against the storms and sorrows that were filling up her life. But he was like one of the cassia trees outside whose flowering golden clusters defied the seasonal rains only to be beaten and later scattered, mere petals in the wind. He felt just as helpless.

Though he was barely fifty, Burland looked so bent and forlorn at this moment that his hair appeared grayer, his facial lines grimmer. His blue eyes that could twinkle so generously had dulled unhappily and were swollen and irritated so that anyone would have guessed him to be much older. He had heard the wail of the baby just minutes before, but no one had approached him to reassure him that Mariana had safely survived the ordeal, and it seemed to him that already an eternity of waiting had gone by.

Burland's heart soared with elation when at last Carmen bustled out, flashing a grin against her dark skin. He turned to face squarely the woman whose devotion to Mariana had made her dear in his eyes.

"She's doing well, Señor Boorlan. She's doing well. The baby is adorable—a sweet, tiny girl."

Inside the simply furnished bedroom of the pension where Mariana lived and where Helena was born that tumultuous afternoon, the oil lamps flickered at the onslaught of every draft forced inside through the shutters by the raging tropical storm. While the slashing rain had temporarily mitigated the heat of the Isthmus, the humidity inside gave the room an unpleasant musky odor, dank and oppressive.

In a corner an old-fashioned altar left over from colonial days and rescued by some devout Isthmian raised up a painstakingly carved wooden crucifix surrounded by glass jars containing limp gardenias and jasmine. Their wilted petals were already brown, drooping unnoticed in the darkness in which the small altar stood.

At the opposite end of the room Mariana's bed was positioned at an angle from the corner. Quietly, lost in the generous proportions of the bed, Mariana herself lay with her precious bundle wrapped snugly by her side. Her jet-black hair lay in disarray over the white linen pillow. She stirred at last and awkwardly propped herself on her elbows, managing to raise her head in spite of the persistent fatigue that washed periodically over her. She gazed down once more in awe at the miniature features of her sweet Helenita, as she called her baby lovingly in Spanish. She smiled at the fineness of her tiny nose, remarkable for a newborn child, and at the golden fuzz of her hair and the darkness of her eyes. Sadly, they were not at all blue like Edward Buchanan's, but were as black and shiny as beady little marbles.

Mariana turned her head toward the door as Carmen came bustling in with Burland Jones in tow, dispelling with her energetic charm any gloom that might still have lingered in the room. Carmen was wearing a starched apron that was beginning to cling to her calico skirt in the oppressive humidity. Her salt-and-pepper braids were piled up on top of her head and lent her an aura of great dignity that made her look tall, darker than usual, and quite formidable. Her vitality appeared overwhelming to Mariana, and it struck the younger woman at that moment that she could always rely on her friend, for Carmen undoubtedly had strength enough for both of them.

"Look who's here to see you, Mariana, and the baby, of course!" Her voice boomed with happiness and pride. A shutter creaked and a new eddy of wind forced its way in as she sailed onward, Burland lingering more shyly behind her. He was holding his native straw hat in both hands, twirling it around and around, ill at ease yet not unhappy, judging from the look in his tenderly glowing eyes. The light from the oil lamp near the bed fell on him and turned his silver hair to gold, mellowing the strained features of his face. To those who knew him well it would have been obvious that he was embarrassed, perhaps because he was playing a role that rightfully belonged to another man. Nevertheless he made a brave effort to overcome his sudden shyness and breathed in deeply to ease his tension.

He didn't notice the dampness or the litter of the usually orderly room. He was oblivious to everything but the woman who lay serenely within the pool of lamplight, whose large velvet-brown eyes were fixed softly on his. Then, because his love for Mariana was greater by far than his pride, it was suddenly easy to forget that these were not his wife or his child, and he

11

approached Mariana rapidly, kneeling down beside her bed, hovering so closely over her that he felt her breath on his face. It evoked in him an indescribably painful yearning that had in it a quality of joy. Joyful pain, if that was possible, he thought to himself fleetingly. Then, paradoxically, a surge of frustration and anger spoiled the joy of his more tender emotions. It was anger directed not at Mariana, whom he loved, but at the haughty and arrogant southerner who had abandoned her to defend her life as best she could.

"But she has me," he thought bitterly as the imposing image of Edward Buchanan flashed before him.

He forced a smile when Mariana, with typical maternal pride, invited him to look at her child. As his eyes traveled from Mariana's delicate features, where lilac shadows under her large brown eyes accentuated her pathetic frailty, and fell upon the miniature creature bundled at her side, all resentment vanished instantly. He was overwhelmed by the miracle of the child's presence and rejoiced in the fullness of love and the beauty of innocence.

Lightning lit their tiny world as it streaked, outraged, over the Isthmus of Panama. Thunder rolled and cracked menacingly. But no longer did they have the power to disturb the sense of peace and fulfillment that surprisingly pervaded the unpretentious room.

The days and weeks passed swiftly. Mariana posted yet another letter to the father of her child in care of their mutual lawyer, Benito González, whom Edward himself had contracted. He had planned his leave-taking well and not unkindly, insisting that Mariana would need the protection of a reputable, bilingual lawyer in matters pertaining to the money he would leave behind for her as well as more he planned to send.

But Mariana awaited only the loving words she was sure Edward would be sending to her when the news of the baby's birth reached him. What did it matter that he had not married her before he left? Could she really blame him? Why, he was of such high birth, and she was only a simple girl not even accepted by the aristocracy of her own people. At moments during her avowals of love, however, Mariana burst into tears, for taunting thoughts threatened to answer her questions with bitterly clear words. Yet the memory of Edward's handsome and cherished being still had the power to overwhelm her each time she studied her child, and she would grasp her tightly to her bosom, gulping away the tears that threatened to betray her real suspicions.

Christmas came, and with it the dry season. In the evenings the sky was richly laden with blinking stars, while on the ground many new flowers dared to display their flamboyant beauty. The bright magenta bougainvillaea had crept from the inner courtyard up the wall, spilling lavishly onto the street side, while the tree hibiscus was already intensely yellow, each blossom drooping slightly with the weight of its gold. It was pleasant to walk about in the late afternoon once the breezes from the sea began to pay their nightly visit and cooled the land.

One evening just after New Year's Day, Señora Carmen sent an errand boy to Burland's house, urging him to come as soon as possible. Burland was not there. The note she had written was placed under his door, and by the time he came home and found it, it was already night.

He hurried to the stand at the Parque Santa Ana where he knew carriages were always available for hire, and from there he sped to the pension through the dark-shadowed cobblestone alleys and unpaved streets which led into the old walled part of Panama City. His heart felt tight in his chest. Carmen's message that Mariana had simply walked away from the pension and disappeared before Carmen was aware of it left him in the grip of a cold fear. Because he loved Mariana so unselfishly, he was attuned to her moods, and he had sensed the depth of her despair at the apparent indifference of the father of her child.

When he finally arrived at the pension, the guests had retired for the night, and lights burned only in the kitchen and in the dining area adjacent to it. Burland pounded on the main door to the courtyard. As soon as the houseboy lifted the latch, he swiftly entered the lighted kitchen.

"What is it, Carmen? Have you found her yet?"

Tears were glistening in Carmen's warm chocolate eyes. She was so distraught that she didn't even notice that Burland, in his nervousness, had spoken English to her instead of his usual broken Spanish with the strange garbled accent of the Americans.

"Oh, Don Boorlan," she cried, "I left Mariana unattended because I thought she was much better. I sent the boy out to look for her, but he just couldn't find a single trace of her in this area."

Burland thought for a moment. "Did she mention Gringo Town to you at all?"

"No, but come to think of it, she did say something to me this morning about meeting the train from the Atlantic side when Mr. Buchanan should return, and the station *is* in Gringo Town. Don Boorlan, do you suppose she might have decided she should go there?"

"I'll have to try in that direction."

He turned on his heels and strode away, determined to find Mariana. The streets were almost deserted, swept by a balmy night breeze that came in over the low seawall. He crossed the simple cobblestone plaza on which the pension stood, and his heavy boots echoed as he headed toward the wall on the hill near the market that served the inner city. He took the bay street and descended the hill to Gringo Town, the American business sector that sprawled out in its accumulation of bars and restaurants but which had lost most of its bustle and intensity since the California Gold Rush years.

As he reached the other side of the market with its lingering stench of fish and overripe fruit, the bay came in sight again. The moon was reflecting a path on its waters, and millions of stars bathed the streets in a blue-white light, revealing in the distance the frail outline of a girl. She was sitting against the low side of the stone parapet looking away into the horizon. Several feet below the other side of the wall the waves were slapping against the rocks.

A few couples ambled along the sidewalk that bordered the inner city along its length. From time to time one or another of the couples glanced curiously at Mariana. Probably a young woman waiting for her lover, they thought.

Burland arrived at Mariana's side without her hearing his approach; yet she was not startled by his voice.

"Mariana." Burland spoke as tenderly as he could. "I've come to take you home now. Come."

He lifted her gently to her feet, and held her around the waist, pushing gently in the direction of the hill. They were silent all the way to the summit, but then she turned to him and whispered, her eyes very large, feverish, with burning tears of bitter realization.

"He's not coming back, is he?"

"I don't think so, Mariana," responded Burland, fearing that a lie, even one motivated by kindness, might have a worse effect on her in the long run. He kept his voice as gentle as he could.

They crossed the plaza in silence. The boy opened the door, and Burland and Carmen put Mariana to bed as though she were a little child. She fell asleep with tears still glistening on her soft cheeks.

BOOK I

*The Land
and
the Sea*

Chapter I

Helena's fine woolen skirt and the generous folds of her heavy cape whipped gently about in the salty cold breezes that swept the deck. The sun had managed to overpower the curling mists that had lingered persistently since dawn, but she was unaware of its light on her face. Her mind was in a bewildering disarray, but one thought was clear—she would soon have to face the uncertain realities that lay ahead now that her life had changed its course. She wanted to face them, and yet she did not, and her reluctance to confront them led to an inner restlessness, an agitation matched only by the endless motion of the sea before her.

Myriads of tiny waves blinked at her as the sun began to sparkle even more brightly on their surfaces. During the last hour or more, ever since the ship had pulled away from the coast of France, the sun had been struggling to push through the gauze of early-morning mist, but Helena was only vaguely aware of the sudden success of the warm rays. She was locked away darkly in her own thoughts. More frightened and lonely than she had ever been before, she was now fully acquainted with the painful meaning of the word orphan.

Sorrow, confusion, a deep sense of loss: They had been dragging her into emotional anguish ever since Mama died. And now she was finally and irrevocably alone on the ship that was to carry her back home. Home to what? To whom? To Carmen, who was old and very sick? To Uncle Benito, whom she really did not know very well? To Rosario Pérez, her mama's business partner, who fluttered about in a panic for every little thing? Helena felt the depressing shadow of a thought that they would not be able to comfort her.

The mist had finally evaporated. It was an unexpectedly sunny day after all, but Helena was still only barely aware of her surroundings, so withdrawn was her mood. Her line of thinking was now hovering over the uncertain wisdom of small and great decisions she would soon have to make, but the thoughts were unclear, intermingled with sadness one moment, trembling with hope the next. Her eyes roved unseeing over the white miniature crests that the huge beast of the ship continuously churned. Her slender, solitary figure looked small and vulnerable on the almost abandoned deck.

She did not notice the stranger or the expression of raffish surprise and admiration on his handsome, darkly tanned face. He stood casually near the last of the tiny groups of travelers who had lingered outside on the deck after the anchor had been pulled up, and he was leaning on the railing, his weight on his forearm and elbow, his shoulders turned to the sea. His head was pulled back, and the droop of his eyelids gave his expression a quality of lazy, nonchalant indifference.

His rimmed hat slouched defiantly over his forehead, cocked at a blasé angle, and shadowed the sparkle of his eyes that today were greener than gray or brown. In spite of the hat, however, nothing missed his gaze, for his eyes had been trained long ago to take in every detail of his surroundings. Charles de Thierny, alias Charles Terny, did not miss a single particular about the slender girl who stood apart from the others. His eyes glowed with pleasure and fascination as they absorbed the intriguing form of the young woman with the serious expression turned almost in profile to him. She seemed very young, and Charles wondered casually how she happened to be on deck without a chaperone in sight. Certainly the lass was not more than eighteen or so.

Charles was accustomed to seeing beauties of that age surrounded by bevies of "protectors" and chaperones as well as beaux. Without exception chaperones riled him, and he had concluded that it was because they gave their wards an aura of eligibility for marriage that chilled him. It was a relief to gaze at a pretty girl without the disturbing presence of an older female companion, or of an overeager-to-please mother —the scourge of French and English societies; his experiences with them had been harrowing. Not so secretly he feared their persistent ways, and feared, too, that one day one of them would succeed in trapping him one way or another into marriage. Once, perhaps—it seemed so long ago—he might have wanted to settle down with a wife, but now he most assuredly did not. It was truly a breath of fresh air to be able to gaze, at his leisure, upon unattended beauty and youth, and he was enjoying himself immensely just leaning on the railing, inhaling deeply the cold briny air, and studying the delightful creature on deck who did not seem to know he was alive.

He could always enjoy a pretty female, but he was disappointed and tired of the cloying, possessive women who seemed to clutter his life. They depressed him. His last affair had been difficult to end, not because he had become less bored by it than by the others, but because Yvette had been insistent and clasping until the very last moment. Surely she must have sensed that he was finished with their little fling. And anyway, his well-honed instincts had warned him that she was more bent on turning him into a malleable creature like her other lovers than she was in winning his total love or commitment. All her lovers had wound up at her feet, and she had cast them all aside. She had a reputation by now of possessing a touch of sadism, of raising hopes to dash them brutally down. He was not interested in ending up like the others in Yvette's love-life. She had wanted to own him, to command him, and he would be damned if he would let any female control him. He had to admit, however, that Yvette knew how to use her body—to her own advantage, of course, but still, to pleasure a man expertly. Their last meeting had been a tryst of caresses that would have been delightful except for her blasted insistence that he remain at her side in spite of his plans for traveling to the Isthmus of Panama on an important mission for the French government.

Why did women always want to make something permanent out of a liaison that was strictly physical? Considering that she was a married woman, to Charles her reasoning had seemed warped, even taking into account that they were still under the distorting influence of passionate embraces, but to her it made perfect sense that he should remain in France to spend his every waking and sleeping moment with her. Damn! He could still hear the whine of her voice the last time he had been with her.

"Charles, how can you even think of leaving me now that I am going to be alone? You know that Jean is leaving for Africa soon. I won't be joining him for quite a while, and we could at last be free. I can't believe you would be so cruel as to abandon me just when everything is looking so rosy for us."

Her long and slender fingers had trailed through his chest hair, while those of her other hand had lingered provocatively over his buttocks.

Charles had preferred not to answer. She had flirted relentlessly with him from their very first meeting, even in front of her husband, who consistently ignored his wife's suggestive remarks and the flirtatious glances she directed at every man but himself. One evening Charles had succumbed to her very sensuous charms, the night her husband invited a group of men who had served in various capacities in North

Africa to a party at his home. Their wives were markedly absent, and Yvette was present only to greet the gentlemen and excuse herself. When she welcomed Charles, however, she motioned him aside and whispered an irresistible invitation, giving him very clear directions to her boudoir. Charles had kept his arms crossed as he listened, and then he'd straightened suddenly, his eyes glinting in amusement at the daring, indiscreet Madame Lamère. He towered above her, and the attractive curve of her nose was turned so as to avoid the disturbing glitter of his eyes, full of green, brown, and yellow specks, eyes that could stare with malice or with tenderness. Surely, he thought, her embarrassment was not unbecoming, but he was cynical enough to believe it was yet another fine piece of acting, impossibly authentic. She simply knew how to flirt, to play the coy one from time to time, to lull her man into thinking that it was he who was the seducer, and not she. Well, what did he have to lose? He knew her kind, and he would merely be on guard. Besides, she was already married, after all.

For her part it was true that she had started out to ensnare the affections of the handsome Charles de Thierny. What woman would not be interested? But what at first had seemed an easy task had proved much more difficult. She had the feeling that at this point in her game she was no longer the seducer, that indeed he himself had finally decided to try a taste of Yvette Lamère. Goodness knew, she had tried many a trick to capture his interest. Was he perhaps, she had wondered, the kind who leaned toward men, like her husband? But no, it couldn't be, for all the comments she kept hearing about Charles de Thierny indicated that he was definitely a ladies' man. Was she then perhaps losing her own beauty, her youth, and her allure? Charles de Thierny began to fascinate her even more, for how could he resist what so many other men found irresistible? The yellow pinpoints in his eyes mesmerized her, but also made her feel unsure, something that no other man had been able to do for a very long time.

The reason for the party was soon obvious to Charles. Jean Lamère, the host, a very ambitious man, believed in making the right contacts. He hoped also to cull information from his guests which might eventually assist him in his new government field-post in Africa. He would be leaving soon to take up his duties in North Africa, and eventually Yvette would join him. But not until he knew who the key men in his new post were so that her assistance could be channeled advantageously. She was usually very adept at helping him with his promotions and his successes, and though he knew quite well how she accomplished this, Jean Lamère felt no pangs of jealousy or conscience. On the contrary he was pleased. His marriage to Yvette had been intended solely for the purpose of assisting him in his career. Besides, his sexual preferences lay with those of his own sex, and he had barely managed not to be revolted by Yvette's voluptuous feminine curves during the first few weeks of their marriage.

He had been freed of the responsibility of making love to her soon after, however, for instinctively Yvette had chosen one lover and then another. She had been an instrument for his advancement from the very beginning, albeit unwittingly at first. But her insatiable appetites fitted her well for her sordid duties, and she was not long in discerning a reward system at work: her husband was especially nice to her when she treated certain important men generously enough that he profited in some way from her charms. Her jewels and furs bespoke a doting husband; only a few astute observers knew the real reasons for such extravagant generosity.

Charles had guessed very quickly what the situation was, and though he was at first repelled by such commercialism, he had finally deduced that Yvette was stubborn from time to time and took on a lover or two who appealed to her personally, without regard to his importance in her husband's schemes for power and advancement. He had decided that her husband was not particularly interested in the sort of information Yvette could pry from him. His own field posts had been of an entirely different nature from the humdrum, backstabbing, bureaucratic government jobs overseas in whose atmosphere men like Jean Lamère thrived so beautifully.

In all of Yvette's experienced love-life, she had never met a man quite as virile, as alive, and as masterful as Charles de Thierny. Never before had she felt excited about a man for so long a time as she had about Charles. Perhaps it was because she sensed that he was giving her only a very small part of himself, and that this time it was she who was a plaything and not the conqueror as she was accustomed to being. And she was right. Charles enjoyed the expert touch of Yvette's hands, and for a few weeks that affair raged on with hedonistic joy. Finally, as far as he was concerned, the relationship settled and was beginning to bore him. There was no substance ever with women, he thought cynically. Were they all as empty headed as Yvette, as thoroughly selfish and absorbed in themselves and their beauty as she was?

Nevertheless that last time in her boudoir could have remained a perfect erotic memory had it not been for her irrational attempt to hold him on a more permanent basis. She had hinted once more of getting a divorce, an incredible offer of which Charles wanted no part. She had clung to him and kissed him in provocative ways to make him stay, and had succeeded shamelessly in arousing him once more. Her hands slid over his broad, naked shoulders as he stood half dressed before her, enjoying her suave gentleness and her moist red mouth. She was a very pretty woman.

In spite of his earlier resolve to leave her, forget her, and get on with his plans for traveling to Panama, his hand reached softly toward her, and, playfully, his knuckles grazed her along her small dimpled chin. Women were pitifully transparent creatures, he sighed, but he found their inherent charms difficult to resist, which explained why no matter how callously he thought of them, Charles was tender with his women. He began to caress her in earnest then, nibbling at her ear, kissing the hollows of her throat while he spoke ardent words to her, stroking the curves of her back and well-rounded hips and kissing her very red mouth until her lips were slightly swollen.

Her fingers, in turn, soon unbuttoned his pants again very discreetly and slid caressingly inside to find the curling darkness around his already turgid male length. The trousers soon fell to the floor. She turned her prettily proportioned features toward him, and he bent down and slipped his arms, strong and gentle, around her waist. He kissed her hard on the lips. Her mouth parted under the pressure, and his tongue entered suggestively, pressing more and more urgently as her hands stroked him. Her full breasts brushed against his abdomen, and he gently cupped one. Yvette was very small and had to stand on tiptoes to reach his mouth even though he had bent far down in order to touch hers. It was difficult not to react to her ceaseless and delightful manipulations.

She pulled him toward the bed that still lay in disarray from their earlier bout of lovemaking, and gently pushed him to its edge so that he was in a partially reclining position. Her wild golden hair fell on his chest, and he followed its movements as her head went down to find the maleness of him. Charles groaned as her lips found the place of fire and her tongue twirled around it with the most ardent art. His heavy but well-groomed hands went to her massive golden hair and pulled gently on her, turning her face toward him. Her eyes were half closed, mesmerized with passion and lust. He pulled her over him as he lay back on the bed. His sunbronzed hands supported her by the hips near the small waist that threatened to slip from his grasp, for her slender figure had begun to writhe and undulate with uninhibited movements. When he entered her, she was wild with desire and with anticipation of the moment of splendid release they would reach together. A cry of ecstasy was followed by breathless moans as they arrived at the summit of their passion.

Afterward they lay very still with panting breath, and then finally Charles laughed softly as Yvette's eyes twinkled with satisfied happiness. She was a hot one, Yvette. He gave her a peck on the nose and left her on the bed while he went once again to the basin in the well-appointed room to wash himself. If it were up to Yvette, he would spend the entire day in bed. She was insatiable! He shook his head in mock wonderment, but had to admit that she was the best mistress he had ever had. Yet something was missing now, some of the mystery and the excitement of the beginning of their affair. There was very little to know about Yvette. She was just a luscious body, a lovemaking machine. The image was amusing to his engineer's mind, and it led his thoughts to wander almost immediately to his appointment with the minister of foreign affairs and some special members of the Panama Canal Commission, which had been set up to handle all activities related to the forthcoming construction of the canal. By this time Charles had slipped on his coat. As a simple precaution he never left it downstairs in the hall when he visited Yvette.

"No! *Mon chéri!* Don't go yet. Stay a little while longer," wailed Yvette. Her lips were contorted in a practiced pout that men adored. She sprang out of the bed, her hair unruly and beautiful. Though she was small, her proportions were generous, and her very full breasts contrasted with her tiny waist. Her blue

eyes were bright with determination, for she wanted
to possess Charles's body and soul, and the task was
appearing more and more difficult every day. His
magnificent body was healthy and reacted easily to
her machinations, but his mind? Did he ever give her
a single thought except when his body felt the urge to
possess her, touch her, and consume her with his fire?
She doubted very much that he ever did. Yvette
sighed and slipped her arms around him very tenderly.

"Oh, Charles! I wish you would stay."

Charles smiled down at her but at the same time,
and with determination, he pulled her arms away and
held her apart from him by the wrists.

"You know I can't, *ma chérie*," he answered as he
bent his lips to hers. He pulled away for a moment
and then brushed her forehead with them again. "I
have a million things to do before my trip to Panama.
I'm afraid I am already late for one appointment."

His frown dismayed Yvette, and she let him go for a
moment. He took advantage and disappeared out into
the hall before she could slip her negligée on. She
knew he would show himself out the door, for the servants were well paid and extremely well trained.
When Charles or any other man came to call on
Yvette, they disappeared as soon as they had let him
in and the lady of the house had greeted her visitor.

The front door clicked shut. Suddenly the house
was very still. Charles had left.

Now the remembrance of Yvette quickened Charles's
blood as he gazed distractedly in the direction of the

beautiful blond passenger on deck, but still he did not regret having given up the affair. More than anything else, he was relieved that he had left Yvette forever.

His eyes roved back to focus on the unknown blonde. There was a fleetingly familiar air about her; perhaps it was her small stature that reminded him of his once-favorite mistress. Or perhaps it was simply that his imagination had been stimulated along with his impetuously healthy appetites. He looked with even greater intensity at the young woman, keenly noting several small details even from a distance of several yards.

In spite of the protection of a hood, the wind had blown out of the girl's bonnet some tendrils of amber hair, the color of wild honey. In contrast the darkness of her eyes, now fixed unmovingly upon the waters, lent her the charm and vivacity of southern and sunny places.

Probably French, thought Charles, with dark eyelashes and blond hair. And indeed, her amazingly lovely eyes were generously fringed by thick, long black lashes that almost entirely shadowed the expression of her eyes.

At the same time Charles thought of his own coloring, which so effectively allowed him to veil his ancestry whenever it was convenient. Mentally laughing at his easily made conclusions about the girl's nationality, he continued to think about the complexity of his own family tree and the physical inheritance that allowed him to pass for almost any European type he wished to be, and even for other racial groups. He considered this a physical advantage for someone in his line of work. His chestnut hair was rich and wavy. His eyes were neither too dark nor too light, with green and gray flashes amid warmer brown tones. If he could be from anywhere with such coloring, then of course, the girl could, too.

By God, she was a beauty, really. He held his breath as the blonde turned her face more fully in his direction, as if to leave the railing. Her face formed a perfect oval that framed the two incredible orbs of black light that were her eyes. She walked toward him quickly. He must have straightened up to tip his hat too late, for she glided past him without even a glance in his direction.

"Well!" thought the irresistible Charles de Thierny. "Did she see me or did she not?" Either way, her aloof unawareness piqued him. Surely she must have felt his burning stare. Charles was somehow disappointed when he realized that she had not. Quickly, however, before admitting the slight to his ego, he hardened himself and called himself a fool for considering the incident at all. Even if the girl had merely feigned in some femininely twisted and flirtatious way to be aloof and proud, now was not the time to become involved with fancy virgins and pressuring mamas. Certainly the fact that they were headed for the Isthmus of Panama was sufficiently dangerous for him. He warned himself mentally that he had best keep his charms to himself. One foolish adventure, and all his plans could be dashed to the ground. Of course, there was no harm in admiring the wench from afar, especially since the voyage promised to be long and boring. Perhaps he should be overjoyed that she had paid no heed to him, whatever her reasons.

He, too, went below to the salon, where a hectic game of cards was already stirring the bold blood of the young bucks. With casual elegance, his movements fluid and graceful in spite of his large size, Charles sauntered to one of the tables where a flushed young fellow was taking his leave, apparently already the victim of heavy losses.

"Gentlemen, may I join you?" Charles's French was impeccable.

"Mais oui, monsieur," replied the happy winner of the previous game.

The men concentrated on the flashing cards. As the piles of coins and bills seemed to dwindle away from the previous players to be collected in an ever-increasing pile before Charles, terse groans from the losers reached the ears of the ladies who sat in the anteroom of the gaming salon. It was an unwritten law, silently observed, that no women could join the men aboard the ship in their games of chance.

One pair of coal-black eyes rested on the shoulders of Charles from the open archway, but unaware of their fleeting perusal, he paid no heed.

The following day dawned sunny, though the rays of the sun were tempered by the winter mist that hung like a gauze curtain in the air. As the mist evaporated, the light fell more intensely on the rippling, restless surface of the sea. Charles's arms bore down again upon the railing. A vague sense of loneliness, which perhaps had to do with the vast and endless sea around him, pervaded his spirit.

Would his life come full circle once he reached the tropical Isthmus of Panama? Would his honor, which he treasured fiercely—perhaps even more than his personal freedom—but which had been smirched and trodden upon since the first day of his life, at last find its restoration in that emerald land of Colombia? He sighed impatiently, recognizing the futility of such questions. No one could read the future, and hell!—maybe he should bury the past. But the past gnawed at him, and he knew once again that only public and private satisfaction could ease the hatred that had spoiled and embittered what should have been the best years of his young life.

As he turned to go back inside, he caught a glimpse of a hooded figure. Her hand rested lightly on the rail, and as on the day before, she stared long and hard out to sea. There was something vaguely vulnerable about her—perhaps it was simply her youth—and yet her chin held a small tightness of determination, and she stood erect, with the inbred grace of the aristocrat, and with the same pride. What a delicious creature the blonde was! The embraceable sort of small woman he preferred, who kept herself aloof and apart but who, once in bed, was the wildest.

Now why was this young French girl—no, wait. He must not assume she was French. And if she were, what would she be doing on a boat to Panama? Only vigorous and adventurous Frenchmen and a handful of dowdy matrons accompanying their less sedate husbands to South or Central America were going to Panama these days. The voyage of Ferdinand de Lesseps, the head engineer of the Panama Canal project and the acclaimed builder of the Suez Canal, would come later, and only after that, if the treaty with the government of Colombia became a reality, would there be numerous female French travelers to the Isthmus, willing to accompany their fathers and young engineer husbands to their new posts at the canal building zone.

He waited many minutes more, and still nobody approached the young woman. He was puzzled, for it had never occurred to him that she might be traveling alone. Such cases were unheard of in the year 1878, especially if the girl under consideration was a member of the higher classes. In spite of this young woman's unfashionable appearance, it was obvious that she was of genteel stock. Yet he was not mistaken about his suspicion that the girl was unchaperoned, for as he continued to spy on her casually in the days that followed, Charles noticed that no companion was ever at her side. Her meals were taken in the dining room, it was true, but he was convinced that her fellow diners were not of her private party, for the girl's aura of natural elegance and grace did not fit in well with the common types of the other diners. But Charles could not know that the chaperones arranged for the young woman had been delayed indefinitely in Paris because of illness, nor that it had cost her much pleading and persuasion to convince the nuns of her convent school that, as the captain was an acquaintance of Uncle Benito, she should be allowed to travel under his direct responsibility.

Observing and fantasizing about the life of the *petite blonde,* as he came to call her in his thoughts, became the only source of real entertainment for Charles, especially when he tired of gambling with the other male passengers, who left the girl alone for reasons of their own. As the first few days of the voyage passed, the gamblers began to relax and their comments finally became brazen enough to clarify what those reasons were.

"My God! This must be the most desperately boring voyage I have taken in my entire life!" vowed a dapper young fellow with a whiskey glass in his hand.

Charles did not pay much attention as he shuffled the cards.

"I say! No wonder sailors are such animals once they get ashore, eh?" another player volunteered. General laughter ensued.

Charles nodded to the fourth player to cut the cards, and, chewing a bit on his elegant and simply carved pipe, he began to deal. He listened with only one ear to the men until he caught the word blonde. Then he paid full attention to their somewhat lewd conversation, although he did not join them in their witticisms.

"I'd like a try at her myself, but you know how it is, my man. All I need is another mad mother on my heels! I'll just cool myself down with excessive alcohol."

The other men laughed good naturedly at the cocky

talk of their comrade in boredom. Even Charles managed a smile, but it irked him somehow that *la petite blonde* should have been noticed by the other men also.

"What worries me," said one of the spectators around the players, "is what I would do once she surrendered to my unquestionable charms!" A muffled snicker went up at this, for the speaker was perhaps the least attractive of the adventurers on board. His buck teeth and large round head gave him the appearance of a huge rabbit.

"If I could only be sure that I could pass her on to one of you after a lovely affair, I would dare anything with her!" cried out another player who wanted to enter into the spirit of the bawdy conversation. "But she looks too virginal for that, and who needs a woman clinging along, forever enraptured by my persuasive fingering? Besides, who knows who might be waiting for her at port? All I need is some angry old man with a fine weapon at my back as he nudges me down the church aisle. Aieee!"

Though the men were enjoying themselves as they toyed with Helena's dignity, Charles felt a tinge of disgust at their insolence. It was true that the men were of the same general breed of adventurer as he was, though they appeared infinitely amateurish and uninitiated into the realm of high adventure which he had penetrated years before. He recognized, too, that, as crudely as they might have put it, their reasons for not tangling with affairs of the heart at this time on board the ship were basically his own reasons. Yet he could not place his relationship to the unknown blond

37

passenger on the same level with that of these other men.

Charles had discovered long ago that a man in his profession made himself vulnerable when he did not concentrate on the dangers of the task before him. His own missions were always full of perils. This one he had so willingly undertaken would be no exception, and it might indeed prove more dangerous than most.

Not only were there practical temporary reasons for his avoiding the attractive blonde, but her social position and her role on board the ship mystified him and left too many questions unanswered, all of which could result in serious complications for him. Certainly she was young, apparently inexperienced, and normally, on land, at home in France or in England, he would flirt with her as he did with the other debutantes, with nothing more in mind than giving and receiving a thrill. But beyond that he would not go. If one thing about young women frightened him, it was the thought of getting trapped into marriage. His taste for freedom had developed to the point that he practically panicked at the thought of being tied down by any female.

Another reason for Charles's reluctance to approach the young and attractive blonde and sweep her off her feet, as he felt sure he would be able to do if he wanted to, was the confinement of the ship, which, in his view, increased the danger of unpleasant developments in any romance. On board a ship even a flirtation could turn sour. The trouble with most women was that they did not seem to know when an *affaire de coeur* was over. Even though the blonde aboard the *Amélie* was extremely pretty and had attracted his attention inordinately the moment he first saw her, what would he do if his conquest of her was successful and she turned out to be as insistent as Yvette but without Yvette's experience in pleasuring the male? Charles shuddered. Where could he possibly escape her clinging and cajoling? The thought of being incarcerated on a boat with a love affair gone stale was difficult to contemplate. So Charles preferred simply to enjoy the beautiful stranger from afar, and tried to remain exclusively in the company of the men aboard, where she apparently took no note of him.

Many of these men were actually headed for California, planning to disembark at Colón, the Atlantic port of Panama, and from there ride the Panama Railroad to Panama City. At that Pacific port they would board one of the ships that sailed along the western coast of America to the promised riches of California. Though gold was no longer the cry of the adventurers, it was still to be made by the farsighted entrepreneur who understood the needs of the boom state of California. Among those needs were many skills, it was true, such as wine making, tailoring, teaching languages, practicing European cuisine. But the skill of finding and marrying rich heiresses was uppermost in the minds of many of the Frenchmen on board, and Charles knew why. The parvenus who owed their fortunes to the golden years of the fifties often wished to inject refinement and a certain touch

39

of class into their families by marrying their daughters to polished young Europeans who could perhaps even lay claim to a title of nobility, authentic or not.

Charles knew the intentions of many of the young, already hardened Europeans with whom he played cards aboard the ship. He despised their mercenary approach, though he admired their courage in throwing their luck to the winds of fortune. He himself knew that to be alive was ever to seek the thrill of high adventure and the grandeur of conquest.

Perhaps that was why he had contrived this opportunity to carry out his vendetta against his mother's family in Panama. It promised to be the best and most satisfying adventure yet, even better than some he had dared in the years he'd spent in North Africa. More important, he would cleanse his honor and avenge his years of orphanhood. He would find the way.

Again, Charles found himself pushing these thoughts away. They were for another, more propitious moment. Now they only served to frustrate him. Still, he couldn't help thinking about vengeance, in spite of his efforts not to become obsessed. The moments and hours of introspection forced upon him by the inactivity of the trip kept him turning the business over and over in his mind. Only the form of his revenge remained to be determined, for he had decided that if he was ever to have peace of mind, his vengeance should be absolute, devastating, even if his own blood should be spilled in the process. There would be no turning back.

When Charles was not playing cards or conversing with the passengers, he spent his days thinking about his revenge and speculating about the *petite blonde*. He was careful not to get deeply involved with any- one on board. He had discovered that in his field of work it was far wiser to keep a low profile.

One night in his cabin he dreamed that the golden coiffure of the blonde had come undone and her hair had cascaded over his body, and he felt hot and trem- bling in his sleep. He began to look at her with re- newed curiosity, as though the dream had made them more intimate. Once he caught her eye passing fleet- ingly over the spot where he was standing, but he de- cided that she honestly did not notice him, that she was neither intentionally snubbing him nor flirting with him, and that, in fact, she remained aloof and distant principally because she was totally unaware of his very existence. This certainty riled him even more than he cared to admit.

One day, on coming unexpectedly upon the *petite blonde* in the company of the ship's master, Captain Desmoulins, Charles found himself disturbed by a strange feeling not unlike jealousy. The pair of them were speaking quietly together on a settee in the salon next to the game room. Apparently they did not see him go by the wide archway that separated the two rooms. Only a few of the men were already in the game room, and one or two ladies in the small salon where the blonde sat talking so earnestly with the captain. Charles passed by them and entered the game room, pretending to ignore them.

A few days from the Isthmian city of Colón the winds took on ominous strength. It was not the season for hurricanes, but nevertheless any storm at sea could prove dangerous and even fatal. The squall broke just after dinner, during which the passengers had held uneasy conversations interspersed with long silences. As though he were responsible for *la petite blonde*, Charles kept his eyes on her, and saw that her beautiful, well-formed face was twisted with fear. He knew then that storms frightened her abnormally, and he decided to keep her in sight. She might need someone. As far as he knew, the captain, who was nowhere in sight this evening, was her only friend. Or perhaps he was her lover. Some instinct, however, told him that this was not the case, and he banished the ugly thought.

The boat began to toss about wildly on the sea, and *la petite blonde* excused herself from the table, as did many of the others sitting that night in the dining area. Charles followed her at a discreet distance. He would see to it that she arrived at her cabin safely. For some reason he felt real pity at the panic written on her face. She began to run down the passage, bumping from time to time into the bulkheads as the ship continued to lurch its way into the Caribbean.

A few other passengers were also progressing erratically down the hall and finally made their way to their staterooms. The blonde continued farther, however, passing by Charles's own quarters. Then, as Charles turned the corner of the passageway, he was just in time to see the girl stumble on an uplifted corner of the goat's-hair carpet that was meant to muffle the noises in the corridor. She hit her head abruptly on the rail of the curving steps that began precisely where she had tripped. Charles was too late to catch her to prevent the sharp blow. Nevertheless a fleeting sense of relief and self-satisfaction overtook him; his premonition had proven true. If the girl had been alone . . .

He bent quickly over her, picked the slight figure of this mysteriously unsociable beauty easily up into his arms, and momentarily, not knowing what else to do, pushed open the door of his cabin not far behind them. He never bothered to lock his cabin, for he carried on his person what few valuables he had brought with him. The large amount of money he would need in Panama to outfit his men he was to pick up from the French consul in Panama City. He laid her on his bunk bed, which had already been turned down by the steward during the dinner hour. She was totally unconscious, and her black lashes fell on pale and almost translucent skin. Her lips were parted and the tips of two perfect front teeth gleamed like pearls. Her usually rosy color had drained from her face. He removed her bonnet, and studied the small bloodied cut on her forehead. It did not look serious, but he was briefly worried about a possible concussion. He would take her to her own cabin when she awoke, but in the meantime he would try to get the ship's doctor. He pulled off his jacket, already moistened by the slight effort and tension of helping the girl, and, leaving her in the bunk bed, he ran out to fetch the doctor.

He had no luck at all. The physician was nowhere to be found, for he was extremely busy treating and reassuring the many seasick passengers and Charles kept missing him. The captain was also unavailable, engrossed as he was in the survival of his ship, which was careening wildly from the summit of one wave into the hollow of another. Charles cursed each time he lost his balance as he traveled the length and depth of the vessel trying to get professional help for the victim of the storm—*la petite blonde*. He made a mental note that in future voyages he would cultivate the friendship of the ship's captain from the start. He had failed to become intimately acquainted with Captain Desmoulins, perhaps because of the turmoil in his heart, and now the captain was, of course, not able to help by sending even a steward to assist him with the girl. He felt frustrated and disgusted, and his lips contorted accordingly. He was not used to caring for women who were ill or frightened. What did he know about distraught girls who had no business traveling unchaperoned?

Charles staggered hurriedly back to his cabin and pushed open the door. The *petite blonde* was standing there, swaying visibly, with a puzzled expression on her still-pale face. When she recognized the intruder, she stiffened. Her black eyes opened wide and looked immense in her small face. The ship was trembling like a frightened beast beneath them, and the blonde grabbed on to a beam that formed part of the bunk bed.

"What do you want?" she asked in a faltering voice, obviously thinking she was in her own cabin. She put her free hand up instinctively to her head, where the dramatic if not dangerous cut left blood on her hand. Her first impulse was to cry out at the sight of her blood, but something about the stranger before her held her in check. In spite of herself she trembled, while silently berating herself for being so cowardly and frightened. It was not just the storm and the creaking of the ship that was causing her distress, she suspected.

She had seen him before, yes, gambling in that devil-may-care manner that attracted her admiration regardless of the fact that such appreciation was bold and somehow wrong. Even when he was still, there exuded from this man a dangerous tension, a preparation for defense or attack. He gave the impression of potential dynamism, of an untamed beast pretending unconcern. When he walked, his muscles flowed and rippled with grace visible even beneath his clothes, muscles like those of a restless jaguar in captivity. She had seen one once in Panama with Burland Jones, pacing in outraged frustration and snarling viciously in the well-thonged bamboo cage that held him. But her sense of propriety, instilled in her by nuns and other well-meaning adults, forced her to feel ashamed about her unconventional interest in a gambler. Besides, she felt uncomfortable about this man, and her impulse was to avoid him, even though she had often felt a certain magnetism about him. With her eyes she had frequently sought him, only to turn them away as quickly as she could. There was no reason to distrust the stranger, but her instincts told her that she had something to fear from him. She was uncannily ill at ease in his presence, much more so than with the other male passengers aboard the ship, although they, too, made her feel awkward and aware of her inadequate training in social banter and urbanity. As a defense Helena had assumed a cold and isolated pose of contempt for all the gamblers, and especially for this one.

So she *is* French, thought Charles, as he noted her perfect accent, marred only by the un-Parisian idiosyncrasies characteristic of those raised in the mountains.

"I am Charles Terny, mademoiselle," responded Charles also in what he assumed was her mother tongue. "Englishman of sorts. . . . I had the honor of rescuing you when you fell outside my cabin during an extremely rough moment of . . ."

As he spoke, the boat lurched wildly once again, and the two lost their balance, colliding with startling force into each other's arms. The impact knocked Helena's breath away.

The moment stood suddenly suspended. The gentle odor of camomile rose from Helena's hair up to Charles, while its silkiness innocently caressed his chin. His arms tightened around her instinctively to steady her, then remained cradling her small and slender body with decisive firmness. He felt an almost overwhelming desire to crush her violently to him, to kiss the pulse in the soft, delightful flesh of her throat, to smudge with his lips the dewy film of perspiration that had formed on her brow and had mingled with her blood.

At the same time Helena's face fell into the linen of his shirt. The masculine scents of lingering tobacco, leather, and starch from his shirt invaded her half-dazed senses. A hitherto unknown excitement stirred from deep within her, a reeling dizziness that swept away everything except her feelings. She clung to the sudden luscious sensation that she was enveloped in protection, safe in the hollow of these arms, that she was no longer one solitary lonely girl, that she could easily take root in this very spot and remain there forever. But she was brought back to reality by just as violent a premonition of danger. Bewildered by her confused emotions, by her lengthy and daring stay against his body, Helena brusquely wrenched herself from his arms.

"I thank you very much for your kindness, monsieur, but I am quite capable of taking care of myself," she retorted, her voice trembling, her expression perhaps sharper than she had intended. She continued to sway, although she was not sure if her movements were the result of the convulsions of the ship or of her heart throbbing violently in her breast. "I am sure I can reach my cabin in safety," she added with discernible acidity when Charles did not answer.

Her lack of polite gratitude triggered a flicker of anger in Charles, and a flicker of satire as well. His mouth formed a suddenly mirthless line while his brow knitted in displeasure, which he felt a right to show. After all, he didn't have to see that she was safe. He was nobody's chaperone! Silly girl!

As they stared each other down, however, Charles's eyes softened and some other strange intensity swept his gaze. To Helena the yellow-gray flecks of his eyes seemed to expand suddenly as in a sunburst, only to be overtaken by the depthless darkness of his pupils. It was fascinating, hypnotizing.

Charles's first grim expression faded; his eyelids drooped ever so slightly. He was entranced by this inexperienced, proud girl in spite of his intention to be hard and to impress upon her the fact that he had helped her as he would have done even the ugliest woman aboard the *Amélie*. He had wanted to show a nonchalant attitude toward her exceptional beauty, for maybe it had gone to her head. But he found it difficult to show he was unimpressed.

Could her trembling response have been to the very same wave of heat that had washed so suddenly over him at their touch? Her lips were especially gorgeous . . . the lower one slightly pouting and moist. . . .

They stood facing each other only a few inches apart in the tiny cabin. Her determined chin trembled somewhat. The sudden glint of what Helena took as sardonic hardness in Charles's intense eyes frightened her more than the emotions she had just discovered in herself. She realized that she was alone in this strange man's cabin, and she sensed danger. Her eyes darted from him to the door. Then, after what seemed to her an interminable anguish, his speckled eyes relaxed, and he stepped aside to let her pass.

Before she was fully aware that the path to the door was free, he spoke again.

"May I have the honor, mademoiselle, of introducing myself again, more formally. I am Charles Terny, and I'm traveling to Panama City. I am sorry if I have embarrassed you by bringing you to my cabin, but it

was the only place I could leave you when you hit
your head and passed out. I then attempted to bring
succor"—and Charles emphasized this last word pe-
dantically, thus dismissing with irony the importance
of the accident—"but the doctor was nowhere to be
found, and your friend the captain," he drawled, un-
derlining the word *friend* with barely discernible malice, "was too busy to come."

His odious impertinence riled Helena immediately.
This man was insufferable! And what did he mean by
proposing that the captain was her *friend?* Was he
making detestable insinuations? Helena suddenly
longed to leave the cramped quarters, where inevitably
she must remain close to this totally disturbing and
observant man who apparently thought himself very
clever and who had been spying on her. Or had he
talked to the captain about her already? The audacity!
She stepped in his direction to leave but, remembering
her bonnet, stopped.

Charles took advantage of her flustered hesitation.
To add the finishing touches of arrogance to his self-
introduction, he bowed very formally from the hips,
clicking his heels in a dashing military style that Helena correctly interpreted as mockery. As he did so, his
eyes narrowed appraisingly, and his gaze fell insolently over her body, a wicked smile appearing on his
face.

Strangely, though, Charles suddenly lost his cynical
designs and felt instead another momentary thrill that
came, he knew instantly, from the proximity of her
body and her sweet, youthful scent. His mocking
smile turned into a softer, enigmatic one directed a bit

49

toward himself, perhaps, because of his ridiculous weakness for pretty girls. It gave him unexpected pleasure just to have her near. She was soft and lovely, and in spite of his first intention to vex the girl and bring her down a peg or two from her high-and-mighty pedestal, Charles immediately fell victim to this aura of delicate sensuality which he had missed in following her movements from afar. Although she was small, she exuded some rare quality that foretold a passionate woman, and the glimmer of fear and anger in her eyes, as dark as forest pools, added a mystery that excited him.

Though she had kept her golden hair hidden as much as possible in her bonnets and ribbons, it had rebelled against its prison, and lovely silky wisps had made their sortie into freedom. Now set free at last, piled carelessly on top of her head, her hair caught the lights of the lanterns which the steward kept lit in all first-class cabins and corridors of the ship and which flickered with every harsh movement of the still-tossing vessel.

Helena overcame her fright at his bold perusal, and anger took over as she replied in a curt voice to her dubious benefactor, "Again, thank you, monsieur." Then she gathered her skirts, picked up her bonnet almost as an afterthought, and pushed past him to the doorway. Once outside, she stalked down the hall as decisively as she could with the careening of the vessel, without once turning to look back.

She could still feel Terny's stare burning into her as she turned the corner at the far end of the passageway. She lay back flat against the wall and caught her breath. Her ears were still ringing from the stunning events of the past few minutes, and she was close to tears from humiliation and fright.

How dare he! How dare he look at her like that! Just because she had fallen against his chest. Just because she had remained in his arms from dizziness. Just because . . . She didn't want to go on rationalizing the undeniable thrill she had experienced as she rested her face against his shirt, smelling his man scent. The thought made her blush; she felt embarrassed at the indignity of her own surprising weakness. She was puzzled and distressed by her momentary and unexpected surrender, and she had no ready explanations to justify it. She vaguely sensed only that the man was irritatingly powerful. He was probably one of those conceited men who thought his good looks could turn any woman's heart, and that he could treat women as vilely as he wished without risking the loss of their admiration. True, he was the most handsome man she had ever seen. He was obviously cruel and heartless, too. Couldn't he tell that she was young and alone and . . . and . . . pitiful?

Though she was feeling sorry for herself, there was nothing pitiful looking about Helena. Her cheekbones gave her the elegance and distinction of a much more mature woman. Her lips were sensuous and her eyes luminous and full with the promise of passion. She was striking from afar, in spite of her petite figure, and even more so up close, for her whole being breathed innocence and seductiveness at the same time. Her voice was musical, but pitched huskily low and gentle to the ear.

Helena's instinctive realization of these things about herself must have been behind her decision to stay away from the men on the ship. She was dressed as austerely as the nuns had taught her to dress in France, but if her purpose was to hide her great beauty, her efforts were to very little avail, although from far away the hood and bonnet managed to mask somewhat her splendid coloring and exquisite features.

She reached her cabin, wiped her forehead with cologne water, and winced as the alcohol in the cologne burned the cut. Still, she was relieved to see that the cut was not serious. It must have been her nerves that had caused her to faint. She had certainly suffered worse accidents in her wilder days of childhood and even at the convent, where it had taken much patience to teach Helena to sit still and be ladylike. Inevitably her active search for suitable sport had led her to innumerable spills, cuts, and bruises. Her tomboy activities had given her a notorious reputation, even earlier among her mother's dearest friends.

Helena smiled wanly as she recalled her unruly childhood, certain that her wild ways had led to her poor mama's desperate decision to send her abroad to be educated by civilized and cultured French nuns. Ironically Helena had finally even considered joining the convent, but the sisters had wisely resisted her impulsive suggestion, perhaps convinced that the tomboy still left in her would eventually and disruptively seek to escape. They wanted no rebels in their nunnery! Helena had acquired this reputation for toughness, determination, and rebelliousness in spite of the

fact that she also possessed certain paradoxical and ul-
traweak signs of feminine cowardice, which shamed
her, of course, such as her fear of storms and even of
too dark a night.

Helena's reminiscence of her childhood escapades
was interrupted as suddenly as it had begun by another erratic movement of the ship that was carrying
her back to Panama. She caught her own faraway
stare in the mirror, where the hint of a smile still lingered. It faded, however, as she began to feel the
swift pounding of a headache and realized forlornly
that the ship was still trembling from the storm. She
sighed and, resigned to her cowardly mortification,
sank down on her bed. The ship was still tossing mercilessly on the waves when she finally undressed and
fell into a restless half-sleep.

Chapter II

Sometime during the night Helena was lulled into a deep and refreshing slumber from which she did not awake until sunlight streamed through the porthole. She felt the itching heat as she threw the coarse linen sheet off. She sat up and stretched, covering her yawns demurely.

Her chemise, thank God, was of gauzy batiste, and cool enough when she could open the porthole, but now the thin material was clinging to her in spots, damp from the moisture that had begun to form on her skin. The graceful swell of her small uplifted breasts was outlined in the pale yellow of the nightgown, through which showed the darker shade of two rosettes. She decided to open the porthole before dressing. The storm last night had made it impossible to leave it open while she slept.

Stepping into her slippers, one of which she had to

retrieve from under the bunk where the stormy movements of the ship had hidden it, she leaned toward the porthole and looked out. The sky was tinted a bright flamingo pink, but the brilliance was already receding to give way to the tropical sun which continued to rise with its usual swiftness. Helena felt a sudden delicious languor as she watched the colors turn and fade through the huge kaleidoscope formed by the porthole.

She felt very much alive, her nerves tingling with a strange anticipation. Nevertheless her fingers instinctively reached for her forehead to check the state of her small wound. It was already healing, and she dismissed the fleeting worry. Still, there lingered the premonition that something in her life was about to change. The terrible feelings of despair and depression that had pervaded her life the last few months had magically begun to dissipate and she was thankful for this flicker of hope, determination, and gladness. She felt much more like her old self.

The news of her mother's death had struck her hard, the death of the beautiful Mariana whom she had loved so well—her mother of the warm and tender doe eyes and the dark and silky tresses that contrasted so startlingly with her own light hair. In spite of the muted joy she had just experienced, tears suddenly burned behind Helena's liquid black eyes. One moment she remembered the caressing tones of her mother's voice, and the next, memories of her advice and admonishments flooded her mind. She felt the sting of tears of sorrow and regret that she had not been a better daughter, a less troublesome child.

Any day now the ship that was carrying her home would anchor in Colón, fifty miles across the Isthmus from Panama City. The train had seemed so swift four years before as it had snaked across the Isthmus, bringing her with a screech of metal to the dock area where she would board the ship to France. She recalled Carmen's tears and her mother's desperate embrace when the nonpassengers had been forced to leave the ship, that day so long ago. Helena had remained on deck, pitifully waving a white scarf. Tío Benito had been there, too, with his wife, Tía Alejandra. Good friends, gentle and well-bred, her chaperones for the duration of the voyage, they had waved gaily as they looked forward to their European tour. But Helena still remembered the wrenching of her heart as the sight of her mother and Carmen, waving madly, had blurred before her because of the tears that streamed from her eyes.

There had always been something wistful about Mama. In spite of her business sense and the couturier enterprise that she had run in Panama, there had remained a hovering sense of tragedy about her mother as long as she could remember, and Helena knew it was caused by the irrecoverable loss of Edward Buchanan, her father. The tall, dashing blond gentleman had swept the dark-haired girl away with his passion for her, and then abandoned her utterly in his death, which had played the final hand in the bittersweet love affair.

Her father, a civil engineer graduated from West Point, and scion of a great southern family, had accepted a high position with the railroad construction company, but he had left it early on, caught up in the gold fever of the early fifties; then, on his way back from California, he had settled again in Panama. He had left Panama before she was born, to join the Confederacy in the War between the States. Helena had lost her father in that holocaust. Almost as deep as her sadness, however, was her wish to be certain that if he had lived, he would have come back to her and to her mother. Somehow it seemed that eventually he would have left them, that aristocratic adventurer, even if there had been no war, no excuse for the final parting. This suspicion hurt Helena more than the knowledge that he had not married her mother, and sometimes when the truth of it threatened her in some brutal moment, she felt a strange and throbbing ache, as if she were bereft of all love, unworthy, unsure, and a vague, unreasonable guilt would wrap itself around her and not let go.

Helena did not remember exactly when she first knew she was only the natural and illegitimate issue of that affair. Perhaps it had come to her from the words whispered behind her back whenever she found herself in groups of young girls from school. Or perhaps her mother had made too many obvious efforts to protect her from the seemingly malicious whispers of the girls' parents. Thankfully, the memories of oblique references to her fatherlessness rarely haunted her now. But even when they had been constantly on her mind Helena had considered her father her very own. It was true that she could not legally bear his name, and that she had suffered frequent impulses to hate him, but somehow it had seemed futile to hate the dead, and she could never bring herself to such a state of mind. Instead, she found that she admired him through her mother's words of praise and love. It was from him, her mother told her, that she had received her golden hair, her fine, perfect features.

Nevertheless, in spite of her secret, sometimes fierce, pride that she was her father's child, Helena preferred to put the circumstances of her birth away from her mind, to guard her thoughts. She told herself almost casually that it did not matter in the least that she was illegitimate, but this was only a claim that salvaged her pride. Deeper still, Helena hid the knowledge in her heart and was reluctant to bring it out and scrutinize it.

But sometimes the memories rushed over her and pained her in various ways. According to a letter her mother had received in care of her lawyer from her father's commanding officer in the Confederate Army, one of his last wishes had been that, in case of his death, Mariana be notified. While he was still living, he had failed to write her mother a single message; had he perhaps intended finally to set her free with the knowledge of his death? Helena wished her mother had not loved him so much, for, difficult as it was to admit it fully to herself, Helena felt that her mother had been somehow mentally affected, transformed by her tragic love and left unhinged, so that she had lived from then on in a vague stratum of uncertainty and bewilderment, a condition which others could sometimes discern, Helena better than anyone.

Even after her father's death her mother had continued to pine for him, and had refused to marry Burland Jones, though she did mourn that kind man when he, too, was killed by outlaws in Panama about a year before Helena was to leave for France. Helena had been deeply shocked by Burland's death, for he had been like a father to her. Her gratitude and love for him still burned within her, though she had finally overcome the first edge of grief. And now, this. Her mother gone, too.

Suddenly aware that these sad thoughts were about to overwhelm her, Helena deliberately pushed them aside, desperately tried to dispel them, to make the pain recede.

Once she had gained her composure, she began to wonder about some less personally touching details of the day on which she had left Panama for France and of the place where she had last seen her mother. Would the town of Colón, the dock, and the commercial district look the same as they had the last time she had seen Mama and Carmen? Would the swamps, the hills, and the jungles still appear bent upon swallowing the railroad and any and all vestiges of man's labor and attempts to civilize the wild domains of tropical nature?

The metal road had been built from the tears and sweat and blood of countless men from every part of the globe. It was impossible to imagine how many lives the twisting highway had touched in some way, for thousands upon thousands of men had come from every corner of the world, from as far away as China and Europe, to bend in toil and to construct the dream of American engineers. The macabre belief had sprung up that for every railroad tie laid, some man had given his life, a victim of accidents, of the uncontrolled use of drugs brought by the uprooted—often addicted Orientals—or of the raging tropical diseases that were the scourge of Panama.

How difficult it had been to build that railway, and how herculean the task of keeping the jungle at bay. Would the rails be tarnished and warped from the merciless climate? Did the boards still rot easily, fertilizing the ground for creepers and other tenacious tropical plants so that the undergrowth crept up with almost visible speed, trying to cover the tracks? It was an endless job of maintenance to keep away the encroaching wilderness.

Yet already there was serious talk of the French Canal Company. Was it true that Ferdinand de Lesseps himself would come to the Isthmus soon to begin excavation? What a fabulous dream-come-true it would be for the Isthmians if the French triumphed! Of the resultant financial success Helena was certain, in spite of the discouraging words her mother had once or twice uttered about the tremendous disappointments endured by the Panamanians after the railroad had been finished by the Americans. In Panama dreams of enormous wealth had been perhaps too grand and unrealistic. But this time it would surely be different. Already de Lesseps's Suez Canal in Egypt was a great and prosperous achievement. Like the development of the untamed desert, that of the jungle was sure to bring positive results to the men and women whose existence depended on trade and on the blessing of their great natural resource—the land itself—a slender isthmus between two great continents, placed as if by design in the middle of two vast and important oceans. True, in Panama there had always been some talk of disappointment.

If the French should come to build the canal, as was rumored, there would eventually be a great need for a French school, and, in fact, for any good and solid place of instruction, the thought of which excited her. The boys, of course, would probably continue to go to Bogotá, to St. Bartholomew's, for secondary-school instruction, that is, the sons of the well-to-do, while the older boys would be sent to France and to England for university studies, and sometimes even to the United States. But the school Helena dreamed of founding and administrating would cater to the girls, who, it seemed, were often neglected in this respect.

Perhaps her own personal dreams to succeed in her mother's business as well as to strengthen educational facilities for girls in Panama were too grand, and like the dreams of the Isthmians at the time of the building of the railroad, would also fall flat to disappoint her. Helena stubbornly pushed the discouraging thought away.

With her daydreaming Helena had not noticed how high the sun had already climbed. She would miss breakfast! She suddenly realized how hungry she was. She had not been able to eat a bite at dinner the night before and had taken only a little red wine before despairing and running to her cabin.

She grabbed one of her drab dresses, the one she considered the coolest, shuddering inwardly at the thought of the forthcoming torture of the woolen cloth against her delicate and perspiring skin. If only she had a suitable dress to wear on board the ship! There had been no time in France, after the news of her mother's death, to acquire more than the one cotton dress she was saving for her arrival in Panama. She did not dare to touch it for fear it might get stained. It was almost impossible to properly wash and iron it aboard with the few primitive facilities available, and all her other dresses had been ideal only for the perennial chill of the French mountains.

She piled her hair high on her head and plopped the dullest bonnet imaginable over it, tying the gray ribbons under her chin. Then she slipped into the light-gray woolen dress. The passageway was deserted, and she turned and locked her cabin, slipping the large key into her reticule. She caught herself humming a little tune. For the first time in months she enjoyed a moment of anticipation and lightheartedness. During the night her cares seemed to have evaporated, and she reasoned cautiously that it was probably due to the relief of having survived the frightening menace of the storm the night before.

She made it to the dining area just in time. The waiter, whom everyone called Ramoncho, a sour little dark man who refused to speak French to the passengers whenever the boat was headed west in order, he said, to train them to learn Spanish, brought her several pieces of toast and a huge café au lait that satisfied Helena immensely. Ramoncho treated Helena with special care—never, however, admitting to his partial treatment with visible friendliness. He was determined to remain outwardly embittered and enjoyed his dramatic role to the hilt. Secretly, though, he loved hearing the Spanish words the young woman directed to him whenever she ordered her dishes. Her accent and intonation were definitely not European, yet they were soft and gently rolling, redolent of the Andalusian dialects that had found their way to America.

After her breakfast, which she finished practically alone at table, for everyone fled the heat of the room as soon as they could, Helena stepped up to the deck and stood in the doorway. Her plans to find shade on the deck had not taken into account the astounding brilliance of the sun in the perfectly blue Caribbean sky. Its light, sparkling off the waves, hurt her eyes. It reflected, too, off the grains of sand and salt that covered the wooden planks of the deck so that they looked like diamonds generously strewn about. The sight only made her itch more. She would not find shade in *this* sunshine! She had forgotten how white and hot the light could be in the tropics.

She turned to escape to her cabin, longing to tear the woolen dress off and be relieved of its torture. In her haste she did not see the man and ran straight into him.

"Well, well, if it isn't the young lady I rescued only last night. We have a knack for bumping into each other, don't we?" His voice was more sarcastic than friendly.

Charles Terny! That terrible, insolent man! Had he been following her again?

63

Helena pulled herself away from his immense chest, only to stagger backward, almost falling through the open doorway. She grabbed the doorframe and Charles Terny pulled her forward at the same time. As soon as she had regained her balance, she twisted her arm out of his grasp. She felt embarrassed and humiliated, but could not understand why; in her momentary bewilderment she could only think of lashing out with some rude remark.

"I would be most grateful, Monsieur Terny, if you would leave me alone! I don't need your help."

She wanted to say much more, to put this man who was so incredibly sure of himself in his place. But no smart remarks came to mind. Nothing! He stood looking at her with absolutely no change of expression on his face. The same twisted smile, the same cocky demeanor that she could not understand or cope with. It was exasperating!

"By all means, Mademoiselle . . . ? You told me your name, mademoiselle, but I'm afraid I have forgotten what it was."

"I didn't bother to tell you, monsieur, as you will most certainly have no need of knowing it in the future!" retorted Helena, feeling a small measure of triumph at the recovery of her voice. "And now, please, if you will excuse me?"

She brushed forcefully past Charles Terny and quickly clattered down the metal steps that led to her cabin. Behind her she heard a sudden peal of jovial laughter. The man was insufferable! She ignored the flush of blood that rose to her face.

By the time she arrived at her cabin, she was

drenched with sweat from the exertion, and was sure that she had developed a rash from the intolerable wool. Her hands trembled lightly as she turned the key. She stepped inside, banged the door shut, and threw her reticule wherever it might fall. She ripped her dress off in desperation, and it crumpled into a heap on the floor where she left it. She felt a tremendous sense of relief and sprawled naked on the bunk bed. She would cool off first and then put her things away, perhaps read one of her books the rest of the afternoon. But it took longer to cool off than she had expected. Her thoughts were in disarray and her lack of serenity did not allow her to relax. On the contrary, her body tensed, poised for something which she could not imagine. That terrible, terrible man! He was certainly no gentleman!

Finally, slipping into her chemise again, she sat up in a chair placed to catch the tiniest whisper of breeze that might venture into the cabin through the porthole. She opened her book and read. Much to her disgust her concentration was queerly affected, and the image of strange speckled eyes laughing at her kept intruding all afternoon.

Chapter III

Only a few short days were left before the ship would be anchoring in the Caribbean bay of Colón—the Atlantic port of Panama. Although most of the passengers were beginning to feel that their trip was over, Charles was only now finding it truly interesting. Regardless of the complexity of his plans for his stay on the Isthmus and the time he needed alone in order to sort out his plans, the appeal he had first felt for the blond fellow passenger had blossomed unreasonably, in spite of his determination not to allow such a thing to happen.

Perhaps a streak of arrogance and conceit that ran through Charles had something to do with the sudden obsession he was suffering with regard to *la petite blonde*. Charles was not accustomed to having his handsome virile person scorned and evaded. He took for granted the power of his magnetism and rugged good looks, and, in truth, he would have had to be quite dull witted indeed if he had not realized how generously he had been endowed by nature, from the perfectly chiseled features of his manly face to the muscular perfection of his body.

Charles was in a half-wakened state, stretched out on the bunk bed with no clothes on. The rocking of the boat was soothing and made it difficult to wake up completely, especially as the thought lingered that there was really nothing to do on board ship. By all rights he should have been bored to the brink of frustration by now, and yet, curiously, he continued to feel relaxed and unhurried, in a thoughtful mood, enjoying these moments of complete freedom to think and to dream. It was not yet as miserably warm as it would be in a half hour or so when the sun came up. He yawned and placed his arms under his neck, stretching his long muscular legs.

He must have dozed, for when he awoke, his eyes fell on the sunshine streaming through the porthole. The light reflected off the tiny particles of dust in the air, motes which had beguiled him in his childhood. He could almost hear himself ask his father over and over again what the shiny particles really were.

"Papa, I don't believe they are little pieces of gold scattered by the fairies, because, you know what? I don't believe in fairies anymore. That's for babies, and I am almost eight years old! Please tell me what they really are, Papa."

The Baron de Thierny chuckled good naturedly,

and assured Charles that the next explanation he would surely believe, because it was the very best one he knew.

His father's answer was always different from the one he had given before, and Charles suspected early and with delight that they were explanations the Baron de Thierny enjoyed making up for his son's gratification and happiness.

His father had died some years ago. The baron's life had been hampered by envies and subsequent rumors about the validity of his title, his ideas, and his dreams. Yes, the Baron de Thierny had been a dreamer, but his schemes of grand enterprises were oriented toward seeking glory and fame by doing something historically positive, and he had hurt no one with his attempts to find engineering and development projects grandiose enough to match his aspirations. His greatest fiasco had been attempts to organize a Panama Canal enterprise just about the time that Charles was born. But greater still than this public failure had been the disgrace and pain in which he had had to leave the Isthmus of Panama with his newborn son and a wet-nurse more than thirty years before.

Charles's father may have had to bow his head in shame at that moment, but he could never be ashamed of his dedication to the raising and education of his son. Charles had been given the best schooling available in France and in England, the lands of the baron's ancestors. His tutors had been extremely well chosen, and except for the carping of the baron's resentful wife, a harmonious and congenial atmosphere had surrounded his youth. Charles had grown up sensing the quiet dignity which his father possessed beneath his outer and sometimes eccentric search for glory and renown.

Would the baron have approved of his son as he was now? Would he have approved the intentions his son had developed and planned to carry out, the avenging designs that haunted him? In spite of his self-assurance Charles could not avoid occasionally asking himself these questions. He was certain that the more obvious mission upon which he had embarked would have met with the baron's approval. But what of the other mission—the mission to destroy his mother's family in every way possible?

He had discovered the true story of his birth from his father's own lips, during one of their frequent sojourns at the English estate which the baron had inherited from his British mother. The words still echoed in Charles's mind as they had when he'd just turned twenty-one—too young an age to cope coolly with such dismay and shock and bitter disappointment, but not to learn to hate with devastating intensity on account of the evil done his own mother.

"Son, you are legally a man now."

Charles had remained respectfully quiet, a little embarrassed by the deliberateness with which his father was addressing him, the moment bristling with bad news.

"I have never told you fully the story of your birth. . . . I want you to forgive me for not doing so. . . . I just couldn't before. You were too young. I had to keep your origins a secret from yourself, but now it would be a mistake. . . ."

"I don't understand, Papa." Charles felt suddenly on the defensive, a little resentful that any secrets had been kept from him. After all, he had considered himself a grown man for a few years already, and his father's patronizing words irked him.

"I've always known of my illegitimacy, and it hasn't made a bit of difference as far as I am concerned."

Almost simultaneously Charles realized that enough pain had touched him in life already to make him admit the hypocrisy of his words. So, instead of complaining or defending his position, Charles merely changed the tone of his voice.

"In short, Father, I have no complaints." He flashed a youthful and attractive grin which showed off a row of even white teeth against a face tanned from continual horseback riding and hunting, his favorite sports. "Frankly, I'm better off than anyone else I know." His conclusion had a ring of triumph in it, but its forced sureness did not fool the old man, who returned a smile of benevolence with an element of compassion in it, too, as if he could see beyond to some crushing suffering, some unavoidable defeat that Charles could not in his youth and inexperience possibly visualize. The old man started to say something, changed his mind, and finally uttered other words that he felt he must also say.

"Son, I only hope that the truth will not embitter you."

The baron closed his eyes as if in fatigue, but he was merely mustering up courage to go through with the ordeal of voicing the horrible truth he must reveal to his son. When he opened them again, he noticed that Charles had not budged, and that he was still gazing intently at his father, waiting for the explanation he had promised. Damn it! If only there were some way to avoid wounding his son! But the world was getting smaller, and too many people knew the truth already. Charles might find out in some other way that would hurt even more. No. He would have to go through with the story, the tragedy that surrounded his son's birth. He began.

"God! When I think of what might have become of you if I had left Panama before I did, or if I had not loved your mother enough to stay as long as I did. . . . You were so wretchedly abandoned!"

"Father! Abandoned? I don't understand. If my mother died at childbirth, how could she have abandoned me? *You* certainly have not left me." Charles had leaned forward on his chair and clutched his father's arm. The old baron closed his eyes for a moment as the painful remembrances of the past assaulted him.

"That is the story I would have had you believe while you were growing up, that your mother died in childbirth, for a child and a youth should feel his origins are as unblemished and gentle as possible. No one should have to cope growing up with ugly loathings that might warp his mind and keep him from producing the best his spirit is capable of producing." The baron sighed resignedly. "But you are a man now, and you cannot remain vulnerable to your past by ignoring its truth. It would be to your disadvantage now to keep up the fantasy of your birth."

"Tell me, Father, quickly. I need to know."

The old baron heaved another sigh full of misery and began his tale, his face betraying the pain that wrenched at his heart.

"Your mother was the only daughter of a very distinguished Colombian couple, members of the highest aristocracy, descendents of the conquistadores. They were also extremely wealthy. Her father, Don Jaime González Calderón y Rico, was a younger son, and he had settled on the Isthmus to further his fortune, which he would then not have to share with his numerous brothers and sisters as he had had to do before with their common inheritance. Don Jaime had once served a tour of duty for the government of Colombia on the Isthmus and had seen the possibilities even then for increasing his interests in shipping, in transportation, and in almost every other major business there. It was after he was already a wealthy member of society in the Isthmian capital that I met your mother. Lucinda was the most ethereal and beautiful creature I had ever seen, the embodiment of my ideal, the woman I had yearned for in all my youthful, unsatisfied dreams.

"Her hair was laced with golden streaks from the brilliant sun of Panama, and her eyes, like yours, were hazel. She sparkled . . . her gaiety and her tenderness. . . . But I had found her too late, for my marriage had been sealed—another of those convenient matches made so cruelly even today—and I had nothing honest to offer her—not even my undying devotion and love." The Baron de Thierny bowed his head discreetly to hide his eyes—so light a gray that they appeared almost colorless—for they were stinging with bitter tears. Charles sat motionless, not daring to interrupt for fear that his father might leave out even the most insignificant detail in the story of his birth. He already knew much about his mother, for, as long as he could remember, the baron had often spoken of her—the only woman he had ever truly loved. Charles had idealized his mother and cherished her memory through his father's words even into adulthood. Still, he never tired of hearing her story. Only now a startling new element was being introduced. His father's anxiety and his strange words left him nervous, anticipating some cruel surprise.

"Somehow your mother discovered that we were kindred souls, and fell in love with me, much to her misfortune. It was impossible to keep us apart. . . ." His voice breaking from the torment, the baron tried to regain his composure, to finish the burdening confession. "I, for one, have never forgotten her, not one day of my life, and you are of her flesh and therefore dear to me beyond all else. Lucinda, I know, has surely forgotten me. . . ."

"Father! You speak as if she were still alive!" Charles cried out in shock.

"She may very well be, son, though there were rumors that she had died. All I could ever find out for certain—and that even after very expensive investigations—was that she had lost her mind, that she had remained incoherent and insane, and that her physical health had completely crumbled from these ravages of her mind."

"Insane! I don't . . ."

"You see, son, the things that were done to her, such a sensitive soul, were just too much to bear, and she broke down under the pressures. But for your sake, let me finish. I don't think I can go on much longer."

Tears of the deepest distress had gathered in the old man's reddened eyes, but Charles tried not to let the obvious pain his father was undergoing distract him from understanding every word.

"You said you were very much in love," Charles prompted his father.

"Yes. Very much in love, deeply, passionately. I could not resist the desire to have and to hold her, even at the risk of causing her later pain. My greatest anguish came from the fact that I could not marry her so long as my wife still lived. As you know, in the days of my youth all marriages were arranged, and the inflexible spirit of many a father totally ruined the chances for happiness that his children might later discover for themselves. This was my case.

"I selfishly took what Lucinda, perhaps because of her inexperience with the pains of this world, offered me in complete trust, though I did have the decency to warn her of my situation. But our love was immense and sweeping, and our passion so great that I was willing to and indeed was planning to run away with her and to live with her in simplicity, disclaiming my place in society in England or in France. Nevertheless, I was terrified for her sake when she tearfully announced that she was to have my child.

"She begged me to take her from Panama immediately. I knew her father was famous for his arrogant and inflexible pride and sense of family honor, and I feared the worse for her, but before I could take measures to lead her safely to Europe, I had to make more definite immediate arrangements. So I convinced her to wait for a few days.

"How could I have known that already a maidservant who suspected her condition had betrayed her to Don Jaime?

"Don Jaime snatched Lucinda quickly away, impervious to her beauty and delicacy as she begged him to allow her to disappear with me in Europe, to remain anonymous and never use the family name. They could pretend she had died, she begged.

"But Don Jaime had a hard heart and dragged her with the help of her brother to the mountains of Boquete, to the isolation of their practically inaccessible coffee plantation. There you were finally born and then, unbelievably cruelly, you were snatched from her side, entrusted to a wet-nurse, transported by ship from Pedregal on the coast, and deposited at the steps of my residence in Panama City."

Charles's moan was barely audible. He was almost in a state of shock, afraid to listen to more, afraid not to. His father's words seemed to hammer without mercy into his brain. He grabbed the armrests of the chair and tried to sort the words out, to weigh the meaning of the devastating revelation he was hearing.

"I received a warning that if I did not leave immediately, I would be killed and the baby would be abandoned without protection, for he would never be recognized as a member of the proud González clan, of the purebred conquistadores of the noble blood of Spain, whose honor, they claimed, had never been smirched without blood being shed to restore it." The baron's voice was full of bitterness. Too agitated to remain seated, he rose and approached the window which looked out onto the formal gardens that graced his impressive English estate. His hands were thrust into his pockets, and his shoulders seemed to bend with the weight of his grief.

"As if to make certain I would take the warning seriously, I was ambushed and severely beaten by thugs in the service of Don Jaime. I was a proud Frenchman at heart, and still such arrogance and such determination for revenge were hard for me to believe. But I knew that the threat of death would hold, and I didn't want to leave you both motherless and fatherless.

"I finally abandoned the Isthmus and took you to France. Only later, when my wife finally acceded to my wishes, did I bring you here to England."

As the baron finished his tale, he turned and met his son's face, which having first turned pale as if drained of some vital force, was now flushed with the violence of total anger. The baron had never thought to see such naked pain and hatred in those hazel eyes, for he was more than aware of the immense devotion and love of which Charles was capable. Neither did the old man ever realize to what extent the piercing disillusionment was then glazing over every tender capability and motivation of Charles's spirit.

Though the baron was unaware of it, Charles's love for him and the idealistic love he had developed and nurtured for the mother he had never seen remained the glimmering lights deep in his soul that strove to keep out the encroaching cancer of hate. The devotion to his mother's memory grew into an almost mystical love, while his loathing for his maternal grandfather and for the wicked brother of Lucinda González became absolute.

Charles was ready even at that first moment to risk his life in the quest for vengeance. He could think only of lashing out in a cruel and violent manner, to smite down the pride of that family and leave the members whimpering at his feet for mercy and forgiveness. Only then would he feel catharsis; only blood could wash away the congenital dishonor he had suffered. Ironically, Charles had more Spanish blood in his veins than he realized, for he was acting on the philosophy of honor that was inbred into the Castilians and which he could not help but inherit; the impulses that had motivated his own grandfather to condemn his only daughter to the desolation of insanity.

He realized, nevertheless, that he could not launch his plans for revenge immediately.

First, he had little knowledge of warfare and survival. Second, although his father had not forbidden revenge against the ones who had quietly destroyed his mother, Charles suspected that the baron would disapprove most vigorously if he knew of any plans along those lines. For this reason Charles refrained from confiding his intentions to his father. Once the baron had voiced his disapproval, Charles thought, he himself would be deliberately disobeying if he acted against those wishes, and Charles had rarely disobeyed his father and never when it concerned something so terrible as the decision he was now contemplating. Charles suspected, too, that in this instance the baron would be crushed if his only son went off wildly to kill and be killed.

And though the reasonable qualities of his father's character sometimes irked the impetuous Charles, he recognized that his father had suffered enough. He had been so badly beaten in Panama by his grandfather's hired thugs that he still suffered painful kidney disorders, not to mention the hurt that he carried in his soul for the loss and the suffering of Lucinda.

For his part the baron did not make Charles promise to forget any ideas about revenge, for he never imagined that the tale would have such a sanguinary effect on him. Moreover, the young man seemed to want to avoid further discussion on the subject. The baron prayed that this was because Charles wanted to forget. It was the best possible solution, he thought, his heart heavy.

As for Charles, something happened a few months later that set back even further his timetable for revenge.

He met Ferdinand de Lesseps.

* * *

The Thierny family house in Bellevue, near Paris, was brightly lit to welcome the man whose dream of so many years was soon to come true. De Lesseps had sacrificed, had politicked, and had slaved relentlessly for twenty years to convince the Egyptians and his own people that the grandiose ditch could and should be constructed. Carriage after carriage drove up to the Thierny house on the road to Versailles, and deposited the most fascinating men and women of the epoque to join in welcoming the white-maned lion of Suez.

One quiet conversation alone with de Lesseps later in the evening had sufficed.

Charles was thrilled and inspired to the point that he decided then and there that as soon as he finished his engineering training the following year, he would join de Lesseps in Egypt. If he waited longer to do so, he would entirely miss the opportunity to learn firsthand about the building of canals, a subject which had always been of such particular interest to him as well as to his father.

Charles suspected, too, though he discussed it with no one, that he would also be preparing and toughening himself for what was to come the day he voyaged to Panama to exact payment—blood or otherwise—from the enemies of his parents. His disillusionment at the extent of men's cruelty had certainly not reached its lowest point, but his former naiveté was gone. He sensed that he must learn to protect himself before lashing out blindly against enemies he did not really know.

So Charles kept his hatred under wraps, to be summoned when the time came—like a calculated tactic of war.

In the meantime he devoted himself zealously to the missions assigned to him by the great de Lesseps. Later, after the Suez Canal was finished, he decided to remain in the secret service of France in North Africa, to stay away from the European continent for a while, because his father, finally succumbing to his painful kidney disorder, had died in France. A great numbing ache penetrated Charles at the death of his father. In the end he tried simply to fill the void by throwing himself intensely into his work.

He developed an addiction for the Spartan life of adventure he was leading, though eventually he returned to France and England to manage the valuable properties he had inherited. Though illegitimate he was the sole heir to his father's personal wealth, and in spite of the impossibility of inheriting the title, the family name of Thierny was admired. The doors of glamorous and aristocratic homes were opened graciously to the young gentleman of the bronzed and fluid muscles and the eyes that sparkled mischievously when confronted with the womanly wiles of marriageable daughters and their *mamans*, in Paris and London. Skillfully Charles avoided the snares of many a lady of society bent on capturing, if not his heart, at least his fortune.

But because of the disdain that prevailed for the gentler sex in the desert areas where Charles had lived and worked for some years, he had begun to look upon women with something less than respect. He had found them soft and yielding, conniving and sly, petty—in short, full of despicable traits which repelled him and kept him from forming lasting liaisons with any of them. It gave him pleasure to see and to possess them, but none of them fulfilled his ideal of what a woman should be.

For a time Charles had no ties to stay his flight and did not wish for any. He was free to do with his life as he pleased. He wished only to ply the seas and cover foreign lands, to risk his life and outwit the fates, and to cherish the feelings of triumph and conquest after a job well done. He felt spiritually sinewy, hard as a warrior. He had managed to ward off skillfully every blow to his body and to his sensitivity. At least that's what he thought. He was not completely aware of an insidious brutalization of his spirit. He had begun to take for granted the harsh and unrelenting cruelties of the war games that he played. Charles had lost the sensitivity and tenderness of his youth. Perhaps the loss had begun the day he'd discovered the true secret of his birth. Skirmishes and intrigues had further hardened him. He no longer dwelt on these changes, nor did he realize the extent of his cynicism, but in the early stages of his metamorphosis he had often wondered at himself, almost surprised that he no longer felt moved by tender ideals, longing to be unembittered as he once had been. The hardness with which he had begun to see the world repelled him. This had been earlier, however, and now he rarely thought about it. Instead he concentrated on developing a tough outer crust of recklessness and bravery. The inner insecurities remained hidden.

Charles returned periodically to his duties with the

French government with the understanding that eventually he would be assigned to a government post in Panama. Not knowing the true motives behind Charles's request, the bureaucrats in Paris decided Charles was quite eccentric, for what normal person could possibly want a post in that hellhole? Of course, Charles did not need the post for financial reasons, but he felt that some sort of official standing in Panama might lend him protection should anything go wrong in the blood feud he anticipated.

During his missions for the government of France his life was frequently in peril, not only in the course of his spying activities and during actual combat, but by disease and other dangers that lay in store for adventurers such as he. Once he had spent several weeks in Algiers in a military hospital recuperating from a dreaded fever that a young doctor, Alphonse Lavéran, traveling aboard Charles's ship on a voyage from East Africa through the already completed Suez Canal, had diagnosed as yellow fever. He shuddered involuntarily as he recalled the hell he had been through, though the period of his delirium was a mere vague dream. The worst part had been the raging nausea that had threatened to tear his insides to shreds, and the unbearable, throbbing headache.

"You'll be all right now, Monsieur Thierny. You are a very lucky man!"

The voice had penetrated from some source far away, then approached rapidly through timeless space, until his eyes fluttered open and focused unclearly upon a kind, sunbronzed, and intelligent face.

"Who are you? Where am I?" he asked weakly.

"You are in a hospital in Algiers, and I am Dr. Alphonse Lavéran. I was on your ship. Do you not remember me at all?"

Sudden recognition in Charles's eyes answered Dr. Lavéran's question.

"Of course, Doctor. You said it might be yellow fever. . . ."

"And it was. But you are going to be well now soon."

"Your diagnosis . . . how did you know?" Charles closed his eyes from exhaustion.

"It is my special interest, monsieur—yellow fever and malaria. I have spent several years studying them, and I think I know what might cause them or bring them into the blood—small insects like the mosquito—and not the swamp airs as most doctors believe."

Charles was not fully aware of the end of the doctor's explanations, for he had drifted off into a deep sleep.

Charles survived, thanks to his good physical condition and the intelligent care which he received at the hospital, and finally he regained his strength and former vitality. Not a trace of his suffering remained; according to Dr. Lavéran that was characteristic of the disease. During the period of his convalescence Charles observed with deep apppreciation the devotion of Dr. Lavéran to his patients and to his scientific investigations. Over each bed there was some type of mosquito netting or gauze. After seeing to each man in the ward, he would hurry on down to his laboratory; his favorite work was there waiting for him. Charles and the doctor became friends, and together they discussed diseases that were native to tropical and semitropical soils and which seemed to spread and kill en masse in places like the Isthmus of Panama. Quinine seemed to help against malaria. Nobody knew why, but it helped. And it was common knowledge that yellow fever struck only once, either to kill its victim or to immunize him forever against its scourge. Charles pondered his luck, for it surely must be his destiny to reach the Isthmus of Panama, immune and protected to a greater degree than anyone else he knew.

Charles was given the job in Panama instantly. The officials in charge realized the great advantage their man had acquired with his immunization against yellow fever. Besides, Charles had volunteered for an almost thankless job that carried a salary ridiculously low when one considered the risks. No man would have accepted the job unless he desperately needed the money or wanted, incredibly, to visit Panama very much. For most people the place was merely another of those infernal pits crudely carved from the jungle. Then, too, Thierny was a trained engineer whose opinions would be of value after his first mission of reconnoitering the Isthmus to eliminate dangerous situations for the builders of the new canal who would be going there. Charles was a graduate of the world's most admired school of engineering, L'École Polytechnique, and he had vast experience in the practical hardships to be found in diverse tropical territories. He was exact, hard, and intelligent.

Charles, too, felt he was the most appropriate candidate for the position. In the desert he had learned to survive, to fight and endure. The sun there had browned him as dark as a nomad, and he had learned to wield their weapons with as much treachery as they did themselves. His favorite fighting piece was a barbaric desert weapon, a whip which slipped away to reveal a screwlike dagger imbedded in the handle. Having admired its ingenuity, he had brought it along with him to Panama, if not to use, at least to remind himself that treachery like that hidden in his whip could be waiting for him at the least expected moment, and that he must not trust anyone at all.

The Americans as well as others might not take the probable success of the French as graciously as they wanted the world to believe. Traditionally the Americans had coveted an Isthmian route for themselves, rightly suspecting that for them such a resource would bring untold advantages in the growth and expansion of their immense country. Charles admired the Americans, but he saw his destiny tied up with that of Europe, and he wanted the French to succeed in this enterprise that already, for him at least, promised to be a great adventure. Above all, the man involved in the planning of the canal, Ferdinand de Lesseps, had to be protected, for on his talents depended the success or the failure of the French canal venture. Preparations for personal bodyguards, as well as for loyal workers and supervisors, if any were available on the Isthmus, plus other needs, formed part of the responsibilities now invested upon Charles. Once the time for de Lesseps's arrival approached, he was to work closely with the French consul at Panama City. Until then he was on his own.

To prepare the way for someone as important as Ferdinand de Lesseps, Charles had to leave for his base of operations more than a year before the commencement of the project itself. This was partly to avoid suspicion, partly to study the territory where he would have to carry out his duties, and partly to hire people he could test and trust. For these duties he needed time, especially where transportation was sometimes an insurmountable problem. He needed even more time on this particular mission, for he was determined to avenge the irrevocable pain dealt to his father and his mother. That his own father had been unable to rescue her from her fate had been enough of a warning to Charles that he had to prepare with care his own attempts to avenge his parents.

Now he was ready.

Charles became aware of the uncomfortable heat gathering damply on the sheet beneath him. He stretched one last time before getting up from the bunk and slipping into his clothes.

He took out from one of his drawers some of the fine tobacco he had purchased in London before his short trip to France, and pressed the small pouch into his coat pocket. The coat was unbearably warm in these seas, but it would make him appear more distinguished and serious and not quite as blasé and reckless as he looked in his blousy-sleeved shirt. He did not want to give the impression that he was an irresponsible romantic version of the devil, as one of his lady friends had once called him.

He headed for the captain's quarters, where he

planned to deceive or bribe for his information. He succeeded in doing both with total ease and no pangs of conscience. Only in his private affairs did the thought of dishonesty resuscitate in him the old conflicts of right and wrong instilled in him by his father. The years of struggling in the spy's world of deceit, where truth could frequently cost a man his life or jeopardize the aims of his government, had affected him so that if an affair should concern sleuthing of any kind, his values automatically underwent a change. This faculty made Charles de Thierny at times a most unscrupulous and determined man, a very dangerous man.

The captain's smile was white against his deep tan from years at sea; a generous scattering of freckles matched his bright red hair and lent him an easy charm. Charles found it difficult to believe that such a man could run his ship with the iron hand and will needed to keep men in line. But the ship ran smoothly, and the men apparently bent their wills to his without question. It was a mystery to Charles, whose own ways were more forceful and who had a difficult time controlling his impatience with the incompetence and laziness of others.

"Bon soir, Capitaine Desmoulins." Accepting the captain's friendly gesture that he take a seat, Charles swung himself into one of the two heavy chairs in the cabin. A small table lay bolted between them. "Merci, monsieur," he added.

"To what do I owe the pleasure of your visit, Monsieur Terny? It is not often that I can share the company of a man of your talents."

"You know of me?" Charles's expression could not hide his surprise at the captain's words.

"What man of adventure like myself would not recognize the man and the name of one such as you, monsieur, even if you have chosen for one of your mysterious reasons to anglicize that well-known name?"

Charles began to protest his unworthiness, but the captain held up his hand.

"No, do not deny your fame, Charles de Thierny. My family, monsieur, is well known in Paris, and most of my brothers are nicely settled members of the bourgeoisie. Only I have bothered to stay in the original family business of plying the seas." His eyes twinkled with good humor. "I'll satisfy your curiosity by reminding you of one of your young admirers among the frilly, white-gowned debutantes of our society. Surely you remember my youngest sister, Amélie?"

Charles was taken off guard, and incredibly, he felt the sting of a blush. How the hell could he tell the good captain that he did not remember Amélie Desmoulins any more than he did the other giggling young ladies of Parisian society? Not one of them managed to hide the utter excitement of the manhunt to which their elders pushed them. Even the veneer of sophistication which they thought would fool the older bachelors was not enough to hide their avid desires to entrap a husband. Charles was not impressed by these fair young things, but on the other hand he did not wish to hurt the captain's family pride. On a sudden inspiration Charles beamed a flashing smile.

"You don't mean the flaming-haired Amélie Desmoulins? The charming little redhead? She is your sister?"

"*Mais oui, monsieur. C'est elle. C'est la même.* Of course, she is the baby of the family and is much younger than I am. My father's second marriage, you understand, and the only daughter."

"Well, I can understand why you are proud of her."

"Yes, yes, I am. You see, I never had any children of my own, and, well, Amélie is so much younger that she could easily pass for my own daughter. Yes, I'm very proud of her. She has spunk, and she's extremely intelligent."

"Yes, I noticed."

The captain was not sure, but he thought for a moment that Charles de Thierny's comments sounded a bit wry. Nevertheless the man seemed to remember Amélie quite well, and this satisfied him.

His pride assuaged, the captain turned to his guest. Some port was served. Charles brought out his pouch of tobacco, then handed it casually to the captain.

"I hope you enjoy smoking, monsieur le Capitaine. Please accept this small gift," he said.

"Thank you," answered the captain. "Ah! From England, I see. I hope you'll join me in enjoying its wonderful quality."

They filled their pipes. After a pause during which Charles drew with some concentration on his, he reverted casually to the subject of women. "Ah, yes. The charm of the gentler sex. But you know what they say, Captain Desmoulins. 'Lucky at cards, unlucky at love.'"

The captain scoffed visibly at Charles's meek admission of failure in the field of love. He knew only too well the truth of the matter. It was incredible that the man even remembered his freckle-faced, skinny little sister whom, even though he loved her, he knew to be wanting in physical appeal and allure. He had seen for himself how the most beautiful flowers of his native city fawned and clawed for the attentions of the man before him. A tinge of jealousy fell upon the captain.

"I suppose, Monsieur de Thierny, that you have already enjoyed the gentle smiles of some of the members aboard our ship." It was a question more than a statement, prompted by some deep need to let the other man know about his own interest in young and beautiful women.

"As a matter of fact, Captain, I've noticed precious few women on board. I have been rather busy with the plans my many duties entail. Since you are aware of the nature of my work, I see no point in trying to deceive you. I simply cannot afford to become involved. Besides, I have not yet seen what you would call a beauty among the ladies here."

"Well, then, sir, with all due respect, you must be blind! Have you not yet seen our Miss Helena? Why, I vow . . . a precious blossom like that one from such a small isthmus, eh? She could compete favorably with the fair women of any country."

"Did you say Helena, sir? A dark-haired beauty she must be if she is from the Isthmus of Panama."

"Oh, no!" exclaimed the captain. "Her hair is golden and her skin as white as gardenias. I must say that her eyes are very dark, however, and only serve to set the contrast with her fairness. How could you have missed her?"

"I don't know, except that, as I said before, my duties . . ."

"Bah! Don't speak to me of duties. I myself am duty bound by her family, responsible exclusively for the chaperonage of the girl. It was a relief to find that she prefers to remain below in her cabin. Otherwise I might have had my hands full. The first few days she did stroll about a bit. I was rather busy, of course, and trusted that no one would be immediately aware that the girl was not properly chaperoned."

"Hmmm," thought Charles to himself, "you certainly didn't chaperone her properly; in fact, she has been in a vulnerable position ever since she got on board!" The thought made him realize for one moment his part in making the poor girl feel even more vulnerable; he should also feel guilty.

Aloud he said: "Well, Captain, you have certainly piqued my curiosity. I'd like to see if the girl is as pretty as you say, though I must confess that I have very little time, and I would not want to impose upon you. Does she ever dine with you?" The question was loaded, for Charles knew full well that the girl had never appeared at the captain's table. "Very smart of the captain," he thought, "so as not to draw undue attention to the girl."

"No, but perhaps before the trip is over you shall have the pleasure of meeting her at my table. I plan to invite her there the last evening at sea. You yourself are invited as of now, monsieur, to dine at Miss González's side, in fact."

Charles choked on his port. Quickly regaining his lost composure, he replied in a steady voice. "That is, indeed, generous of you, monsieur. I accept the invitation with pleasure, and I promise to behave myself perfectly with your ward." Here Charles forced a twinkle to his eyes so as to give the impression that he took the whole conversation lightly. "Even if she is as gorgeous and irresistible as you say! And now, though this conversation has been very entertaining, I beg your leave. I realize that your duties, including those of 'chaperone'"—and Charles's eyes sparkled mischievously again—"must indeed tax your strength. Good night, sir." He rose to leave.

The captain rose simultaneously, smiling at the unexpectedly pleasant mien of his passenger and guest. He had heard so much about this bold adventurer, but actually the man was pleasant and unassuming. The captain extended his hand in a hearty handshake, then allowed Charles to pass through the narrow door into the long corridor.

Once alone in his cabin, Charles let himself fall limply into the cabin's one chair to ponder the startling information he had come upon.

As the importance of his unforeseen discovery sank into his mind, it suddenly made blood thunder in his ears and sear his face. He felt a numbness enveloping him, deadening all sensibilities except the bitter taste of hate.

González! The hated name that brought blood into his eyes! The family that had destroyed his helpless mother, even though she, too, had been a González, deserving therefore of all their pity and mercy.

How he despised them! Every one of them. Now he hated this wretched girl, too—if she really was a member of that family. She probably was, he thought, disappointed and strangely thrilled at the same time. The Isthmus was small, and though González was a common Spanish name, his father had told him once that it was not particularly common in Panama.

Well, it made sense that the girl was a González. Even her coloring fit the description his father had given him of Lucinda González, his own mother. Besides, blondes were not numerous in the population of dark-skinned peoples that abounded in Panama.

Charles was now reluctant to admit to himself that only a few hours before the girl had fascinated him. Now he loathed what she represented. Still, he made an effort not to make hasty conclusions about her identity, although he was determined to verify his strong suspicions.

For the remainder of the trip Charles avoided Helena. If he noticed her, he pretended not to see her and continued in the opposite direction. It was too soon to have a confrontation yet. Nothing was to be gained by it now, and he was repelled by her beauty in a strange and painful way.

She, too, avoided meeting him or even seeing him, but her reasons were different from his.

Chapter IV

In the few days that followed, Helena remained mostly in her cabin, although the now even warmer air below stifled her in spite of the open porthole.

She made many excuses for seeking the solitude of her cabin, but deep in her mind she knew that she was simply afraid of the indefinable emotions that Charles Terny might arouse in her if they should have another encounter. She did not know how to interpret her brazen concern with the man, and she was puzzled, too, by her attraction to the reassuring strength of his maleness and, in contradiction, the jealousy she felt for his apparently limitless self-confidence. He seemed so implacably self-assured, and she felt so small and lost.

The few times she ventured out to feel the freedom of the Caribbean breezes on her face, on days when the sun did not beat down on the ship with sultry insistence, she did not meet the dreaded man. Once or twice she saw him pass fleetingly at the end of one of the corridors, but he never saw her. Her sigh of relief each time, however, was mingled with a curious emotion she would not admit as disappointment. She harbored the feeling that something had been left unfinished.

Still, her more sober thoughts dwelled on her plans for setting some order to her new life in Panama. Where would she live once she arrived in Panama City? Helena wondered. The unpretentious chalet of stone and mortar inherited from Burland Jones seemed more like her home. Mama would not be there, however, and she was afraid of the loneliness that she sensed might have taken over the once cozy atmosphere. Nevertheless, she was reluctant to live with Uncle Benito just yet, and the little house seemed the most likely place to stay. Of course, she would have the proper chaperones. She had had enough of being completely on her own among strangers.

She would live in the chalet in Panama, right outside the walled part of the city. It was not the most elegant neighborhood, but it was near the Santa Ana church and its lovely park, and close enough to the inner city to be acceptable esthetically. Besides, she loved the house and that was a good enough argument for wanting to stay in it.

Still, Helena could not deny that another, more powerful reason played a role in her determination to remain in the chalet—her desire for independence. She had craved it for as long as she could remember.

Somehow the idea of being her own boss excited and thrilled her, in spite of the doubts and uncertainties that assailed her. When independence seemed too close at hand, as it had on the ship so far, it became an uncomfortable reality. Independence meant making so many decisions—alone. It was exasperating, for, notwithstanding the burden of such responsibilities, the pleasures could be so rewarding, she was sure, and that made it difficult to know exactly which she wanted—independence or security.

Lost in her thoughts and reveries, looking seaward, Helena grasped the railing with her slender hands and leaned her body against her outstretched and taut arms, cutting a lonely figure.

The unexpected breeze of the afternoon drove away the clouds, exposing the last hot rays of the sun, and it did not rain after all. The humidity that remained was worse than if the sun had shone brightly. Helena wiped her brow where beads of sweat had already formed. It got so hot in this part of the world! She would go below; on the way she would leave instructions with the steward to bring her food to her cabin in order to avoid once more the stuffy atmosphere of steaming food and sweating bodies in the dining hall.

A few people were still strolling about casually on deck. Her eyes sought the figure of Charles Terny in his customary white shirt. The shirt was no more than an ancient design of the peasants, yet it looked so dashing, so masculine, with a twist of tenderness and softness about it that was very appealing. On Charles Terny the loose opening at the neck had revealed wispy brown and golden curls of hair that contrasted shockingly with her own silky smooth and rosy breasts. And he was so deeply tanned, this Charles Terny. Except for his elegant features, he could pass for a native from the Isthmus. The deep tan of his skin acted as the perfect foil to the dazzling white of his insolent grin. His wide shoulders had loomed magnificently above her, threatening ominously to overpower her. His eyes were piercing in the intensity of their light; but she remembered them darkening when he'd narrowed them at her.

As she caught herself daydreaming in this fashion, Helena shook her head and told herself how foolish she was. What experience did she have with men? Her absolute lack of it was probably why she found him exciting and different. He was the first man she ever remembered even touching her in the slightest way, except for Uncle Benito and Burland Jones, of course. She had no way of comparing him to other men of his age. And yet, even during the gambling after dinner, she had noticed him above the others instantly, almost as if she had known him or seen him before in her life, an extremely remote possibility. Helena chided herself again, admitting reluctantly that she would probably be drawn to the subject again anyway.

The last evening out at sea the captain invited a few distinguished members among the passengers, including the charming "Englishman" who had presented him earlier with the delightful tobacco, to sit at his table.

Though Charles was prepared for the seating plan,

the same could not be said for Helena. She had entered the dining room first, and had been seated to the right of a nearly deaf gentleman, when Charles Terny approached the table. There had been no name card at his place setting, a detail he had taken care of easily about a half hour before the dinner was served.

Even before Helena had a chance to realize that he was there, she had begun to feel misgivings about her acceptance of the captain's invitation. Now, looking up at the gentleman who was preparing to seat himself on her right, she was overcome by a wave of dismay and surprise.

But her good breeding and her courteous upbringing did not allow her embarrassment, when she was confronted by Charles Terny, to be expressed other than as a deep crimson blush.

Terny murmured greetings to everyone at the table and bowed slightly as he did so. Then turning toward Helena as he sat down, he said very distinctly, "Good evening, Miss González."

She replied with a flash of astonishment in her black eyes at his audacity. He had dared to investigate her and look up her name. Or had he simply read her place card?

She determined quickly not to satisfy his curiosity one iota more by giving him any further information about herself. She would just let him stew in his ill-gotten misinformation! At the same time a flurry of indignation flooded her as she wondered if the captain had told Terny anything personal about her. It was hard to believe that the seating arrangement tonight was a mere coincidence. She had been appalled at the lightness with which the captain had overseen to her safety during the trip and realized that the man did not take his duties as chaperone seriously at all. Her thoughts were in disarray as she realized suddenly how alone she truly was, with no one of substance to make sure that she was respected.

Remembering the manners that the nuns had so patiently instilled in her, however, she nodded civilly and very coldly at Charles Terny.

The dinner was otherwise uneventful. The heat became more intense, and some of the ladies brought out fans which they employed with casual elegance between courses.

"If the weather is warm here, mademoiselle, what can we expect on the tropical soil of Panama, eh?" The rich baritone voice of the man next to her penetrated in spite of her resistance.

"I wouldn't know, monsieur. What is trouble to one person may be pleasure to another. Personally, I find the climate so far just perfect." Her eyes flashed angrily at him. His clouded for an instant as if to absorb the intentions of her unwarranted barb. Then they narrowed in disapproval, and a smirk began to form on his lips.

"You must, of course, find it cool and comfortable. Your clothes seem to be rather on the warm side, I see." His eyes roved insolently over her breasts, his expression shaded from the rest of the people at the table who were busy eating or chatting by now, so that no one was shocked by his cynical treatment of the young lady.

Helena blushed again, realizing that she was at his mercy for the time being. Strangely enough the idea assailed her that her gown must appear plain and puritanical even among the rather dowdily dressed ladies aboard. For heaven's sake! How this man was irritating her! She pretended she had not heard and picked up her wine cup as decisively as she could. It was too hot to drink wine, but she felt the compulsion to do something with her hands. She really should say something to defend herself. But what? Certainly she had never before carried on light conversation with a man—or what should have been light conversation; her words were riddled with inexplicable resentment. Something about Charles Terny disturbed her deeply, and her usually sharp wits were paralyzed.

She was glad when Charles Terny seemed to lose interest in her and turned, instead, to make an announcement to the guests at the captain's table.

"Mesdames et messieurs, Captain Desmoulins has asked me to convey to you his regrets that he will not be able to accompany you at dinner. Troubles of a mechanical nature are keeping him away, but there is nothing to fear concerning the safety of the ship."

This last assertion appeased most of the guests, it seemed, for apart from a murmur in response to the announcement, no one asked any questions.

It was now unbearably stuffy in the dining room, making the guests silent and languid. Helena was grateful for the lack of conversation, for Charles Terny could not annoy her with his sarcasm while the other guests could hear every word. She was glad, too, for the chance to regain her self-control. She was almost sure her nervousness and uncertainty had passed unnoticed.

Unknown to Helena, Charles Terny had noticed every detail of her reaction to him. He was glad when she blushed and dropped her fork, and he celebrated his triumph with a sardonic smile.

Unfortunately he found no occasion to verify her possible family connections or status and could not bring himself to question her outright. Had he done so, their story might have been totally different.

The next morning the sun rose amid tropical hues to welcome the insignificant little ship venturing into the harbor of Colón.

Helena felt flutters of excitement and apprehension. She was still bothered by the insecurity of her position. Without close family on the Isthmus, how would her mother's friends accept her? She sighed, realizing that there was nothing she could do about the situation until she was met by Uncle Benito at the dock. This courtesy was in itself encouraging, for the Gonzálezes could easily have sent someone else, perhaps a trusted servant, and not have bothered with the trip across the Isthmus by train, and with the necessity of making arrangements to wait for her on the Atlantic side, perhaps for days, if the boat was delayed.

She packed her frugal luggage. Though it did not take up much space, it was terribly heavy. Most of her baggage consisted of treasured books and notebooks which she hoped would be companions to her in the days to come. They represented the totality of her possessions acquired during the last four years. The baggage was taken above to where piles of other suit-cases and trunks were waiting. All her pieces were tagged, and then Helena felt free to watch the final docking of the ship.

By now the sky was a very clear blue, marred only by a few delicate clouds that floated aimlessly about. Daylight fell generously on the docking area.

Colón had originally been a swampy islet close to a swampier shore. During the construction of the rail-road, however, it had been filled in to create a decent port facility from which to cart the necessary building materials. Now it made arrival in Panama much easier and more pleasant.

Helena leaned on the ship's railing and looked out at the bustling activity of the port, which was now coming sharply into focus. A few small wooden, box-like buildings served as warehouses and offices for the shipping companies. During the construction of the railroad in the early 1850s this terminal had re-mained isolated and strictly official, but gradually the port had encroached upon the fenced-off areas and now shops could be seen near the actual official buildings. The line actually ran from the dock down Front Street, the only main thoroughfare of Colón; al-though, to avoid confusion and accidents involving the unloading of freight, the passenger terminal had been relocated a few blocks away. This area provided the first glimpse of the real Panama that Helena had caught in four years. A shiver of relief rippled through her. Not much had changed.

Her cotton bonnet covered the golden tendrils of

her hair and shaded her somewhat from the bright morning sun. Though Helena pretended to appear austere and sure of herself, she looked like a prim young maiden waiting for someone to rescue her from her uncertainty. From her incredibly tiny waist billowed the dress she had been saving for the disembarkation. It was a simple cotton dress, following the strictness of the taste she had acquired from her beloved nuns in France and which she had always more naturally favored. A light gray, with a stiffly starched white collar, the dress had long sleeves that covered her arms completely. The stiff white cuffs almost hid her hands, permitting only her long and graceful fingers to show.

At last she could distinguish the faces of those below, and with a sudden start of joy she recognized her host as he stood waiting for her. She waved, forgetting to remain sedate and proper. Her beautiful smile, graced by perfect teeth and one solitary but deep dimple on her left cheek, was answered in kind by the waving gentleman below.

Benito González stood out easily everywhere he went, for he was as massive as the volcano in Chiriquí. His appetite was renowned among the Panamanians both for its size and its discrimination. He ate huge quantities of food, but only of the best, or so he boasted. Doña Alejandra, his wife, asserted on many occasions, however, that though the man ate truly enormous amounts of food, to her mind his reputation for discernment had always been exaggerated. Most of their friends had arrived at that same conclusion, but out of fondness for him, they pretended to be impressed by the gourmet nature he claimed to possess.

Uncle Benito's outline, though immense, contained the inherited distinction of his class and his aristocratic ancestors. The features of his face, although somewhat deformed by the excess weight he carried, were fine and proud. His eyes were light and danced with various shades that blended into green most of the time. When Helena looked into them for the first time after she disembarked, she received a fleeting sensation of déjà vu. But in her joy at seeing his friendly and warm smile she cast the momentary thought away. His hair was light and sandy, though now silvered in places. He stood out prominently in the crowds of dark-skinned Panamanians around him, and many people looked at him with a degree of awe and respect, they knew not why. His imposing figure simply demanded it.

Unknown to Helena a pair of intense eyes, steel-gray now in their turbulence, narrowed as they observed her eager greeting. Charles Terny looked away angrily, turned resolutely on his heel, and sought out one of the stewards who, he knew, was Panamanian. Perhaps the steward would know the identity of the man on the wharf below.

"Sí, señor, I will try to find out for you. I myself am from Colón and do not recognize those from the capital."

As soon as the ship was anchored, the man took off on his mission. He was to find out the relationship of the man to the girl as well. The first few passengers began to stream down the gentle slope of the ramp, and soon they were swarming below on the dock. Charles observed, his eyes like those of an eagle studying his next prey, how Helena González embraced the man of the wide girth with the enthusiasm usually reserved for family. His jaw tightened, and the muscles of his face flexed.

He followed the movements of the heavy yet imposing man as he led the girl toward the commercial area of the dock and signaled to a handsome open carriage, apparently one of the better public vehicles available at the area beyond the immediate docks.

A young, neatly dressed footman, obviously in the escort's employ, lifted the girl's frugal though heavy-looking luggage onto the back of the coach where a platform had been installed for that purpose. Just as the obese man was helping Helena González climb into the carriage, Charles felt a tug at his sleeve.

"Excuse me, señor, but you did not hear me call to you," apologized the scrawny steward, who had returned from his errand.

"That's quite all right." Charles waved him aside, impatient for the information.

The dark-skinned Panamanian's brown eyes shone maliciously; he was quite sure of the ideas Mr. Terny had concerning the beautiful blonde.

"She is very beautiful, señor, yes? But if you prefer something a bit more fleshy, heh, heh, nobody around here can accommodate you better than yours truly!"

Charles instinctively suspected that in Colón he could get some terrible disease by just breathing the air. He had always taken precautions with his mistresses, but he was damned if he would fool with the whores of this miserable port town. Maybe in Panama City he would find himself, through the consul there, a discreet woman to assuage his drives.

When Charles Terny did nothing more than grunt dispassionately in answer to the steward's offer, the man shrugged his skinny shoulders and decided that he might as well tell all that he had discovered and get on his way.

"Yes, well," he began and cleared his throat. "The lady is Señorita Helena González, and from what I found out, the man who is here to meet her is a famous lawyer, a Señor Benito González. He is the girl's uncle."

Charles gave the steward an additional tip and turned his attention immediately, and without a word, to the arrangements still under way on the dock.

Helena's pretty but unfashionable skirt billowed about her as she sat in the open carriage. The bonnet could not hide the rebellious curls around her now-smiling and kittenlike face, and the sunlight was caught in them. She was pushing one side of her ample skirt toward her more closely so that her Uncle Benito could fit on the same seat. On the other seat across from them were some of the smaller bundles that formed part of her luggage.

Charles de Thierny leaned heavily against the railing and peered caustically in Helena's direction. He did not see her beauty now, however, or the grace with which she moved her arms.

His thoughts were focused on another beautiful face that he had dreamed about for many years, that of his mother. He imagined that gentle and lovely face warped and distorted by the gruesome mental anguish brought upon her by the cruel and callous selfishness of two men—one of whom was below, enjoying the renewed fondness of his niece.

Benito González had been his mother's brother.

Burning anger continued to possess Charles as the scene unfolded mutely below. His fists clenched on the railing, and his very soul trembled with rekindled hatred.

Perhaps it was a travesty of love which he could not have understood at that moment, but for some reason the hatred he had been feeding and preserving stubbornly all these years now came to focus, not only upon his wicked uncle, but upon the golden-haired figure of the innocent girl below on the dock. And because he had felt strong physical attraction for her, a subtle shame at his foolish weakness nurtured the hatred he was feeling now, and it doubled in its intensity. All merciful thoughts about Helena were wiped out in that bitter moment. He would get his revenge after all. Now he knew what he would do. . . .

Chapter V

A frown marred the usual silkiness of Helena's forehead as she bent over the papers on her mother's desk. Again and again she had gone over the books and the bills which, upon her mother's death, had fallen to her.

There was no other inheritance for her, it appeared.

As she studied the papers once again, Helena came to the conclusion that her mother's dressmaking establishment and the sewing school adjacent to it were on the verge of bankruptcy. No wonder Uncle Benito had seemed so worried about her plans regarding the business. She smiled wanly at the thought that the dear man had been brave to let her discover by herself the harsh realities now facing her. Isn't that what she had wanted all along, and what she had led Uncle Benito to believe? Well, she certainly had all the independence she could possibly handle now!

The train trip to Panama City had provided some very disappointing revelations for Helena. Her mother's business was in bad shape, Uncle Benito had warned her, but he had not volunteered all the details. He had told her, too, that Panama's economic problems appeared insurmountable.

Taxes had been raised unwisely to incredible heights, and inheritance tax was killing many businesses like the one her mother had started. Most schools had been closed down in desperate attempts to save an already depleted treasury. The economic conditions were terrible. Only the French could save them.

Some of the last bills that had been paid before her mother's death held Carmen's signature, which meant, of course, that Mariana's old friend had saved her from total bankruptcy for a while. Tears of gratitude stung Helena's eyes. Carmen must have known that Mariana had stubbornly been sending her last funds to her daughter in France so that her education could continue, yet Carmen had paid bills which she could ill afford. She had been old and sick, and her little boardinghouse could not have been bringing in much money during these last few years of financial instability before her own death.

Benito had left the news of Carmen's death for the day after Helena's arrival. He was afraid even then that Helena might not hold up under the distress of so much misfortune at one time, and he tried to break the news gently. But no amount of gentleness could soothe the stinging pain. Carmen, too, was dead.

The thought of her sadness filled her eyes with tears again, and she wiped one or two hastily away. There was no time now for crying. She had to get on with the business of putting her affairs in order, not only for her own sake, but also for the sake of Rosario Pérez, her mama's faithful friend and business partner, who stood to lose much, too.

Helena recalled the signs of terrible decay and poverty she had seen in Colón. From the ship she had missed the details of the devastating situation of her people. Later, on land, amid the color and shouts of the vendors, there had risen the stench of poverty, and Helena had been deeply shocked by the sight of abject misery. Ragged children and gaunt women had huddled in corners everywhere.

Somehow her years in France had filtered from her memory the once familiar contrasts of Panama, and only images of beautiful sunsets and gulls swooping over the bay had remained with her throughout her stay in France. It had been a harsh awakening to see instead black and lanky buzzards swoop boldly into the streets to pick and fight over the piles of refuse and garbage that were strewn along the muddy gutters. The sight had revolted and depressed her, although she remembered that the ugly birds were a blessing in disguise. They were the unofficial, and sometimes the only, street cleaners of the Isthmian cities of Colón and Panama.

The sight of such poverty and filth had wrenched at her heart and had made her feel guilty for having forgotten them. She wanted desperately to do some-

thing for her people, but what? Perhaps her ideas for
establishing a French school would somehow help,
but the project, which had seemed so glorious to her
in France, seemed pitifully inadequate in the face of
so many overwhelming problems.

Now, at her mother's desk, the rush of memories of
the train ride across the Isthmus fled, and Helena was
confronted once more by the stark reality of her financial situation.

She stared at the bills and, just for a moment or
two, felt a great urge to cry. But she must not let go.
She felt a tide of stubbornness rise within her, and she
jutted out her chin and pouted her lower lip in sudden
determination. She was faced with a serious problem
here, one that threatened to be insurmountable. Never
before had she had to deal with financial problems of
this magnitude. Of course, there was an easy way out
for her, but that would be letting Rosario down miserably. She knew that Uncle Benito and Aunt Alejandra
were sincere in offering to let her stay with them, for
her aunt had greeted her with tears in her eyes and
had begged her to accept their home as hers with the
same generosity with which they had offered her the
use of their name and family connection, for they had
rightly suspected that Helena might have to travel
alone. Being old acquaintances of Captain Desmoulins, who was aware of their power and prestige, they
had been sure he would take his responsibility for Helena's safety and comfort more seriously if he felt she
was their blood relative. Now Helena made them both
promise to wait until she had first attempted to solve
her problems as best she could. She was most reluc-

tant to give up in despair without at least trying to fend for herself. She planned to sell everything she could in order to pay off as many of the debts left by her mother as possible, and then perhaps accept the invitation of the Gonzálezes to come to live with them at their mansion by the bay.

She had been tempted to leave her worries and join the elderly couple in their luxurious surroundings right away, for the González couple was astonishingly wealthy, and the economic depression had affected their life-style very little. Their home, though centrally located in the walled area of the city, faced the city and in the back looked out with a series of terraces onto the sparkling Bay of Panama. Footmen and maids hovered over the couple and their guests to see that their every wish was granted. What a contrast it made with the humble stone cottage that now belonged to Helena and with the misery that reigned in the streets! Helena did not resent the Gonzálezes, however, for they were well known for the many charities they supported. Benito's enterprises were often run at a loss, but he would not think of firing a single one of his workers and did everything he could to stimulate the economy which had been so badly handled by the government.

Amid Helena's financial problems and the ideas she had for solving them was pain, as well, that had to be resolved somehow, pent-up emotions that had to be released. Helena had felt their pressure building up, and all her efforts to control herself and behave in a grown-up and civilized manner had only buried them. Her mother's death, relayed to her from far away, had never seemed final to Helena because distance had made it seem unreal. Now she thought how frail her mama must have been at the end!

A lump of suppressed sorrow and love clogged her breast as she recalled her days by her mother's side, the days when Mariana was always there—frail and delicate—yet always strong enough for Helena to run to for protection from the trivial upsets and heartbreaks a little girl could suffer, and from the loss she had borne at the death of Burland Jones.

Helena tried to put these dolorous memories from her, and allow her more practical nature to take over. It was not easy, however, for Helena's heart was deeply saddened and disturbed, and her little world had been completely and cruelly disrupted by her mother's death.

In her sadness, however, there was no real bitterness, a happy fact attributable perhaps to her generally secure childhood. Except for the deaths of her mother and earlier of Burland Jones, Helena could not recall any truly unhappy or scarring moments in her life, which had been filled with love and during which she had sensed the admiration of those she loved best. Her life later with the nuns in France had been filled with a peace and harmony that contrasted with the insecurities and upheavals of the present.

For a time after her mother's passing away, the spiritual teachings of Helena's faith had failed to comfort her, and she had felt mistrust of and detachment from the nuns and their religion. Fortunately the teachings she had so easily absorbed earlier gradually reasserted themselves, and she began to understand the need for death on this earth. This new understanding provided nevertheless only a small amount of comfort, for she had been on the other side of the world and had not had the consolation of holding her mother's hand close to her as she took her last breath. Her mother had been snatched away as if the hand of God had plucked her up and let her vanish into thin air.

Her thoughts revolved about these tribulations, and also touched upon her own young determination to leave a meaningful mark on this earth, to do something worthwhile to help her country.

Helena gazed absentmindedly about her in the eerie light cast by the oil lamp on her desk and by the rays of the suddenly fading sunlight. The whitewashed walls gleamed bare about her, softened only by the shadows that were cast upon them. Only the rich red tones of the mahogany table and the verdant luxury of tropical plants adorned the room. But it was pleasant, and right now as quiet as a church. The delicious cooking odors that drifted in from the old flagstone kitchen reminded her that Doñita, the cook, was there and that she herself was not alone, although Rosario had left that afternoon, as she did on Fridays, to settle her affairs in her own small cottage where her aging mother and her other spinster sister remained. Thank God for Rosario! She was a jewel of a friend. Without her, Helena mused, none of her plans for enjoying some measure of independence, even if for just a short while, would have been possible. Without a decent and trustworthy chaperone no girl of seventeen could live with respect.

Some months before Helena would have risked her reputation, but the unpleasant incidents on board the ship with that impudent Mr. Terny had left her with a sense of insecurity that she had not felt before. She wished she could forget the man completely, but somehow the memory was taking more time to fade away than she had hoped. Anyway, she felt better having the assurance of Rosario's presence in her home. Good, sweet, and very proper Rosario.

With a hint of a smile Helena pictured Rosario as the little brown seamstress had appeared when she greeted Helena at the door of her mother's modest stone cottage near the Santa Ana Park.

Rosario had remained skinny all of her life, and gave the impression of a restless little bird with a protruding and squacky beak and an energetic way of walking and moving that tired people just from watching her. She was dark skinned and had the tight curly hair that prevailed among the populace of the port cities of the Isthmus. Like those of a true daughter of the Isthmus, her locks rebelled at every effort she made to straighten them.

It was not to her discredit that Rosario tried to conform to the ideal of fair white beauty and silky straight hair shared by most of her compatriots. Though a sizeable portion of the population had inherited rougher, swarthier, even negroid features, the ideal beauty of the culture had nothing to do with them. Secretly, or at least quietly, the masses craved the beauty of the fair and admired and spoiled them, catering to them out of sheer delight.

Rosario was no exception, and she was thoroughly charmed by the blond radiance of her former partner's daughter. She had felt the flattery of being loved by Helena before she left, still a young girl, and the subsequent tenderness on her part had embellished the memory of the young woman in Rosario's thoughts. So it was that Rosario, her dark and bony arms wide open in greeting, had welcomed her partner's daughter with tears streaming down her prematurely withered cheeks.

"Let me look at you, my darling girl," she had exclaimed, her voice tremulous with emotion. "Oh, my! How proud your mama would have been to see the fine young lady you have become!"

"Tía Rosario, you are much too kind." The two were momentarily locked in a warm embrace. As they separated, their eyes brimming with tears, Helena put her arms on the shoulders of the little seamstress and exclaimed:

"Anyway, you look wonderful yourself. I'm glad to see you. And you really haven't changed a bit, *gracias a Dios*! And thank God, too, that you are with me, Rosario. What would I have done if you, too, had been snatched away from me?"

Before Helena had a chance to break into tears at her own words, Rosario spoke.

"And thank God you have only grown up and not grown different. You are still as sweet and beautiful as ever, only more so. I believe, my dear, that there is no other on the Isthmus that could possibly compare

116

to you. Now, come in, *querida,* and let me help you with your things. My, my, how your poor mama would have been proud to see you."

A little twinge of pain struck Helena as she entered the cool and simple living room. The red mosaic tiles didn't shine as much as they once had, for the years had finally taken their toll on their hard surfaces. But the walls were resplendently white, and the green leafy plants in the corner formed a striking and refreshing tropical bower. The old hammock that had hung across the opposite corner for years and in which she had often sat swinging gently when her mother had company, had disappeared. Only the rusty iron hooks remained, waiting perhaps for someone to buy a sturdy new hammock.

The wicker chairs with the cotton-stuffed cushions remained grouped around a simple mahogany table which Panamanian artisans had manufactured. The wood had not been allowed to dry sufficiently and the table had warped slightly, but it was carefully polished nonetheless and the beautiful tones of the reddish wood caught Helena's eye. She recognized the room and knew she had returned home at last, but in spite of these feelings, the house was too quiet and cold, a tomb of memories. All Rosario's merry and loving words could not erase the fact that this place housed only the remnants of a loving family.

Sadness overcame young Helena, and she yearned to hear the softness of her mother's voice and feel the security and love that she had always received in her mother's arms.

117

Rosario's welcome had aroused in Helena a series of mixed emotions. For a few days she had felt a strange and lonely sadness that she could not shake off. Yet no flood of tears came to release her from her sorrow as slowly she came to the realization that she would never see her mother again.

In her great wisdom Rosario had insisted on making Helena a few gowns, appealing thus to the inbred feminine pleasure of dressing correctly and beautifully, a sure method of distracting her young friend.

"Now, Helena, you know you cannot wear those gowns you had made in France. Your blood has become thick in that cold climate, my dear. You really could faint from those heavy materials. Don't you remember how some of the gringa ladies used to pass out from the heat when they first arrived in this hot place? No, indeed, you must have some white or black-and-white dresses made of the lightest cottons. And no solid black for you either, child. I don't care *what* anyone says!"

Helena laughed gently at Rosario's intense concern, and her own musical voice and cultured accents fell pleasantly on the little seamstress's ears.

"You're right, Rosario, I really do need some clothes. Perhaps you can help me fix up some of mother's things, for I don't think we can afford to buy anything new."

Taking the opportunity Helena decided to discuss the financial straits of the partnership more fully. She realized that Rosario had to be handled carefully, for once she panicked her naturally nervous state made her useless.

"I've been looking over Mother's books, and I know now that she tried to spare you as much trouble as possible, Rosario. She didn't even let me know about some of the financial difficulties the business was in. Apparently she used up Burland's bequest on my schooling long ago, and was practically using all her remaining funds and her earnings to keep me in France. She always had such strong feelings about my being educated abroad."

Rosario knew what had prompted Mariana to send her daughter abroad. She had wanted to avoid, for Helena's sake, the cruel disapproval of the closed society of Panama. Her exceptional beauty would not help her against it. On the contrary, the jealousy of the legitimate world would place Helena in the painful position of aspiring only to being some rich man's mistress. Now, at least, she had grown up away from mockery and disdain; she also had the refinement and education which on the small Isthmus of Panama meant that she could hope for a decent, if not greatly advantageous, marriage. Rosario, having silently approved of Mariana's plans for Helena, had suspected long ago how costly those plans would be.

"Helena, are you trying to tell me that we are broke, my child?"

Helena's sudden blush of embarrassment was all the answer Rosario needed, but instead of the faint-hearted, panic-ridden reaction the young woman had foreseen, Rosario's voice was calm and gentle, devoid of dismay, her slightly nasal tones of the Isthmian dialect soothing Helena.

"We are broke, aren't we? I thought as much, but

119

your mother kept reassuring me that I had nothing to worry about. My part of the money seemed to keep coming in as usual, with very little difference to account for the slowing down of business. I am not blind, my dear, but part of the bargain was that Mariana would handle the accounts. Had I been able to do something about it, I would have insisted on sharing the losses as well as the gains we made in previous years. But how could I say that your mamá was deceiving me? I wouldn't have hurt her for the world, even if it were for her own good. Instead, suspecting the real straits she found herself in, I have been saving half of my income, pretending that life was already miserly with me, so that one day I could help Mariana instead. She was the best person I have ever known, Helena. She always gave of herself, and in the most unselfish way I have ever witnessed, for she suffered much."

"Oh, Rosario, how wonderful you are! I didn't want to tell you either, but I had no choice. We have to sell everything, even the house, just to pay back the debts. If there was anything left over, I planned to give it to you. I, at least, have a place to turn to now, for the Gonzálezes have begged me to go with them until . . ."

The statement remained unfinished, for Helena felt a sudden shame that she should have to look for a suitable marriage partner so as not to be a burden to Uncle Benito and his wife. She had always dreamed of a love match, and the sudden calculations on her part for marriage embarrassed her. If only she were a man, and did not have to depend on the security extended by some total stranger! Rosario broke the short silence.

"Well, let us not dally and talk about things we can do nothing about. Instead, why not plan a wardrobe? It will certainly make me feel better to see you in a proper setting, and in gowns that won't make you ill just from this heat."

Helena had discarded her woolen gowns, but the one cotton dress she wore and aired out at night was beginning to look sadly worn. The humidity did not allow it to dry well enough when she washed the bodice, and its dampness was uncomfortable and made her feel the heat even more.

Both Helena and Rosario had failed to look through all of Mariana's trunks, and now, when they did, they were amazed at the number of unused dresses that had been folded carefully into a large flat wooden case under another chest.

"Why, of course, Helena," exclaimed Rosario, "this is part of the last collection of gowns designed by Mariana before she . . . died. Apparently she forgot to tell me she had brought some of them home to work on a few details. I do remember her telling me that a few had turned out a bit too frilly for some of the young matrons, and she wanted to modify the adornments. How lucky can one get?"

In spite of herself Helena, too, felt a tingle of excitement as she viewed the rainbow of gowns made of the coolest materials. How clever her mother had been to take the latest fashions and modify them for the people and the climate.

A startlingly beautiful pale-green gown attracted her attention, and she and Rosario took it out to try it on Helena. Only some stitching at the waist would be needed when once again Helena felt comfortable wearing colors. For the time being, however, she would have to seek the lightest shades of black and gray or the black-and-white patterns that were popular. One smart though simple gown seemed to fit the need perfectly. Of pinstriped cotton, it had an over-skirt that was split down the front and gathered into a delightful bustle at the back of the waist. The slender curves of Helena's long, graceful legs were barely discernible through the front of the underskirt where the stripes ran up and down. A small bodice, also of striped material, was sewn so that the stripes met in a V-shape and formed a peak at the waist, accentuating its smallness. The neckline was also V-shaped. Nestled in the gentle bustle that fell in folds almost to the hemline was a huge red organdy rose with green silk leaves. The effect was stunning, especially when Helena and Rosario discovered a delightful red parasol that matched the rose.

"All we have to do to this one, my dear," exclaimed Rosario, "is to remove the red trimmings and not use them until later. If it were not for what people might say about you, and knowing that your mama would have been as delighted as I am to see you in that pretty gown, I would allow you to wear it with the red trimmings. But . . ."

Rosario did not have to remind Helena of the damage that the vicious tongues of Panamanian society could unleash, especially if the victim were worthy of envy for any reason. And Helena's stunning beauty was indeed worthy of envy.

Therefore Helena wore only the simplest dresses, but from time to time the two women worked on the beautiful, exclusive gowns of lusher shades that Mariana had left behind, the meager but delightful inheritance of her beautiful honey-haired offspring.

Rosario was more than pleased, for she had a natural talent for clothing women according to proportion and coloring. With Helena home, her creativity was aroused. The girl was amazingly well proportioned, with a straight and flexible back that seemed to sprout from the tiniest waist. Her hips were round and firm but small, and her legs were slender but curvacious. Her best asset was her beautiful bosom. Her neck rose proudly and delicately from the whiteness of her throat. Rosario eagerly looked forward to the day when she would design and sew gowns worthy of Helena.

Now, even as Helena sat wondering and worrying about finances which no amount of waiting seemed to solve, she felt some inner feminine security in the knowledge that she looked her best, that her clothes were elegant and well made.

As Helena sat at her desk, her mind flooded by the recent memories of her arrival on the Isthmus, she realized that a month had passed since the boat had left her in Colón. She was still thinking over and considering the possibilities for arranging her business affairs. Soon, perhaps, she would be able to sell the house, the factory rooms and machines, even if at a great loss.

The creditors had been kept at bay because Benito, a well-trusted and respected lawyer, and an immensely wealthy man, had reassured them as far as eventual payment was concerned. Besides, he had begged the creditors to give Helena a bit of time to get over her bewilderment and her sorrow before he could influence her in the right direction.

But it was now time to pay up, and Helena was beginning to feel the tremendous pressures of setting her affairs in order. Only after they were settled could she accept Benito and Doña Alejandra's invitation. They had plans for her, it was clear to see, plans to settle her with some rich relative or friend so that they could claim they had done her a great favor and at the same time not have to put up with her for too long. This bitter interpretation of the Gonzálezes's intentions was not fair, for Helena had absolutely no proof that the Gonzálezes felt anything but tender regard for her. But Helena was experiencing the first bitter moments of her young life, and the emotion was difficult to contain.

Well, at least she had some time before a husband was "found" for her. She could hardly hope to find one immediately, for she was not allowed to attend social gatherings. The period of mourning, though less strict for unmarried women, was still a formality that must be observed, and besides, Helena's young heart was in true mourning anyway.

Outside, the sun had completely disappeared. Helena had not noticed, for a lamp had been lit at her mother's desk and at the entrance, and the pool of light on the papers before her had remained relatively constant. The house lay quiet except for the clanging sounds of a few utensils in the kitchen which reached her ears from time to time.

When Rosario left Friday afternoons to see about her mother and her sister, Helena stayed at home, and the old cook, who still continued with her after years of serving her mother and whom Helena had called "Doñita" as long as she could remember, remained with her.

Doñita was unusually quiet in her kitchen, but the delicious aroma of vegetables and eggs wafted through the air. Helena's hunger reminded her that Rosario would be there for supper any minute now, but she was startled nevertheless by the loud knock at the door.

"I'll get it, Doñita," she shouted in the direction of the kitchen.

Assuming that Rosario might be loaded down with packages and bundles which contained her clothing for the next week, Helena headed quickly for the door, the skirts of her pinstriped dress swishing at her ankles as she went.

"Hummm," she wondered aloud, "Rosario must have come in a public carriage." She could hear the sound of horses snorting and pawing restlessly outside, probably fresh horses, and for a pleasant change, healthy ones, she thought, from their frisky sounds.

Helena quickly undid the chain, unlocked the three small metal bolts, and called, "Just a minute, Rosario."

The door swung open from the outside almost the instant it was unlocked. She saw the dark flash of shadowed men at the door, their figures looming in frightening rapidity toward her. The events that followed remained shattered in her mind in confusing shards of light, as if a kaleidoscope were working black-and-white patterns before her. Their rapid succession paralyzed her.

Her eyes, opened into a dark abyss, remained fixed as Rosario was flung, apparently unconscious, at her feet. For an anguished moment Helena remained as rigid as stone, but some automatic compulsion set her into motion and she cried out as she bent down to help her old friend. She was too late, however, for in that instant and with amazing agility and strength, a pair of arms lifted her away and out of the door.

Before she could scream, Helena found a gag stuffed into her mouth. Her arms were pinned to her sides with a reckless, painful pressure.

The door of a darkened carriage was open, and she was pushed inside and quickly shoved into a corner. The door slammed shut, even as, in a lash of sudden fury, she kicked the man seated before her; but her captor pushed his leg before hers to pin her shins to the area below the seat.

Helena's eyes were wide with fright and indignation. She struggled helplessly against her captors as they pushed her harder into the corner to control her. She found herself looking up at the massive forms of three men whose features she could not distinguish, although the moonlight revealed their light-colored shirts. The acrid smell of burned wood peculiar to peasants rose to her nostrils. In the city, even when folk smelled somewhat of smoke because their clothes were pressed with coal-heated irons, the smell was different, not as pungent, perhaps because it was combined with other odors. Inexplicably, the detail of her abductors' smoky odor seemed to take precedence for a moment over all other thoughts and, as if disembodied, she wondered curiously why these peasants could possibly be doing this to her. It was totally incomprehensible. It had all happened so fast.

They had her completely pinned down now, and though her muscles still strained against their grip, she could not budge an inch.

Suddenly she wanted to scream out—not so much for help as for relief—though the gag threatened to choke her. Her whole body began to shake, but this torture of nerve and flesh gave way as the blessing of unconsciousness spread over her.

Already the carriage was moving swiftly away through the main cobblestoned thoroughfare and on over the unpaved city streets where people were still about, scurrying home before the dangerous hours of the night overtook them.

Chapter VI

When Helena regained consciousness, the carriage was swaying and rocking crazily over huge ruts in the road. It was now completely dark, and she could only hear the terrible creaking of the coach and the pounding of the horses' hooves.

As a surer sense of reality penetrated her brain, she began to take in her surroundings, groping to ascertain her situation.

Her hands had been tied before her so that they rested on her lap. Her position made it difficult for her to hold her balance, even though she was pinned to her seat by the bulk of the man on her left. The gag had been removed, but she made sure that no sound escaped her lips. Let them think I'm still unconscious, she decided.

Suddenly she was aware of the reek of liquor. Memories of violent stories told by the maids at Carmen's pension and in her own mother's kitchen vividly assailed her, and she felt afraid. She knew from these stories that men under the influence of alcohol could be unreasonable and extremely dangerous.

She tried to think why she might have been kidnapped. Perhaps for ransom, but that seemed pointless, too, because surely she was too poor to pay any. She decided that her captors must have made a mistake. What would they do when they discovered their error?

Helena was innocent enough not to worry about any possible abuse carried out on her person. She did consider naively that her pennilessness might incur the wrath of her kidnappers when they discovered it. What terrified her, however, was that then they might leave her, perhaps tied up, to be discovered by the police or to die in the wilderness.

It was too dark in the coach for the men to notice that she was conscious, and no one paid her any heed. Soon the carriage slowed down and finally stopped. The door was pulled open by someone from outside, and the sounds of the stomping and snorting of horses became immediately louder.

Helena was pulled out by a new set of rough, strong arms as her unidentified companions tumbled out hastily from both sides of the vehicle.

Spanish voices echoed in the dark with the accent and nasal qualities of the Isthmians, marked by the hesitancy of speech and limited vocabulary of the Cholos, the Indians from the mountains. This, of course, explained the smoky smell of her captors, for all Indians smelled of smoke.

The speech of one man among the others struck her as being strange, for it was that of a cultured man. His intonation seemed to mark him a foreigner. Yet there was something familiar about the resonant quality of his voice, even though it sounded muffled and slightly slurred. She could not imagine whom it could belong to, however, and quickly put aside her questions to concentrate on her physical predicament.

By now her captors had realized that she was totally conscious, and without giving her warning, one of them picked her up and placed her on the back of a mule, leaving her hands tied. Helena felt hot indignation at the way she was being hauled and shoved about, but from the ease with which her kidnappers handled her, she realized there was no use protesting. She would only leave herself open to verbal abuse and ridicule.

The foreigner gave instructions to the driver of the carriage in a commanding tone. He seemed completely at ease; his attitude was almost flippant.

The driver turned the vehicle around expertly on the narrow gullied road, which was little more than a cow path, and was soon speeding away.

"All right, muchachos," said the man with the cultured accent. "Let's get into camp as quickly as possible. Pablo, you take Miss González directly to my tent and see to it that she does not leave it for any reason."

As Helena heard the name González on the lips of the stranger, sudden recognition flashed through her mind. Of course! This was Charles Terny! Then, as it dawned on her that he had kidnapped her for ransom, she felt a great urge to laugh at the irony of it all. He must have mistaken her for a wealthy González and now assumed that a goodly sum would be paid for her rescue. If he only knew how little he would get! But her small smile of triumph remained unnoticed in the night.

Very soon, however, she was afraid again—terribly afraid—for he would soon realize that she could recognize him, and he might not set her free, even if her captors convinced Uncle Benito to pay her ransom.

Her usual clarity of perception and thought by now had left her, as had her strength of will. She had been through too much in the last few months. Now this new and frightening experience was proving extremely difficult for her to handle.

She began to tremble in spite of her attempts at self-control. Her thoughts were in great disarray. Still, not a single word left her throat. She could think of nothing to say, could make no intelligent protest. So she said nothing.

As soon as Charles Terny gave his order, the horses and mules began to move. Helena could hear the sound of the ocean, which seemed to be getting louder and louder as they progressed down a rocky incline. Vegetation was sparse here, and flat slates of rock covered much of the ground. The beasts had to step gingerly; the pace was slow. It seemed that hours had passed before they reached a sandy beach along which they then made their way. With her hands tied before her Helena found it very difficult to keep her balance atop the mule, but now the movements were even, for the sand was smooth and hard. The tide must have just gone out, leaving the sand wet and packed.

She heard one of the men say to Charles Terny: "Patrón, from now on it's an easy ride. We'll be there in no time at all."

The Indian received a grunt for an answer, a sound that startled Helena, for it no longer seemed to express a single cultured quality of the odious Charles Terny.

Helena still said nothing. She was numb with fatigue, not only from the nerve-racking events of that evening so far, but also because she was not used to riding. As a child she had displayed great talent for riding and jumping—a talent her mother had encouraged; but it had been years since she had been astride a horse.

In spite of the strenuous emotions and the ride which had brought her to the brink of exhaustion, Helena's pride welled up, and she decided that she would disregard Charles Terny as much as possible and not deign to address him at all, especially not to make one sound of complaint. In spite of his good looks and apparent veneer of culture and education, he was little more than a dangerous animal and not worthy even of her disdain.

At last, in the density of the evening sky, several tall black silhouettes appeared. As Helena studied them, she realized that they were buildings. This surprised her, for she had not expected such a spectacular skyline this far out in the bush. Certainly, now that she thought about it, no country village or even city that she knew of boasted such high structures, except per-

haps Panama City with its beautiful cathedral. It was
indeed strange, these edifices so far out in the wilderness. But as they left the beach and reached the first
walls, Helena realized that the buildings were crumbled and in complete decay.

The undergrowth was thick in places and threatened to choke and cover every wall of the ruins. The
lacy tentacles of coconut palms reached down from
the skies, silhouetted even in the darkness, and pure
white sand on the strand below reflected what little
light the slender moon gave. Smaller varieties of
palms filled in every gap they could find as the path
left sandier ground and climbed inward from the
beach.

Helena held on as well as she could, though the
thongs around her hands had already chafed her skin
raw. The dank smell of rot reached her among the
cleaner odors on the breezes from the sea. Some
swampy marsh must be nearby.

The mosquitoes were unbearable, but their bites
only bothered Helena physically and did not frighten
her; there had been some talk that yellow fever was
carried by insects, and not by the rotten breezes such
as she was beginning to scent now. Either way, Helena had nothing to fear, for she had been the victim
of yellow fever when she was ten years old, and luckily she had survived.

Yellow fever was almost always deadly. If a victim
reached the black-vomit stage of the disease, his
chances of survival were very small indeed. She had
been lucky that hers had been a mild case. She barely
remembered the details of her illness except that her

mother had hovered above her day and night, and that as she had regained total consciousness after the high fever, it was her mother's anxious face she had seen first. It had taken long months of convalescence for Helena to regain her strength, but at least now she had the security of knowing herself immune to the dreaded disease.

Helena wondered, but only very vaguely, if Charles Terny would be lucky enough to survive the sicknesses that hit foreigners even more devastatingly than they did the natives. It was not so bad now during the dry season, but the rainy season was another thing.

A new waft of swamp odors assailed her, and her thoughts returned instantly to her surroundings. They were practically under a huge tower that loomed like a menacing giant over the group.

Then it struck her where she was. This had to be Panama Viejo, Old Panama, the ruins of that old colonial city which Henry Morgan, the English pirate, had burned to the ground over two hundred years before. Nobody came here anymore. A new city had been built miles away, and no one had any use for the old ruins. The road that had led to them had fallen into disuse and finally all but disappeared. Only a few daring adventurers and engineers like her father and Burland Jones had camped within the vine-covered walls of these beautiful ruins. Though Helena had heard only vague reports about their existence, they had been enough to interest her in the history of Old Panama so that she had read about its tragic but romantic fate and knew the story well.

It was with Burland Jones that Helena had learned many things about Panama, for though he was a foreigner, he had come to Panama many years before, when the railroad was being constructed, and he had worked as a member of Ran Runnel's vigilante group, which had dedicated itself to eliminating or capturing robbers and bandits who raided the line of construction and the overland route. Consequently Burland knew much more about Panama than her mother, who had been born and raised there, the daughter of a Spanish immigrant and a Colombian girl who had come to the Isthmus with a wealthy branch of her otherwise humble family. Uncle Benito, too, had been instrumental in educating Helena, though much more indirectly than her mother and Burland Jones. Between the two men, Helena had come to know the country from different angles and points of view. Uncle Benito lived the life of the aristocracy, and Burland taught her to appreciate the simpler beauties of the Isthmus, to recognize the various kinds of fruit trees, and to know the geography of her homeland. Even more important she had learned to see the Isthmians and their customs not only from the viewpoint of a compatriot, but also with the more discerning, more objective eye of the foreigner.

Now the horses and the mules pushed through what must have once been a carriage entrance.

In spite of Helena's misery and fear, a little unexpected thrill ran through her as she found herself inside one of the ruined convents or public buildings. Most private houses, she knew, had been burned because they were made mainly of wood, but the cathedral tower and some of the religious and government stone houses had resisted the voracious fires set by the English pirate in his desperate search for gold.

It was with a sense of irony that Helena now viewed these tales of former glory, for Panama was in a pitiful economic state at present and resembled in no way what had once been a splendid jewel of the Spanish dominions.

Her thoughts of history were rudely interrupted, however, by the so-called Pablo, who lifted her from the saddle and set her down brusquely on the ground. Helena felt her legs wobbling under her dress of black-and-white pinstripes. It was one of her cooler and simpler dresses, for the afternoon had been quite hot and it had not rained for days. Now, however, the breezes, cooled by the sea and the night, had penetrated the thin material of her gown, and Helena felt a chill in the middle of her back.

She did not have time to dwell on her physical discomforts, though, as Pablo guided her with surprising politeness to a tent whose outline was barely visible in the dark. The flap was held open for her, and she stepped inside without a word.

Inside, Pablo lit a lantern and placed it on a small wooden cratelike table. His Indian features came into focus, and Helena noticed his *montuno* native shirt on which some fighting cocks had been embroidered. To his left she saw a cot which appeared relatively comfortable, especially as Helena was thoroughly exhausted. The floor of the tent had been covered with reed and rope mats. The air inside was still warm from the earlier heat of the day, but the opened flap let in a cool draft.

Pablo motioned to the cot, and assuming he meant it was for her use, she sat on the edge, her hands still tied before her. Without warning the Cholo Indian unsheathed from an embossed natural-color leather scabbard that hung at his side, a short wicked-looking machete, the Isthmian equivalent of a hunting knife, and came closer. The weapon glinted ominously in the soft light of the kerosene lantern. Helena shut her eyes tightly and braced herself for death. So this was the way it was going to end for her! The Cholo cut the rope which bound her hands, and Helena felt herself slump down on the couch.

The man left immediately and the light from the lantern continued to cast a quiet glow inside. Helena had opened her eyes quickly and now concentrated on the gentle light and refused to faint. Then, somehow, as the minutes drew slowly on, Helena's terrible apprehension began to wear off and her tense muscles relaxed somewhat. The muted chirping of crickets and the noises of the jungle night began to lull her to sleep. What did she have to gain, anyway, by staying awake? She tossed her hair to one side, for most of her simple coiffure had come down. She laid her head at one end of the narrow cot and made herself as comfortable as possible.

She heard the men outside a little distance from her tent as they greeted and talked with those who had stayed behind in the darkened camp. Someone had built a campfire, she understood, but she was too tired to go and look outside. From the men's words and shouts Helena surmised that they were unsaddling their horses and preparing for the night.

Apparently they meant to keep her here in this tent. She looked about her, almost indifferent to what she saw. She wondered if they would be eating supper this late and realized she should be hungry. Yet her stomach felt queasy and unreliable. She found it difficult to concentrate her thoughts on any one subject, even on her own discomfort, and soon she drifted off into a fretful and unsatisfying sleep.

Helena wrinkled her nose. A feather was flying about her face, trying to get into her mouth. She could feel it tickling her cheek and wedging itself between her lips.

She turned her head drowsily, her eyes still closed, and a tired sigh escaped her lips. A warm, almost hot breath of air caressed her throat, and in that state of half-consciousness she imagined seeing the handsome profile of a vaguely familiar figure hovering over her. She could feel gentle fingers on her shoulders and a flurry of touch at her breast, a delicately stirring sensation which was just a passing dream. Or was it?

Her eyes flew open. Charles Terny's fingers were lingering on her mouth, then immediately went over the curves of her bosom, insolently seeking to cup them. Her reflex was to grasp his hand quickly and fling it away.

"What the . . . ?" She sat up instinctively, as fierce as a cornered tigress. Her audacious response surprised her, however, and she sat very still and rigid, waiting for some impossible explanation.

Without answering, Charles Terny bent even more

brazenly to her, his knee on the edge of the cot, and took her lips in a hard, grinding kiss. Helena flayed, slapped, and pelted the shoulders of the swaggering brute before her.

"Come on, Helena," he accused her almost gently, "relax. I can't be gallant if you insist on bruising me so violently."

Charles Terny's voice was slurred, his breath reeking of alcohol, but it was obvious to Helena that he had enough of his wits about him to know what he was doing, and her fury was only augmented by his cruelly ironic remark. Bruising him indeed! As if she could believe that her blows had penetrated the hard layer of skin that covered his seemingly invulnerable muscles.

"Leave me alone!" she hissed, at the same time levering her hands on his chest and shoving hard. Charles's body did not budge, and Helena was overcome with sobs and tears, genuinely frightened now, for she had suddenly realized the extent of her weakness and that of his strength. He was a huge man, towering shamelessly over her, brazen to the core.

"Don't cry, girl. I don't want to hurt you any more than necessary, but I won't abide resistance. I've made up my mind, and I'm in no mood to be thwarted. And anyway, a little coyness and hard-to-get play goes a long way, my dear. . . ."

"Do you honestly believe I'm playing some kind of game?" she whimpered incredulously, as she again swept his long tanned fingers away from her cheeks. His hands just reattached themselves to her shoulder, and though she was angry and sorely tempted to insult him, to spit in his face, some deeper fear made her hesitate. She was trying to feel for the extremes to which she could go in her treatment of the callous blackguard who was abusing her so barbarically. Liquor was thick on his breath, searing her each time his lecherous leer approached her. He was drunk, all right, but not enough to claim all innocence of what he was about.

"Come now, *ma petite*. Too much shyness is not becoming to a woman." His clothing was rumpled, and his shirt was carelessly opened to the waist. None of the handsome male neatness he had displayed on the ship from France remained.

Helena made a grimace of disgust, her upper lip curled to one side in utter disdain. Suddenly he grasped her about the arms and pulled her up strongly and easily, as if she were only a small animal or a rag doll. Helena whimpered a protest, but soon his mouth was on hers, bruising her again with a hard kiss. She moved her face from side to side but had very little success in freeing herself because the brute had swiftly grabbed the back of her hair at the nape and held her in a viselike grip. He forced his tongue into her mouth, ravishing it voraciously.

At last he freed her as vehemently as he had lifted her off the cot, and in shock Helena realized to what extent she was at his mercy. He began feverishly to undo the back buttons of her dress, while she stood rooted to the spot, unable to move. He had almost succeeded in slipping her dress off, when she finally regained her senses and screamed and twisted around to scratch him viciously in the face. But he was too quick for her, and grabbed her hands before she could hurt him.

"Don't fight me, you little minx! I'm going to have you one way or another. You might as well relax."

"Stop it, you . . . you animal! You're a disgusting animal. I hate you!" she screamed at him.

"You hate me, do you? Well, that's just what I want. Exactly the emotion I mean to elicit from all you Gonzálezes sooner or later. You will pay, by God!"

Helena kicked at Charles, but her skirt got in the way of her futile gesture. He laughed at her, and in furious retaliation she spit wildly in his face, even as tears of humiliation, frustration, and fear stung her eyes.

While she wriggled and moved unceasingly, he brought her around to stand against him with her back to his loins. She could feel his hard body against her back and her buttocks where the dress had been released to below the bustle. He pulled her arms behind her and nudged her forcefully, propelling her toward the cot. All the while she tried to step on his toes and hurt him any way she could.

He threw her recklessly on the cot. Had she been a large woman, the bed might have fallen apart with the force of her fall, which knocked the breath out of her. Her attacker whipped out a piece of rope, and before she could regain her balance, he lashed it several times around her wrists, tying her hands once more.

His steely eyes, reddened and wild from drinking, glowered down at her in the light of the lantern. Before she could scream again, his hot heavy breath seared her mouth. At the same time he managed to grab the shoulders of her dress and, with one violent jerk, tore it off, leaving her bosom bare.

Helena's bewilderment was such that she lay still for a moment before beginning her useless struggle once again. Her hands were tightly tied and the skirt of her dress tangled her legs so that they were totally ineffective weapons.

Horror filled her finally, horror such as she had never before imagined even in the worst nightmares of her youth.

Had the man gone completely mad?

Her body began to tremble uncontrollably, and finally, as his lips stopped painfully crushing her tender mouth, she started to scream, to let out in one abandoned expression the pain and humiliation she was feeling. Even this outlet was denied her, however, for before she could inhale deeply, Charles Terny placed a gag in her mouth and began undressing her hastily with a determined expression on his face. He even took off her buttoned shoes, shoving her down each time she tried to get up or take the gag out of her mouth.

Helena's chest began to heave. She felt she would never get enough air.

Then Charles Terny stood up before her, blocking out the light of the lamp with his towering height.

The violent look of lust which he directed at his naked blond victim chilled her even though she was not completely sure, in her great inexperience, exactly what he would do to her. She sensed that it would be something savage, something to do with her most intimate self.

He whipped a cord off the crate table and tied it around the narrow cot so that it pinned her down. Her hands were still tied and lay helplessly on her smooth abdomen.

A horrible heaviness invaded the pit of her stomach, a fear that made her want to retch. She had not eaten in many hours; only an acid and burning bile rose into her throat.

She stopped struggling. Her blood ran cold, then hot, and she felt as she had in girlhood nightmares, that running and running would get her nowhere.

Then, amid the shadows and shafts of light inside the tent, Charles Terny deliberately took off his own clothes, all the while keeping his bloodshot eyes on the girl.

Helena also, for some incomprehensible reason, could not take her eyes off him. Her eyes remained immense and dark, fixed with fear and apprehension. She could not move. She felt apart from her body which lay so disgracefully in the view of this strange man whose hate could carry him to such unwarranted and unbelievable extremes. Helena did not bother to wonder why he loathed her so strongly.

The muscles of his shoulders glistened from the fine film of sweat he had worked up in his attack. Then he flung his boots in a corner and stepped out of his riding breeches.

Helena closed her eyes tightly. She had never before

seen a naked man and overwhelming shame invaded her at her momentary fascination at the unabashed brutality of his revelation as his organ sprang from his loins.

Suddenly he straddled her. As his heated length brushed her thighs, Helena was sure that he had branded her with a hot iron. Then callously, in his perfect but slurred French, he suggested: "If you don't struggle, it won't hurt as much."

All this time Helena cursed the gag in her mouth, for she could make no defense at all—not even with words to plead with this madman, might he rot in hell!

Suddenly his lips, reeking with the smell of liquor, were seeking places in her neck and bosom that no man had ever dared to touch. She felt repulsed by his shameful abuse and arched her back in frustration, though her movements were limited by the rope that pinned her to the cot.

Still he kept on, humiliating her beyond endurance. Helena thought she would die. If only she could faint. She could not withstand this mental torture, for physically Charles Terny was actually no longer hurting her.

Then his mouth moved down, roving over her abdomen and finding the silken muscles of her thighs. Helena kicked up her knee in a gesture of protection and hit the side of his head.

Enraged, Terny made a snarling sound as if to signal that he was now determined to abide no more resistance on her part. With his bare hands, his muscles bulging, he snapped the cord that held Helena to the cot and pushed her onto the floor.

Helena found herself rolling, her hands and wrists still bound, on the mat of rushes that covered the ground inside the tent and under which the edges of the tent were tucked so as to keep out crawling animals.

As she lay battered and sprawled, still at last, she gasped to catch the breath that the sudden fall had shaken from her. The gag had slipped but she could not scream. Only futile gasps escaped from her mouth.

The air all around her appeared diffused with lights and shadows that leered at her obscenely and tormented her. She heard sounds of anguish and fear which were her own, though they seemed to come to her from a great distance.

Suddenly Charles Terny was upon her, shutting out all traces of light and thrusting only darkness before her.

She struggled, more feebly now, her eyes clenched tight to abet her strength.

His hands reached her thighs and pulled them determinedly apart. She had no strength left to close them in protection against his entry, and he mounted her swiftly. He found his mark, and she went limp with pain after the first excruciating moment.

The roughness of the mat below seared her delicate skin, tearing fiercely and treacherously into her from behind at the same time that her assailant thrust himself into her body and possessed her with all the desperate cruelty of his revenge.

Chapter VII

Daylight had come. Birds were chirping innocently outside in the already warm air of the camp at Panama Viejo.

The smell of acrid wood-smoke and brewing coffee drifted through the balmy air and overpowered the odors of the nearby swamp and the sea.

Helena groaned on the cot inside the tent. Her eyes opened suddenly as she arrived, it seemed, from a long distance away to find that light had diffused through the tent.

Her body ached everywhere, and she felt as it must feel to have endured the tortures of fire. She felt sticky from the dirt and sweat all over her body, and she had a momentary impression that the heat of the tropics had scorched the skin of her back. She raised her hand to her head and was almost astonished to be able to do so. Her hands had been untied, at least.

She lay on the cot for a long time, closing her eyes for fear of seeing objects which would remind her even more painfully of the unspeakable horror and degradation of the previous night.

When she opened her eyes again, her gaze fell upon the heap formed by her badly torn dress, near the foot of the cot. She felt a sudden urge to clothe her body.

She stood up staggering from the cot and realized the full extent of her nakedness and soreness. Her head spun dizzily, but she managed to remain on her feet. She took a step in the direction of her clothes.

A violent jerk of the tent flap made her raise her eyes that were smarting with tears of frustration at her own helplessness, she who had once been known as the fearless tomboy with the will of iron.

A pair of glinting hard eyes, eyes of steely gray, met her own-shadowed liquid eyes.

An irrepressible sense of shame and anger overpowered her and left her trembling with an emotion she could only recognize as intense hatred—the hatred of the weak and vanquished before the violent and powerful.

Helena stared at Charles Terny, her hands instinctively covering her bosom.

Curiously, though, she was past all petty fear now, for she preferred death to the torture she had endured. She was too tired for fear, too tired to struggle against the brutality of the man before her. Helena was in a state of shock, beyond emotion. She remained standing quietly, her thoughts suspended, barely breathing, so that she appeared to be a statue made of delicate rosy marble.

With the opening of the flap a shaft of light had penetrated the gloom and had fallen upon the cascading golden hair of the girl standing there, nude and still.

Charles held back a gasp, for the sudden glory of her beauty hit him hard, perhaps as violently as he had taken possession of her body the night before.

Helena's face was dolorously paralyzed. Quiet tears streamed down her cheeks, leaving behind tiny rivulets of smudge and dirt that lent her the defenseless air of a small child. Her long golden hair fell below her waist, tangled and wild in its disarray. Gravity forced down the thick and fine strands of ripened gold, and they tried in vain to protect their mistress from the prying eyes of the man who had so brutally dishonored her. Her body was uncovered, a thing of grace and beauty. Her young breasts were full of the immediate promise of ripeness, and because her protecting hands were small and delicate they failed to hide the youthful upward tilt of the two roses of flesh, provocatively sensual in their salmon hues.

Charles stood still for only a moment, though it seemed an eternity to them both. Then he turned on his heel and went back out, only to reappear almost immediately with a pan of water and a small rag.

Helena was still standing there, her arms covering her breasts. Though she had suffered a personal hell, she still possessed an aura of serenity and beauty. Charles suddenly felt a pang in his chest as an unaccustomed feeling of guilt flooded him.

He approached Helena silently, avoiding her eyes, and knelt to place the pan of water before her, wincing in spite of himself at the sight of the bruises caused by his fingers and of the caked blood that had tainted the whiteness of her thighs.

As he rose to leave so that she could wash herself in private, he barely had time to catch her crumpling body. Helena had fainted.

The darkness that enveloped her was sweet. Her mother's gentle face looked lovingly at her, singing a lullaby and refreshing her body with delicately scented towels. Mama! Mama! Why did you leave me? There was no direct answer, but still the face smiled and cooed at her, loving her from beyond life, reassuring her that things would work out. No they cannot, Mama. They cannot work out. I see no solution. Everything is ruined. . . .

At last a few rays of light penetrated her mind which was closed in protection from the conscious world. Hazy and later unremembered images floated in and out, until finally, after a dreamlike effort, her eyes fluttered open. She saw that she was again lying on the canvas cot. Her hair had been arranged and combed completely behind and above her so that it flowed like a stream to the floor.

She smelled some sort of alcohol rub, of bay leaves, she thought, and knew that someone had cleansed her and had laid her carefully on the bed so that she could rest comfortably.

She lifted the muslin sheet that covered her body and saw that her bloodstained legs had been wiped.

The embarrassment of having been exposed so rigorously to the scrutiny of ministering foreign eyes made blood rise scarlet to her face, where it stung and threatened to bring tears of rage and self-pity to her eyes again. But what was the use of crying now?

She lay immobile for a long time after re-covering herself with the clean sheet. She tried to concentrate on little things, for the crime that had been perpetrated on her she could not endure to think of. She listened to the chirping of the birds and the croaking of the frogs. There were other strange sounds, too, which she did not recognize—cries of the jungle animals which were new to her. She had been gone too long from Panama. She heard the roar of the ocean, the swelling and the crashing of waves upon the sands. Salt was in the air, and the stimulating faint smells of iodine and tropical ocean life.

The iodine, the faraway smell of decay, these she remembered from her childhood. Curiously, she had missed these odors intensely when she had arrived in France. Their memory had somehow intensified her longing for her homeland, and these smells of the sea had remained to her the symbol of home ever since. In France the mountains had introduced her to another physical reality which she had also come to admire, but always deep within her had remained the lingering nostalgia she had first felt for the sea of the tropics, its beauty and its immensity, its rhythmic beckoning and mystery, and its lure of freedom and open space.

Helena turned her head suddenly, hearing voices near the tent. She recognized bitterly the tone of Charles Terny's deep voice. Without warning he swiftly stepped inside, filling the tent with his presence. He blocked out so much light that his face remained in the shadows for a while. His legs were apart and his hands were on his hips in a gesture of grandiose defiance and menace.

His white shirt was billowed like the peasant blouses of France and the collar formed a V-line on his chest. His shoulders were square. Helena remembered in spite of herself how she had once, it seemed so long ago, fallen into his chest and felt the towering masculinity of his formidable build.

Charles Terny looked like a pirate standing there glowering at her. She could sense more than see the expression on his face as he scowled angrily. All he needed was a slashing wicked scar, but even without it, she had the sudden thought that perhaps it was Henry Morgan come back to life who stood there, with his boots and his pants outlining the muscles that she knew bulged beneath the tropical cloth. How she hated him! No wonder the Spanish had sworn revenge on Henry Morgan, for like the Golden City of long ago, she, too, had been scourged, brutalized, and, as far as her society was concerned, dishonored and destroyed.

A sense of betrayal engulfed her. She had suffered so much unwarranted cruelty. How could God let this evil thing happen to her? She had a vision of complete desolation before her. The image of a sweet and caring God that she had nurtured in her school days at the convent in France was so cruelly shattered that she momentarily forgot all the other lessons which her religion had also taught.

Along with the humiliation of being sexually possessed against her will, was that of having failed miserably in judging the danger to which she was susceptible in everyday life. She had felt too secure and had reached out to grab her measure of independence without thought to public opinion or to the real dangers to which she might expose herself. She had been arrogant enough to think that her good intentions and her exemplary personal life were enough to win her protection against the evils and the passions of others, and it was not so. This cruel deception and disappointment added to the bitterness of her present moments. Everything was wrapped up and interwoven with the violence she had undergone. She only knew that she felt utterly abandoned, and that somehow she was partly to blame.

But worse than all these regrets was the feeling that all was lost for the future. How could she ever again pick up the pieces of her young and torn life in a land that would forever scorn her and cast her aside in shame as though her suffering had been brought about completely by her own doing? She would be better off dead, she thought, and she prayed that she would die. Wrapped in the rush of her gloomy thoughts, she was startled when Charles Terny spoke at last, and was surprised to hear a noticeably soft expression in his voice.

"What am I going to do with you now, young lady?" She winced at his endearment.

"Why don't you use that knife at your side and kill me with it for a start?" She spat the words out in spite of her determination not to address him at all.

His retort in turn was delivered with a barely controlled sneer.

"Oh, but my dear girl, that would defeat the purpose of my revenge! No, I want you alive, very much alive, and a very large embarrassment to your dear family!"

Helena found it difficult to match his sarcasm.

"What did my family ever do to you that you would want to hurt them? Anyway, I haven't got any family! And don't call me or them 'dear'!"

My God! Was that the best she could do? She fumed at her inability to defend herself, even with words.

Charles just laughed low and continued:

"Well, that means that at least we are not really close cousins, dear Miss González, and my revenge won't include any serious incest!"

His thoughts were that Helena must be the daughter of a cousin of his mother's, for she had had only one brother and no sisters. That would make Helena at most his second cousin, close to the González's hearts—especially as his uncle was practically her guardian—and still blood relatives, and close enough in the public's opinion to be able to disgrace or honor the clan according to the events of her life.

"What do you mean? Are you insinuating that we are related? How dare you? Are you mad?"

She had risen on her elbow, and only when Charles Terny's eyes, which were now closer and visible to her, fell on the uncovered column of her neck and her shoulder and on the gleaming mass of golden hair that had fallen to one side, did she hastily cover herself with the sheet and lie back rigidly on the cot. Her face was livid with a crimson blush as she realized that the sheet did little to hide the revealing curves of her slender form.

"No, I'm not a madman, and it's too bad that you must be the one to pay the first penalty. But I intend to see that all of you pay. This is only the first installment. Your family's evil deeds must somehow be cleansed, and only blood can do that now."

"What could my family ever have done to you? My mother died penniless because of her kind and unselfish heart and my father . . ."

Helena's words were cut brutally short. Charles had raised his hand as though to slap her across the face. His voice rasped hoarsely as he tried to control his anger. Helena was taken aback and heard his remarks without speaking, shrinking from his sudden fury.

"I don't care to hear the story of either your mother or your father—and especially your father or whoever of the two it was gave you your name. It's your name I curse, and if it's the last thing I do, I shall see it dragged through the mud. Do you hear? And there is more I have planned as well. Nothing and nobody is going to stop me!"

He glared at her just a moment longer, as if to make sure that all the hatred in his eyes had penetrated deeply into her brain.

Helena was totally bewildered, and she felt a wretched twisting in the pit of her stomach that made her nauseous. She finally found her voice.

"But I'm not a . . ." Her voice trailed off as he turned brusquely away and stalked through the flap of the tent.

Helena could hear the drawing of his breath outside

as he inhaled deeply of the damp and salty air. A short while later Charles Terny returned to her side, looking much more relaxed—as if he had changed his mind about something, and had perhaps made a decision. He began to speak, then paused as Helena continued to stare straight ahead of her. Suddenly she blurted out again:

"You've got to let me explain. I'm not of your family; I can't be."

Charles scowled at her, and although he was again in much the same maddened frame of mind as when he had threatened to slap her, he again thought better of hitting her and clenched his fists by his side instead. By this time he was no longer shocked at his own brutality and his complete loss of control where Helena was concerned. Something about her drove him to these wild lengths and he wasn't sure, but he had an inkling that it was not only because he hated her, but because he was disappointed that he must do so. Of all people, she would have to be a member of that odious clan that had destroyed his mother and stolen his birthright from him. He had been forced to despise her. A doubt about the justice of his method of revenge flickered in his mind, but he found it impossible to allow it to intrude seriously at this stage.

"Save your breath, and don't try to explain anything to me about yourself, because nothing will make any difference. I don't want to hear any more or you will find that your troubles are just beginning. Do you understand? I care nothing for the bitch of your mother nor the son of a whore of your father."

The words cut Helena to the quick. At that moment

she thought she had never hated anyone nor could she ever loathe anyone again with the black intensity that overwhelmed her.

Nevertheless she kept her chin up, and refused to answer him, but her silence let him know not only that she understood exactly what he wanted—to refuse to listen to the truth that might make a difference—but also that she held herself above the lurid insults he had hurled at her. She gazed at him directly with her piercing black eyes, and enjoyed a tiny moment of triumph when he averted his own.

As for Charles, he sensed that he could never acknowledge a mistake as grave as the one that Helena seemed about to voice, but the incipient doubt brushed only lightly over his thoughts. Stubbornly, in self-deception, he refused to hear what she might cry out to him.

"Look, there is no use pretending you don't hear me. I know you feel pretty wretched, but maybe from now on you will obey my will without question and not have to suffer needless violence. Last night . . . well, I had to get drunk to go through with it. . . . I probably hurt you as I had not intended to do. But now you know, anyway, that what I want, I will get. Save your breath and don't get hurt. It's very easy. Just do what I say.

"And now I'm saying that you will have something to eat. The boys are cooking up a decent *sancocho*, and when Pablo brings you the broth and some of the vegetables, I want you to eat all you can. We're breaking camp and moving along sometime soon, I suspect.

You're going to need your strength again. I'll also be giving you quinine."

At the flicker of fear in Helena's eyes he hastened to explain: "It's to protect you against malaria. And you'd better pray that you don't get yellow fever! I cannot help you with that."

Helena hid her suddenly sly look. Let *him* worry about getting yellow fever himself!

"I brought you some clothes—no frilly skirts, please."

He had laid a bundle on the crate table when he first came in, and now, without another word, he strode out of the tent.

Helena lay defiantly in her cot and made no move to get dressed.

A short time later the Indian Pablo came into the tent carrying a deep tin plate. The vapors from the food made Helena realize how hungry she really was. As soon as the Cholo left, she wrapped the muslin sheet around her tightly, and stepped over to the desk. With the wooden spoon by the dish, she ate every morsel. She wanted to die, but a slow death by starvation seemed self-defeating and degrading.

She got back into the cot without even touching the bundle of clothes. Before she could think much further, a lassitude had crept into her system, and she was asleep, as if she had been given an herb. Whatever the reason for her sudden relaxation, it did her wonders, for when she awakened she felt much more invigorated, almost like her old self again. Only when she moved was she aware that her body was still sore and that the inner part of her thighs burned agonizingly.

From outside the tent the strumming of a guitar fell gently on her ears. On a bongo someone beat softly the rhythms of the Isthmus, a syncopation that invited feet to dance during gayer and happier seasons.

She suddenly wanted to escape the enclosure of the tent, even if only to see the location of the camp. As she undid the bundle of clothes that Charles had left on the table, she realized that it was men's wear he had brought her, a combination of European and native attire. The pants had simply been cut for the length of her legs, and a short length of rope—too short to hang herself, she thought fleetingly—was to be the belt to hold her pants around her small waist. The shirt was of rough linen, much like Pablo's native one, except that the embroidery was simpler and more geometric. Rough leather sandals finished the outfit. Her feet were tiny, and Helena wondered if the slippers hadn't belonged to a child. They were much too small for the flat feet of the country women and they certainly could not accommodate those of the men.

She opened the flap and was greeted by a brilliant sunset such as she had never seen before. The sky was ablaze with intense hues of pink and gold. A refreshing breeze was rushing in from the sea, flirting wildly with the leaves on the huge banyan trees nearby and making them flutter in response.

The camp was surrounded on three sides by decaying stone walls in whose craggy surfaces grew myriads of vines and weeds. In some places the stones were barely visible. Even the once-magnificent church tower with its gaping holes was covered in twisted green tendrils of jungle vines.

Helena took a deep breath and remained quietly unnoticed for a few seconds. Charles saw her, however, and rising from the large stone on which he had been sitting as he listened to the music, came in her direction. She scowled as he approached her, but he pretended not to notice her aggressiveness or disdain.

The delicacy of her bone structure, the porcelain fragility of her flawless skin, fully disclosed in the mellowing sunlight, only angered Charles, for they contrasted sharply with the strength and hardness of his own fierce brutality and brought to mind the valid grounds that existed, and which he refused to consciously acknowledge, for genuine remorse.

The somewhat confusedly recalled violence he had unleashed the night before on a very inferior adversary mortified him, for somehow in his prideful intentions and plans to dishonor Helena González, he had never assumed he would meet such ferocious resistance as she had returned. For the first time in his life he had had to force a woman to surrender her body to him, and his swaggering self-esteem had thereby been dealt a stinging blow. Coupled with the humiliation that plagued him, was his determination to loathe his victim. Yet, some other uncomfortable emotion kept rising within him, too. Though he was incapable of consciously recognizing its nature because of the hatred and pride boiling within him, he indirectly acknowledged that difficult-to-concede shame and remorse by deciding that he'd be damned before allowing Helena to suspect that he wasn't for a moment doing anything but what he had cold-bloodedly planned. He was determined, precisely because of his loss of control the night before, to show Helena a man in supreme command of his actions.

His tactic was to pretend a lightheartedness and blasé self-confidence he was far from feeling. He unfurled from the deepest recesses of his personality all the calculated gestures and mannerisms his war and espionage training had instilled in him, banking on them and his enemy's youth to hide his sullen bitterness and the remote silence of his guilt.

Had Helena been able to see beyond the cool composed exterior of the man, she would have been shocked indeed by the turbulence of hatred and confusion he was suffering, but because she did not know him very well, she failed to detect the tension in his stance and voice.

"I see you caught a little nap. It has done wonders for you. I must admit I didn't think you would grace these horrible clothes so beautifully. Come join us by the fire. The men are brewing coffee again for the guards to drink during the night. When it gets dark we can't let it boil again or the smell of the coffee might give us away. So come and have a hot cup if you like."

The man chatted away as if nothing in the world had ever linked them in intimate violence. Helena was outraged, and simply because she was too astonished at his nonchalant manner, she didn't know how to react to it, so she let herself be guided like a child to sit on the ground in front of the rock that Charles used as a chair.

The ten or twelve men that formed Charles's band

pretended there had been no interruption and kept on playing, listening, some of them smoking. Helena was amazed that they were all Cholos and wondered how Charles had managed to surround himself so wisely. It was known that if one gained the loyalty of Indians, one was protected as if by the gods. By the same token, one disloyal act turned a man into their sworn enemy, to be destroyed in quiet revenge—sometimes when least expected. Everyone knew these things. So she resigned herself immediately to the fact that she could never hope to enlist the aid of Charles's men on her behalf to help her escape.

The sunset lasted almost a half hour longer; its changing colors fascinated Helena and distracted her from the sad fact that she was a prisoner among trees and waters.

The men began to wander off to prepare for the night and to sleep in smaller tents which Helena noticed were not of native materials. Charles had probably provided them, she thought.

Three of the men stayed behind, apparently the first shift of guards.

Without turning her head Helena sensed that Charles, too, had risen and was ready to retire for the night.

"Shall we go, too, Helena? I'm tired, too tired to remain away from my bed any longer, and of course, you can't stay out here alone." He put out his hand to help her stand up.

"I won't be alone," she snapped. "Your men are still here, some of them."

He laughed as one does when a child says something naively funny, though his laughter was tainted with bitterness and ridicule.

"Come, Helena, you don't think I consider them men enough to guard you! Why, it would take six of them at least to hold you down. . . ."

She interrupted him and asked sarcastically:

"So you consider yourself worth six men, do you? Or did you find the extra strength in your liquor last night?"

The mocking laughter in his eyes vanished for only a moment before Charles regained control of himself. At great cost he managed to crinkle his eyes in a poor imitation of a friendly smile while his mouth formed an insolent and rigid grin.

Helena suddenly realized that her abductor's wrath lay just beneath the surface of his momentarily polite veneer, and she was taken aback by the unreasonably fluctuating reactions she was provoking in this man.

Terny began to say something at last, but then apparently thought better of it and simply grabbed her right hand and pulled her up.

"Buenas noches, muchachos." He waved to his three guards. One of the men was already putting out the fire.

"Buenas noches, Patrón," they chorused back.

A couple of lamps had been lit. Pulling Helena along, Charles swooped down and picked up one of the lanterns.

He felt Helena pull back when he opened the flap of the tent, but with a resolute yank he jerked her inside.

"Well, let's see how our sleeping arrangements should be, Helena. I don't want to be selfish and use my cot alone, but on the other hand it doesn't seem quite fair that you should use it all the time either."

Helena stared ahead and said not one word. She had not failed this time to detect the sarcasm in his voice. She felt the dreaded sting of tears at the somehow petty humiliation caused by the needless cruelty of his remarks. Did he believe her so truly stupid that she would not recognize the mockery? And why should she care what he thought of her?

Charles paused only a moment and then chatted on as if he were wholly content to be talking to himself.

"Now, why didn't I think of it before? I happen to have bought two lovely bedrolls in Panama City."

He strode over to the entrance and called out to one of the guards.

"Hey! Jaime! How about bringing me the two new bedrolls over there in Pablo's tent?"

He turned his head, while he waited, to look at Helena, who stood stoically rigid as stone. The girl was stubborn, thought Charles. He reluctantly caught himself admiring her gumption, and turned again to see Jaime coming toward him loaded down with the bedrolls. Charles murmured his thanks, and Jaime returned to his post.

"Yes, indeed," exclaimed Charles enthusiastically. "These will do just fine. This way, my dear, neither one of us will feel offended by not having the cot to sleep on."

He began humming a little French tune as he spread out first one bedroll and then the other.

163

Helena felt a flash of new anger as she noticed how close together he'd laid the mats. Not that there was a huge space in the tent, but there really was no need to place them in contact with each other.

"All right. You lie down quietly, now, and you will be safe tonight." His voice sounded tired and resigned for a moment which Helena thought immediately afterward she had only imagined. Charles clarified himself. "I don't care to repeat any scenes."

Like an automaton, propelled by fear which invaded her again, Helena lay down quietly, with as much dignity as she could muster. She turned on her left side and closed her eyes.

Soon, Charles's body was next to hers. This time he had removed only his shirt. She stifled a scream of protest as she felt him place his arm over her side. Her eyelids fluttered open and fell upon the furry covering of hair on his arms. The white unblemished skin of her own arm where the loose sleeve of her oversized peasant *montuno* shirt had rolled up, gleamed smooth and silky in contrast to the sun-bleached covering of his bronzed arms. Then he cuddled up to her, and she could feel his breath in her hair, near the lobes of her ears that tingled suddenly at the brushing of his lips. She had no doubts that this insulting proximity of his body was meant to frighten and humiliate her further.

She held her own breath, the tension was so great within her, and finally, after an eternity, she relaxed as she realized that Charles Terny had fallen asleep. The lamp was still burning.

Chapter VIII

The days after they left the camp at Panama Viejo followed each other in a blur. The mules trod along at a jagged pace, loaded down with equipment needed to make camp each evening. Helena got the impression that most of the trappings carried by the mules were for the benefit of Charles Terny. The Indians seemed to use little of the paraphernalia.

The sturdy ponies which also formed part of the train were ridden until an edge of foam appeared along the saddles. They were a breed distilled by time from horses that had escaped from the Spanish conquistadores three centuries before and had survived the rigors of the tropics. Some of the men rode bareback, a sure sign of inferior rank. Pablo, stocky, silent, and smoothly brown, rode abreast of Charles more often than not. He was the only one to speak his thoughts at all, for the others remained taciturn to the point of appearing sullen, at least until the evening songs stirred their throats into a symphony of sound. Every evening, before darkness engulfed them in the sudden tentacles of short tropical dusk, the Indians stopped at their instinctive hour to prepare for a new campsite. Every night for a week saw them await the morn at a new spot, much to Helena's unhappiness, for she was emotionally and physically sapped almost beyond endurance. Once or twice she felt the urge to ask what their destination might be, but the occasion to approach the Cholo, Pablo, never arose. She was too exhausted to shape such an opportunity herself, and some secret pride made her unwilling to let Charles Terny witness her curiosity.

After her first impulse to find some miraculous way to escape, she had come to realize how futile those efforts were. The Cholos would certainly never side with *her*.

Another fear discouraged her from running away. There remained the embarrassing threat of dishonor before society. Should she manage to return to Panama City, what would become of her? If she remained hidden away for a while, perhaps her predicament would be forgotten and upon her return, should she return, her uncle would help her rake up a dowry to join the convent in France. Surely no respectable man would accept her as his wife now. Not if she knew her people. The convent would not be bad. She had aspired to reach for its gentle security before. It was not an unpleasant thought. But escape seemed so difficult. The main obstacle, of course, remained her inability to defend herself. If she could only get hold of a gun, or even a sharp knife. But she had nothing. She would just have to wait until the opportunity arose.

Curiously, in her innocent world it never occurred to Helena that she might become pregnant and that the possibility loomed greater the longer she stayed at Charles's side. Somehow his cruel assault had wiped away all thoughts of babies and more gentle things concerned with sex, and though she was not completely ignorant by now, her immediate worries were for her violent loss of virtue and reputation.

She was also bewildered by her sudden awareness that she was weak, vulnerable, not at all the mistress of her destiny as she had previously held it her prerogative to be—hers as much as any man's. She had insisted on independence, on being treated fairly in a world of men. All her growing years she had yearned for what seemed to her the unfair freedom of the male, who, like her own father, could camp and hunt and test his strength against the dangers of nature and man unhampered by the criticism of his peers and family. But Helena had not considered seriously enough the advantages of brute strength. Now there was no consolation for her in fact that the glens and bowers in which they made camp were without exception of unbelievably wild and luxuriant beauty. She was, instead, scornful of the scorching sun and the penetrating noises of the night, the mosquitoes and the snakes, and was not enjoying the challenges of the wilderness at all. What under other circumstances would have been alluring to her and stimulating, only seemed to point out and accentuate to her the weak-

ness of her female sex and the frustrating dominance
of the male creature who had made her a captive.

To make matters worse, her body felt hot, tired, and
sticky from the strenuous exercise of riding the brown
mare she had been assigned. On the fifth day she
managed to overthrow her pride enough to beg her
captor the privilege of a bath whenever it was possible to stop at a stream.

"A bath? Certainly. It's fine with me," assured
Charles Terny. "There is only one stipulation, and that
is, you take a bath only when my men are making up
a new campsite. You cannot hold us back. As you can
well imagine, any delays caused by your presence
would be unwelcome. Anyway, I don't intend to pam-
per and coddle you, my sweet, for it might go to your
pretty little head."

His casual scorn of her, especially after she had broken down and actually asked a favor of him, set her
blood afire with hate, and her thanks was to glare
just as coldly at him. It infuriated her no end when
the low rumble of a mocking laugh escaped him.
Turning on her heel Helena stalked off to sit near the
Indians, who had already begun to hum and warm up
to their tunes.

Nevertheless, in spite of his odious remarks, Helena
noticed that every day after her request, campsites were
made near brooks and pools big enough to wade in
and even near small waterfalls that fell into depths
banked by great mossy boulders. Usually, the hour
being much earlier than Charles would have wished
or chosen for setting up camp, she realized that he

was actually holding his trip to a slower pace than he had planned. Helena felt absolutely no remorse for hampering his pace, and only seemed to hate him the more for this inconsequential sign of gentility.

The first day she bathed, she took a rag and a tiny bar of soap which he had given her of his own accord. She felt almost happy as she wandered into the secluded bower over the babbling brook that was to refresh her. The water ran cool and clear, darkened only by the shadow of the trees and an endless variety of palms that seemed to seek protection under their shade, too. Helena had always loved the wilder plants, and in her childhood had delighted in taking them home and domesticating them. The only trouble with some of them, she had found, was that once their roots took hold, their growth choked away the vestiges of the frailer garden varieties, taking over the available space without scruple. She laughed inwardly as she remembered her mother's admonition that her tomboy's ways were threatening to do the same thing to her—to strangle all signs of domesticated gentility in her. She had always suspected that her mother's wish to send her to France had had in it a bit of the desire to see her daughter tamed and properly reared. "Poor Mama," she thought. "If she could see now, dressed like the most miserable Indian, scratched insolently by jungle plants and bushes, raped and disgraced, at the mercy of a brute without a remnant of decency, escorted against my will to God knows where, unhappy . . ."

169

She stripped and laid her manly clothes on the driest boulder within reach. Then, with one graceful leg poised to feel the coolness of the water, she finally stepped within its ripples and stooped to splash the delightful drops into her face. She was beginning to feel a sudden rush of freedom when a metallic sound made her turn her head to the right and slightly behind her. There on a boulder sat Charles Terny, a rifle near him as he rolled some tobacco into an unusually small cigar wrapped in light-colored paper.

"Just what do you think, monsieur, that I desired your company while I tend to things that should remain private?"

Her voice was hard with anger.

"Now, madame, do not fret, for God's sake. I'm only here to protect you. Do you think I would risk your coming alone into a brook in the middle of the jungle? Even with a gun I might be too late to save your hide if a viper should get to your pretty slender legs. Those boots I lent you are no guarantee that you are safe. Besides, while I'm here guarding you, my men are busy making camp, and I shall be the sole witness to your ablutions. I shan't budge from here, so just enjoy yourself and say the word when you are finished."

What a sassy and smart-tongued cad this man was. And yet there had been a note of protectiveness in the midst of that possessive obnoxiousness. It flashed into her mind that his presence did in a way fill a need for protection—but protection from what? From vipers and spiders and scorpions? Or protection from rape at the hands of other men? Without any knowledge of its history Helena glimpsed for one moment the cruelty, the implied threat, that had stood between men and women since the beginning of time. The price of safety. But the flash of insight left as quickly as it had come, leaving simply a residue of bitterness at her own basic helplessness at the hands of Charles Terny.

Without a further sound she reached for her clothes and put them on over her still wet and gleaming skin. She stepped out of the rocky creek as gracefully as she could in order to maintain a semblance of dignity and slipped on the enormous leather boots that Charles had insisted she wear for protection against the deadly snakes that crawled about on the Isthmus. By the time she reached the camp, the alluring smell of brewing coffee and other delicious food assailed her nostrils, and not even the indecency of Charles Terny blunted the edge of her appetite or of her newfound and newly earned enjoyment of her surroundings after her refreshing bath.

Only when it was time to return to the tent did dread begin to penetrate and dispel her fleeting contentment. Charles Terny had begun to assert himself again some days ago in small ways by right of superior strength, and Helena was frightened by a multitude of hates and strange sensations—and this just as she had begun to think that he would not touch her again after his initial assault in Panama Viejo.

During the last five nights, Charles had not forced himself upon her. During those days Helena had tried to make herself as small and unobtrusive as possible, praying fervently that the madness that had seemed to overtake him would never again return. She ate in silence and withdrew into herself, concentrating on the

impersonal details of her surroundings. She had begun
to hope that the words of revenge which he had spoken had referred exclusively to his assault, and that
this great violation of her rights had sufficed for his
purposes.

His motives continued to puzzle her, but she was
beginning to feel that certainly he must have made a
mistake. Yet she knew very little about her origins and
she had been away from Panama for a long time.
Could her mother have been guilty of some terrible
deed that would call forth this obsession for revenge?
Was it possible that her mother, sweet Mariana, had
once hurt another human so violently that he would
want to pay back in violent kind? It did not seem
probable that such was the case, and yet doubts began to assail Helena, adding to the turmoil and confusion of her soul. It seemed beneath her dignity to ask
Charles Terny point-blank the reason for his revenge.
He did not seem the least interested in clarifying his
motives to her, and anyway, though his words had
been too distorted and vague for her to make sense
out of them, she was not willing to let down the bar-
riers of her deeply hurt pride to engage in conversation with the hardhearted man and discuss the details
and purposes of his "revenge." As far as she was concerned, it was too late anyway.

Whenever the thoughts of her injuries came to
her, and they came often, Helena's eyes glowed with
dark contempt. She redoubled her efforts to show him
her scorn, but the exercise of scowling and narrowing
her eyes at him only succeeded in accentuating the

lilac shadows under her smoldering eyes. This evening of the fifth day, however, more than hate, a nervous flutter of fear began to grip her, as if she sensed again some vicious threat. Oh, God! Don't let him touch me!

As soon as the music had begun, Charles let his eyes that glowed more golden than gray in the firelight linger a long time in the direction of Helena González. She did not raise her own dark eyes to his. Had she done so, she might have found herself confused entirely, for the lust that shone in Charles's gaze was tempered by another light that in her inexperience she would not have easily deciphered; it was a small gleam of admiration.

They retired early to the tent—as usual, at the insistence of her captor. Helena lay down on the bedroll and covered herself with a heavy sheet that had been provided for the night. The evenings were beginning to send warnings of a gentle chill. She had noticed, too, that the group seemed to be always in view of the mountains. Helena had decided that they were heading west, which meant that if they were at the skirts of the mountains already, then the sea was south and the mountain ridges were to the north.

Suddenly, she realized that Charles Terny was stripping off his clothes.

She shivered, and a small feeling of repulsion swept over her. She lay very still and closed her eyes, for he was undressing in plain view, apparently on purpose.

He lay down beside her and firmly rolled her over to him, as he said in a voice grown husky with desire:

173

"I want you, Helena."

He held her to him and then kissed her, relishing the moist and tender mouth beneath his own burning lips. For all their softness, however, Helena's lips did not yield to that kiss.

She opened her eyes to glare at him, but Charles saw no glare. Instead, his glowing eyes, dark with passion, fell into the bottomless pools of Helena's black eyes. Their strange depths so captivated him that he was momentarily confused, and wondered fleetingly just how much of his revenge was an excuse for the sheer taking of his pleasure with this girl. Charles dared not trace any further the sudden doubt that flickered across his mind. He refused to linger on ridiculous self-made accusations, and his mouth roved down to the graceful base of her throat where he uttered and murmured intimate sounds Helena had never heard before.

Motivated by some passionate desire, he raised her up and stood her next to him, perhaps to undress her more efficiently. He eased off her *montuno*. His fingers, now browned intensely from his last few weeks in the tropical sun, ran a gentle line over the healing skin of Helena's back.

A shiver of fear ran up her spine, in defiance of her mind's orders to maintain complete control of her every emotion.

It came as a surprise to hear a distinct note of softness in Charles's voice.

"I forgot about the mat, *ma petite blonde*, that night. I was too drunk to think clearly of your welfare."

Her eyes flinted fire at his words, flames of anger. Her welfare. Bah! But she held her tongue.

He purposefully turned her from him, and pressed his mouth on the already healing welts. Where they fell, a strange and incomprehensible message was relayed to Helena's brain. She felt the compulsion to relax against the hard muscles of his frame, but the thought of succumbing as a child might to the sweetness of a chocolate bonbon shamed her, and she felt, too, the strange element of some primeval fear of surrendering to the enemy.

Charles slid his arm around her slender waist and turned her around to face him, mistaking the blush of shame for a glow of passion. It puzzled him suddenly that she remained limp and unresponding. Helena's own gaze froze upon the cross of brunette hair turned golden by the sun that covered his chest. Somehow, instead of repulsing her, the curling wisp mesmerized her.

Now his lips were finding hollows and pulsating places in the graceful column of her neck.

She groaned in pain, for in spite of the wide-brimmed Panama hat that Charles had placed on her head for the voyage, the merciless rays had somehow burned her tender white skin.

"Forgive me." His words faltered. "I didn't mean . . . I didn't realize that I . . ." The murmured words clumsily escaped him in spite of himself, while he continued to touch her and caress her.

The tenderness of his unintentional remarks was drowned, however, in the irony of the situation, for

Helena had been hurt too much already by her captor.

He pushed her gently down onto the bedroll and slid his mouth over the tips of her breasts. Much to her shame and chagrin, the peaks bristled with some automatic sense of excitement and stood suddenly erect and saucy.

Still, though her body was betraying her, Helena kept her will and checked all nonautonomous responses, holding her muscles in languid disdain and the stare of her eyes straight ahead.

He began to kiss her hair and groped clumsily at the makeshift belt at her waist. She did not help him at all, and lay as passive as a dead fish, limp in his arms. He gave up on her trousers for the time being and simply lifted his head to caress her breasts again.

He found the hollows beneath them and licked them and sucked very gently until he thought he would have to evoke a response. But he was wrong, for Helena continued to lie still, staring into space.

His own rising desires, however, spurred him on, and with amazing newly found agility he slid the trousers off her legs and forced his engorged flesh against the soft mound between her thighs. Helena felt the heat of his phallus and poised herself to resist the pain, but curiously, the hardness did not even burn as it slid inside. Charles enveloped her shoulders in his mighty arms when he felt the warm moisture enclose him, and feeling a terrible and shamefully unexpected tenderness for his victim, he held her even closer before he began the eloquent thrusting and receding of his heated length.

Thousands of thoughts began and raced unfinished through Helena's mind. There was no pain, no pain at all—only a swelling titillation that she could not deny, though she tried. She managed to control, by tightening her buttocks, an almost irresistible urge to match Charles's movements, not realizing, in her great inexperience, that this unwitting caress only heightened the by now raging pleasure of her captor.

When he rolled away from her body with a groan of satisfaction, Helena remained very still. Charles turned toward her, thinking that perhaps she would give him some sign to ease the momentary pang of guilt that he felt. But all he saw were silent tears rolling down her temples.

Suddenly he was angry.

"Holy Virgin, girl, you might as well enjoy it, because I'm going to have you every night for a long time. I told you I want no one to doubt that you have lain with me."

He stood with the agility of a jungle cat and washed himself with the water in the basin which was now left every night on the little crate table.

Then he put on his pants once more and went to sleep, this time without holding Helena in his arms.

Chapter IX

It was a long time before Helena could fall asleep.

The buzzing of jungle insects and the rustling noises of the night formed a backdrop to the thoughts and emotions that whirled about in her mind, and which left her without a single solution to her problems.

The next morning, after a quick breakfast of reboiled yuca, the camp moved on. That night Charles not only took her once more, but let neither her tears nor her total lack of response bother him, it seemed, for he even kept his arms around her shoulder and her waist as he fell asleep.

As she lay meekly under the relaxed weight of his bronzed arm and the muscular leg he had thrown over her own graceful limbs, the dread assaulted Helena that she might not be able to keep up her indifference for as long as she had thought possible.

She tried to conjure up a sense of grimness through which to interpret the images that flashed through her mind in spite of every effort she made to block out Charles's lustful pawings. But the grimness didn't come. Instead she found that a small measure of pleasure infected her memories.

Charles kissing her with lips that suddenly lost their determined line and turned sensuously loose upon her body. His hands, no longer harsh and cruel, exploring places that were beginning to rebel against her forced indifference. The fine and silky texture of his rich brown hair brushing against the tips of her breasts while his mouth lingered on the expanse of her firm young belly. The hard feel of muscle against her legs, and then that other hardness that no longer tormented her physically, but called to her temptingly instead, inviting her to let go her hatreds and partake of his pleasure. But no! She couldn't, she would not.

Wouldn't she then be on his level, approving and rejoicing in the violation of her honor and the scorning of her rights?

And though under no circumstances had his first ravishment forced other than his physical self upon her, this seduction he practiced now threatened to cause the capitulation within her of all the attitudes that Helena considered right and decent.

In anguished frustration she could only accuse herself unfairly. To what depths had she sunk since she had left the protected purity of the convent in France? Closing her eyes from sheer exhaustion, she felt the trickle of tears; but soon, sound asleep, she felt them no longer.

The routine of their travels began again the following day with the packing of the tents immediately after breakfast.

Someone had caught tasty catfish from the stream, and as they fried on a pan over the fire they gave out, along with the mugs of coffee, an enticing aroma.

Soon the train of riders was on its way, beginning to climb the skirts of the mountains where their slopes were gradual and the paths pleasant. The jungle was beginning to lose some of its impenetrability and the open fields were of shorter grasses with edges less sharp than those of the hardy grasses of the more tropical savannahs. Their rate of travel seemed more rapid now that nature allowed them easier passage.

Still, they climbed one hill and small mountain after another. From the summits they could see hundreds of lumpy green hills covered with grasses and scraggly bushes spread beneath them in a vast panorama. Clumps of trees held silent meetings here and there, dark and mysterious, lording their superiority over the vulgar weeds that clung desperately to the poor, thin layer of topsoil. Beds of incipient rivulets and ravines were being hewn by the general erosion of the rounded hills. The red soil, whose eye-catching color signified barrenness to the local tribes that tried in vain from time to time to squeeze from it a crop of corn, peeped brightly through the light green of the tough, sparse grasses.

The evenings were cooler now, and a thin blanket was added to the coarse sheet that had already been provided for Helena. During the day the coolness was not as noticeable except in the fact that Helena, the men, and the beasts did not perspire as freely from their strenuous efforts. More than before Helena felt sure they were heading in a westerly direction.

She knew from her experiences in France that most people thought of the Isthmus as running north to south, when actually it curved in such a manner as to run almost from east to west. This accounted in part for the strange angles at which the sun seemed to rise. It was a puzzling experience to see it rise and set in the Pacific at places along the coast.

She smiled vaguely as she recalled the astonished look of admiration of her classmates and teachers whenever she gave a lecture on some small point of history or geography concerning Panama. Europeans were so prejudiced and ignorant about her Panama that she could not imagine how they could possibly come to it and build a canal, as it was rumored they might soon be doing. They had no idea of the real dangers here, and yet they had the wildest notions about a few threats which they considered very frequent and very terrible and which were, in fact, very rare. One of these (she smiled even more) was the danger of headhunters. How much that story had inflamed the imagination of her friends in the convent in the mountains of central France!

The pace of the caravan through the hills was too fast for Helena, and she felt worn out. She asked the Indian named Pablo, once, when finally she was able to approach him without Charles witnessing their conversation, in what region they were traveling, and he said: "We're almost to Santa Fe."

181

Santa Fe! How far away from civilization and Panama City that was! Nobody but Cholos lived up there in those mountains. What in the world did Charles Terny want to do in Santa Fe?

Helena knew better, however, than to believe Pablo's unqualified statement that Santa Fe was close by. The Indians, as was true of most of the people from the interior of Panama, were notorious for their vague impressions of time and space. A mile was just a stone's throw in their opinion, and a league might be just a little ways down the road. Nevertheless Helena did realize that Panama City had been left far behind by now.

The thought left her desperate, for if she did manage to escape now, it would be almost impossible for her to even find her way back or survive, even if she could perhaps guide herself by the sun. They had traveled so far already! And worse than that, she had absolutely no weapon for protection and survival.

Nevertheless she felt an instinctive obligation to discover all possibilities for escape, and while Charles was seemingly unaware of it, she carried on short but enlightening conversations with Pablo, whose Spanish dialect was pure enough to be understood. A few days later she managed to clarify something that was puzzling her. In a friendly tone she asked:

"Pablo, I know that Santa Fe is very far from Panama City, but it seems to me that we have taken an unusual amount of time to reach even this far. Why is that?"

"Well, now, that is easy to explain," Pablo ventured, pleased that the captive beauty had deigned to address him on a more friendly basis. After all, even if she was white, she was only a woman and not the *patrona,* either, not his master's wife, but a woman like any other in his tribe. Her indifference and then, worse, her arrogance were hard to bear, for neither he nor his men had harmed her. Nor would they dare, he thought sheepishly as the commanding figure of Charles loomed ahead. The man not only radiated power, but was also invaluable to his tribe, for he had promised help in acquiring arms and ammunition for the people of Santa Fe, to hunt and to defend themselves from the scavengers that infested the hills every time there was a new outbreak of hostilities between the Liberal and the Conservative parties. He and his men could not afford to antagonize Terny by molesting his private captive.

"We have had to avoid several areas used for camping by the guerrilla forces of the Liberals and the Conservatives. They have been active in these hills. Though most of them are friendly enough to us they might not be so friendly if they spot two foreigners here among us. *El patrón* gave us orders to avoid all groups, especially any having to do with either of the parties. So you see, we have had to take long detours. Normally we men from Santa Fe make it in half the time or less, and we rest at some of the villages along the way."

Pablo's explanation left Helena even more despondent, for if she tried to run away, there would be the additional danger of marauding bands of hostile and aggressive men. The thought of falling into their hands made her shudder. She was no longer innocent of man's lust and violence. She had no real choice but to remain under the dubious protection of Charles Terny.

So Charles Terny knew that he could use her as his mistress now with great freedom, she thought bitterly. No one in this wilderness, in this sparsely settled interior of Panama, could possibly be interested in aiding a Europeanized child of a foreigner to escape from the man who had deflowered her. Possession was nine tenths of the law and this extended to the possession of females, too. Helena had always sensed the laws of machismo about her, and she suddenly knew that all was lost. She was the complete victim, not only of Charles Terny, but of her fellow countrymen as well.

Her shoulders sagged in sudden dejection. She felt empty and beaten, and her heart cried out in anguished protest at the thought that all this had been caused by her own stubborn insistence on being independent, of living alone and finding her own way in life, that this had happened to her because she had not been willing to fit complacently, humbly, into the mold that had been carved out by the species for all members of her sex. An involuntary sob welled up in her, heaving its way up her throat, humiliating her even more when she almost choked as she tried to hold it back.

That evening she could not eat any supper, and she fell asleep restlessly, her brow somewhat feverish.

As if he sensed her state of anguish and self-reproach, Charles left her alone that night, and the night after that, too. When she wasn't looking in his direction, his eyes would find her, a gleam of admiration creeping into his expression. The girl was brave and didn't give up easily, he thought. Somehow he no longer found satisfaction in making her suffer the humiliation of his forced lovemaking. But immediately he would consider his original hatred and knew he must keep her with him, even if he no longer planned to force her.

Indeed, the next time that he advanced upon her, his intentions had changed to the point that he sought only to raise within her a deep sense of pleasure, and to this end he began a campaign of physical lovemaking designed to melt the hardest woman.

The first night he began by caressing her face, her hair, her ears, almost as one would a beloved child. Then a new note of intensity was introduced and Helena shivered in fearful anticipation of her fall.

His mouth tugged gently at her flesh and roved scandalously unrestrained over gleaming feminine and gentle muscles.

The new tactic of Charles's tongue to search her out became suddenly more frightening to Helena's spirit than the brutal and searing rape of that night in Panama Viejo that now seemed so long ago. This new violation was that of her innermost resources, the sanctity of her willpower, the image of herself; and her body, accursed traitor that it was, was allying itself with this man whose every effort seemed bent on making her scream not with pain but with the indignity of delight.

Charles turned her gently onto her stomach. He pressed her buttocks with his groin, cradling her within the arch of his own body, kissing her nape while she lay in that defenseless position, gently massaging and kneading the dimpled curves just above her well-rounded buttocks with long aristocratic fingers that knew what they were about.

Helena groaned, totally frustrated in her determination to remain aloof. Charles's lips gave her no chance to recover from the accelerated racing of her blood through her veins. He forced her somehow, guiding her expertly, to kneel against his own kneeling body, her legs encased on either side by his own bulging thighs, and while his lips continued to caress her shoulders and her neck, his hands slid tenderly to cup and feel her breasts. Helena closed her eyes, not realizing that the slight slump of her body and the small whimper that escaped from her lips was a clear signal to Charles that her blood was afire. His fingers found their knowing way to the furry mound between her slender legs, touching her in places Helena had never suspected could make her feel outside herself. She was suddenly, irrationally, transported by sheer animal pleasure, by a quickening of physical want, an indescribable ache that could only be assuaged by the ruthless body on which she was leaning.

While her eyes drooped with lust and her mouth slackened to reveal the tips of her teeth, Charles turned her and arranged her slender legs around his body, kissing her on her soft, parted lips, lingering there while his hands continued their wanton roving.

Helena was not aware how, but Charles managed to

penetrate her with his enormous phallus until all else was naught except for the thrilling throbbing within her, the alternate thrusting and withdrawing of his body.

Helena's own body writhed beneath the touches of his hands, his fingers, his mouth, and finally, having lost the battle, she was overcome by spasms of sheer physical release which, if it had been coupled with inner tenderness, would have made her cry for joy.

But her cry was the lament of a wounded dove, a poor dove betrayed and demeaned beyond her spiritual endurance. In the aftermath Charles mistook the plaintive cry for that of the fulfilled woman, not realizing that once more he had alienated Helena's sensitive and generous spirit, that he had not been attuned to her feelings and thoughts. He remained puzzled by the colder distance he sensed, and that night he fell asleep with a touch of bewilderment at her totally indifferent attitude.

Helena, too, had remained inwardly confused, for she was shocked by the intensity of passion deep within her which had been revealed to her this night.

They were beginning to climb the mountains in earnest now, and creeks and rivers cascaded from time to time down to the Pacific.

Helena was saddened at moments as she felt herself fall into a maelstrom of change over which she seemed to have lost control completely. Try as she would, she succumbed to certain emotional waves that emanated from her abductor, and as they trekked into slightly different terrain at the end of the mountain range, she felt dazed, as if she had lost touch with reality.

The horrible temptation she'd experienced one night as they camped later than usual sufficed to let Helena know that she had changed very much about many things, and especially about her feelings toward Charles.

That night, when the oil lamp flickered in the tent, Helena had come upon a strange whip with a braided lash on it and a handle covered with leather of natural color. It was elegant yet cruel looking, and she let it fall almost as soon as she picked it up from where it had lain near a sort of duffel bag that Charles Terny carried. As the whip fell, it made a strange sound, and at the same time the handle popped off slightly from the lash. Helena thought that she had perhaps broken Charles's whip and bent again to pick it up to see how much damage she had done. To her surprise the handle came off completely, revealing a treacherous dagger with a blade almost like a giant screw. She quickly reattached the handle, and as a cold sweat began to pour from her, replaced the entire whip as closely as possible to its original position.

Later that night, as Charles came into the tent to sleep, Helena remained quiet and still, pretending that she was already asleep. It was not long before she heard the relaxed rhythms of Charles's breathing. Then she got up as silently as she could, as stealthily as she knew how, and made her way slowly toward the whip that she had discovered earlier. Slowly she grabbed the handle and freed it from the lash.

Clutching the dagger tightly, she walked carefully toward Charles.

His face was in the complete relaxation of sleep, lashes thick and shadowy on his rugged face. He looked entirely vulnerable, completely defenseless. He was at her mercy. Helena began to lift the dagger high above her so as to bring it down with as much force as her small frame could manage. But down the dagger would not come. It was as if her hand had been frozen in midair, or as if a giant behind her were holding her wrist tightly and preventing the weapon from descending in a brutal sweep and murdering the man who had used her as a pawn in his own personal game of revenge and hate.

Finally, she let her arm fall gently to her side. She turned quickly and sheathed the dagger in the whip, leaving it crumpled and twisted on the floor, looking like a poisonous snake.

She slipped back onto her bedroll on the floor, and shut her eyes very tight, considering how close she had come to killing a man. At the beginning, Helena knew in her heart, she would have been able to murder Charles without a qualm. What kept her from doing so now? She searched her soul, though not too deeply, for her inner wounds were still raw, and it was difficult to face her suspicions squarely. When she finally fell asleep, it was a restless sleep.

She did not notice that Charles's even and relaxed breathing had halted, to be replaced by a sharp intake of air at the moment she had replaced the dagger in its sheath. When Helena was finally asleep, Charles got up and went to where she had handled the whip.

Looking down at the treacherous weapon—which he had kept with him as a reminder that he must trust no one—his brows lifted in surprise. Then he walked the few steps to where Helena was sleeping, and stared down at her face for a very long time, pondering what she had almost done.

Helena never knew about Charles's discovery, and so she remained ignorant of the fact that he, too, was aware of the innermost changes of her heart.

It was still warm enough during the day, especially with the strenuous activity of the journey, to enjoy the refreshing baths Helena was allowed in the privacy of little pools. She had become accustomed to being watched by Charles, her guard at such moments.

Usually he would sit on a rock, his boots finding leverage in the crevices, one of his legs stretched out before him while he bent the other leg to support his arm and sometimes his chin. Often he smoked the small cigars he rolled for himself.

One day they arrived at a most inviting spot. The roar of a waterfall not far away made Helena's eyes sparkle with anticipation. As soon as the Cholos began to busy themselves with the setting up of camp, she slipped off without asking Charles's permission.

Here, at the slightly higher altitude which the travelers had reached after climbing the last few days, the vegetation had assumed new qualities that delighted Helena. Unlike the sweltering, oozing, insect- and reptile-ridden nightmare that the floor of the sea-level jungles could be, here the massive mahoganies, breadfruit, palo marias, and spectacular fanned palms created a splendid roof over passable and relatively low brush. A thousand varieties of tiny ferns and mosses coped here with each other. The rays of the sun that forced their way by sheer tenacity into the private domains of this greenery spotlighted an orchid here or there hanging for dear life onto its powerful host. Brilliantly colored or velvety dark, the butterflies fluttered quietly about, like the souls of flowers.

After Helena entered fully into the canopy, her eyes gradually became accustomed to the dim light. The lush and enclosed beauty of the place, where the roar of the hidden waterfall created a seductive background, quickened her pulse. Sheer glory. The purest essence of beauty.

Hidden from her, feasting not only on the background in which she was framed but on her golden beauty as a beam of light caught her, was a pair of hazel eyes in which flecks of green and gray glittered with admiration, then darkened with the rush of total desire and lust.

Helena felt a shudder run through her that had nothing to do with her awe of this beautiful place, a tiny moment of fright or of some incomprehensible hesitation. But she shrugged it aside and scoffed at her premonition. She pressed on, seeking the source of the roar of water.

When she arrived at the fall, she gasped at the marvelous sight. A graceful waterfall about twenty feet high had created a deep pool that shimmered in the sun before its waters ran away again in search of the ocean level. Great tropical trees interspersed with strange varieties of ferns and fan palms surrounded the pool, as well as huge moss-covered boulders, some of them with smooth flat tops that reflected the bright light of the still-warm sun.

Helena slipped quickly out of her clothes and waded excitedly into the refreshing water until it was deep enough to swim. Her long hair floated to the top as she played in the pool by dipping her body with little carefree dives under the water.

A feeling of joy invaded her, a feeling she had not experienced for a long time and which she had thought, after her kidnapping, she would never feel again. It was simply the joy of being alive and in tune with the beauties of nature. God was good, after all, and maybe, somehow, she would someday be able to pick up the pieces of her shattered honor and start again.

Her thoughts swung almost startlingly to Charles Terny. At his hands she had suffered more than she had ever thought possible. Yet, instead of bitter hate, a sudden and treacherous sense of vague regret came to her. What a loss! If only his heart had been of a kinder nature to give substance to his handsome and raffish expression and body. Or if she had met him properly before he went mad with the wild desire to use her for revenge.

Sometimes as they lay close in the tent at night, his arms and legs imprisoning her, Helena had relaxed enough to wonder about him and his life. But somehow, in spite of his surprisingly passionate and tender lovemaking, a wall of reserve and hate that Charles Terny kept around himself, as well as her own pride and hatred, dissuaded her from questioning him. Besides, she had no wish to arouse his anger and disdain, not even to satisfy her sometimes burning curiosity, or to let him think that she cared about him.

Actually, at those moments, Helena felt ashamed, for his embrace no longer left her feeling a sense of disgust, hard as she tried to conjure up those hates and keep them. In his arms, held by his sinewy and heavy muscles, she felt a new sentiment that made her blush. After all, Charles Terny was her ravisher and she could never forgive him for what he had done to her. Never!

She dived in again, relishing the freedom of her body in the water. As she surfaced, her face radiant and refreshed, she gasped, swallowed water, and sputtered to catch her breath again. The face of Charles Terny, wearing a sheepish grin, was before her.

"Hello, there! Mind if I swim with you?"

He was treading water, and the muscles of his massive shoulders gleamed beneath the surface.

With sarcasm in her voice, Helena retorted harshly: "You never have asked me permission for anything you wanted before."

She slid deep into the pool, not hearing his burst of amused laughter.

He caught up with her underwater and pulled her up with him above the surface. He looked at her mockingly, the shimmering colors of his eyes boldly piercing into the black depths of hers. Slanted rays of the sun showered a thousand lights into her eyes.

Then an emotion, something like a little pain in his chest, made him avert his eyes and avoid her stare. He let her go and slid into the water, kicking his muscular legs to get away and swim for just a while.

Soon Helena no longer felt like swimming, and she headed for the edge, thinking about many things.

What a strange man Charles Terny was. It seemed to her suddenly that much of his meanness was a sham. But why would he want to appear in such a negative light? What hates had warped his mind so violently?

She kept on swimming, reached the shallower edges of the pool, and rose to walk out.

She still thought of Charles, the image of his face, the changing gray of his eyes and his cocky demeanor which was impossible to shake off. She would soon have to try to tell him the truth again—that she was not a González—for his hatred of her suddenly distressed her acutely.

She reached the flat boulder where her clothes had become warm from the sun. Deep in her reverie, she had not heard Charles come up behind her, and she almost lost her balance as he slid his arm with a strange gentility around her waist, his hand alighting on the smooth and gently tanned surface of her young torso. With his other hand he lifted the wet masses of her hair the color of wild honey and kissed her tenderly on the nape of the neck.

A tremor ran through Helena. She clung to the thought that the sun must be going down and the air turning chilly.

Charles was murmuring her name over and over again, a strange new note in his voice, and he was still holding her so that her back was to his muscles and his loins.

She felt the smoothness and yet steely strength of his body. Her own seemed to have lost its healthy vigor, and a mysterious languor had taken its place.

Charles turned her slightly and picked her up easily. He laid her carefully on her clothes, which together with the layer of moss that grew there formed a very thin cushion. His kiss was a gentle pressure on her lips, which parted of their own accord. He leaned back to take in her beauty.

His fingers trailed the path of his eyes as they wandered from the tiny waist upwards. He took in the fine skin, like the purest silk, and the swell of her breasts, fine and gracefully formed, inviting to the touch. . . .

"Helena . . . Helena . . . You'd drive any man to a frenzy with wanting you. . . ."

"Charles . . . please . . . don't do this to me . . . I . . ."

But she could say no more, for Charles's mouth had swooped down and ground hungrily across her lips, stopping her cries of protest against this final contest of their wills.

Her lips were parted and short little breaths escaped from them. Her eyes, half closed with desire, were impossible to resist. Her graceful arms reached around him to bring him closer. He bent above her, his knees supporting him on either side of her body. Gently he bent again and grasped a handful of her golden hair, bringing it to his mouth and kissing it passionately, then almost at once roving to the warmth and beauty of her throat.

"I have to make you mine, Helena . . . all the way. Give yourself to me. . . . Let me take you completely." His voice was hoarse with pleasure and excitement.

Helena groaned as a feeling of lassitude overpowered her completely, and a fire seemed to concentrate itself where she could receive him.

Now Charles was kissing her wildly, while with his large but gentle hands he sought and found the weaknesses of her body. Helena moaned in ecstasy and arched her throat back as if inviting him to partake once more of its beauty. He took full advantage of the offer, and his whispers of desire huskily announced how much she was thrilling him at last.

His experienced caresses no longer caused her resentment. Instead she was suddenly aware that she was his, and that the fire of this moment was like some tempestuous and purifying flame that was transforming her heart. Within the fleeting kaleidoscope of her thoughts and emotions surged a strange mixture of wild desire and tenderness. Instinctively, she relaxed her thighs and reached to help him.

Understanding her wishes, he allowed room for her to part her legs and readjusted himself so that his thrusts would penetrate her as deeply as he longed for them to do. He wanted passionately to blend into one flesh with her, to possess her thoroughly, to deposit all that he was deep within her until she would never be able to forget that she was his.

Heedless of everything but a savage exhilaration that suddenly raced through her veins, Helena, too, plunged with abandonment into the passion that consumed her. She laced her arms about Charles, entwined her slender legs about him, and pulled him against her.

Then she felt herself melt and flow into him in an intense and lasting fire that obliterated all except sensation after sensation as he curved and thrust, taking her with a strange and loving fury.

Chapter X

"Patrón, Patrón!" It was Pablo. His rifle was at his side, and he wore the sash that held his ammunition. With his straw hat on he looked prepared for violence.

Charles leaped away from Helena, cursing under his breath for having been caught unprepared to defend himself. When he saw that it was Pablo, however, he relaxed enough to notice that his man had a startlingly agitated expression on his usually impassive Indian face.

Helena sat up brusquely, trying desperately to cover herself with the clothes under her. Charles turned to help her, not disguising his sudden humor at the sight of the beautiful Helena struggling with her clothes and her embarrassment. She gave him a caustic look in return, as if to accuse him of humiliating her in this small way, too.

"What is it, Pablo?" Charles tried to keep his voice

calm, as he sprang to another rock lower than the one on which he had just made love to Helena. There he slipped on his rough pants and boots and listened to Pablo's excited voice.

"Bandidos, Patrón! Pedro just rode back into camp. They have burned down a whole village. There, over that ridge toward the sea."

Charles turned to look in the direction that Pablo was indicating. Great billows of black smoke were rising over the horizon, but the wind was blowing the smoke away from them, which explained in part why he had not smelled it. He had been so absorbed in Helena that he had failed quite miserably to detect any signs of danger. He should never have become so involved with his captive. After all, it was revenge he wanted. Why, then, did he let her haunt his every waking moment as if she had cast a spell over him? He turned to glance at her as she sat waiting as if for instructions, trying to cover herself more fully.

"Helena, get dressed as quickly as you can. There's danger, and we have to head for camp!"

This was enough for Helena, who already felt vulnerable in her nakedness. She had slipped her *montuno* shirt over her head, and hesitated just a moment before standing up. Her slender legs were still gleaming with water from her swim, but the shirt was long enough to cover her upper thighs, much to her relief. She slipped the pants on quickly, and tied the rope she used for a belt around her waist. The sandals were on in a moment, and she was gracefully fleeing the big boulder where she had just surrendered to the man she ought to hate with all the strength of her passionate nature.

For a long time afterward Helena wondered what might have happened to the relationship between Charles and herself if Pablo had not chosen that moment to warn his master. Their encounter on the rocks above the pool had been so intense, so full of vitality and strange energy. She had never imagined that physical love could be so splendid.

As she reached the men below, Charles grabbed her arm and pulled her along briskly.

"We don't have a moment to lose! Pablo just told me that bandits are in the area. Probably looking for arms. They just burned a village to the ground."

Helena did not answer, but stepped along beside Charles as quickly as she could, trying not to delay their return to the camp.

When they arrived, the men were in a bustle of activity. The mules were half loaded, and tents that had been almost pitched had been torn down again, and were being folded hastily to load them onto the mules. Helena found that she was the only one who had nothing special to do. The others were so thoroughly organized, taught by Charles and aided by their natural instincts for self-preservation, that in no time at all the camp was swept clean of any artifacts that might have given them away. Only because the grass had been trodden and beaten down could one deduce that men had been there a short while ago.

Every Cholo had his cartridge belt swung across his chest and was fully armed. Helena wondered fleetingly if she could somehow get hold of a weapon herself. If the opportunity for escape arrived, she decided at that moment, she would willingly take it. She simply had to make an effort to leave. If she kept on reacting the way she was doing to Charles Terny, she would soon be a degraded slave, totally at his mercy, and the thought was grim and difficult to bear. Those moments on the rock above the jungle pool had let her know just how close she was to falling into his trap.

"Everybody on their horses!" Charles ordered. "You, too, Helena." Then, lower, in French, he added, as he approached her: "In case we have to fight, Helena, don't let them know you are a woman. Put this cartridge belt over your shoulder so you won't look too different. And this rifle, too."

Helena felt a slight moment of elation. She, too, was well armed, even if she wasn't sure how to use the gun. She slid up onto her pony. She would keep her eyes open. With Charles worried about the bandits and defense, the chance for escape just might present itself; she might flee forever from his influence and the paradoxical feelings she had for him.

Helena did not have long to wait for total confusion to reign. Just as the caravan had begun to file down the path, several men on horseback appeared. The afternoon sun glinted off the metal of their weapons. The cold, marble planes of their cruel faces and their well-aimed guns shocked Helena.

"All right! Everybody throw your guns down!"

It was the leader of the gang who spoke. His fierce black mustache drooped in the heat of the afternoon, and his great straw hat barely shaded his cruel and glittering eyes. He spat a brown, evil-looking spurt of tobacco juice to one side, and rode up to Charles Terny, whom he had immediately recognized as the leader of the group.

The men had not yet thrown down their weapons, when suddenly Charles picked up his Arabian whip, which he had wisely thought to carry by his side, and wrapped it in an instant around the neck of the bandit chief. The man let out a strangled yell, and fell off his horse. Everyone was so shocked by the swiftness of Charles's movements that they remained as if paralyzed. Then pandemonium broke out as everybody ran or rode for cover.

Helena, who had remained alert in case she could escape, disappeared into the bushes close behind her.

Still holding the handle of his whip, a weapon rarely seen in Panama, Charles slid swiftly off his horse and held the bandit leader in front of him; he then loosened the lash from around the bandit's neck. The man coughed desperately as air rushed back into his throat.

"One shot from you men and your leader gets his throat jabbed!"

Amazingly, the whip with which their chieftain had been tricked had fallen away, and there, protruding from the handle, was a gleaming, twisted dagger with a very mean point. Nobody moved, except Pablo and Pedro.

The two Cholo brothers had instinctively come together behind Charles and made a quick plan. With two or three of their men they had circled immediately behind the enemy and suddenly they appeared, pointing their guns at the bandits whom they had found clustered in hiding behind bushes and palms.

As they all came back into the clearing where Charles and his men had been ambushed, Charles seized the opportunity, and was gratefully relieved that he had chosen his men well.

"All right, all of you, you are totally surrounded, and you are my prisoners. Disarm these men, Pablo. Do it yourself. They are not to move or to throw a single weapon down themselves."

Still restraining the bandit chief by the arms, pinning them behind his back, Charles watched as the men were disarmed one by one. There were only about ten of them, but they were enough to burn and destroy one small Cholo village in the hills.

A few of the bandits were also Cholos, but signs of dissipation unmistakably marked their faces, and they did not look nearly as healthy or alert as Charles's own followers. They were probably renegades, then, victims of the city who were no longer accepted by their tribes in the mountains. It was not difficult to turn to a life of crime when one was rejected and starving. The French consul in Panama City had briefed Charles well, and the sight of these Indians did not surprise him.

"Now, get in a row with your hands on top of your head. We're marching straight ahead."

Pablo looked across the space toward Charles with a puzzled look on his face. Why was the *patrón* going toward the burned village? Not a thing had been left there, as he himself had reported after Pedro's return from the fire.

Charles walked behind the bandit chief himself, while the other men held their guns pointed at the others. The horses were brought up in the rear by the younger members of Charles's group. The long procession stumbled down the hill to a small creek behind the ridges of the waterfall where he had been with Helena less than an hour before.

Helena! Where was she? He had not kept track of her in all the commotion. Without taking his eyes off his prisoner, Charles yelled, "Pablo! Have you seen my blond prisoner?"

Pablo scanned the heads of his own group and those of the bandits. No graceful slender figure with wisps of golden hair peeping from under a hat was to be seen.

"No, Patrón. I don't see your prisoner anywhere."

"*Merde!*" mumbled Charles. She had gone, the little minx! Escaped into this inhospitable wilderness. Did she think these bandits they had just captured were the only ones in the hills? *Merde* a thousand times!

Strangely enough his only thoughts were for her safety, though he did not reconcile himself graciously to that fact. Not even a remote remnant of his original hatred came to him. That such a petite wisp of a girl had bewitched him should have made him want to roar in angry defiance. Instead he found himself worrying even more about her. Where could she have hidden?

First, he would have to get rid of these killers, and then he would go in search of Helena.

* * *

When Charles Terny pulled out his whip and with incredible swiftness and sureness unseated and almost throttled the bandit chief, Helena reacted very quickly, too. She scrambled off her pony into the bushes, still holding the gun that Charles had given her. She had often thought about escape and her self-induced aggressive determination had guided her almost automatically toward safety. There, covered by thick fronds of palms and other tropical vegetation, she decided very quickly on a course to follow.

She backed off slowly so as not to arouse suspicion from Charles's men, who were also hiding in that same area. She heard Charles's warning to the enemy that he would kill their leader if they moved to use their weapons. She had to admit, though still reluctantly, that Charles had been magnificent, half naked on his horse, bringing down his opponent with lightning speed.

As soon as Helena was back far enough from the rest of Charles's men, when she could no longer hear the voices of victors and captives, she broke into a jog, then ran headlong as fast as the vines and plants of the forest floor would allow her. Fortunately, at this altitude the jungle vegetation had thinned out somewhat, and was lush only near the waters of the small river.

She headed toward the smoke of the village that the bandits had just destroyed. Surely no one had been left, for the village must have burned in its entirety. She knew that the little settlements in the mountains were tiny indeed, marked only by a few palm shacks. Often the Cholos moved from place to place, sometimes in search of better hunting or because of small wars between their groups. Those who had white men's guns were usually the strongest and biggest bullies, pushing their weaker relatives farther and farther into the mountains. The village site would be the last place Charles Terny would look for her, she thought. Why should he go there now?

Out of breath, Helena stopped for a few minutes, panting wildly as she tried to regain her strength. Once more she picked up her gun and trotted off downhill, keeping in sight the strands of black smoke that had thinned out considerably by now.

The village was a good two miles away, although at first she had thought it only about half a mile. Going downhill was almost more difficult than climbing uphill. Many times she stumbled, scratching her face and forearms with fine little lines that bled and stung as the blood mixed with her perspiration.

A strong waft of acrid smoke reached her suddenly. She pushed aside a few more palm fronds, and came upon the most appalling sight she had ever witnessed. What remained of the village was nothing but ashes and one or two badly blackened huts at the opposite edge of the forest clearing. Apparently the wind had carried the flames in another direction, thus sparing the two lone shacks that seemed to gaze sadly over their vanquished comrades.

Helena could make out several thoroughly burned mounds—bodies of some who had first been shot, then burned into cinders by the raging fire. She felt a tremor of fear and disgust at what the bandits had done to these innocent people. She hesitated about going into the circle of consumed flesh and burned hovels, but decided that it was the only sensible thing to do, for luckily, two huts remained. She could hide in one of them. If Charles Terny got his way and really captured the bandits, he would not have time to look for her right away. He would never think to search for her here.

She walked resolutely across the center of the burned-out village and stepped into the shadow of the first shack she came to. She stumbled into a thickness at her feet, and opened her eyes wide with incredulity at the sight of a bleeding and torn torso whose head lay in greater shadow about two feet away, horribly twisted and splotched. She gasped as she tried to control her nausea and fright, but when a whining sound seemed to come from the head on the floor, she could control herself no longer and let out a long, shrill scream that reverberated through the clearing and into the quickly darkening forest.

Charles was feeling quite bitter about Helena. He had trusted her with the weapons for her own good, in case he should be vanquished by the bandits. She would then have had a chance of escaping. But the thought that she had run from him instead was humiliating, especially after their shared moments of love on the magnificent boulder where he had taken her so completely not one hour ago. She was exasperatingly beautiful, full of fire, hardheaded just as he was, but delicately feminine and totally artless. She was herself, a woman such as he had never thought to find, natural and intelligent and—as it appeared now more than ever—impossible to tame and control. Had she, perhaps, been simply a challenge? Well, she was gone now, hopefully out of danger. He would look for her, but only with luck would he find her. Without a knowledge of the area, she might have taken off in any direction. Perhaps Pablo or Pedro would be able to track her down for him.

His prisoners remained silent as they trudged down the twisted Indian path, slippery with dust and treacherous with roots, until finally it was level enough for Charles to mount his horse.

Charles was determined to confront the bandits with the evidence of their deed. Even if he could not absolutely prove their guilt, he was determined not to take chances with them. He had to assume that they were killers. The safety of his men and his woman came first.

As they reached the village clearing, Pedro exclaimed: "We are here, Patrón. This is the village."

"What's left of it," thought Charles bitterly as he saw the destruction.

Just then an outcry so piercing that the hair on his arm stood on end directed his attention instantly to the two remaining shacks on the other side of the clearing, and he was astounded to see Helena come rushing out, fear painted on her face as if all the devils in hell were chasing her.

She stopped suddenly in her tracks, realizing that men on horseback were staring at her. Then, with of the wilderness and had not a tinge of revenge about it. It was survival, not sadism.

The woman of the village did not flinch once as the murderers were shot. Their eyes, in turn, reflected a certain stoic resignation that Helena had not expected to see in men about to die violently. She thought that perhaps it was due to the constant company these men kept with death. What was one more life, after all, even if it was their own?

For a fleeting moment Helena envied their resignation, realizing that she herself would have fought desperately to the end, suffering immensely and uselessly the whole way.

Nevertheless, in spite of her thoughts, Helena's tears did not stop flowing. Even after the dead men had been piled up in the two remaining shacks, and fire set to them, and the Indian woman had been mounted on a mule with her child to be settled in the next village, they flowed on unchecked, silent streams down her face.

Charles swung up behind her on his pony Chocolate and crushed her to him. They rode off on the sturdy Isthmian horse as she cried bitterly in the dark.

mingled dismay and relief, she saw that it was Charles. Surely whoever was in the shack behind her would not harm her now. But she was again a captive of Charles Terny.

Charles broke into a canter and in one moment crossed the middle of the village.

"Get up here," he growled.

He bent down and picked Helena up savagely from the waist, plopping her in front of him on the saddle. She trembled with fury and fear and did not dare to utter a sound. She felt debased, crushed. He had won again!

"You little fool! Do you think the likes of these murderers would have helped you if you had come upon others just like them?" He tightened his hold across her middle, hurting her. Helena gasped for air, and tears of helpless frustration stung her eyes.

At that moment Pedro stepped out of the shack which Helena had just exited screaming in panic. Behind him he pulled a woman carrying a bundle in her arms.

"Look what we have here, Patrón," the Cholo ventured.

Charles swung his pony about, his eyes so fierce that the poor woman flinched when his gaze fell on her.

She threw herself and her child in front of Charles's horse, and cried out in a mixture of Indian and Spanish: "Spare me, Patroncito. I am innocent. My whole family has already been killed. What harm can one helpless woman do to you?"

"Tell her not to worry." Charles directed himself to Pablo, who in dialect and Spanish addressed the woman. When she saw that Charles's eyes had softened, and that he held the now sobbing girl in front of him with a certain protective gentleness, she became greatly calmed. Charles asked if she could identify the men who had burned the village and asked her, too, how it came about that she had been spared.

"I was not in the village when it was attacked—by these men with their hands on their head. They had been here before, searching for arms, but we had none, señor, not this time." She pointed casually at the murderers. "After they set fire to the huts, they ran off, leaving behind no witnesses, or so they thought. But I was just coming back from the creek with my baby and some water when I heard shots and hid behind trees and bushes. If you don't believe me, Patrón, the jug fell and broke in my haste to hide, and the pieces are still back there in the woods somewhere."

"I believe you," said Charles quietly.

He got down from his horse, leaving Helena on it, but not before he had slipped the cartridge belt off her and grabbed away her gun. Helena angrily clamped her lips shut. Charles was deliberately making a public display of her.

Charles walked rapidly over to Pablo and gave him swift instructions regarding the prisoners. Helena heard and gasped in surprise and terror. The bandits were to be executed down to the very last man!

"No!" Helena broke the stunned silence that had followed Charles's orders.

No one paid attention to her protest, however, and

the prisoners were lined up one by one, thei[r] tied behind them. Everyone but Helena see[med to] agree with Charles's cruel decision, for as h[er] roved in terror from face to face, all she sa[w] deadpan expressions that belied no protest [or dis]agreement. How could they just stand there a[nd let] these men be killed in cold blood without a sembl[ance] of a trial? What sort of justice was this? She [would] plead with them, she would make them listen t[o her.] She would not be an accomplice to this mass mur[der.]

"Stay on your horse, Helena," Charles warned[.] "You don't know what you're saying. I cannot let t[hese] murderers off. They are the scourge of the hills, [and] they would do this again if they had the chance. T[hey] destroyed a whole village because they could not [find] the arms they thought had been entrusted to the [vil]lagers by leaders from the city for terrorizing the po[p]ulation of the Isthmus. If I let them go now, they w[ill] continue to kill innocent folk without a qualm. Y[ou] just stay put!"

His last command had an edge of steel to it, [and] Helena sank back into the saddle. She averted [her] eyes, but at the sound of the first shot, she loo[ked] morbidly at the carnage that greeted the dusky sile[nce] of the night.

Bitter tears sprang into Helena's eyes. Her arm[s were] too heavy to wipe them away, and she allowed th[em] free rein.

She could not guess how wretched Charles was f[eel]ing, but he knew he had to be strong and that to s[ur]vive he must execute the bandits. It was simply jus[tice]

Chapter XI

Pablo and Pedro were brothers, and to everyone but the other Indians they looked like twins. They had become the self-appointed leaders of a band of young Cholos who had rebelled in the Council against the opinions of the older, more patient members of the tribe in Santa Fe, who persisted in their naive belief that help for the tribe would be forthcoming from the rulers in the capital. Knowing that power over the tribe, in the miserable state in which it now existed, was an empty power, the younger bucks decided not to rebel openly against the elders and had, instead, taken off for the capital to seek help for themselves. But they had met with misfortune after misfortune until they finally landed in jail. There they had met Charles Terny.

Pablo and Pedro had taken to Charles right away.

After securing their freedom in Panama City he had point-blank informed them that he expected something in return for his help. That was understandable and honest. One did not give away money or help without some intelligent reason. The reasons might vary, but they were always there, even if the giver himself was unaware of them.

The Cholos believed Charles, but now they were not so sure about his motives. There seemed to be more to his plans than what he had told them in the Panama jail. At least, though, he had dealt fairly with them insofar as he had made it definitely clear that he was hiring them to work in return for their freedom, aid for their people, and an additional wage as well.

For one thing, the Cholo Indians were puzzled because of Helena. The use of force to get a wife was understandable, and common. But Charles apparently had brought the girl for some other unfathomable purpose. The two brothers had often talked about the mystery, and finally had given up trying to decipher it. But they continued to wonder in silence about the subtle changes in Charles's attitude toward the girl, and they were thoroughly puzzled by her stubbornly aloof contempt of him.

"You know, Pedro," asserted his brother, "now I believe what old Tomás told me once long ago when I laughed at him and his troubles over that young wench he took as wife. He said that there comes a time in every man's life when a woman begins to be the source of all his troubles."

"Don't I know it!" laughed Pedro. He was considering his own young wife whose childlike ways and black eyes were all he could think of sometimes, especially now that he had been away so long. "But I don't believe the *patrón* realizes that he is letting this woman get under his skin. He'd better get rid of her before it's too late."

Unlike Pedro, who took the whole thing in a lighter vein, Pablo was genuinely worried. Women to him were an enigma and consequently a source of irritation. Their wily ways disturbed him tremendously, and he didn't trust a single one of them. He preferred the company of men where troubles were more open and came only from the unruliness of their nature or of their surroundings, from things a man could learn to eliminate or control. As was to be expected from a male who thought in this manner, Pablo was the best hunter and tracker of the village, a man's man, and the men universally recognized his superior strength and cunning. The women, too, respected him, possibly because they sensed his immense distrust of their sex. This made him invulnerable to their flirtations and created about him an aura of seriousness of purpose and great dignity.

Pablo was puzzled now, however, by his own mixed feelings toward Helena. This white woman who had come into their midst so suddenly and for no logical reason did not fit the expected pattern of female behavior. She was cold and reserved, yet spoke with unashamed directness, like a man. She made no false or provocative moves to entrap the sympathy or admiration of the men. Soon Pablo's amazement became approbation, and he began to experience pangs of some hitherto unfelt emotion whenever he saw Charles take

Helena into his tent. There was no real passion in his pain, however, for he was impressed mainly by Helena's mind and spirit, as though she were a revelation from another world, perhaps like a fairy or some other fantastical creature. Though her physical attractions were many, they were not what pulled Pablo toward her. Tenderness, respect, and a protective instinct were really what drew him. Pablo came to regard Helena with a love that would have astounded the men who knew him, for it was the antithesis of macho love.

In his newfound sensitivity Pablo began to realize something of what Charles felt for the girl, an immense guilt or overriding obsession and passion that he could not or would not admit to himself. And because he was grateful to Charles for his help so honestly given and for his manliness that did not demean his followers but made them proud to be his men, Pablo began to wish that things would work out for both Charles and Helena, even though Helena was the most self-disciplined and arrogant woman he had ever known, a woman full of fierce pride, resembling in this way not the women, but the men of his tribe. He had no doubts that Helena would kill Charles in revenge if she ever got the chance, which, of course, was strange and admirable in any female, let alone a white woman.

Pablo kept his eyes on her in curiosity, admiration, and distrust, but he never admitted his feelings about Helena to anyone, not even to his brother.

The Indians hardly spoke during their travels, except for practical purposes, as when camp was being set up. But their lonely, nasal litanies in the evening, and the strumming of the primitive guitar, filled Helena with self-pity and self-doubts. Only the fascinating resonance and the syncopated rhythms of one or two alien bongos the Indians had adopted from the Negroes on the coast, obliterated to some degree the sordid struggles of her mind and body.

"I find them fascinating myself," commented Charles, as though Helena had spoken her thoughts out loud.

It was the evening of the day after their lovemaking by the waterfall and the execution of the bandits. The intense moments on the mossy boulder had left Helena dismayed at the discovery that she could be aroused by Charles to such a height of passion, and that she could so willingly give herself to any man, let alone to *him*. Then the afternoon of blood had shocked her into a state of numbness that only now seemed to be lifting.

When Charles made his comment about the bongos, he gave the impression that he was reading her mind, and Helena felt totally vulnerable, menaced to the core of her being by that possibility.

"I'll learn to hide my emotions if it kills me," she thought. "Somehow I must prevent him from taking over my soul and my mind; I cannot let him get away with this!" And she swore defiantly to herself that she would harden her heart until it was impenetrable, safe from Charles Terny.

Without realizing it Helena was beginning to change, and craftiness, a quality unknown to her until now, was beginning to assert itself. Until her physical and mental surrender by the waterfall, the essence of

Helena's innocence had survived intact, in spite of her physical ravishment. Now she began to think of all sorts of little ways in which she could hurt Charles, even to the point of hiding her loathing and coming out with it when he least expected it. Anything to ruin his day. She knew that he wanted her to take pleasure in his pawings, and she relished the thought of using this as a weapon against him.

But that night and each night after, her body betrayed her mercilessly as Charles caressed her, intent on bringing her, arching and crying out, to the level of his own penetrating desires.

So it was that Helena grew sullen during the day, full of self-loathing, abhorring the encroachment upon her spirit that Charles had begun in earnest. Though he spoke words of fire and murmured compliments about her beauty as he brought her to climax, not once did he say he loved her. This fact did not escape Helena's notice. She continued to feel used and degraded in spite of the very considerate and tender caresses with which he began his nightly overtures. As their intensity increased, Helena could only cry and moan and whimper, amid the waves of pleasure that swept her away.

"He has enslaved me," she thought desperately, "in spite of all my efforts to remain aloof. And yet I hate him with all the strength I have in me." This last thought was not as sure as the first one, for actually Helena caught herself doing little things that no complete and true hatred would motivate. She would pick up his discarded shirt, or his hat, and place it where it would not be trampled on in the tent, or she would unconsciously see that his plate was generously filled, sensing that his body craved much more food than hers. Once he answered her suggestion that he serve himself the last of the *ñame*, a thick and tender root that was quite tasty when boiled with a little salt.

"Are you sure you don't want it, Helena?" answered Charles in what Helena interpreted as a mocking tone of voice. "You seem to be losing a lot of weight. You could use a fleshy root or two."

Helena raised her flashing eyes to his, letting them blaze angrily.

The sight of the wispy petite figure glaring at him in such seething and challenging anger over such a small incident suddenly made Charles burst out laughing.

"What! You dare to laugh," Helena cried. "You dare to stand there and . . . and laugh? Damn your conceited black soul! I'll scratch your eyes out!"

She lunged at him, flaying her slender fingers viciously at his face, a veritable virago.

Charles's laughter dwindled to a grin as he caught her wrists in midair.

"I'd rather kiss than scratch, my beautiful Greek fury."

He brought her toward him and tried to kiss her lips, but she twisted her face from side to side. He merely chuckled.

Helena was furious. Charles seemed to delight in making her appear ludicrous and unimportant. He treated her like some empty-headed little ninny. Couldn't he ever take her opinions seriously? He insulted her instead, and that after she had succumbed to her better instincts and unselfishly thought of his welfare—the welfare of her enemy!

Her voice sounded raspy as she assaulted him with her only available weapon—her tongue.

"The trouble with you, Charles Terny, is that you are old! You're so afraid you're getting decrepit that you have to prove otherwise."

Charles looked at her in disbelief, as if to make sure that he had heard correctly, then threw back his head and laughed with such diabolical self-assurance that Helena gasped. For a moment she felt sure she was in the presence of the very devil himself.

"Yes!" she kept on, undaunted. "And don't look at me so surprised! You are old! Old beyond your looks, and you think that just because I'm so much younger I haven't got a lick of sense in my head!" With that she dealt him a blow on the shin with the tip of her hard leather sandal.

Charles grunted a muted "Ouch!" and released one of her wrists to rub his shin. Keeping his hold on her with the other hand, he asked, "Who said that's what I think? On the contrary, if I may be so bold as to observe, I believe you have not only sense—but taste! Good taste. Which, of course, is why you find me so irresistible."

"You conceited . . . dog! Stop making fun of me or I'll . . ."

Helena stopped in mid-threat, realizing the absurdity of her position. After a moment's hesitation she wrenched her wrist free and turned quickly, walking away with determination, her head high. "Oh!" she exclaimed between gritted teeth.

Charles was still chuckling to himself. He yelled after her: "You are a most strikingly handsome woman when you are angry, madame!"

Helena did not acknowledge his remark and stalked straight on to the tent. Not knowing what else to do, she went in and pouted for the rest of the evening, though not before great tears of disgust and frustration had gathered in her eyes.

The thought of Charles's mocking claim that she was scrawny came back to her. It was true that her limbs were very slender now, but they were strong from the vigorous exercise of the daily riding. She had never been in better physical condition, but she supposed she did look a bit too mean and lean for a woman. She had heard her mother and Rosario comment often enough that skinny girls were not attractive to men, and she supposed then that, like most men, Charles preferred sedentary women with voluptuous breasts and hips. Well, as far as she was concerned, she would stay as skinny as a stick. She felt fine. She didn't care a bit about his pleasure. Indeed, she had been slender enough when he ravished her anyway!

Leanness had had the opposite effect on Charles's body, for the fact that not an extra ounce of fat clung to his limbs or belly made him all the more attractive. He looked almost like a centaur as he rode the sturdy Chocolate. Helena had begun secretly and hesitantly to admire the triangle formed by his angular shoulders that tapered down to sculptured narrow hips. In fact Charles had grown so lean that he had developed a slightly infantile habit of pulling his loose trousers

221

up every once in a while, a gesture that reminded Helena of a young boy.

Where the sun rarely touched him, his skin gleamed white at night in the tent, but his chest, arms, and back, which were often exposed, had turned a deep golden brown. His coloring was accentuated by the furry covering of hair that appeared generously all over him but especially on his chest, tapering wickedly downward and disappearing from view where his pants began.

Other qualities made him attractive, too: the way he held himself tall and straight, the gentle resonance of his voice when he spoke to his men, the undertones of a man accustomed to being obeyed, the easy manner with which he swung himself onto his horse, the fleeting flash of a rare but devilish grin that contrasted white against his sun-darkened face, the cocky posture of his Panama straw hat.

"I must be going crazy," cried Helena helplessly in her heart. "I can't go on like this." And the thought struck her that she could perhaps end this ordeal by making him listen to her whether he wanted to or not as she revealed her true identity and the fact that she was an orphan, with no family against whom to vent his anger. "For better or for worse, I must tell him," she decided.

But some vague and indefinable emotion kept her from speaking the truth. Many times by the campfire she began, but decided against it almost immediately. She sensed vaguely that the truth at this point could so release Charles from his hatred that he might also lose all sense of responsibility to keep her alive. At present he allowed her to exist merely because he could satisfy his lusting pleasure with her, but above all because alive she remained a symbol of the central object of his revenge, the representative of the González clan.

She finally prepared for sleep, her worries lingering into the night when Charles joined her once more in the tent.

Helena often styled her hair in braids now. It was, she discovered, a practical way to keep it from falling rebelliously out of her straw hat. She had no idea that the whimsical, almost childlike beauty of her features framed by the golden cords and curls on her head were too much for Charles to resist.

At night in the tent when his lips had aroused in her first a bitter-sweet longing, then a self-torturing fire, her mouth would pout, her lips slightly puffed, gently bruised by his kisses; her eyes would close halfway, drooping with the weight of her desire, and the tips of her teeth would catch the light of the moon that seeped through the tent or the light of the glowing kerosene lamp.

The vision of this delicate, delicious creature lustfully surrendering her body beneath his, moving her hips to meet his thrusts, was enough to drive Charles mad, and he undulated over her with increasing joy and renewed determination that she would never belong to anyone but him. He arched over her to murmur sweet encouragement, then pressed his lips wherever the urge led him, sliding his mouth over the curves of her young, slim body. He wanted to brand her with the sensations she aroused unknowingly in him and which seemed to escape from his innermost self through his kisses. He couldn't get enough of her.

The band of Indians, the handsome foreigner, and the golden girl were now climbing treacherous mountain paths. Theirs was a slow pace, for not only did they continue to avoid guerrilla bands, Liberals or Conservatives, but were further slowed by the rains that had unleashed their fury upon the lands of the Isthmus, and the miserable paths that they followed were practically obliterated in a mire of slick mud.

The mountain heights and pounding rains affected Helena as the storm at sea had, arousing in her overwhelming fears of which she was ashamed. Before falling victim to yellow fever in her childhood, she had scoffed at people who were afraid of such things. But since that time she had had many nightmares in which the sea dragged her from the beach, and in which fathomless abysses opened up to swallow her. And always there was falling rain. Now Helena felt as if her nightmares had come alive, and she was stiff with terror. For a long time she did not cry out her endless fears of falling into the deep ravines they were skirting, but finally one night in Charles's arms, as they were lying in the tent listening to the ceaseless rain that had accompanied their lovemaking, she blurted out: "Is this torture of possible death part of your revenge, too? Do you delight in seeing how frightened I am of slipping down into the ravines?"

He looked at her in surprise. "No, the thought never occurred to me. Are you afraid of heights?"

The tone of genuine interest in his question alerted

Helena even more to a vaguely changing attitude she had begun to notice in him.

"Yes, and you might as well know it. I love the mountains, but not climbing along their edges. It's frightening, and I can't help it, you know. I'm not some hysterical female."

"I know, my dear," reassured Charles. "In fact, I think you are a very brave young woman."

His patronizing tone infuriated her even more than would his thinking that she was hysterical. Her nerves were raw, and the tension brought about by the treacherous climbing of mountain paths swimming in red mud made her physically ill.

"Brave or not, you know I'm at your mercy. I wouldn't doubt for one moment that you would torture a defenseless girl, to finally push me into an abyss!" She practically spat out the accusation, and at the same time drew away from him in disgust.

He glared at her, his lips pressed grimly. "Whatever else I may be, Helena, I am not a murderer."

"Is being a murderer so much worse than being a rapist, monsieur?"

"There are a lot of things worse than rape, madame, especially if the victim enjoys it."

The enormous unfairness of his statement shocked Helena. Her pupils dilated, and she opened and closed her mouth in astonishment.

"How dare you!" Her voice was husky and low, full of contempt. "How dare you accuse me of such perversity!" Her nails crisped into his face and dug into the stubble of his beard, marking him with red lines.

He rolled over on her, and pinning her arms above

225

her, kissed her on her red and very delicate lips, as though he were sucking the most precious essences from her. Then his direction changed and his tongue forced itself into the sweetness of her mouth, ruthlessly seeking to possess her with all the lust and passion of which he was capable.

Bewildering thoughts raced through Helena's mind. Was Charles right? Had she descended to such low levels that this forced sex was what she longed for? No! She longed for something else, though what it was she could not define. Still, Charles was somehow involved in all these vague yearnings.

Charles had continued to touch her and kiss her. Helena caught her breath and then found herself returning his kisses, opening her mouth moistly, allowing him to penetrate there and thrilling to the fondling of his hands as they touched her palpitating flesh. Her thighs parted as her arms encircled his back and then caressed the huge expanse of his shoulders.

Then he was mounting her and swiftly penetrating her, bringing her to an oblivion of all senses except the climbing of her passion until her body exploded into a million delicious and dizzying pieces of light that shimmered downward like the drops of a tropical rain.

Charles's face, still contorted from the physical ecstasy he, too, had enjoyed, served to quicken in her a sense of power over him that had begun when she felt for the first time that his taking of her had changed from pure lust and desire for revenge, to something else in which these played a smaller part. She experienced a sudden surge of strength, and took a strange delight in it.

Then her old feelings of self-recrimination flooded over her, turning to hate once again, and she lashed out: "What would you do if I were not what you think I am, if I were not really a González?"

Charles withdrew from her quickly and impersonally. An impenetrable mask fell over his eyes, but he could not hide the pain in his voice.

"What do you mean?"

"I mean," answered Helena icily, "that you have wrought your revenge on a perfect stranger. My family name is Canales, monsieur, and I am not even remotely related to the Gonzálezes of Panama!"

There! It was out, the truth that might once have saved her from his ravishing hatred had she suspected then what he wanted of her. Now the same truth might very well make him abandon her or murder her far away from the protection of those few loved ones that remained to her.

Charles stood as still as a statue, except for the expansion and contraction of his chest. His legs were apart; his nudity was splendid in its starkness. The glow from the lamp made shadows appear above the swelling of his muscles, shining on the bulges and giving his face a frightening and eerie cast. He looked like a magnificent, heaving savage.

"Madame," he began, his voice quiet and controlled, with an undertone of wrath like the threat of a dagger, "tomorrow is our last day on this trek. We should arrive tomorrow evening at Santa Fe, unless it rains more than usual."

With that he strode to the basin, washed himself, and slipped his clothes on. Then he left the tent, his pouch of tobacco in his hands. A gentle rain was still falling.

Helena remained silent on the bedroll, astonished at his control and bewildered by it, too. There had been no hint of what he intended to do with the information she had so suddenly and without warning provided, only his terrible eyes seething anger through the frightening wall he had suddenly reerected about himself. He had totally ignored her words and spoken callously, instead, of trivial details regarding their voyage. He was so cold blooded. Was there nothing vulnerable about this man? Could she not hurt him at all, ever? She had to confess that he had certainly penetrated *her* defenses. Hadn't he been able to tame her so that her senses were atuned to some wild longing that shamed her and merely left her anticipating the hungry caresses of the man she hated with all her heart? It was degrading.

Even as she lay still on the floor of the tent cursing her situation, the muscles of her legs tight and sore from the vigorous climbing and riding of the last few days, Helena's mind was suddenly filled with the memory of his embraces and caresses. Try as she would, she could not rid herself of these images. Finally her eyes closed from sheer exhaustion. Early in the morning Charles Terny awakened her.

He was shaving outside the tent when she emerged washed and dressed, and she wondered fleetingly why he even bothered to shave in the middle of the wilderness. She remembered, too, that amazingly, as heedless as he was to proprieties, he took time out each evening to trim and clean his nails. They were never jagged or dirty. In spite of the calluses that had developed on the palms of his hands, his long brown fingers remained remarkably well groomed and aristocratic.

He seemed to avoid her, so she did not dare broach the subject of her revelation of the night before, though the question of his decision burned deeply inside her. What, indeed, would Charles Terny do with her now? She was hardly useful as his instrument of revenge, since she wasn't of the González family anyway. Obviously he had expected her to be part of that family all along. Would he then consider her altogether useless, an embarrassing encumbrance or a reminder of his criminal lust? How and when would he get rid of her, and if he left her alive, what good would it do, for how could she ever pick up the shattered pieces of her life?

At mid-morning the skies began to gather into great dark clouds, rich and pregnant with the threat of more rain. Helena noticed Charles's anxious looks, though she was relieved by what appeared to be the tranquil plodding along of his Cholo followers. To her dismay, however, the Indian Pablo interrupted the quiet struggle of the group as they made their way up the treacherous side of a red clay mountain, which was sparsely covered but whose sharp-edged grasses managed to hold the soil together.

"Patrón, I believe we'll have to make camp as soon

as we get to some sheltered part of the hills. Looks like a real storm brewing."

Charles surveyed the gray skies with one sweep of his eyes, then said, "No. We press on. If we hurry, surely we'll make it to our goal all right. We're so close now."

"As you say, Patrón. There is only one section of the next mountain that worries me, but if we can make it past there before the rain, all will be well."

"Let's go, then."

Charles waved the men on and spurred his mount forward. They would have to walk the dangerous ridges ahead. Remembering the slippery mess of some of the paths they had maneuvered already, he only hoped these would not be worse. Perhaps it would be wiser to wait, but his goal was Santa Fe, and the mystery which that forsaken place held for him was gnawing at his heart. The sooner they arrived, the sooner he would be at peace.

The storm broke with unrestrained fury precisely halfway through the worst path that they had yet to traverse. The Indian refuge of Santa Fe had been chosen well indeed, for the slippery mountain ravines and inclines formed a natural fortress at this point. They could not turn back, and only here and there along the muddy red path could two men walk abreast. Sheets of tropical rain obscured everything from view except the rusty clay of the slippery path just ahead of each traveler and the cavernous black of the ravine to the left. Rivulets of red-tinted water began to gush suddenly from the mountain wall on the right through crevices eroded in the soil. The instant waterfalls hit the path below with amazing force, denting the surface and making it even more dangerous.

Charles left his mount in charge of one of his men and allowed several others to pass him until Helena arrived at the spot where he was standing.

Without a word he stepped behind her, not seeing the sudden flash of growing fear and doubt that crossed her eyes as she carefully treaded the mud and slime ahead of her. The rain pelted their faces with relentless energy.

On the right a few scraggly bushes and roots lent support, but unfortunately the vicious torrents and waterfalls that had formed in the eroded red clay between the wild plants threatened to push Helena's fragile figure off the path. To the left the deep cut of the mountain yawned, frightening to behold, like the gaping mouth of a huge monster. Each step could lead to death. Helena was terrified not only with the thought that nature could claim her as a victim, but that this was, indeed, a propitious moment for Charles Terny to get rid of her and the embarrassment to him that she might prove. One little push on that slippery path and . . .

Then they knew that they had made it, for the path became rockier and the cliffs on either side gave way to gentler slopes.

Charles stopped once he was certain all the men and the beasts had arrived upon safe ground. He slipped his arm, strong as a band of tempered steel, around Helena's fragile waist and held her close to him. She turned her face toward him, numbed by tension, and blindly and instinctively sought the refuge of his arms. She was almost unaware of the pressure of his lips upon her hair and the gentle murmurings he made proclaiming his relief that she was safe.

"My God." His voice was just a hoarse whisper. "If anything had happened to you back there, I . . ." Then he faltered, as though suddenly realizing what he was saying. His body tensed, and Helena pushed herself away gently, having felt the sudden stiffening of his arms.

In spite of Charles's attempts to subjugate his naturally loving impulses toward Helena, their eyes found each other, and something entirely new to their relationship, something ethereal and strange, passed between them. But the moment was lost almost immediately as the excited and triumphant sounds of the men intruded.

"Patrón, we made it," Pablo shouted, "and now only a mile more and we shall be there, even ahead of schedule!"

The rain was still falling, but more softly now.

"Help Miss González to mount one of the mules," Charles ordered. "Pedro, you and I will go ahead as before."

As Charles strode away, his poncho dripping with water, Helena wondered at the name he continued to use as hers. González. She knew so little about the Gonzálezes. During the last mile of the trip she tried in vain to recall any stories she might have heard about that most prestigious family—stories that would help her to fathom the mystery behind Charles Terny. But none had come to mind.

He had once mentioned that he was an Englishman of sorts, yet he spoke flawless French. Of course, that was not uncommon. She herself had received extra instruction in English at the convent. Her Spanish was as Panamanian as that of any well-educated Isthmian, except that some of the nasal qualities of Isthmian Spanish had disappeared from her voice because of her long absence from Panama. So it wasn't actually strange at all that an Englishman should speak perfect French.

She had yet to hear his English. Would she ever? It was difficult for Helena to believe that Charles Terny would not abandon her, though she now sensed that he would not kill her as she had thought he might. Apparently he had been relieved that she had not hurt herself during the storm.

Strange thoughts assailed her tired mind. She was relieved when the last rays of the afternoon sun pushed through the broken clouds and the sounds of children and dogs and the smell of wood fires reached her.

They had arrived at an Indian village in the mountains of Santa Fe.

Chapter XII

Many weeks before, when Doñita had hobbled out from the kitchen into the small living room of the house near the Santa Ana Park, her dark little eyes had grown large with shock and fright.

Rosario lay on the floor in a crumpled heap; the door of the house swung piteously open in the breezes stirred by the oncoming night. There was no sign of Helena.

"My God, Rosario," Doñita cried out in dismay. "Rosario, get up, please. Oh! What am I to do? What happened? Helena! Helena!" But Helena was nowhere to be found, and the old woman continued to tug at Rosario with all the force of her aged and enfeebled body, crying in vain for Helena's help.

Finally, gripped by a terrible premonition, she left Rosario, and rushed to the door to look for Helena up and down the cobbled street. She saw nothing but dark and deepening shadows.

She closed the door and ran again to Rosario, who still did not stir. On close examination, however, Doñita decided that Rosario was still breathing. Her parched and bowed legs carried her quickly to the kitchen, and she came back, huffing and puffing, with a small pot of cool water and a clean dishcloth. Mopping the brow of the unconscious seamstress, she finally achieved positive results. Rosario began to moan as she regained consciousness.

"Oh, my head!" She made a move to touch the back of it. "Ouch!"

"What happened? Where is Helena?" Doñita said as she helped Rosario rise from the floor. She supported her with her body as much as her brittle frame could hope to do, then half led, half dragged Rosario to one of the wicker chairs and allowed her to fall as softly as possible into its arms.

"I don't know. I don't know. Oh! My head. I think I'm going to faint again."

Grabbing a simple straw fan from the mahogany table that Helena had been using as a desk, Doñita waved it in Rosario's face.

"Breathe deeply, my dear," she added, not knowing what else to do.

"Help me to my bed," whined Rosario, and without another word Doñita again stumbled off with the younger woman toward the smaller of the two bedrooms.

A crucifix over the bed, and the simple accommodations of the room, had once given it the basic austerity and penitent atmosphere of a nun's cell. But slowly, as Rosario's personal accoutrements had been brought from her own gaily decorated house, the small room with its iron-barred window that had once been Mariana's had taken on the air of gay disorder that matched Rosario's personality.

In spite of the scatterbrained impression she made, however, Rosario had wits quite capable of dealing with the most unusual problems. Mariana had discovered the true nature of her friend many years before, and Helena had recently begun to recognize these hidden qualities as well. Doñita had always known about them, and she followed Rosario's instructions with unbounded faith. In fact, Rosario knew how much Doñita depended on her for reassurance and security. So, as she lay painfully down on the narrow hardy bed, she began to give orders to the bewildered and ancient cook.

"Now, Doñita, not a word of this to anyone, do you hear? No one is to know that Helena is gone. But you will go now, if you please, and hire the neighbor's oldest son to send a message to Don Benito. He is to come here immediately without waiting for any further explanation."

As Doñita began to question the wisdom of leaving Rosario alone so soon after her accident, Rosario herself interrupted her imperiously. "Go now, Doñita. Do not waste a moment!"

Within minutes, an astoundingly short time for the hobbling old woman to carry out her mission, Rosario heard the pounding of hoofs along the cobblestoned street as the neighbor's boy rode full speed toward the González mansion at the edge of the Bay of Panama.

The arrival of the message did not come as a total surprise to Benito González, for he was still trembling from the shock of an unfolded note that wavered in his hand.

After all these years!

Could the dead come back and haunt the living? Was it true, then? Or was this some joke misbegotten by a sick mind?

Helena! Captured and dishonored!

The note boldly stated the deed as fact. In partial payment for the destruction of the life of one Lucinda González, his sister.

Oh, God! That tragedy so long ago had haunted him relentlessly for years, until eventually the ashes of those terrible days had scattered in his brain and lost their strength. But now this vile message had brought his shame before him once again. Ugly memories came forth, writhing and moving into his conscious mind like devils performing a lewd dance.

He had been young and inexperienced then. He had not known his sister well, only well enough to want the best for her.

When Lucinda had finally confessed her love for the Baron de Thierny and also the fact that she was carrying his child, he had not reacted in the compassionate way he should have, mainly because he had been confused and bewildered by the shocking revelation of his own sister's illicit love.

Young, idealistic, and naive in spite of his years abroad, Benito, too, had been a victim of his father's indomitable pride and unbending sense of family name and honor. Don Jaime had been driven not only by honor, however, as Benito now realized, but also by a dictatorial impulse to maintain control over his offspring until his dying day. He never did mellow in this respect, and even on his deathbed one of his greatest fears had been that Benito would not continue to act in the submissive manner he required. The old man had been determined to go through with the heartless scheme to punish his daughter's shame, her disobedience. Benito himself had been a coward, afraid to bring the wrath upon himself by disagreeing too energetically with his father. It was true that Don Jaime would eventually have carried out his plans for his daughter, and no one this side of hell would have stopped him. But Benito did not even have the meager consolation of having tried.

Now, out of the shadow of the past, came Lucinda's own flesh, her son, seeking to revenge himself upon the head of the cowardly brother whose fear of being disinherited had made him abandon his sister to her own fragile defenses. And how poorly she had fared. Even the recollection of the bitter past was difficult for Benito to endure.

Now his cowardice had created a new victim, for Helena was totally innocent, not even a member of his family. The idea of the crime perpetrated upon her was horrible. It made Benito ache inside as nothing had hurt him since his sister's tragedy.

To make matters worse Benito felt that he had been careless with Helena's safety and reputation. Instead of giving in to her childish wish to be independent, he should have insisted that she stay with Alejandra and himself, where she would have been safe. He recalled his weak arguments to Helena the day they rode back on the train from Colón. Her reasoning had proved stronger than his doubts.

"I really am terribly appreciative, Uncle Benito, but I simply could not impose myself on you or Tía Alejandra. After all, I won't be alone, for as you know, Rosario Pérez will be staying with me. She has always been like a close relative to me, and in fact often supplanted Mama when Mama was too busy with the business to attend to my needs."

It was true that Rosario, though of humble origins, paid more heed to propriety than anyone Benito had ever had the pleasure of knowing. No worry there. And Helena was adamant about testing herself in the business world.

"No, really, I wouldn't think of going to live with you now. Not until I have seen for myself whether or not I can handle all these problems. Perhaps, though, I shall fail miserably. . . ."

"No, no, my dear, you mustn't say such things, for I know from the letters of praise your poor mother received from the mother superior that you have a keen mind and that your character is strong and good. There is no need to worry on that account. It's just that there are so many problems in Panama now, problems beyond your control which may make your task quite difficult. In fact, it might be worthwhile to go over a few of them now."

Helena was concentrating all her attention on Benito. She looked startlingly lovely as she sat facing him.

"I would be most grateful, Uncle Benito, if you would inform me about Panama's political and economic situation. After all, I was only a child of thirteen when I left, and I had never really worried about such problems while I was growing up. Mother did write me a few things, but very little about the business, except for the actual designing."

Benito sighed. He did not wish to disappoint the young woman. "I'll try to gather my thoughts so that I can outline only the most important things, Helena. No use cluttering your mind with too much information all at once."

Helena smiled. "All right, Tío Benito. Please take your time." She'd turned her attention casually to the tropical green landscape that was clipping along from her window at an even and monotonous pace. The windows were all slightly open, and a not-too-rough breeze disturbed and teased the curls about her face.

In Benito's heart welled a deep sense of admiration for the delicately beautiful girl with an apparently iron determination. She reminded him in this way of his wife, Alejandra, whom he cherished and who, in spite of her smallness and her gentle ways, was woman enough to contradict him when he was wrong.

Benito returned to his reflections. He was worried for Helena's sake, for many factors of life on the Isthmus were beyond his or her control, and yet could affect her seriously and suddenly. Then, once he'd made up his mind to speak his piece, Benito's voice rang out with great resonance.

"Well, then, let us begin at the beginning." Benito cleared his throat, preparing to lecture the gentle blonde in much the same style as his professors had lectured him when he was a lad in school in Bogotá.

Benito remembered Bogotá well. It was the closest center of learning to which an Isthmian of means could send his sons to study, and his father had sent him there at an early age. Later he had been sent to England to study law and philosophy. All those years away from his family rankled Benito, for he had never been allowed to get close to the members of his family. Now, before this young lady who could pass for his daughter, he was not sure what was right and what was wrong. His wife was barren, and being a man of great decency in that respect, Benito had never sired children elsewhere. Should he perhaps be stricter with this young woman? Should he allow her to live in her lonely house with only Rosario Pérez to guard her? He certainly felt responsible for Helena, yet extreme harshness or inflexibility had never been his way. He had seen the cruel results of self-righteousness and had sworn never to fall into the traps of exaggerated codes of honor as his father had. No, he would simply explain the situation to Helena, and be there if she needed him. She was intelligent, and though she had been a wild little child, her reputation as a gentle and proper young lady had preceded her impressively. Rosario and the maids would provide enough protection for the girl's reputation.

The rest of the two-hour trip they chatted about Panama and exchanged ideas and stories, so that by the time the train rolled into the station in Panama, Helena felt completely at ease with Benito González, and he felt proud that the young lady should pass for a member of his well-known and respected family.

He imagined suddenly, too, that he had found at last, rolled into one, the daughter and son for whom he, and especially his wife, had often yearned.

Now Benito knew that he had made the wrong decision concerning Helena's welfare. He had been miserably mistaken. He should have paid more attention to his doubts and brought her to his home. He could have introduced Helena to society, found the beautiful creature a wealthy husband right away, and solved all her problems instead of waiting for her to take care of as many of the business finalities as she could. Besides, he had known from the beginning that the couturier business could not be saved, no matter how much money he might pump into it. The markets had disappeared, and without a demand, no business could exist; it was that simple. But he had been reluctant to handle all the loose business ends himself and perhaps rob Helena of her opportunity to enjoy the bit of freedom and chance for experience she seemed to crave.

And this had been the result! The beautiful and innocent girl he had taken under his protection had been seized, and disgraced at the hands of a man who cried justice—an eye for an eye, cruelty for cruelty. Benito shuddered. Poor little Helena!

Benito González was in this state of turmoil and self-recrimination when the urgent message came from Rosario Pérez. He bade the messenger wait outside as he ordered his own impressive carriage, and within minutes the small convoy was reeling toward the Parque Santa Ana, the young messenger galloping ahead on his Isthmian pony.

Rosario was sitting up, a damp cloth on her head, her feet propped up on one of the other wicker chairs, when Benito González entered the little store house.

"Rosario!" he cried. "I didn't realize that you were hurt! How did it happen? How did they get Helena away from here?"

"You know she is gone?" asked Rosario incredulously.

"Yes, I received a note—you might say a sort of ransom note, except that it is too late to do anything but wait."

"Then what do those men want with her? I hired a carriage home, and at the door several men accosted me from nowhere. Oh!" Her head was still throbbing madly, and her stomach felt queasy again. A wave of nausea washed over her. "I'm going to die, Don Benito! Please explain to me quickly!"

In spite of his tribulation, Benito never ceased to admire the complexity of the little brown woman before him. He never knew whether to take her statements seriously or not.

"The madman behind this abduction simply asked that my wife and I get on the next boat to David and from there gain our way to Boquete to our coffee plantation, where he will eventually give us back Helena and . . . that's all."

"But what possible gain could he have from this? Did he not ask for a single penny?"

"No, my dear, not one cent. But her life is in danger

243

if we do not follow his orders immediately. I'll see now about that, and also about a doctor for you."

Benito was extremely tired from the activity and confusion. In his carriage, racing to the doctor's home, his breath came harder and harder.

He returned shortly to Rosario, where he was relieved to learn that she would survive her slight concussion very well; she was not going to die as she had so dramatically announced to him. Then he hurried back to his sprawling water-side mansion to work busily on the papers he must put in order. Restitution. Yes, that was it. This time he would make amends for the error he'd committed in the foolish years of his youth. There would be no more innocent victims because of his error. No more. This time he would be decisive and brave. Compensation. Forgiveness. Peace.

Much later he finally left his desk in the elegant European-style library of his home and went upstairs to bed. The next day he would make arrangements for passage on one of his own ships for himself and Doña Alejandra to Boquete.

Chapter XIII

The big lonely house stood back like a wooden relic of some decaying past. The path was overgrown with weeds, but still usable, and led directly to the front door. A large porch whose floor was built of short wooden planks practically encircled the house. Helena imagined that the plaintive call of some relentlessly tortured life reverberated from the structure of unpainted wood, but actually all was quiet and peaceful. Only the sounds of scurrying small animals and birds broke the eerie calm.

The hair along the base of Helena's neck stood on end, and she was afraid of an unknown misfortune; feeling perhaps a warning of evil things to come or an echo of those already past. The mood passed away as quickly as it had appeared, however, and she turned to concentrate on Charles Terny. What in the world were they doing here at this weird, almost unholy place? She was puzzled and apprehensive.

Charles hesitated as he approached the looming house. He breathed in the smell of decaying wood and noted the desolate, yawning windows that opened onto the veranda. A malicious breeze loosened a shutter on the second floor, and it began to pound against the wall.

A signal from Charles to Helena and Pablo brought them to his side. Despite his earlier valor Pablo's pupils were now dilated with fear. Helena was tempted to laugh—nervously, to be sure—at him and at herself, but the pained and enigmatic look on Charles's face stopped her. The brown of his flecked eyes was deep, his brow knitted, his lips almost quivering. Helena was suddenly at a loss as to what to think and was only mildly surprised that she yearned to comfort him. This was the kind of irrational reaction he often inspired in her.

Perhaps they were no longer to stay together. He had made every effort to be polite and distant to Helena ever since she had blurted out the truth of her identity. He almost seemed embarrassed by his mistake. The only words he had spoken had referred to some change of plans and the fact that they would no longer continue on to Boquete overland. This was to be the end station of their voyage. He had explained that soon they would be returning and that she would be safe. He acted gentle enough. He was certainly a changed man from the one who had treated her so violently amid the ruins of Old Panama. It seemed that now it was he who needed her support. What a complex man, and what a strange place this was.

"Charles . . ." stammered Helena, unconsciously using his given name instead of her usual cold "monsieur." "Are you all right? You look as if you have just seen a ghost."

"I think I have."

Helena was more puzzled then ever at his quiet answer.

"Are we going inside? Does someone live here?"

"The Indians who lived here have fled, and they avoid this house and its evil past. No. No one lives here anymore. I thought perhaps . . . When I arrived in Panama I even thought that by some miracle my mother . . . might still be here . . . alive. But her death was finally reported and filed in the official records in Panama City a few short years ago. It was the first place I searched, of course. When I came across her file, I realized then I would eventually find only her tomb . . . or at least this place where she lived out her last years. . . . Somehow I had to see for myself."

"Your mother! You mean your mother lived in Panama? Was she English, then, or French?"

"My father was French, Helena, but my mother was Panamanian."

He turned to face her squarely. "My mother was the sister of Benito González."

"Don Benito!" Helena cried out in surprise. "But you hate the Gonzálezes. You told me so!"

"Perhaps I hated them too much, Helena. I used you to get back at them. You, an innocent. . . . I think this wicked trick of fate was meant to teach me that I was wrong to seek revenge by hurting and lashing out so violently. I have only hurt an innocent girl—even if you had actually been a González, which you say you are not."

"That's true, but I love that family and wish them only well. I can't imagine what Don Benito could have ever done to you that would have caused your hatred. He's such a kind gentleman."

By this time Pablo had eased away from them to the edge of the small field that had perhaps once been a lawn. He was obviously more comfortable away from the house. Charles glanced up toward him and waved him away, then turned his eyes upon Helena's uplifted face.

"Come with me and see the house where she lived her last few years. I'll tell you the whole story."

Grasping her hand, Charles led Helena up the creaking wooden planks that still served as steps to the veranda. Charles ripped off the rotting nailed board that barred the door, and the two halves of the double door swung inward, freed at last after years of bondage.

He stepped into the shadows of his mother's last dwelling place with Helena in tow, and they both gazed around them at the dust-covered ghosts of furniture that still haunted this place. When Charles finally began his story, his resonant voice faltered here and there. His fingers traced along and swept away from the surface of tables and chairs the dust of many years.

Helena listened in respectful silence, not once interrupting what she intuitively sensed would bring relief to Charles as he unburdened his heart of the hatred he had kept locked up inside it for so long.

When at last he had finished, Helena could think of nothing to say. Her astonishment, dismay, and sadness at his tale had left her weary. She followed him silently into the other rooms.

Only sparse furnishings remained, and in what must have been his mother's room, a crucifix high on the wall hung as a mute witness to the madness that had overwhelmed the young woman.

"After my birth in Boquete they brought her here. There were too many neighbors in Boquete close enough to discover that the aristocratic Lucinda González Calderón had become a raving lunatic." Charles's voice betrayed the bitterness he felt. After a little while, enough time to gather up his inner resources again, he continued, filling in the story with facts he had learned from sources in the Indian village of Santa Fe where they were now staying.

"Here, where isolation was complete, she was abandoned to her fate. Only the nanny who had raised her remained with her, but she died long before my mother did. When finally death came to release her, she too was alone. The Indians who cared for her, some of whom still live in the village below, were afraid of her. They considered her madness a powerful source of magic and avoided her almost as much as they later avoided the house. She was buried without the blessings of a priest."

"Was her grave marked?" Helena's question was soft and sympathetic.

"I don't know for sure, but one of the old Indian women who lived here told Pablo that there is a small cemetery nearby where she was laid to rest. She died many years ago . . . my mother. . . ."

Charles and Helena looked back only once as they headed away from the house, leaving behind the decaying structure that had housed the sacrificed victim of González pride.

An unexpected feeling of well-being overcame Helena as she walked beside Charles, her hand in his. Because his sorrows and his mother's tragedy seemed so great, there was no place in her thoughts for the hatred she had been nursing all these weeks. Instead she was swept along by her natural feelings of sympathy and understanding. Serenity and quiet resignation settled over her.

Charles led the way, his heavy boots crushing the green grasses that had long since taken over what had once been a narrow gravel path. He was looking for the cemetery and had apparently been informed of the general direction in which it lay. His footsteps were sure, and soon his arms were swinging along simultaneously with Helena's in graceful arcs.

In spite of the enormity of the tragedy which Charles had related to her, Helena could not help but feel relief. Finally she thought she understood what had motivated Charles on that desolate black night when she had suffered the searing pain of his revenge. She felt vast pity for him. And paradoxically enough, at this moment, with her hand in his, life did not seem as menacing as before.

In a desolate grove of trees stood a small, humble cemetery. In the center a gorgeous tombstone of the whitest Italian marble dazzled Helena and Charles with its brilliance. It was a totally unexpected sight.

Helena stopped as Charles's hand left hers. He walked as if mesmerized toward the beckoning tombstone, resting abandoned among the weeds. After a few seconds he collapsed before it on his knees. A great sob racked his body; he bent his head.

Helena followed her impulse to comfort him this time, and came to stand beside and behind him, her hand coming to rest on his heaving shoulders. She read the writing on the tomb.

> In memory of my beloved sister,
> Lucinda González Calderón,
> Who suffered much in life.

So Benito had erected this monument to his sister's memory! The final blow to Charles! His mother dead, but honored by the man whom he had always held responsible for her misery, who had remained in his twisted thoughts the embodiment of evil. His hated uncle had somehow managed to install this magnificent tombstone in the desolate mountains of Santa Fe. If in doing so he had not been able to assuage his conscience or mitigate the horror of his part in the crime, it still remained an act of love. Santa Fe was almost inaccessible, and because no one ever came to these properties anymore, only Benito González could know of his own effort to make up in some way for

251

his youthful failure toward his sister. Thus his effort to honor her after death had merit, for he had not gone through such gallantry for the sake of what others might think or say. Surely Charles realized this now.

And he had, of course. But more importantly, he had found out something in the Indian village. He had been too ashamed to confess it to Helena. But he had felt the lash of his conscience on hearing the old Indian woman.

"Patrón, did you come here sent by Don Benito? He used to come here before, when Miss Lucinda was still alive. He don't come here no more. Is he still living, Patrón? I still remember he used to bring so many things for us Indians, things to wear and guns to hunt. But ever since Miss Lucinda passed away, not even the priest comes."

After the first wave of surprise followed a sense of dismay. Still, Charles had questioned the old woman further. He discovered that Lucinda's brother had indeed made the trip to Santa Fe several times to see about her, leaving her in the mountains because the climate there was healthier than in Panama. Apparently he could do nothing more to aid his sister, for it was too late. Lucinda would never get well again, and nobody but the Indians wanted to imprison themselves in this isolated region to take care of a sick insane woman. Even though the cruelty that had been showered on Lucinda could not be taken back, his uncle must have long ago felt the weight of his guilt and tried to redeem the terrible mistake. A regret swept over Charles, weakening his defenses.

After a while Charles looked up, his eyes red. Like an angel in the roughest clothing, Helena stood hovering over him and he was suddenly and painfully aware of the physical similarity between Helena and the portrait Charles had built in his mind of his own mother.

As they returned to the house, Charles was very quiet. Helena dared not break the silence, though she longed to ease his suffering, but words seemed too banal for such purposes, and she merely did her best to keep up with the swinging gait of Charles's long legs. At last the back of the abandoned house came into view. Charles and Helena continued around it and followed the direction which Pablo had taken earlier. Once or twice they looked back at the house.

"How terribly lonely and frightening it looks." It was Helena's soft and musical voice, its husky tones full of sympathy. Charles was suddenly grateful that she was with him. Whether deliberately or not, she had been a comfort such as he had not known since his father was alive.

He had no intention of doing it, but somehow he found his arms around her and her face uplifted with large sad eyes seeking the thoughts behind his own gray-and-green eyes. Then his mouth gently found her lips, and he brushed them, and returned to them a little warmer and moist, more tenderly pressing than he had ever kissed any woman before. Barely audible groans of sweetness escaped from his throat, but in that moment of ecstasy Charles suffered cruelly, remembering unwillingly the ruthless crime he had perpetrated on his young victim. For God's sake! Helena was not even eighteen years old, and he had already ruined her life.

He pulled himself from her own gentle embrace, and discreetly avoided the strange purple lights of her eyes, holding her arm as he led her to the horses. His brown gelding and the gentle mare she rode were tethered at the edge of a small forest that began here. He lifted her onto her horse, still avoiding the possibly overwhelming wonder in Helena's black eyes. Then he sprang onto his own, and they cantered off on their return to the Indian village.

After about two miles the vigorous exercise of riding and skillfully maneuvering the ponies around trees and through narrow paths along the sides of the hills had relieved their tension. Soon they came to open spaces again, and Helena broke the silence.

"Why did you not seek your mother's house when you first hired the Indians here?"

"I didn't hire them in Santa Fe. Actually they got into a row in Panama City where they had gone in a group, as a commission, I would say, to buy new arms and ammunition with which to hunt. They were so frustrated with their lack of money that all they managed to do was get drunk. I happened to be in the area on the lookout for men for my own work and had just returned from Boquete where I had tried to find out more about my mother. So when I met up with these men, who were precisely from Santa Fe, and when the police came to lock them up, I thought of a fine way to bind them to me. I bailed them out, or in another way of speaking, paid the police to leave them in my custody. The police did not have any in-

terest in me, considering me just another foreigner,
and one willing to take the unruly louts off their
hands, and for money, too! They didn't question my
motives for wanting to do what I did."

"I wondered . . ." Helena's voice disappeared as
the horses loosened some rocks with their hooves. The
clatter alerted them to the fact that the path was already getting more definite, a sure sign that some
form of steady traffic kept it so.

A mile later they approached the primitive Cholo
village, where Charles had commandeered and paid
for one of the better-protected huts.

The hut was thatched with the dried leaves of various types of palms found in this cooler region of the
mountains. The walls were a mixture of hardened
mud, cornhusks, and twigs, and had a pleasant appearance. Within these walls Charles had deposited
the bedding, no longer close together on the floor, but
discreetly apart. And here they had dwelled for two
nights before they had set out to verify the tales about
Lucinda González.

Now, as they finally arrived at the village they
found it in an uproar. The entire population, it
seemed, was swarming about in panic, voices and eyes
straining in the direction which, from their vantage
point on the brown ponies, Charles and Helena saw
was across the empty space which served as the village square.

There one of the men—he looked like Pedro, though
his furiously distorted and pained features made him
barely recognizable—was being dragged to his hut, as

though he could not stand on his own feet. Was it possible, thought Charles, that so early in the day Pedro had already imbibed so much chicha that he was totally drunk?

With the mystery of his mother's death weighing heavily upon him, Charles had not bothered to ask after the welfare of the families of his Indian followers, a fact which he now regretted, thinking that perhaps his men were shouldering burdens he might have eased.

And now as they rode into the village, through the hysteria of some of the women and from the grave, wavering voices of the men, he made out that Pedro, in a fit of jealousy, had just murdered his wife, Lastenia, a sweet, black-eyed Chola with creamy brown skin and firm round breasts that she had pushed proudly forward against her long loose-fitting cotton dress. Even Charles had not failed to notice her brilliant smile among the wives who had scurried to meet his party on their arrival two days before.

Unwittingly leaving Helena in anguish to handle her panic, Charles slipped quickly off his horse as soon as he discerned the figure of Pedro's brother, Pablo, whose grief-stricken face was as contorted as that of the murderer's. On approaching him, Charles grabbed Pablo persuasively and led him away from the excited and mobilized villagers who were pressing the murderer toward his own hut. Those who could fit, Charles saw as he looked over his shoulder, entered with him, and the rest milled about outside, clamoring with questions, answers, and laments.

Closeted with Pedro's brother in a nearby hut,

Charles learned that Pedro had arrived in Santa Fe, immediately taking his woman with him to their hut. He had discovered only this morning that she had been seen in secretive, unbecoming intimacy with one of the men who had stayed behind; this man apparently had seduced her during Pedro's long absence in Panama City. Now the woman was pregnant, it had been rumored, and Pedro had wrenched a desperate confession from her acknowledging her error. In his rage Pedro had dragged her by her sleek coarse black hair to the dwelling of the lover and there he had challenged the treacherous buck to a duel down in the cañada.

When Charles expressed a wish to know the details, Pablo, by now morbidly excited like the rest of the villagers, led him to the edge of a steep hill nearby, and down into the ravine. Along the bottom flowed a lazy creek which now, fed by the rains that had been pouring down every afternoon, was a perpetual torrent of muddy water. Thin bamboo canes called *caña* grew here abundantly along the banks, and in clusters up the side of the hill, and hid from view any violence that either nature or man could perpetrate in the clearings between the various groves. It was here that the bloody scene had taken place.

The spot where Lastenia had screamed for forgiveness and mercy was still drenched in blood. It would only be washed away in the rains later that day. Farther on was another great swath of blood, and it was there that Pedro had slashed his wife's lover to death with a machete. Lastenia had been decapitated with one sweep of the blade of the long fighting machete

257

which the Cholos normally used only to slash vegetation. The machete, whether short or long, was the prized possession of every Indian, and it was continually sharpened on hard stone, wetted with water, then sharpened once more. It was deadly.

Pedro's last words to Lastenia before he cut short her hysterical pleas for pardon no one had heard, for all had kept away from the duel, knowing that to incur the wrath of the husband was folly. When at last Pedro had begun stumbling dazedly up the sharp embankment, friends and relations of both victims and even of the dishonored husband had clambered down the steep hill. The bodies had been removed in horror and buried hastily on another hill downstream away from the village. Pedro would never consent to their burial in an honored fashion, so the hasty job was done to avoid further scenes of violence. While the interments were being carried out, Pedro stood noisily outside in the village square, shouting obscenities while gulping great draughts of chicha laced with *seco,* the dreadful white lightning of the mountain peasants. It was then that the villagers had decided he must be controlled.

By the time Charles returned to the village from the ravine, the citizens had settled somewhat, and the uneasy silence was broken only by the curses raging from time to time from Pedro's hut. Only a few men still stood outside his door to make sure he did not once again disrupt the dignity of the village.

Helena had been peeping continually out the door of the hut she shared with Charles, totally bewildered by the tale of blood she had finally understood from some of the women. How could Pedro do such a thing? The girl he had so viciously murdered, whom he had once loved no doubt, was young, lonely, barely a woman except in the physical responses of her body. It was not her fault that she had succumbed to the wiles and snares of an insistent seducer. Didn't she herself know the futility of struggling against a determined man? The woman who had befriended her had told her the story, and even beneath the current of criticism for what Lastenia had done by falling in love with another man and betraying her husband, there had been an obvious understanding and even some sympathy. But none of the women dared display that sympathy to the males of the tribe for fear that their own honesty would then be questioned.

At least once every generation there took place in these mountains the decapitation of an unfaithful woman, sometimes even of one simply suspected to be so. Helena was shocked to hear that the rumors of such violence which she had heard in her childhood were true. Now she hoped to hear that Charles would act as a judge, a harsh one, and spurn the righteous mentality of the men by severely punishing Pedro, thus putting a damper if not an end to such barbarous crimes.

When Helena spotted Charles returning from the cañada, she gathered her courage and walked briskly, half-trotting across the clearing of the village to meet him.

"What do you plan on doing about this . . . this murder?" she blurted out, her breathing labored from the strange constriction in her throat. Upon Charles's answer hinged the resolution of her own conflicts, for their recent closeness in the plateau above the village had bewildered Helena as much as the horrible crime which had taken place in the village that day. When it came, his answer was like a swift knife.

"I don't plan to do anything, Helena. These people have their own way of judging their crimes, and I for one do not plan to interfere."

"You don't plan to interfere? You don't plan to interfere?" Helena's question seemed to echo from the pits of her heart, and her bitter disappointment at Charles's answer went unnoticed by him only because he was too concerned with what he would be hearing from Pedro, toward whose hut he was headed.

Charles felt that as leader of these men, he actually must become involved even if to a small degree in the affair, if only to maintain that niche of leadership which he had earned with so much difficulty. He did not intend to lose his advantage, his position of command, the paternalistic pedestal on which his men were beginning to put him. But to pit himself against the age-old customs of the villagers was to lose their faithfulness, which he intended to have at all cost for the good of his own country. Furthermore, he knew he could not change these people's attitudes by forcing his own sense of justice on them.

Not realizing that Helena was in anguish at the callous words he had spoken—words which only pointed out to her the vulnerability of herself and of all women—he strode decisively into Pedro's hut.

The hoarse cries of the inebriated Cholo soon quieted down, and from outside, where Helena remained standing in shocked stillness, the sound of the men's voices in the hut became eventually only a loud murmur of unintelligible words.

So. This white male, this supposedly cultured and educated creature, was not prepared to defend in any way the memory of a young defenseless Indian woman who had unjustly been slaughtered in a jealous rage by the man who had sworn to protect her. So. Charles de Thierny continued supporting revenge in its most brutal forms, not bothering to lift a finger to help those in the lowest pits of despair and injustice. Helena covered her face with her hands, sobbed suddenly into them, then turned desperately to run back to the hut.

Two of the women who had seen her talking with the white man, and who—from her reaction on hearing the story of Pedro's crime—could guess what she had been about, came to her and helped her down on a mat of rushes where Charles had earlier laid their bedrolls, and encouraged her to remain there. Soon all three women were sobbing over the violent death of their fellow woman, though Helena was truthfully the only one who felt that the Indian wife's punishment had been totally undeserved. She considered the brutal chastisement and warning one more male method of crushing womankind—using as the excuse for murder the dirty, meaningless avenging of men's so-called honor.

In the meantime Charles heard the wretched story from the dazed and drunken murderer himself.

"I didn't want to kill her, Patrón. I didn't want to kill her. I always wanted her near me. But when I saw her there, even after that son of a *zorra* was dead, bleeding to death from every open wound, I could see that he was taking her with him. I could see it in her black eyes. He had won. He would possess her every moment while she lived. He was taking her with him even in his death . . . and I didn't want him to take her with him." Pedro broke down crying miserably, helplessly, wallowing in mucous and hiccups, in the debris of broken clay pots and artifacts which had once graced the hut.

Charles could not stomach the awful scene anymore, and soon quietly left, passing through the small group of men outside who, in awe, moved apart to give him space. Wearily, he entered his own hut.

Helena was lying on the mat, asleep, tears staining her cheeks. She must have been exhausted, thought Charles. It had been such a strenuous day. Too much had happened. In the gloom of the tiny dwelling only Helena's beauty shone, touched by rays of the afternoon which soon would be no more, for already great black clouds were rolling in from the north over the valleys and plateaus of the mountains. He let himself fall down next to her, and leaned on his elbow so that he could study her. He wanted so much to reach for her, to touch her, but he only allowed himself to grasp a handful of golden hair that lay in disarray about her head. It was like silk, the purest golden silk imaginable, and he felt himself pulled to the golden mass to smother his lips and face in its perfection.

As the first giant drops of rain began to pelt the

Cholo village, Charles remained staring out the primitive open door into the gray sheets that blocked everything from view, thinking about many things.

When Helena woke up after the overgenerous rain, it was Charles who was sleeping, and that night, since they now communicated not at all in the darkness of the enclosure before going to sleep, Charles did not notice the sullenness of her silence.

The next morning, in the earliest hours, Charles left with Pablo and a few of the other Cholos to hunt, aware that deer and wild rabbit would be a delicious treat for the villagers, whose hunting had been sorely restricted by a lack of arms and ammunition.

The men returned after the noonday meal, triumphantly dragging on a sled of palm fronds a magnificent deer, which was soon to be quartered, divided among the families, and cooked with zest and satisfaction for the evening meals.

Charles hurried to the hut to talk to Helena, but found her exhausted once again. She begged to be allowed to rest for a while. Charles attributed her tiredness to the shock and strain of the previous day, though he himself had already put the terrible incident behind him. He could see no sense in dwelling on the brutal revenge that Pedro had carried out. It only caused a restless pain within himself to think about it, but he knew that Helena was very sensitive, and when she asked to be left alone to relax, he acquiesced, solicitous and gracious. After taking out his pipe and tobacco plus a slim cardboard file containing a sheaf of papers on which he worked from time to time, he left her.

He ambled pensively toward the relaxing hammock one of his men had swung for him across the low branches of two guava trees. He smiled, sinking into its folds, for his stature and weight were such that his buttocks remained only a scant two inches from the bare, root-gnarled ground under the trees. The dirt there had been trampled so excessively in this favorite spot of the village that the water of the storm the day before had simply run off down the hill that fell away behind the two handy trees. During the right season one could easily reach up and pluck the delicious yellow-green fruit and munch it while swinging gently in the breeze.

Charles's thoughts, however, could not remain on prosaic details because his mind strayed with insistence to the poetic softness of Helena, who had been able to touch the deepest chords of his heart. He had used Helena vilely. There was no forgiveness for him for that, he knew. But the thought that they would soon separate forever was even more difficult to contemplate. How could he sleep at night and not half-waken to reach softly for her, to feel inquisitively her oblivious form and assure himself of her warm presence? What would it be like to awaken in the morning and not see her stretching in her sleep, then unconsciously snuggling drowsily against the muscles of his own yearning body? Wouldn't he be bored to frustration when he could no longer hear her taunting voice, or her laughter whenever she forgot she was supposed to hate him?

Charles was suddenly aware of the seriousness of his questions. If he were to allow Helena to leave, there would forever be an unfillable vacuum within him. He was not an inexperienced lad who sought the ideal woman of his adolescent dreams. He had savored the flesh of many women; he had known many more, and he knew there was no perfect female anywhere. But somehow, with all her imperfections, her terrible lack of docility, her caustic tongue, Helena was the only one he had ever loved. Hell, yes! He might as well admit it. Back there on the trail, when her life was in danger, he knew that he loved and wanted her by him always, so badly he could tremble from the thought. He didn't just want her body, though he thought of her female curves often enough. He also wanted her admiration, her approval, her devotion—in short, her love.

His mind told him he was worse than a fool, misinterpreting his own lecherous motivations that way, but his heart was convinced that the wisest thing he could do was to be straightforward and, for a change, thoroughly honest about Helena—and honest *with* her as well.

Relieved at having come to this happy conclusion, he finally settled himself steadily into the hammock to work on plans and suggestions concerning his mission, which he had discussed with the French consul in Panama City. He gathered his papers, put them in order, and began to concentrate on the information about Panama which he had been sadly neglecting all the preceding weeks while investigating his mother's whereabouts, and then carrying out his miserable revenge.

The smell of cooking awakened Helena, and though

she felt hungry, some of the odors that assailed her, instead of whetting her appetite, merely disgusted her—uncharacteristically so, for it was the usually pleasant smell of wild onions cooking that she suddenly found distasteful. Her throat felt dry and queasy.

As she sat up on the bedroll, she spied a folded sheet of paper on the floor and reached out for it, suspecting it had fluttered down from the file Charles had taken with him when he left her behind to rest. Some innocent curiosity made her unfold it. As she glanced at the writing, she was engulfed by a rush of pain and bitterness. It was a list, in French, presumably written by Charles, outlining in cold-blooded detail her own abduction as part of the revenge he had since carried out.

1. Prepare carriage
2. Deliver note to Benito González
3. Waylay the girl's chaperone; have Pablo handle the old bat.
4. Pick up the González bitch. . . .

Helena could read no more. The rest flooded over her in memories so full of bile that they made her feel sick to her stomach, compounded as they were with the icy memory of Lastenia's murder and Charles de Thierny's unmoving cruelty and unfairness in the face of it.

The bitterness was so thorough that all the tender emotions she and Charles had only a day or two ago shared on the high plateau near his mother's grave were wiped away in that moment of shame—shame that she had betrayed her self-respect and her pride for the paltry prize of his too-knowing caresses, shame at her so easily won affections. He had treated her with contemptible cruelty, yet his physical attractions had subdued her hatred. No! She would not allow him to escape her true and righteous wrath. Where, earlier, forgiveness, even tenderness, had reigned, now she would fan only the conflagration of hatred that consumed her. The proof was too clear that his streak of ruthlessness ran deep within him.

Her eyes came back unwillingly to the paper which trembled in her hand, and fell on the item referring to her chaperone.

Rosario! In all these weeks Helena had not once remembered that Rosario, too, had been attacked. It proved to her that she had been warped by degradation into a selfish creature, thinking only of herself, surrendering to the physical pleasures with which her captor had seduced her, forgetting her pride and her promise to loathe what he represented, slithering like a slimy snake in ecstasy beneath him. Evil! She, too, had become evil by succumbing to his devil's temptations. Helena crushed the sheet of paper in her hand.

Precisely at that moment a long shadow loomed across the dirt floor of the hut. She looked up at the source of it. Charles. He stood there, tall and silent, his silhouette immense against the light at the entrance to the hut. His voice came softly, low, full of unexpected distress.

"What I have done to you is unforgivable."

The statement was met by a stony silence and the unaltered stare of liquid black eyes.

"Helena, will you marry me?"

This time the silence that followed was only momentary. The retort came out of Helena's mouth before she could phrase it any sweeter, but her voice was steady, carrying not a single trace of hysterics; only an icy edge to it gave away her deep resentment.

"Charles de Thierny, just the thought that you could think I'd accept your proposal sickens me indeed. Did you really think I could marry a man who's done to me what you have done?"

Charles was taken aback. His humility before the girl, though sincere, had been difficult to muster.

"Do you hate me so much?"

"Not only do I despise you, monsieur, but I would never marry a man for the sole purpose of hiding behind his name to save my honor. No. I will face what I must, but at least my life will be my own. I have done a lot of thinking the last few weeks. I'd rather throw myself on the mercy of Don Benito, for as much as you have despised the man for some foolishness of his youth, I have never known him to do an unkind thing. *He* will find some way to protect me."

A twitch of Charles's shoulders indicated how her words smarted. "I deserve that," he stated bitterly. "I cannot blame you for thinking the worst of me. I have acted like an animal—worse, because I used calculation and actually planned this whole revenge. And all under the pretext of cleansing my honor.

"But I will tell you something, *ma petite blonde*. I

realize now that I fell in love for the first time on that ship from France, and that I lost my heart to you, a proud and brave young girl from whom I should have learned many lessons in life. I am not offering marriage solely as reparation. Won't you think it over?"

A heavy silence followed, for Helena did not deign to answer him, thinking bitterly to herself that a man like that could not possibly know the meaning of the word love—guilt and remorse, perhaps, but not love. Out loud she asked bluntly:

"What do you plan to do with me now, monsieur?"

"Stop calling me monsieur, for God's sake! Can't you simply address me as 'Charles'?"

"I can't bring myself to call you that. Don't force me on such a small point."

"I haven't forced you to do anything for a long while now, Helena, and I don't intend to force myself upon you any longer. Tomorrow we turn back to Panama City, and I shall deliver you to your friend, Don Benito. Even if he is still in Boquete waiting for me to take you there as I informed him that I would, it should not be difficult to leave you in his house in Panama and get a message to him by way of the port of David to come back to Panama City and claim you. Once he makes it to David from Boquete it should take him only a few days or even less to arrive in Panama City."

After a pause, in a softer tone of voice, Charles added:

"I suppose you will tell him everything that has happened?"

"No, not everything, unless life forces me again to

go against my own will. If I can help it, I will forget these last few weeks. They have been terrible for me."

"Everything about them, Helena?"

"Yes, everything. What you mistook for pleasure was more painful to my soul than that first night in Panama Viejo. I want to forget *everything*."

Resigned, Charles made his decision.

"Very well, then. Tomorrow we leave early in the morning. I don't want to chance any rain on the bad part of the pass. I shall also prepare a list of addresses and points where you can get word to me should you need me for anything. It's the least you can allow me to do. I trust you will not go to the police about this. I won't let anyone catch me anyway, and besides, I think too much has been done to you already. Let us spare your reputation a public trial. That's no way to punish me. Besides, your scorn is more than enough punishment because . . . I . . . love you."

With that Charles de Thierny turned and strode away, as if his confession had brought some terrible shame down upon him.

Chapter XIV

The waves pounded unceasingly against the black rocks of Punta Paitilla. Streaks of turquoise across the waters weaved in and out amid the gray blue, while away in the distance the lusher islands made a dark-green contrast, so that greens and grays swarmed in Helena's mind to form a pair of disturbing flecked eyes.

"Charles's eyes," she thought simply.

They had made their way back down to the Pacific and soon she would be home, or at least the closest thing to home she had—Don Benito's and Tía Alejandra's and the love and protection of Rosario as well. Confronted by this prospect, she felt more desolate than joyful.

As uneventful as the return trip to the city had been, Helena had felt the constant strain of maintaining an aloof distance from Charles. He had made every effort to draw her into conversation, making her aware that he was bent on becoming her friend, as reparation, perhaps, for the terrible punishment which she had endured. He seemed to take no serious note of nor was he taunted by her unfriendliness, assuming apparently that it was her way of preventing his physical proximity—which was, in part, the truth.

Helena had no realistic idea, however, of the struggle Charles had to make to keep his hands off her. She had continued to bathe in the late afternoons whenever it was possible and, as usual, he kept watch over her. Candidly and deliberately, without shame, Helena stripped and washed herself lavishly in the green forest pools that they discovered, or at the edge of tiny brooks that now with the rainy season were often swollen to a dangerous size. Frequently the water was churned and muddy, and Helena had to forgo her bath. So she took to bathing in the rain, whenever the rains came later than usual in the day, completely disregarding Charles's presence as if she had forgotten how his body could react at the sight of her nakedness.

The first time she decided to use the summer rain as her personal shower, Charles's eyes, shaded by the brim of his hat, ogled her with undisguised lust until he was slightly dazed. He had taken up his post under a large wild almond tree, and while water dripped off the large glossy leaves, he watched in anguished delight as Helena rubbed her body gracefully. The tropical droplets of rain slid caressingly over her silky skin.

Oh! Damn! What torture she was innocently doling

out to him. If she had wanted to revenge herself against him for his previous sins, she could not have found a better way. But he pretended indifference and tore his eyes away from her, wincing as he did so.

His craving for her was tempered by the certainty that his next chance to make her truly his would have to come when she was prepared to admit that she loved him. He would therefore have to woo her, begin from the beginning. By this reasoning he was able to exert control over the yearning that filled him as he watched her ablutions.

Helena didn't appear to notice his inner struggle for control, although she did remark one day with a sarcastic casualness that was not totally lost on him, that he seemed angry after each of her baths.

"Perhaps you shouldn't bother yourself to watch over me, Charles. After all, there is precious little you could do to save my neck if a snake should bite me."

"There's a lot I could do."

"I've learned to take care of myself by now, anyway."

He waved her objections away. "No, no. It's fine. I feel responsible for you."

"Well, I just had the feeling that you resented doing this somehow. That's all."

She looked up at him under her lashes, and for a fleeting moment Charles thought he saw a glimmer of triumph in them. But her eyes clouded over and held no special message.

"I'll stay, Helena."

Helena had few pangs of fear regarding Charles, who now left her alone at night and was extremely

273

respectful. And if he suffered secretly at all because he had given his word not to touch her—*tant pis!* He deserved his frustrations. In any case, he kept his distance and showed no obvious signs of inner turmoil. She began to relax, unlearning her former apprehensions about his intentions. He seemed by now to have lost interest in her physically, much to her relief. Perhaps his new attitude was due to her slimness, for had he not once mentioned that he thought she was skinny? Helena frowned as she experienced a few moments of uncertainty, suspecting uncomfortably that she might have lost much of her beauty during this terrible voyage to and from Santa Fe. However, the practical side of her nature assured her that this was the way she wanted it to be. She didn't want Charles to touch her so it didn't really matter how ugly she might have become. If it helped her to repel his amorous advances of the past weeks, so much the better!

Helena did not realize that though she was somewhat on the too slender side, her breasts had begun to fill out in an unexpected spurt of womanly development. Her golden tan gave her a delicious mellowness that was heightened by her sun-bleached hair, which Charles imagined had captured the essence of tropical light. But Helena was sure that Charles would find it much easier to keep his promise not to force himself upon her now that she was not as attractive as she'd been when he first abducted her. And as long as she could keep him from touching her with his clever, experienced hands, she knew she need not fear succumbing to his will.

But words were something else. Helena had been starved for so long from communicating her thoughts and her ideas, that she was afraid she might fall quite easily into accepting the tacit invitation that Charles extended. Her negative feelings managed to help her from joining joyously in conversation, but in spite of herself, for the first time since her chat with Don Benito on the train from Colón to Panama City, Helena found herself listening to a man, this time to one who candidly spoke of his plans for the future and of his past. And he had lived such a glorious past, she soon discovered, adventuring in the north of Africa, working with the famed Ferdinand de Lesseps, traveling to exotic realms that she could only imagine. His experiences had ranged from the grand houses of London to the ballrooms of Paris to the most wretched and inhuman wildernesses, and they were the experiences she would have wanted to have, had she had the fortune to be born a man.

Whenever he ventured to be kind and relaxed during his attempts to draw her into his stories, Helena felt a tremor of uncertainty; his gentleness made her want to capitulate. But no! This was the man who had brutally raped her—who had ruined her chances for a happy, fulfilled life. She would never forgive him for that! It was important to remain worldly, controlled, and invulnerable before him. Above all she must appear invulnerable. And for that reason he must never know that once, several weeks before, she had longed for him in a strange, confusing way that had nothing to do with his caresses and his advances.

They had been on their way to Santa Fe. She had already succumbed to his pawings, that evening, and he appeared to be exhausted after a grueling day and quite satisfied after he had made love to her. But as had often happened to Helena during those terrible days in the mountains, she couldn't fall asleep right away, for her thoughts and her worries kept circling in her brain—always unresolved.

Charles had forgotten to turn the lantern off before falling into a deep slumber, when abruptly, in his sleep, he kicked his cover off, perhaps because the night was warmer than usual. Helena paled for a moment in surprise, but as she let her gaze fall on his nakedness, instead of cringing before it as she would have liked to be able to do, she felt, the impulses of an irresistible curiosity. Before she was really aware of what she was about, she had reached for his body, her hand sweeping downward lightly, almost longingly, over his taut belly to his groin and lower. His muscles flowed smoothly over his long limbs, gleaming in the lamplight. The dark curly fur that caught the light was fascinatingly masculine, covering his body in varying degrees of healthy thickness. Helena had never seen Charles totally relaxed, so that for the first time his male vulnerability struck a chord of some curious tenderness in her, a mothering protectiveness which she had never felt for any man. She had quickly covered him again, however, as she sensed the danger of this moment for her. Now she must hide her uncertainty and her guilt at all cost, for if Charles knew how deeply he had affected her, she would be lost, would be his slave.

Charles did not give up easily trying to coax Helena into responding to his long-winded tales, but it did consume a great share of his emotional strength to do so, for he was by nature neither a talkative, nor a patient man. But sometimes, as the evenings wore into the night and Helena's drowsiness pulled her guard down, he was rewarded by the sight of the deep and captivating dimple of Helena's left cheek. It would peep out at the most unexpected moments, and especially when Helena smiled, which was not as often as he would have wished.

One night near the end of their return trip, by the fire which had been lit mainly to keep away the savage mosquitoes of the rainy season, and sensing that Helena was in a melancholic and tired mood, he managed with exquisite persuasion to elicit from her some vague facts about herself, but on hearing her hesitant story was sorry he had successfully prompted her to tell it.

"My mother was desolate when she received the news of my father's death, and I don't believe she ever completely recovered her nerves after that. When I returned from France, it was because she had died. . . . Formally, I am still in mourning." She paused as her eyes fell on the flickering tongues of the campfire, remembering something that perhaps she would not reveal.

Charles slapped at a mosquito that had braved the heat and the smoke of the fire, while his eyes wandered guiltily away from Helena. Stepping away and picking up a cudgel near them, he poked quite needlessly into the fire. He busied himself by stirring up the coals of burned wood, and by cleaning his hands, rubbing them together.

In mourning! He had abducted an orphan and by his actions had razed her hopes for a decent and normal life. Would he ever be able to make it up to her? He didn't think so, and he sighed as he came back to her, to hear her speak in her lilting French that had the barest trace of a mountain accent.

Helena's background did not continue to unfold before him by the evening campfires as they wended their way down the mountains and hills and through the jungles, only because she chose not to allow to. He learned to respect her aloof civility, though, for in spite of the fact that it defined only a fragile sort of relationship, it did to some degree protect them mutually from any more emotional pain. He recounted some of his more fabulous adventures, happy when he heard her musical laughter and the huskier notes that pervaded it whenever she forgot to remain in austere indifference, usually when she had been dreamily staring into the evening fire. He learned to take advantage of those moments, and felt not an ounce of guilt for that bit of ruthlessness. He felt a never-before-experienced thrill when he could make her look at him in wonder at those moments as he told of the deeds of his past. He soon realized that Helena had a vivid imagination and that his tales were unfolding in very real scenes before her.

Charles did not confide all, however, and omitted telling about the many deceptions and disappointments he had suffered in his life. Once he thought he had been in love, but that was long ago, and it had not been love after all. Nor did he complain about the efforts of his stepmother to make his life hell on Earth in order to get even for her own frustrations and jealousies where his father was concerned. It was she who had come to Jeannette's family with that terrible secret about his mother's insanity. It had been difficult enough to convince Jeannette's parents that his illegitimacy would at least not affect his fortune, but the new information caused even Jeannette to cast him aside forever. How many tears had he shed? He'd still been young enough to cry over a woman then, but he had sworn he would never cry over another. When Jeannette and her parents were killed not long afterward in a carriage accident, he shed no tears, though he did suffer an upheaval of regrets and bitter memories.

After Francesca, his stepmother, died, Charles discovered how she had come to possess that secret which his father had once assured him had never been violated. Charles found a packet of letters among his stepmother's papers and realized very quickly that they had belonged to his father. Among the letters, which all concerned Lucinda González, there were reports from the private investigators the baron had hired. These letters had fallen into Francesca's hands, and thus, the wicked deeds of the Gonzálezes, the insanity to which they had driven and condemned their own flesh and blood, had been compounded by still more evil and had destroyed his life, for Francesca had used the tragedy of Lucinda to expose and ruin her stepson Charles, relating the secret in all its ugliness to the parents of sweet Jeannette. The discovery had aroused his original hatred for the Gonzálezes to a higher pitch than ever, and he had sworn again in blinding rage that one day he would scourge the González name and family if it was the last that he lived to do. The intensity of his hatred had been staggering.

Charles said nothing to Helena about how all this had soured his life, for he felt embarrassed that she might misinterpret the confession as an attempt to excuse himself for what he had done to her.

Since the day Charles de Thierny had openly confessed his love for her, it seemed to have intensified a thousandfold. This fact he kept to himself, too, however, afraid to lay bare his heart and expose himself to her further disdain.

It was with a sigh of regret that he had finally sighted the Pacific and realized that they would soon have to part.

Now they were almost to Panama City.

Far away from Punta Paitilla, across the bay which was enclosed and sheltered somewhat at his end by the rocks of the point, the vague silhouette of Panama City could be discerned. Fishing vessels were already far out for the day's work, some of them barely specks across the waters.

Helena turned from the scene before her to observe the men as they broke camp. She watched as they folded the bedroll on which she had lain every night during the return trip from Santa Fe. The sparse grass around the tents was still bent from yesterday's rain, glistening like green metal blades.

Charles had kept his word. Not once had he approached her with anything less than courtesy, as though perhaps she were his ward rather than his mistress. His mistress! And yet the title did not disgust her as she hoped it would. Helena was confused by her own reactions. Instead of feeling the surge of triumph she had expected at Charles's spiritual defeat, a strange and restless uncertainty had crept even farther into her soul. Now, when she should be relishing unbounded joy at the prospect of leaving behind this drama of her life, she felt an anticipation of homesickness much like the one she had experienced when she'd left the Isthmus for school several years before.

"What is wrong with me?" she asked herself in bewilderment. But not once would she admit to herself that Charles de Thierny had much of anything to do with the emotions that were wreaking havoc within her.

Charles was busy directing his men. The camping equipment and most of the men would head back to make a new campsite. He and three of his Indian cohorts would arrive there later. Would they decide to camp at Panama Viejo? Helena wondered vaguely, the images of the ancient ruins fluttering tauntingly in her mind. The memories were too disturbing. She looked again out to the waters that twisted and hurled themselves onto the barnacle-covered blackness of the rocks not far below. How magnificent the ocean was! How ceaseless its attempts to woo the land. But the land resisted and resisted.

Helena had always preferred the creeping of gentle waves onto the sand, for the pounding of the sea on rocks and walls, though spectacular, had never offered her solace or the opportunity to participate directly in its beauty. When the sea was calm, on the other hand, and when she was still a child, she had delighted in walking along the sandy beach, collecting shells and watching the tiny crabs that scurried from one miniature conch to another. Burland Jones had often accompanied her, for he insisted she should experience these thrills, and he seemed to sense her need for adventure and exploration.

Helena remained gazing out, sometimes toward the islands and sometimes toward the gray specks of Panama City. A hand on her shoulder startled her.

"Beautiful, isn't it?" Charles's baritone voice vibrated over the sounds of the waves crashing on stone and sand.

"Yes, it is." Helena's voice was lost in a whisper.

"It's time to go now. Come."

He helped her down off the perch of higher rocks on which she had stood, the wind whipping her blond sun-streaked hair about her in disarray. She was beautiful, thought Charles, and he had lost her. And worse than that, he had harmed her. His mouth was twisted in self-recrimination as he led her to the ponies.

He had changed his clothing, and his linen shirt was fine and shone white in the sunlight. Beads of sweat had formed on his sunbronzed brow from the exertion of breaking camp. To wipe away the perspiration he unfolded the finest-quality linen handkerchief with the initial C de T embroidered with the fine black hair of the French seamstress who had made it. His pants were a deep tan color and the cut, even to Helena's not yet experienced eye, was obviously excellent. He wore his taller riding boots, black and polished until they boasted that unmistakable gleam of the finest-quality leather. He cut a striking figure. Somehow Helena was pleased that he looked so elegant.

She herself was wearing a blue calico dress which one of the Indian women had made for her from material Charles had brought for the tribe in Santa Fe. It was a loose gown with small sleeves and a round neckline that fell straight down to her ankles in great loose folds.

Five ponies waited for them, rested and saddled. They would have to skirt the swamp, ride inland about a half a mile, then set out across the gentle hills that led into the city.

Charles helped Helena mount her horse; the three Indians were already astride theirs, and Charles leaped easily to straddle his own chestnut pony. Chocolate whinnied and gamboled his forelegs in restless anticipation of the morning's exercise, but soon quieted down as he felt the master's guidance.

"Good-bye, Helena. I have to leave you here. My men will take excellent care of you and will accompany you to Benito González's house."

"You are not coming with us?" Helena's question was undeniably one of surprise. Did he detect just a small note of disappointment? Bah! Wishful thinking. And if there were some disappointment on her part it would only have to do with the loss of the friendship he had offered and carefully cultivated all these weeks since they had left Santa Fe. He would not risk losing that, too.

"No, I'm not coming along. I cannot be seen in the city until my work is done. As I recently explained, Helena, though my work is ultimately for the good of your country as well as mine, as a Frenchman trying to protect the interests of France, my presence on the Isthmus must remain a secret. The governor of Panama might take a negative view of my snooping around without permission from the central government, and since the treaty for the canal construction has not been signed yet, things are too delicate to risk an international incident. If I'm caught, I could even be declared a spy by Colombia.

"So you see, I did not come to Panama solely for revenge, after all." Charles suppressed a bitter smile. Lines of determination appeared around his mouth once more, set sternly to utter, "Good-bye."

Before Helena could question him further, he slapped her pony, and the foursome moved away in rapid leaps—Helena and her three Cholo escorts mounted on the sturdy Isthmian horses that had so faithfully carried them the last weeks and even months.

Charles turned his own larger steed in the opposite direction, and once, when he glanced back, he sighted Helena's tanned face as she, too, looked behind to catch what she thought was one last glimpse of Charles de Thierny.

BOOK II

*Panama
City*

Chapter XV

Helena and Rosario sat at the breakfast table in a nook overlooking the sea, for the González home, along with some of the warehouses that belonged to the estate, was built in a busy area of the town on a low rocky ledge overlooking the Bay of Panama just a few feet below. A series of terraced floors opened out and supported a potted garden of fanlike palms and feathery ferns. Container after container, all placed in groups whose natural-looking setting vied with the jungle for beauty, graced the terraces that ended in a balustrade marking the beginning of the waters of the bay.

Not far away sailboats and fishing vessels bobbed and dipped as the placid water shimmered beneath them, making them tremble with its touch. The slight odor of putrefaction was mitigated by that of iodine

and offset by the beauty of the gulls as they swooped
and circled gracefully.

Never would she stop admiring this place, thought
Helena. And incredibly, it was hers. She had inherited
every piece of property owned by the González family
on the Isthmus of Panama. Her wealth was so enormous and the surprise and shock of the bequest so
great that even after these many weeks since her return from captivity, Helena felt as if she were simply
dreaming it all.

Her yearning to thank Don Benito could not be satisfied, for even before her own release, both he and
Doña Alejandra had drowned in a shipwreck at sea,
on their way to their coffee plantation in the mountains of Chiriquí in the valley of Boquete. Rosario
had told Helena of the strange request her captor had
made in his note, and then, having put together the
pieces of information, realizing that even though their
death was accidental, it had been predestined, Helena
had burst into tears.

"The revenge, the revenge," she cried out between
sobs. "Lucinda González received her revenge after
all." And amid the tears that flowed and the distress
that tore her apart, Helena told Rosario the whole
story of her bondage from beginning to end, including the history of Charles de Thierny and his family
tragedy.

The kind pats and cooings of Rosario at each new
burst of emotion from Helena as she recounted the
tribulations she had been through acted as a sort of
tonic to soothe the young woman's nerves. The sobs
became less profound and finally turned into gentle

hiccups, among which the cruelty of Helena's situation began seriously to take on enormous proportions in Rosario's mind.

"I just want to forget it all, Rosario, but I don't know how."

"Well, now, darling, don't you worry. Now that it's off your chest, most of it will just begin to seem like a bad dream you had long ago."

"But, Rosario, his face! I see it so clearly. His eyes . . . bearing down on me. . . . And the worst thing is that I can't seem to forget him!" The words began to fail her then, but she continued even though they seemed to clog in her throat. "The . . . rape . . . is almost a blur in my mind, but I see him as clearly as if he were here, following me, making me suffer. If I could only blot that face out of my mind, because I . . . I . . . I hate him!"

Finding that Rosario's previously comforting clucks, instead of soothing her, suddenly irritated her, Helena turned on her heels and ran upstairs to the elegant Spanish colonial bedroom that was now hers. Without a thought to the delicacy of the lace that covered her lovely mahogany bed, she threw herself full-length on it and cried until she had no more tears. She was startled by the sudden and confusing realization that she couldn't say for sure why she was crying.

Even when she remembered that Rosario, too, was mourning the loss of her own mother and her spinster sister in the great fire that had recently burned one third of Panama City, Helena did not stop lamenting her own troubled and turbulent memories. Downstairs

Rosario continued to hear the long echoes of Helena's wailing.

But Rosario did not follow Helena upstairs. She remained instead in a pensive mood at the foot of the massive curved steps that led to the sleeping quarters. She decided she would have to keep a close eye on Helena. She was reluctant to pry, however, fearing that such probing might have a negative effect on the girl's nerves. Helena had been through too much. Her health, both physical and mental, required looking after, however, and she, Rosario, was the only one she had now.

As the days went by, Rosario continued to feel the deep unhappiness that hovered over her friend and mistress. She did not pry, but she did try to encourage Helena to speak about her problems. With an instinctive sensibility, Rosario was sure that Helena's nightmares would vanish if she could somehow verbalize them and get at least some of the hurt off her spirit; but Helena did not choose to unburden herself enough to erase her inner scars.

Helena appreciated Rosario's concern, especially because she suspected that all of Rosario's spritely movements and attempts to care for her were harder on her than Rosario cared to admit. The terrible fire that had rampaged across the city while she was still in the jungle with Charles de Thierny had caused great damage and claimed many lives. The death of her only relatives was a serious blow to Rosario and she had aged visibly in the last weeks. Her body had begun to betray the frailty of age that her spirit would not admit.

In fact, Rosario was more wrinkled than ever, and getting darker, so that sometimes she looked to Helena like a delightful prune. The birdlike motions of her limbs only accentuated the stiffness of her joints. She tired more easily each day, of course, but nevertheless continued to minister as well as she knew how, with sometimes lively and sometimes tender chatter, to the psychological needs of Helena as well as to her physical well-being and relaxation.

It was thus Rosario who first noticed the signs of Helena's pregnancy.

"Child, I never knew you to be disgusted by the smells of cooking food. As skinny as you were, you always did eat like a horse, begging your pardon, of course."

"It's just that I've been through so much. And also, even here by the bay, it gets so hot. I feel more flushed than nauseated, really."

Rosario merely remained silent and thoughtful once again.

One day soon after that comment she approached Helena and asked her, between stammerings, and blushes which only she knew of, for her skin was too dark to display them, how long it had been since Helena's monthly bleeding.

"Why, Rosario, I had almost forgotten. I guess with all my troubles, I was secretly glad that I didn't have that to cope with. I really believe that all the drama I have been through simply affected me. I suppose, too, that the violence . . . Then there was so much forced excercise, and all that horseback riding. . . ."

"Oh, child"—and now it was Rosario's turn to burst

into tears and sobs—"don't you know that the ceasing of a woman's monthly bleeding can mean that she . . . that she's . . . that . . ."

"Well, for heaven's sake, Rosario! What? Surely I'm not going to die!"

"Oh, no! It's nothing like that. I might be wrong, but this could be a sign of . . . pregnancy."

Instead of the assured tone of voice she wished to produce, Rosario's voice faltered and ended almost in a silent mouthing of the word.

Helena heard, however.

The word stunned her, and she stood staring at Rosario as though her feet had taken root. She could not move; she could not think.

"You must try to take it calmly, my dear, for there is naught else to do but have your child. I would like to think of it as a blessing in disguise, a child to soothe the loss of your dear mama and of Carmen and Meester Boorlan, God rest their souls." Rosario was trying desperately to help Helena overcome her apparent dismay and shock.

"But I can't have this . . . this thing in me. I just can't. Isn't there anything I could do to get rid of it? I mean, I have heard that some women lose their babies before they are big enough to live. . . ."

Helena stopped chattering her nervous thoughts when she saw Rosario, eyes huge with shock and disapproval at Helena's words, hastily make the sign of the cross, a gesture that under certain circumstances was made to keep the very devil himself away.

"Helena! Don't even say such things. Do you realize what you are suggesting? Don't even say it! I would never be party to such a thing. My God! What would your poor dear mother in heaven think if she should hear you even suggest this terrible thing?"

"Rosario, I know what you are insinuating . . . that my mother gave birth to me without a husband. But that was different. I have been . . . forced. It was against my will. I could not possibly bear this child." A huge sob racked her as she put her hand to her mouth to keep from crying out her anguish. "I won't!" she finished. And the petite victim of Charles de Thierny burst into bitter tears and ran, sobbing hysterically, up the stairs and into her room.

She slammed the door behind her and threw herself on the bed whose lovely lace coverlet had absorbed so many of her tears since she had returned from her captivity.

After a little while Helena sensed the door creep open, and Rosario's worried brown face appeared around the corner. Helena kept on sobbing as Rosario approached her cautiously. Soon she felt the gentle touch of Rosario's loving hand on her hair.

Helena let herself be pulled about gently while Rosario wisely put her into a nightie. Rosario, it seemed, sensed Helena's need to escape into some world where this pain could not enter so cruelly.

She lay down. She had to lie down for a while. She felt ill. It was the shock, she knew. She must think. She must absorb this new pain, this new assault. Her mind was confused, utterly confused. She could not think this way. She must try to relax. A blessed darkness came over her, a protective sleep that she willed upon herself in some instinctive wisdom.

It was four o'clock in the afternoon when Helena awoke. She lay very still in her four-poster mahogany bed, gazing blankly at the stripes and swirls formed by the iron bars that graced and protected her windows, and thinking, thinking—as rationally as she could.

Charles had won the final battle in his intended war of humiliation. Helena bitterly acknowledged that her body, over which she had once felt the master, had done nothing but betray her since she had met Charles de Thierny. He was the one who had power over it now, having left behind forever his indelible mark in the form of a baby, which, to her utter humiliation, her own body must shape, form, and nourish. As a man, he was able to do this to her, and Helena's rage against the injustice of nature and man knew no bounds. She cursed all men silently, and cursed her weak female condition as well, but her frustration only left her more unhappy and bitter, however determined she remained to refuse to submit with meekness to the abomination of being a woman.

At length she dressed herself, and came down quietly to where she knew Rosario would be waiting, at the breakfast nook that overlooked the sea.

"What do you think I should do, Rosario?" Though her voice sounded unhappy there was in it more of resignation than of rebellion.

Rosario was supremely relieved to notice Helena's calmer attitude, and she sighed gratefully.

"I don't have any specific idea in mind, Helena, but at least you don't have to worry about how to support this child. It almost seems as if it were meant to be, my love, for a González baby will inherit this

González wealth—as he should; Lucinda González was sacrificed, and her grandchild will inherit. It's fair enough when seen from that point of view."

"But I have been sacrificed, too, Rosario, horribly sacrificed!"

"Yes, Helenita, I know how terrible all this must have been for you, but we must also try to resign ourselves to the will of God."

"Keep God out of this! He could not possibly have willingly permitted this awful thing to happen to me. It's more the work of the devil, if you ask me."

"Oh, darling, I'm only upsetting you with my stupid remarks. I don't want you to feel hurt anymore. You have been hurt so much already."

"But what should I do?" wailed Helena, and she wrung her hands as she sat on one of the chairs around the table. She stopped her impatient and anguished movements for a moment, then covered her face with her hands and sat quietly there, as if waiting for advice from Rosario.

Hesitantly Rosario finally suggested, "Why don't you find a husband, Helena?"

"A husband?" Helena looked up in surprise. "And deceive some kind man into thinking that this is his child? Is that much better than ridding myself of the baby before it is much bigger?"

"Infinitely better, my dear. You are not going to deceive anyone. Plenty of men would find not only yourself attractive but also your fortune, and they should be willing to raise your child and give it a name without feeling that they are not getting anything in return."

"Why, I could never do a thing like that, Rosario, not when the father of the child has offered matrimony. True . . . I don't love him. . . ."

"You mean you would rather marry Charles de Thierny?"

"Well, you set me to thinking, Rosario. I just don't want to get another man involved in this tragedy. My pride . . . to beg a man to give my child a name . . . I couldn't do it. It's just not in me. Just as I've decided it's not in me to kill this baby."

"Oh, Helena! I knew you would realize that to have your baby would not be so terrible. After all, you have more than the means of supporting a child. And if he carries your name—and it is a good name—what of it?"

Helena did not seem to be paying attention to Rosario's words, but looked as if she were thinking very hard of what her next step would be now that she had decided that she should, after all, accept her pregnancy with dignity.

Rosario's words had led her to contemplate how far she was willing to go to acquire freedom from public gossip and freedom from private hurt. Coldly, as though she were trying to solve someone else's problem, Helena had decided that she could not destroy this child that she did not want. She had felt a flame of shame at her daring suggestion that death for her offspring could be the solution to her problem. In the end it would not solve her inner turmoil and the painful dilemma of her soul, and these, after all, were what unceasingly tormented her.

"But I've got to get word to him. He did offer marriage. I didn't accept for myself, but for the baby it would be the wisest thing, don't you see? It is a solution. . . ." Her voice faltered as if she were not so sure that this idea was the right one either.

Rosario had misunderstood Helena, and the sudden realization that she seriously meant to wed the criminal who had made her suffer came as an unwelcome surprise.

"Yes, Helena, I do see. I see that you are binding yourself forever to that Charles de Thierny who did you so much harm."

"At first he did, yes, Rosario, that's true. But I've been thinking all these weeks since I came back, that he really did try to make amends. I suppose he didn't want to insist on anything again, especially since he had forced me so violently in order to get his revenge. I think now that he was thoroughly ashamed, even after the first time. But he's so full of pride, and he had made himself such a binding promise. It was an evil promise, but nevertheless, he thought it was a duty to keep his word—even to the point of risking his own life to carry out that revenge.

"Don't you see, Rosario? I would be doing the baby a terrible injustice if he should grow up thinking that his father never wanted him. I just couldn't do that. Or his whole life could be embittered by the thought that he was illegitimate. At the same time I cannot contemplate marrying a stranger to give this baby a name. Oh! I don't know. . . ."

Rosario remained still, somewhat in doubt of the validity of Helena's assertions, but she said not one word that would influence her to take such a drastic

and binding step as to marry Charles de Thierny.
Compulsively Helena chattered on, rationalizing her
motives for seeking him out and bringing him to her
in order to make him renew his offer of marriage.

As the idea loomed larger every day, it also underwent a slight transformation. Finally Helena was certain that marriage it would be, but marriage on her
terms.

Rosario trembled wretchedly. The fact that the sun
was shining brightly in the dirt street before the cantina was only a small consolation, for in this dangerous part of Panama City only fools—like herself, she
thought—dared to tread. The coach behind her was
zealously protected by the liveried driver and a guard,
both ominously armed, whom Helena had suggested
she take along. Rosario made a cowardly grimace full
of resentment. Why did Helena trust only *her* to deliver the message to Charles de Thierny? Why did she,
Rosario, have to play go-between?

Charles de Thierny had wisely left to Helena a list
of places where contact might be made with him, a
surprisingly friendly gesture on his part. This repulsive bar was one of those places. Being inside the city
limits, it was the most practical choice for Helena,
though certainly not the most comforting. It was on
the fringes of Gringo Town, in the worst slum left
over from the desperate days of the gold rush, the
meeting place of vipers, drug users, thieves, and
knaves. It certainly did not speak well for Charles de
Thierny.

To Rosario's mind the slant-eyed Indian who lingered malignantly about the door of the cantina looked like a predator waiting for his next victim, and she hesitated painfully before him, shaking in her buttoned shoes. He looked insolently past her to assess the strength of her armed guards, who, she hoped, were staring in challenging brazenness at *him*.

"Excuse me . . . señor. Do you know if Señor Charles Terny is inside waiting for me?"

"Are you the woman who has a paper for him to read?" was the Cholo's answer. Then he continued without giving her a chance to answer. "Señor Charles said you should give me the paper." He added with noticeable pride: "I am one of his men."

"Oh!" said Rosario in a frail voice, and quickly gave him the note, relieved that her mission was so soon in its concluding stages. "Thank you very much . . . señor." And with that she scampered back into the closed carriage and ordered the driver and guard to get the vehicle moving out of there—and fast!

In the early morning hours three riders disturbed these usually lazy hours of the tropical city of Panama, their mounts making the flint fly off the cobblestones of the inner streets of the town. Soon the three figures on horseback were on the nonpaved streets that led out from the city in the direction of Punta Paitilla. A sudden gust of wind sprang up in response to the newly arrived sunlight and it blew vigorously against the horsemen, ripping off the straw hat of one of them. Golden hair shone, surprised at the treachery of the wind, but Helena Canales, heiress of the

González fortunes and estates, continued to ride undisturbed.

Her mouth was drawn in a determined line, her eyes intensely alert and dark, almost angry. Although she had a general knowledge of the way, she followed close behind the guide whom she had had the foresight to hire. A virile young priest, his cassock hindering his comfort as he straddled the horse and flew into a gallop such as he rarely had occasion to enjoy, followed the guide also, a bit farther behind him than Helena.

Already Father Rafael was rejoicing that Helena had confided so sincerely in him and had assured his success in Panama with promises he had not dared to hope to hear from anyone on this wretched swampy and mosquito-ridden outpost. To think that because of her promises, a fortune would be donated to the Church and that a convent school could, in the near future, count on her support, both morally and financially! And he would get the credit for convincing her to be so generous. In return she expected little. In fact, what she desired was most gratifyingly in keeping with the laws of man and God. He could not refuse her, in all good conscience.

The sun rises rapidly in tropical countries, surging with vital energy in overwhelming beauty, and showering its warmth perhaps too generously over the land. The priest felt the heat quickly enough and for one angry moment resented the cassock and the black garments that his Spanish order demanded he wear. The clothes were fine for Spain, but here they were nothing but a martyrdom.

The city was soon left far behind, but the paths they followed were wide enough to accommodate one rider behind the other with ample space on either side. Should people stop using these paths, though, the sturdy grasses and vines would easily choke them and swallow their traces. Where the riders had to turn toward the sea this was in fact the case, and no more trail was available to them. Nobody lived in the swampy areas near Paitilla Point, and though the point was solid rock and well above water, it was useless for agriculture, and too far from the city for dwellings.

The guide picked his way along the drier rises of land, crossing the creek that ran down the middle of the swamp where the banks were not so soft. If the tide had been in, even at this point such a crossing would have been messy indeed, if not downright dangerous. But the tide had not overtaken the land yet.

About half a mile after they crossed the creek, the three riders reached the solid ground of Paitilla. The grass here was high, and Helena was grateful that she had donned men's clothing, her boots of brown leather polished and gleaming. Even her manly attire had about it that indefinable but noticeable air of distinction which the handsomest designs and tailoring lend. Rosario had insisted that all items of Helena's wardrobe must first pass her approval, as far as design was concerned. She had been so adamant about this that Helena had acceded, but only on the condition that Helena must have the final word about the choices.

Rosario had been a little reluctant to design such

rugged apparel for her mistress, but had soon realized that Helena meant to have them whether Rosario said yes or no. As it was better for Helena to have beautiful men's clothing than ugly or coarse men's clothing, Rosario had capitulated and designed them herself. The choice of materials, the perfection of the cut, and the graceful form of the owner had turned the avant-garde style into a thing of beauty and elegance. The shirt was of the finest linen, with tiny mother-of-pearl buttons set at one-inch intervals down the front. The collar was buccaneer style, a daring detail which Rosario had conjured up, with billowing sleeves that ended in a wide closely fitting band about the wrist where again tiny motther-of-pearl buttons graced the blouse. For cooler weather a white silk and gleaming scarf was to be worn with the shirt, but right now Helena wore it with the first few buttons undone. The heat of the bright sun and the exercise were too great to worry overmuch about modesty. Besides, whether it was because of her newly acquired wealth, or because of the terrible adventures which she had endured, Helena recognized within herself a new and daring streak. It was as if she delighted in flaunting her disregard for convention. Perhaps it was only to protect herself before the possibility of being scorned by society once her secret burden was revealed. What were a few buttons more or less when she had lost so much virtue already that she felt tremulous with anticipation at the thought of this reunion with her ravisher? The priest knew about the rape, of course, but Helena had been reluctant to confess everything she had felt about her victimizer later during their many weeks in the hills and mountains of Panama. She couldn't quite describe her feelings, and she was afraid to voice them, even to herself.

As the guide led them over a small ridge, Helena looked down toward the rocks that led to the sea, and beyond them she took in the pounding surf which only a short time ago had lain dormant and tranquil, gathering its strength quietly until it should be loosed. Now the tide was coming in. Helena's mind took poetic flight. Poor ocean. Would it never know that the land was rooted and determined to remain frigid to his advances? That she would remain aloof to all the passion and cajoling of the seas? The thought gave Helena immense pleasure, even though she had always loved the sea.

They wended their way among the rocky surfaces where a light covering of soil allowed the sawed-edged grasses freedom to grow. Then the rocks were barer. Here they were to meet Charles de Thierny and some of his men, and here, by the sea, Helena Canales was to marry the man who had once abducted and shamed her.

The riders dismounted in silence. Helena did not feel like talking, and she was grateful for the taciturn mood of her companions. The guide moved away discreetly, as he had been instructed to do by Helena. He had been promised extra pay if he would also act as a guard. His guns were ready; everyone knew that bandits still infested areas along the fringe of the city.

Helena's slender figure was outlined in the luminous light that flooded the tropical seas and shores of Panama. She had given up on her hat, and it hung behind her attached only by a slender chord. From time to time the wind tugged at the hat, pulling it away from her and putting uncomfortable pressure on her throat. Strands of golden hair had found their way out of the coiffure, which was a simple single braid at the nape, and they played with the wayward wind. The exertion of the ride had left a healthy glow on Helena's face so that she looked like some bewitching creature, a blend of woman and child that was difficult to resist admiring. Even Father Rafael found himself looking with undisguised admiration at the young woman who had made him her confessor. His thoughts kept returning to the promises that had poured unbidden from the mouth of the young woman whom Rosario Pérez had begged him to visit. Her state of mental anguish was such, Rosario had stated, that she dared not allow the young woman to go to the ordinary confessional at the church. If he would be so kind as to come instead to her home? And what a home! Father Rafael could not help but be impressed with the elegance of Helena's house, its fine mahogany panelings and softly lustrous furnishings made of rare tropical woods. Helena had obviously been brought up in the lap of luxury. From what Rosario had hinted about the generous endowments Helena wanted to arrange for the Church, Father Rafael was aware that she was willing to part with some of her riches, a rare thing indeed for one so young, with so much ahead to live for, and who would perhaps need money for her security later in life.

Then he had heard her confession and had been astonished at the composure with which she related the unfortunate events. Had he detected moments of real guilt, as if perhaps she were not disclosing all her doubts? Father Rafael had heard confessed all the sins in the world long before he had completed the first year of his priesthood, and though he was still relatively young, the wretched depths of human depravity had been so thoroughly disclosed to him by now that what he lacked in experience from age, he made up for in awareness simply from the experience of hearing confessions. Helena Canales was troubled, but not only because she had been raped, or even because she now found herself pregnant. It was something to think about. Perhaps there was some way he could really help her, if he could only guess what was making her restless and unhappy.

Suddenly, on the ridge that they had left behind, three more riders appeared. The new arrivals hesitated as they took in the area slightly below them; then they headed to the place where Helena and her companions were waiting.

Charles de Thierny dismounted quickly, even before his horse had come to a full halt, and, ignoring even the priest, he made straight for Helena.

"Helena!" He took her hand in his and lifted it to his lips, his eyes warm and shining with pleasure. Then he noticed the limpness of her hand and the air of complete indifference reflected in Helena's face. He let her hand fall, and stiffened somewhat, unwilling to expose himself unnecessarily to the girl's blank and unreadable gaze. It made him uncomfortable as hell. After all, it was she who had arranged this meeting. Why then was she so distant, so aloof?

"I came to Panama Viejo as soon as I received your message. I had been in the hills again, and I thought it would be better to be camped closer to Punta Paitilla so as to be here on time and still rested. I thought perhaps you had changed your mind about me, and then I even thought that perhaps you were thirsty for revenge and simply wished to betray me. I must admit I took a few precautions in case the latter should be the truth." Almost before he had said it, Charles was sorry that he had volunteered so much information.

"You needn't have worried, Charles de Thierny, for revenge is far from my mind. In fact I had begun to forget the unpleasant circumstances of our . . . shall we say, time together . . . until something even more unpleasant turned up. In fact, I came out here to accept your proposal of marriage."

Her words fell on Charles like a bomb. He was totally unprepared. Marriage? It didn't make any sense, for the look in Helena's eyes was definitely cold and full of disdain. He didn't trust her.

"All right," he drawled, "tell me what it is. You said something very unpleasant had happened to you. I assume you mean after we parted."

Helena felt a sudden discomfiture. Somehow she had forgotten all the arrogance of which Charles de Thierny was capable. What if he refused to marry her? Doubt assailed her, but just as quickly she recovered her aplomb and decided with brutal rashness that if he didn't marry her, it would be his son who would be a bastard, just as he was. And anyway, being a bastard was not really so terrible. After all, she herself

306

was born of a natural and illegitimate relationship, and it had never really affected her happiness and security. . . . No, she quickly contradicted herself, she did not want her son to be born a bastard. Very well, if he didn't marry her, she would find another man to marry her. With her money . . .

Helena remained quiet before speaking, instinctively preparing a new approach. Her words finally came low and softly.

"I am expecting your child, Charles."

She had no time to finish, for Charles interrupted, immediate and obvious pleasure shining in his eyes and the flash of a white grin on his face. His hands groped for her slender shoulders, and he brought her to him in a strangely rough and yet tender gesture. She remained passive, not daring to look up into his face, afraid she might succumb to his apparent pleasure. Somehow she was disturbed to share his joy. It was just as well, because if Helena had seen Charles's expression she might have misconstrued it to be one of displeasure. Charles's brow had suddenly creased. She would have had no way of knowing that it did so at the black thought that he had perhaps sired this child only by force. It would be wonderful to think that the child had been conceived in love or even passion as on that day by the waterfall. . . .

"When is the baby due, do you think?"

"I don't know. Rosario thinks it must have happened . . . a few weeks after . . . Panama Viejo."

"I see," remarked Charles, a bit too drily for Helena's comfort.

Well, he thought, at least it didn't happen because

of the rape, and he wiped the damned thought out of his mind as quickly as he could. God! How he suffered every time he thought about that terrible day.

"So you think, Helena, that for the child's sake it would be better to marry me, even if, as you said before, I am the last man in the world you would marry?"

"We all have a right to change our mind."

"Do you mean that you love me now?" An insolent grin punctuated his words.

"I didn't say any such thing"—and Helena blushed visibly, her eyes leaving Charles's face and avoiding his intent gaze. There were so many different colors in those eyes—gray, green, yellow, and brown. They were disturbing eyes, especially when they looked at her as if they would penetrate her very soul and the deepest thoughts hidden safely there, thoughts that were better not laid bare even to herself.

Charles shrugged as if to minimize the importance of the situation.

"Very well, I will marry you, Helena, but I have a few conditions."

His voice was quietly controlled, the tension giving it a vibration of danger. Yes, this man was soft spoken, but his will was unbendable, even when he was misguided. Helena stammered out her response.

"*You* have conditions? But I wanted to state my terms. I mean, I didn't expect . . ."

"You mean you didn't expect me to marry a woman who loathes me, even if she has every right to do so? No, Helena, I am not going to deceive myself over this marriage. I know how you feel; at least I know that you do not love me. But if the marriage takes place, it must be on my terms. Now, you recall I explained that for at least a few months more my job here requires secrecy, so my main desire is that after one year from the marriage ceremony, you must let me exercise my husbandly rights in every way. . . ."

Helena began to protest, but Charles cut her short again with a wave of his hand. "Wait, let me finish. There's no use getting nervous because by husbandly rights I do not mean forcing you to myself physically at all. Believe me, I shall never do that again, even if the law gives me the right to do so. Perhaps one day you will come to me of your own accord. But the main thing is to assure myself of a home where my child can grow with both his parents, and where I can show my love for him freely, as he will be able to do as well, for both his parents. I want no split home. Those are my conditions."

Helena's restless confusion while Charles spoke had not disturbed him in the least, or so Helena decided. The unexpected air of assurance which Charles exhibited, and his words and conditions, numbed her. She had been totally unprepared for this turn of events. She turned away from him for a moment, letting her gaze fall on the surf, trying to find a way out of the embarrassing situation into which she had fallen. But the realization hit her that she really had no choice in the matter, no choice that made any sense. Too, Charles was not asking for unreasonable returns. Finally, convinced that she had better accept Charles on his terms, she gave him only one barest glance as she walked toward Father Rafael, who was standing a few

feet away. Father Rafael was obviously feeling awkward before the obvious bickering of the two determined persons he was about to marry.

"Father Rafael, would you be so kind as to speak to
Señor Thierny and me now? We would like to get married as soon as possible." Helena had spoken in Spanish, and Charles noted the softness of her accents, almost Andalusian in the lack of final sibilants and
lacking, too, the nasal vowels which the Isthmians
usually intoned. The marriage ceremony would be in
Latin, of course, but the promises were to be spoken
in Spanish. It was indeed strange and a bit ironic that
Charles had never yet heard Helena speak Spanish.
How little he really knew her, after all, for Spanish
was her mother tongue. She had refused, perhaps out
of rebellion and pride, to communicate with his men or
the Indian women in Santa Fe, at least whenever he
was present.

The ceremony proceeded as if all the participants
were in a dream. The two Indians, Pablo and Pedro,
and the guide whom Helena had brought along, were
the guests and the witnesses, the sponsors of the marriage of Helena Canales and Charles de Thierny
González Calderón. Helena decided right away that if
the child was a boy, she would name him Rafael, or
perhaps, Edward, after her father. But *Charles?*
Never! The priest had reminded Helena in Panama
City of the need for a wedding ring, and she had
brought along a valuable but frivolous ring that did
not look like the simple wedding band which the
priest had intended. Instead a cluster of diamonds sur-

rounding a small but brilliant emerald was produced for Charles to put on her finger. She did not look married at all with that band. The detail of this insult did not escape Charles; he pretended to ignore the taunt. His reaction infuriated Helena, of course, but she fumed in silence.

When the brief ceremony was over, the bridegroom did not kiss the bride. Instead he simply looked at her with gentle tenderness that even the priest did not fail to notice. Helena's harsh stare, however, bespoke the hatred which she felt for this man. The priest knew, of course, the reason for her hatred. Poor child! To hate a man so much and have to bear his child. Well, at least she had money, and that brought consolation to anybody at times like this. The priest sighed. He moved away from the newlywed couple, for he was already aware that after the wedding they were to part. But a few moments of private talk should be allowed them.

"When shall I see you again, Helena?" questioned Charles.

"If it were up to me, never."

"I don't want to be a nuisance in your life, but I plan to drop in from time to time to see how you are doing. And after the baby comes. . . ."

"You will do no such thing. Your condition was that I play the role of wife and mother of your child after one year. That means I don't have to see you until one year from now."

"Perhaps by that time I will be tired of waiting, Helena."

"So much the better, monsieur!" retorted Helena sarcastically.

A wicked grin covered Charles's face.

"I see we are back to monsieur, eh? You are much too formal, my dear."

They were both speaking rapid French again, their voices rising and falling in strange intonations which neither the priest nor the other men understood. But the message of the argument was fairly clear. La señora wanted no part of el señor.

Charles finally must have sensed stirrings of doubt and disrespect coming from his two companions, for suddenly he turned his back to his men and quickly and quietly said, "Helena, I am going to kiss you for the sake of appearances. Your behavior before my men could ruin me; my work here depends too much on the respect and trust they might have for my leadership. You know very well that no Indian or Latin can respect a henpecked man."

And with that he wrapped his arms about her and kissed her passionately, his lips hard on hers. Suddenly his lips softened, and he pressed her more intimately against him. Through the tight breeches of her masculine riding suit Helena felt the hardness of his male body, and a treacherous ache assaulted her own loins and weakened her legs. She tried to force herself to be indifferent, but her body kept pressing against his, betraying the desire which Charles had aroused so quickly in her. As usual she was disgusted at her weakness, but she could not help it. Finally Charles let go of her.

"Thank you, Helena. I will see you soon." His voice

was cruelly flippant. Helena felt the urge to scratch his eyes out. But she was rooted to the spot, her legs almost trembling from a vile mixture of emotions that she was finding hard to control or to understand.

With his words Charles strode away toward his horse, calling out to his men.

"Vámonos, muchachos."

Pablo and Pedro glanced mischievously at the woman their *patrón* had just married, and saw her standing rigidly where he had left her, her eyes riveted upon the man who once had stolen her away into the jungle.

What a man their *patrón* was! Obviously the girl had fallen for him and had fallen hard. Otherwise she would not fight him so desperately. Even if the details escaped them because of the devil tongue in which the two lovers had spoken, the Indians had long ago seen the subtle changes in the girl's relationship with their boss. The overeducated Europeans and whites were always blind to their own emotions.

Before Helena could react, Charles de Thierny and his henchmen were astride their horses, heading swiftly away from the point toward Panama Viejo. Helena turned for a few moments to stare across the waters that were pounding furiously against the rocks by now, and didn't notice that their fury drowned out very efficiently the pounding of her own heart.

Then, having regained her composure somewhat, and with a determined effort, she turned toward the priest and the guide, and spoke so softly that they did not hear her, but understood from her motions that she wanted to go home now.

Memories of her marriage day brought Helena bouts of depression, and she found it difficult to understand exactly why she could not get the pictures out of her mind. Sometimes in the middle of her reveries, too, Charles's image made her feel an ache and a desire that she was able to control and extinguish only because he was not physically present. Self-recrimination, and disgust at her weakness, often followed Helena's daydreams, leaving her in a foul mood, imperious even with Rosario, quarrelsome about the servants' performance, and finally depressed and miserable.

Chapter XVI

Soon after her secret marriage, after a barely decent interval from the day of the Gonzálezes' death and after her reappearance in the capital city, invitations began to arrive for Helena from several prominent families, most of them with sons of marriageable age. By this time Helena was not surprised at her own cynicism in interpreting these invitations as a sign that her wealth now gave her access to many parlors where before she would have been allowed only because of the generous sponsorship of the Gonzálezes, and then only as a sort of poor relation to be snubbed when her sponsors were not looking.

Her personality had undergone a severe transformation during her trek in the mountains with Charles, and by now she was getting used to her new way of looking at life. Along with her blasé cynicism, however, a certain real self-assurance had survived and developed. She had overcome many sudden and brutal obstacles thus far, and Helena felt sure that she would be able to work out her problems in the future with care and reason. But this was only sometimes. On other occasions she was tormented by doubts and guilt and she would purposely allow her harder self to take over and protect her from pain.

Though she secretly scorned the attempts to woo her wealth, Helena accepted the many invitations for several reasons. First, she was curious about the way the prominent families lived, how they behaved. Second, since she had never experienced society, she was afraid and yet challenged by the opportunity to find her way and develop the social graces which she had only learned in theory in school. She had begun to realize that her years abroad had prevented her from understanding her people as well as she would like to, and she was seriously interested in finding out how these people lived, what motivated them, how they perceived life, and what their opinions were.

Later, she would not be able to satisfy her curiosity. She was sure that they would reject her once they realized that she was pregnant, apparently out of wedlock. There were no obvious swellings in her body to give her away. The apparent weight she had slowly begun to put on could easily be attributed to her natural recovery from her first mournful reactions to the news of the death of her mother and, later, of her benefactors.

Before his own death at sea, her "Uncle" Benito had had the foresight to tell everyone who was aware of

Helena's arrival on the Isthmus that she had been recuperating at his vast hacienda in Santa Fe from the
great shock of her mother's death and the bankruptcy
of the couturier business. Little had Don Benito
known, in choosing this location, how close he had
been to the truth. He only knew that Santa Fe was far
away, almost inaccessible. Who would bother to go
there and find out if what he said was true or not? It
had been a stroke of genius that had salvaged much of
Helena's pride and reputation. Rosario, who had
helped to spread the rumor that Helena—well guarded
and chaperoned, of course—had left the city because it
was too painful for her to remain there at this time,
had informed Helena about Don Benito's decision,
made right from the beginning of her abduction, to
protect her reputation.

Helena expected, nevertheless, that eventually her
new hosts and hostesses would begin to ignore her or
even scorn her. She could not hide her pregnancy forever. But then again, the day would·come, according
to plan, when her marriage would be announced—
within a year, Charles had said, for he needed the time
to finish his so-called secret mission—and her child
would have the acceptance, with or without reluctance,
of the entire society of the Isthmus and France. She had
the papers and the witnesses' signatures and personal
cross-marks to prove the legitimacy of her baby. Her
child, at least, was protected in every legal way.

Feeling the pressure of social obligations, Helena
began to toy with the idea of sponsoring a Christmas
party, perhaps one requiring the use of costumes. It
would not necessarily be a religiously oriented affair,

but rather one close to that time of year when the rains would cease and she could expect to use the beautiful terraces of the González home—sometime in December when the stars shone magnificently in the sky. The heavens were so close to Earth at the Isthmus. She remembered how she had felt when she was a child, almost as if she could reach up and pluck the stars, they were so near. The party would be in December.

"Rosario, my dear, tell me honestly. Don't you think the fiesta is the best idea you ever heard?"

"Well, Helenita, if you ask me, it would probably make you feel happy again, at least. So I am all for it."

"I don't mean that, Charo," replied Helena, using a nickname which Rosario found extremely annoying. Somehow it robbed her of dignity, and she sensed that she could not afford to be one bit less dignified than she already appeared.

"I don't understand why anyone would give a fiesta except to feel happy, I must say."

"Well, for one thing, Rosario—and Helena was wise enough to revert back to the more elegant name for her friend, chaperone, and family in one—"it would be the very first time such a party would be given here. I'll be known everywhere for my generous and lavish entertainment, and what is more important, I shall have a chance to avenge myself with grandeur against that odious and despicable man whom I had to marry."

The sudden vehemence of Helena's voice and the lack of sense of her words took Rosario by surprise, and brought out that rare moment of impatience to which she was beginning to feel she was entitled. With obvious irony in her voice she stated: "Why, of course, it is perfectly clear to me how a party would make the perfect sort of revenge against the gentle Señor Thierny, especially if he'll be the only one not to receive an invitation. Poor man. Not to be invited to your party. With his delicate sensibilities! Why, he'll be desolate!"

Helena only made a grimace at Rosario's sarcasm, while her chaperone and former business partner continued.

"Good night, my dear, for I think you need to go to bed and get some rest. You are beginning to prattle." With this, Rosario began to turn and leave.

"No, wait, Rosario." Helena had been lying on the couch, her feet propped up on a pillow to avoid damage to her legs which the pressure of the baby might cause. It was Rosario who had insisted that every evening Helena should relax in such a position. Helena made a movement to get up to stop Rosario.

"All right, Helena, you can tell me." Reluctantly Rosario turned again and sat in the overstuffed chair which she had had moved near the couch. She preferred to humor Helena than to see her interrupt her rest or do things which she had no business doing in her condition.

"Sit down, then. You see, Rosario, you are an important part of the plans for my party."

"Me!"

"Yes, you, and don't pretend that you aren't pleased."

319

Indeed, Helena knew Rosario too well, even after four years of separation from her, not to realize that feeling an important part of the family was the most fulfilling thing in her life. If she could combine this with her vocation of creating beautiful clothes, her happiness would know no bounds.

"Yes, you are perhaps the most important link to the success of this party as well as to my revenge."

"Your revenge!" Here Rosario was not sure if the pleasure of being important compensated for the distaste she had for revenges.

"Yes. But first let me tell you about the party. You see, it will be a costume party. That way I can hide my state. It's beginning to show, Rosario. Pretty soon I won't be able to wear those gowns you have been fixing up for me. Yes, a costume party it will be, with the most lavish background. And it will have to be soon, because it cannot rightly be a Christmas party, what with costumes and all. I want you to spread the word. By the time I send out the invitations, I want everyone to be anxiously awaiting one."

The women talked awhile longer, and when Rosario finally left for her room, it was with the intention of going through with her personal role in the play. She also planned to start the very next day gathering the parts for the costume her friend and mistress would require.

Helena was left satisfied that she would be able to carry out her plans. Her eyes narrowed as she relished the thought of Charles squirming from embarrassment and anger when he found out that she was independent and determined to do what she wanted to do without the least qualm about what his opinion might be. The man did not exist who could tell her what to do or how to run her life. Not anymore. She was rich and she was beautiful, and she no longer need worry about her virtue. She was totally free and that was how she would stay. Her independence and disregard for the gossipy opinions of the neighborhood had proven just how powerful she was. If she wanted to give a costume party before Christmas, that was just what she would do! Everyone would come, of that she felt certain, because they were above all very curious to see how she lived, and because she was very rich. No one would snub her for casual reasons or because she was a bit extravagant in her ways. Her wealth was her magic weapon.

These hardened rationalizations suddenly caused her pain, however. Life had been cruel to her this last year, ever since her mother had died. Nothing but trouble. Her idealism had suffered along the way, and had given way to a spirit of practicality more like cynicism. She sighed. How she had changed! Had she ever really been so naive, so innocent, as she remembered herself to have been in France? What a chasm lay between that maiden and the woman she knew she now was. Though often she yearned to be again as clear and prismatic in her soul as she had once been, it seemed impossible, for that had been too long ago.

The naive and innocent girl who had arrived in a bustle of goodwill and high hopes at the port of Colón so many months before was gone forever. In her place was a woman whose awareness of the sordid faults of human nature had been developing like some cancer eating away at her tender heart and insinuating itself everywhere in her spirit. The new hardness did not make her happy. Nevertheless she was powerless to halt its growth, and found herself feeding it instead. To put away her bitterness she tried to turn her mind to the more frivolous aspects of her present life—this time, the fiesta.

On the surface the party would seem to be an attempt on her part to reciprocate at least once before Christmas the many invitations she had received and accepted to teas, to dinners, and even to soirées of more intimate atmosphere where the male guests were encouraged to gamble and to be themselves.

Helena had already shocked more than one matron when she had actually joined the men in games of chance. She smiled every time she recalled the brashness of that first flaunt of the conventions of Isthmian society, conventions which somehow had begun to seem hypocritical and boring soon after she had plunged into their vortex.

Her brazen behavior was one way of avenging herself. The worse the image she created, the worse it would be for Charles de Thierny the day he showed up to claim her. She wanted no part in glamorizing him.

Her outrageous behavior had quickly given her an avant-garde reputation, but as she never went off with any one man, or ever left anyone's home in any carriage but her own, and as she dressed with singular taste and propriety, she continued to be accepted in her newfound social circle. She knew that the truth of the matter was that as long as she did not truly scandalize society with immorality, her huge fortune would win acceptance for her.

Among the bustling groups of young men who soon vied with each other for even a thoughtful look from the wealthy and beautiful heiress, one suitor seemed more than the others bent on impressing Helena. He was Raúl Santana, the first to try to ingratiate himself with Helena the evening on which she had first defied convention and actually refused to join the ladies after supper and had joined the men instead. It was Raúl Santana who had ventured forward to accept her and ease the tension for her. He was rather charming, and in fact terribly handsome, and his dashing figure seemed to bring admiring glances from the younger girls of the society in which Helena was now taking full part. The mothers of the girls did not seem impressed by Raúl, however, and apparently tried very hard to steer their daughters away from his path whenever possible without seeming too rude. To Helena it soon became obvious that he was not considered a good match, though not one single lady bothered to warn her against him. Later, when she knew more about him, she realized that most of her female acquaintances might have been glad, actually, if she had not seen through Raúl's pretences and had married him, thus ridding all the as yet unmarried females of their social stratum of the danger he posed for them.

Helena had tried, out of curiosity more than anything else, to draw out some semblance of deeper thought and purpose in Raúl Santana's spirit, but all he seemed truly interested in doing was spending money as fast and furiously as possible. Helena decided also that he was as slippery and superficial as the tiny waves of the bay. This perturbed her somehow, for though his hypocrisy was obvious to her, she felt she had to be on guard every moment to protect herself from his wiliness. She knew now that his solicitous preference for her company did not stem from his admiration of her personal qualities of charm or intelligence or from her physical beauty, but rather from her vast and impressive wealth.

Helena had no difficulty learning the story of Raúl Santana's life. On the small Isthmus of Panama everyone's life was continuously tossed about on the waves of rumor and reality, and the gossips' delight was to review each scandalous incident as often as possible.

Don Agustín Santana de Saavedra had been of the truest and noblest blood of Spanish-Colombian heritage. Not so his wrinkled and still lively spouse, a now cantankerous old witch with flaming hair the color of Sevillan oranges. Her claim to a place in Panamanian society had come about solely on the basis of her husband's fabulous wealth and spotless lineage.

In his foolish youth Don Agustín had been ensnared by the beautiful American prostitute Laurie Lee Jenkins, of the flaming tresses. He had met her in Colón after she'd already made the rounds in Chagres, that dirty hole sired by the forty-niners on the Atlantic Coast of the Isthmus before the railroad had cut too deep into the jungles from Colón on its way to the Pacific.

Chagres had been like any typical western gold-seeker's town with all the added disadvantages of a sweltering disease-infested tropical climate. In fact, Chagres had the doubtful honor of boasting the most unhealthful climate on Earth, and this reputation was deserved even if it was impossible to prove.

Among the houses of ill repute at Chagres, Laurie Lee had chosen to work at the House of All Nations, where the girls ranged in color from the blackest ebony to the pale sickly white of powdered second-rate girls from New Orleans. Her life there was profitable but difficult, and having had to resort to wearing a small pistol while she "entertained" her gentlemen callers, Laurie Lee had decided to flee to Colón with her savings just about the same time that Chagres was collapsing from disuse and she from too much use. But she was undeniably attractive, and her voice was sweet and mellow. Her mind had retained its keen edge, and when she met Don Agustín, she found it a cinch to dupe him into marriage by taking advantage of his ridiculous sense of honor and his inexperience. The news of their marriage killed Don Agustín's father, and his mother fled the Isthmus in shame to hide in the mountains near Bogotá where part of her family still lived. Years later she, too, passed away without forgiving her son the terrible stain he had brought them.

Don Agustín, in self-defense, had rebelled and, un-characteristically, had "thrown his house through the window" as the Panamanians described the reckless expenditures he lavished on his wife and the son she gave him. By the time he lay on his deathbed, the fabulous wealth had dwindled to an unimpressive pile and his wife found herself more and more openly the butt of scorn and derision at the hands of the gentility of Panama.

Knowing this basic tale of the Santana family, Helena soon deduced the rest from observation and from bits and pieces of commentary in the social circles in which she moved.

Laurie Lee's son Raúl, accepted by society somewhat more readily than was his mother, had learned early to flaunt his handsome body and face as lavishly as he did his money. Not surprisingly, he was soon impoverished, and the sore lack of funds was embittering his entire existence.

Nevertheless his good looks were a sort of collateral, he felt, and he hoped that his elegant demeanor would eventually allow him to catch some wealthy Panamanian heiress. Thus Raúl kept himself in good physical condition by exercising and riding, and in spite of his hectic nights, his body stood tall and straight, his shoulders broad and strong, and his chestnut hair, though beginning to dull from his sometimes heavy drinking, still retained its fullness. His gray eyes were fringed by heavy, dark lashes, and his lips were sensuous and provocative. The slightly cynical smile he practiced drove the younger girls absolutely wild. Many a wise mother and father distracted their young daughter whenever Raúl Santana strolled into a salon, hoping that theirs would not be the young girl to succumb to his irresponsible attractions. As a result it was not easy for Raúl to find the heiress he so avidly sought.

To further frustrate Raúl Santana, the Isthmus was suffering a terrible economic depression that threatened to last for many years. It thus came as no surprise either to Helena or to the aristocratic segment of the population that Raúl Santana should begin to pay court to Helena Canales.

Helena continued to think, however, that Raúl was harmless to her, for she could read him so clearly. He was not even intelligent enough to hide his shallowness from her. And yet his physical handsomeness could perhaps be put to her advantage if she should ever want to make Charles de Thierny jealous. How or when the thought of such doings occurred to Helena she could not say, but the thought grew and grew until it became a plan. Part of her plan called for the masked get-together.

The idea of the fiesta soon began to run away with itself, for Rosario and every seamstress in town helped to create great enthusiasm over it. Even the initial criticism of the fact that the death of the Gonzálezes had occurred only a few months ago seemed to fade as the young women of the Isthmian families could hardly contain themselves at the thought of a masked soirée in the spectacular home of the much admired and criticized Helena Canales. Just as Helena had hoped, word of the party spread with a velocity surpassed only by the eagerness of the invited guests.

At the ball, Helena planned not only to bedazzle her little world with her beauty, her charm, and her wealth, but in doing so to humble the man she had taken as a husband. She knew that under no circumstances could he allow himself the luxury of demanding his marital and legal rights in public, for had he not said himself that it would be fatal to his mission to be seen and identified at this time? Wasn't he afraid that his actions, though they would actually be for the good of Panama, might be wrongly interpreted as mere spying for France? Hah! She had him where she wanted him. She had not been able to get the marriage on her own terms, and had been again humiliated into accepting his. Always he managed to get his way. But now she would show Charles de Thierny that Helena Canales was not just some simple chit to be shamed, then lied to with false words of love, to be cast into the role of unwed mother among a people who would only make her the butt of their scorn and wicked tongues.

Plans were going along beautifully and according to schedule. Not only was the party promising to be a success, but Helena felt a trembling current of excitement at the thought the Charles de Thierny would soon find out just how strong she really was!

Part of her plan called for Rosario to meet with Charles. She was to communicate to him the message that her mistress was about to become entangled with a certain gentleman known for his quick way with the ladies of the Isthmus. Rosario was to pretend that she disapproved of such behavior, for she was naturally aware that her mistress was married, and to whom. As it was Rosario who had made indirect contact with Charles before the marriage at the request of her mistress, it would only be a natural assumption that, knowing how to go about it, she had taken it upon herself to "chaperone" her mistress a little bit and warn her husband of her impending liaison.

Though Rosario did not confess the truth to Helena more than once, she thought that Helena was being dangerously brazen in her encouragement of Santana's obvious advances. It was a relief to suppose that perhaps her husband would find himself forced into the open and that the secret of their marriage would then be out. That way, by the time the baby was born, probably in February or March, she calculated, the child would have a publicly acknowledged name, and all this subterfuge would come to an end. Rosario just wasn't constituted for such intrigues and doings as the ones in which she was now involved. It would be a relief indeed to see Helena really married, albeit to a man about whom Rosario had mixed feelings and about whose character she had many doubts.

She had only learned of Charles de Thierny by means of the descriptions provided by Helena, but she could "read" between the lines much more ably than the young woman suspected, so that she had a fairly good idea of the man who had first ravished and then loved Helena Canales. Unless the man was a fool, his offer of marriage, made long before he had any way of knowing that Helena had inherited the González fortune, had to be based on his having fallen in love with the victim of his revenge. In Rosario's Latin mind, too, the fact that Charles had had the audacity and courage to carry out a cleansing of his honor at the risk of losing his life, made him a man of valor, though she could not help a personal resentment of him for his brutal treatment of Helena and for the minor, though even more personal, blow on the head that one of his men had dealt her the day Helena was abducted. Hoping that her positive feelings about him were responses to true attributes of the man, Rosario tried to subdue her doubts about the character of a person who would abduct an innocent girl and then proceed cold-bloodedly to dishonor her in order to slake his thirst for revenge. It was so confusing that the little chaperone feared almost as much as she looked forward to meeting the man himself. Once in his presence perhaps she would be able to get a better glimpse of his soul and of his intentions with regard to Helena.

"May the Good Lord help and enlighten me," she muttered under her breath as she stepped into the carriage that was to convey her to Charles de Thierny.

The cantina was wrapped in darkness, and once again Rosario had to repress the terrible fear that her very life was in danger in this repulsive slum. She entered apprehensively. In the dim glow of the tavern's kerosene lamps the flat planes of several Indian faces were reflected. The slanted eyes of the men were further slit by the shadows in the dingy bar, giving them a sinister, hooded quality that frightened poor Rosario Pérez nearly to death. The coach waited outside. Strict orders had been given to the driver, and this time two armed guards, to look out for thugs and robbers. A footman had also been sent along to enter the bar with Rosario, for this was, indeed, a part of the city into which only the bravest or the most foolhardy ventured. Most of the buildings were one level, with dirt floors which, because they were swept out every morning, then trampled all day and night, had become almost as hard as dried clay bricks. The roofs were for the most part thatched with palm leaves in intricately woven designs which showed only from the underside. Tucked under a section of the roof was an attic where some members of the group slept.

Here Rosario was led by one of Thierny's Indian thugs. She found herself trembling again as violently as she had done the first time she had made contact with Charles's men.

Unlike the first time, however, she was now supposed to be on her own. She had already made arrangements with the Indians, and they were to take her to Charles if he should agree to see her. Apparently he was here now, waiting for her.

At the top of the wooden log into which large nicks had been cut to turn it into service as a ladder, Rosario hesitated. Her legs felt weak beneath her clumsy skirt.

A muscular arm jutted out to help her. She could feel the strength emanating from Charles de Thierny as he pulled her up the rest of the way until she was standing on the platform that was the attic floor.

"Sorry that I could not meet you in a nicer place, Señora Rosario."

"Well," thought Rosario with some relief, "at least he seems to be courteous."

As she did not know quite what to say under the

circumstances, she waited for him to speak again. His silence, however, was just as heavy after the first sentence, and finally, out of embarrassment, Rosario began, "It is I, señor, who am sorry that I had to inconvenience you. If my mistress Helena knew I was here, she, too, would be most upset."

"I thought you had come on her behalf."

"Oh, no! I came because, well, I know you are married—"

One of his eyebrows rose as he again seated himself in the hammock that swung from two of the corner posts that held up the shack. Charles was much too tall to stand in this cramped and low-ceilinged part of the bar. He waited for Rosario to continue.

"For some reason, señor, of which I am not sure, you cannot announce your marriage yet, and I feel it is my duty to Helena not to let her make a fool of herself, and hurt your honor, by paying attention to a man whose reputation could well ruin hers by mere association. I'm so afraid, señor, that Raúl Santana is up to no good, and will ruin her life if she doesn't stop seeing him. Now she is giving a masked ball to which she has invited many important people and there is no doubt in my mind that she will dance in front of everyone with this Raúl Santana until all the tongues will be wagging. What will happen when she announces that she had been married all the time? I don't know what to do, and I can't convince her that she is being foolhardy. I even overheard her tell him to come dressed as Henry Morgan the night of the ball. Already that forebodes no good, for she must intend to recognize him immediately."

Rosario realized that she had said much more than Helena had instructed her to say, and that she had done so because she actually did feel worried about Helena's decision. Certainly society judged people by their actions and not by their intentions. Even if Helena's intentions were only to make this man sitting before her suffer—which might not be so easy, for the man seemed very sure of himself—the consequences could be much more serious than that. He had not moved a muscle, however, except for the one that worked his eyebrow.

"Thank you for coming, Rosario, to tell me all this. It seems that Helena once needed protection from me, and now she needs it from herself. You must try to understand her, though, for she has suffered much, and I'm afraid a great deal of it was my fault. She needs an outlet for her hatred of me, and certainly, though she might not have told you, it may very well be that she wished to smear my honor in return for what I did to her. Did she tell you all about me?"

The question took Rosario by surprise, and she automatically nodded yes.

"I figured she had to confide in someone. She's been through a terrible ordeal, and the worst part of it is that she does not believe that I truly love her. After all, I . . . Well, that's all in the past now."

After a long pause Rosario turned as though preparing to leave.

"I just wanted to let you know about Helena. She doesn't seem to understand the danger she is putting herself in with her . . . plans. I should be getting back."

Charles rose cautiously from the hammock.

"Here, let me help you down this blasted ladder. You can see for yourself that I must keep hiding. My life could be in danger if I'm not careful. I need to take care of myself to see that my work here is completed well. Then I plan to take Helena back to France with me."

"Oh, señor, take her back?" Rosario practically wailed the question.

"Not without you to accompany her, of course."

Charles's shrewd answer relieved Rosario, and her dark and wrinkled features relaxed. Just the thought of going to France, to Paris, perhaps, gave her a sudden thrill, for never in her life had she ever thought such a voyage possible for her. Paris was the Mecca of the fashion world! And fashion was Rosario's business and vocation. But the most important thing would be to accompany Helena and the coming baby, whom Rosario already loved.

Very suddenly Rosario noticed that the features of Charles de Thierny were extremely aristocratic and handsome, and that his poise gave him an undeniable charm and attraction which could be very hard for women to resist. It occurred to her that under more fortunate circumstances he and Helena would have made a beautiful couple indeed! Their child should turn out very special if it was born healthy. Very beautiful and special.

By the time Rosario was safely in the coach riding back to the house on the edge of the water of the bay, she was beginning to understand a little bit better the problems of the soul and heart with which her dear Helena was wrestling. Having met Charles, and knowing the violent way in which he had subjugated the proud girl, Rosario could well understand that the very thought of having fallen in love with her abductor could cause utmost pain and self-loathing in Helena's heart.

It could not be easy for her to face what she probably interpreted as the development of depravity within her, or to confront her conflicting emotions of hate and desire. All Helena's previous training—especially the slight prudery she had no doubt nurtured under the good nuns in France—could only threaten her sense of decency before the vile truth of the matter: Helena had fallen in love with Charles de Thierny.

As for Charles, he remained tense in his birdhouse attic, feeling an almost irrepressible urge to smash something with his fist. His turbulent emotions suggested to him old-fashioned jealousy, and it galled him to think that he—Charles de Thierny—could have come to this—actually jealous of a perfect stranger because of a woman. His fists clenched tightly.

The Cholos, who were waiting for Charles downstairs, were startled by the sound of a crash up in the loft. A bottle of whiskey that someone had left up there, perhaps? Then in the strange tongue their *patrón* sometimes spoke, they distinguished sounds and words that sounded uncannily like their own Spanish curses.

As soon as the rolling and hoofbeats of Rosario's carriage had faded completely away, Charles abandoned his retreat, leaving his earlier plans for the day to be finished some other time. He climbed down the ladder; once on the ground he turned toward the door and without breaking his long stride called to his Indian men: "Vámonos, muchachos!"

They poured out the narrow door of the unassuming cantina, leaped on their eager ponies, and clattered away toward the outskirts of the city, disappearing in the direction of their new hideout.

Chapter XVII

The French consul sat behind his desk with his feet insolently propped upon the writing surface. He was puffing contentedly on an ostentatious cigar, filling his private office with smoke in spite of the open window, through which a slight evening breeze managed to penetrate. The kerosene lamp flickered mellowly and gave the tenebrous room a dreamlike quality at the same time that it softened the middle-aged lines on Monsieur Thibédeaux's face. The atmosphere made him feel drowsy. It was so nice to relax like this at the end of the day, he thought, and he heaved a small sigh of contentment.

He reached up to scratch his salt-and-pepper hair, which, much to his annoyance, was becoming thinner each day. Then he readjusted himself for comfort in the large swivel chair from Paris which was his pride and joy. He was so relaxed, in fact, that he jumped violently when the door of the office flew open.

"Gads! Thierny! Can't you do things without being so damned dramatic? You scared me almost out of my skin!"

Thibédeaux found himself standing by his famous chair with his heart still in his throat. His mature figure stood straight, and he was elegant in an affable sort of way, though the elegance of his carriage could not altogether hide his paunch, the result of years of overindulgence.

Charles de Thierny laughed good-naturedly.

"I'm sorry, Jean, it's just·that I didn't think you would be asleep on the job!"

"On the job? Hell, I finished my job hours ago. The rest of my job, as you call it, has been for your sake, and not for your duties' sake, my dear colleague, but for your personal satisfaction. And this is the thanks I receive—insults, fright, a heart seizure! It's a good thing for you that I am not a temperamental fellow!"

Charles laughed again. Jean Thibédeaux was known for his flaring temper and overdramatic personality, his ability to exaggerate and to act out his grandiose ideas about what made living worthwhile. He was as loyal to his friends as he was to his country, to an almost absurd degree. Nobody dared voice the smallest criticism about either when he was around, for he would lash out in long soliloquies of indignant protest that ended either by boring the daring critic or simply appalling him. In his zeal Thibédeaux often created·problems for himself, sometimes offending the wrong fellow with the wrong influences in the French government—the very country he defended so staunchly and unconditionally. In consequence he was often relegated to backwater posts, such as his present one in Panama.

"Sit down, Charles. We have a lot to discuss tonight. Did you have any trouble getting into town?"

"Not particularly. I took the usual precautions."

Charles pulled up a captain's chair which Thibédeaux kept for his visitors. He was wearing a cotton shirt with the sleeves rolled up and a pair of slightly baggy gray pants. He could easily have been mistaken for a native of the city except that he was unusually large and his handsome features were far from ordinary.

"Your wife is fine, nothing new there," reported the consul. "I understand she is giving a huge party of some sort, to which I was not invited, by the way. I have the feeling she wants nothing to do with French representatives in the city. By the way, it was wise of you to tell her that I know something about all this marriage business."

"I didn't tell her. I told Padre Rafael in case anything happens to me. It's quite possible that he has already passed that information on to Helena."

"Yes, well, in any case, it certainly will protect Helena and the child later when you *can* announce your marriage, and also, in case something should happen to you, as you say. You are not exactly playing with children when you deal with bandits and mercenaries."

Charles had finished lighting his pipe and was pulling draughts of air through the sweet-smelling tobacco that managed to overcome somewhat the acrid smell of Jean Thibédeaux's pungent cigar.

"Hey! What is this? A competition? I can hardly breathe in here."

Thibédeaux jumped up and threw open another window. The resulting draught quickly alleviated the smoky congestion of his office.

"That's better; I can't stand people smoking in my office."

Paying no heed to his friend's ridiculous complaint (After all, who in Panama smoked more than Thibédeaux?), and without undue emotion, Charles said:

"I know about the party, Jean."

"You do?" He looked disappointed. Damn! Would he never have original news to give his friend, the famed secret agent, some tidbit of information that would impress him with his own sleuthing talents? Charles always seemed to know things even as they occurred, and here he himself lived in Panama City with his two ears constantly opened in a place where all information flowed freely. Yet Charles, hidden away in the surrounding hills and mountains, seemed to find out the same facts ahead of time. The man was uncanny!

"Our new ambassador to Peru arrived here at noon today, Charles. Do you know him, a Monsieur Jean Lamère?"

Charles stopped puffing on his pipe and looked up at Thibédeaux without hiding his look of surprise. After a moment's hesitation he answered.

"Yes. In fact I know him quite well, that is, his wife and I . . . I mean, I knew his wife quite well." Then changing the direction his comments were taking, he said: "But I thought he was on his way to Algiers."

"Oh, yes! He mentioned some trouble getting in his way of staying there. It was his last post, but apparently he was recalled long before his tour was up. He didn't seem pleased at all about going to Peru. But his superiors at the ministry insisted that he accept the post or resign from the diplomatic corps altogether. Of course, he came."

"When I left Paris I was under the impression that he was to leave for Africa soon and that his wife would follow shortly thereafter."

"By the way, his wife is also here with him."

"Yvette! How very interesting." So that was it! Yvette had a way of getting whatever she wanted, sooner or later. Had she come in pursuit of a renewed liaison with him? It was quite possible. Yvette had far more influence in making arrangements than did her husband. All his superiors were her lovers, some of them quite addicted to her!

A gleam of some impulsive idea shone in Charles's eyes. He had not thought of his former mistress in a long time, and the sudden remembrance of her sensuous, full-blooded caresses gave him an unexpected relish.

Thibédeaux did not miss Charles's reaction to the news about the sensational Madame Lamère.

"Well, Madame Lamère should enjoy seeing you again, Charles. You're looking better than ever, and I'm sick with envy, of course. This damned climate hasn't done a thing for me, but you're overflowing

341

with muscles and there's not a trace of a belly any-where. Gad! How do you do.it?"

Charles's answer was a good-natured chuckle. "Don't hold it against me, Jean. You'll get back in shape when you are transferred back to France, to the Ministry. Surely they don't plan on leaving you in this post forever."

"Maybe they are," answered Thibédeaux with a gri-mace. "I fall into the suspicion once in a while that they are attempting just that. But you're right. When I return to Europe, I'd better get in shape. Listen, I want to get in shape so that when I get a mistress, she won't have to be homely enough to look like she's my wife instead!"

The pair of them roared at this witticism.

When they'd quieted down, Jean continued talking about the alluring Frenchwoman who had come to town with her husband.

"They are staying at the Hotel de las Garzas. I heard that Madame Lamère spent the first hour in the hotel complaining about the primitive conditions. She'll make one hell of a diplomat's wife in Peru. The Peruvians are not much better off in their country than we are here except that their climate is much more pleasant. I must admit, of course, that a better climate eliminates some of the problems we face around here. She must be some hellcat to live with, though."

"Yeah," drawled Charles, absentmindedly, for his thoughts were not wholly on Jean's words, "some hell-cat."

Images of Yvette, nude and gleaming, sensuous and

wild, flashed unavoidably before him. He was full of
sexual desire, and Helena . . . well, she disdained
him too much to bear, too much to hope that she
would soon succumb to his love. He could not wait
much longer for her to overcome her hatreds and her
pride and discover that she loved him as he sensed
that she did.

Charles had come to suspect, much to his chagrin
and at times even despair, that he had already wooed
Helena and had failed miserably to penetrate through
her bitterness. He had not given up on the thought of
eventual success, but he knew himself too well to plan
on remaining physically faithful to her under the circumstances. It might be years before she forgave him
for what he had done to her. The prospect of leading
a monk's life while his eyes and mind feasted on his
enticing wife, was a most unlikely one indeed.

Furthermore, he wanted desperately some emotional tie and outlet that would dull the ache of yearning in his heart. He thought of Yvette, with her feminine tricks that had seemed so transparent to him, and
suddenly he found that they had amused him and
made him forget his cares after all. She had a way of
touching him, of abandoning herself, an unrestrained
giving and taking of pleasure that came to his mind in
a gush of sudden lust and perhaps something else that
was akin to love. He knew it was not love, for he had
tasted that nectar once and he could never know its
flavor again with anyone but Helena. He felt the pull
of primitive passion which his wife refused to let him
satisfy with her, and he regretted with some bitterness
her denial of the love and admiration which coming

from her would have more than made up for his unsatisfied carnal desires.

He would see Yvette.

He snapped out of his reverie when Jean Thibédeaux pulled a sheet of paper out of a folder on the desk and with a flourish presented it to Charles.

"And here is the quill to sign it with, my dear friend. But before you do, I consider it my duty to inform you that I believe you are thickheaded. Yes! Stupid to sign away your rights to her fortune. After all, she is your wife and should remain dependent on you. I think giving a woman so much freedom—independently wealthy indeed!—can only bring her husband trouble. Mark my words."

"Jean, I have heard all your arguments before. Again let me tell you what I think. First of all, I think I am tired of hearing you call me stupid even though I know you are trying to shock me into reacting against my previous decision. Secondly, I don't need the money. Thirdly, I have my own reasons for wanting to give her total freedom at least in this one respect. You won't understand unless I explain intimate details which you are obviously interested in knowing. And guess what?"

"What?"

"I'm not about to tell them to you. So please just let me read this damned thing so I can sign it and leave. I have something I want to do."

Charles adjusted himself on the wooden chair to read the document before him. Should he sign? Was he doing the right thing for himself and for Helena? He had a good idea of how vast her fortune was, and if they had not been legally married, and his child consequently protected, he might not be so willing to give up his rights to handle the wealth. Fortune hunters were numerous, and should one of them succeed with Helena, his child might wind up penniless. But he had impressive financial resources of his own which would one day go to his legal offspring anyway. He had no others.

Strangely enough, when he'd heard that Benito González had died and had left all his money and his enterprises to Helena, Charles had felt a vast sense of relief. For one thing, he would never have to face Benito now. His cowardly relief was mingled, however, with a certain satisfaction in the realization that out of the violence he had perpetrated on the woman he wanted more than any other, at least some positive gain for her had resulted.

Charles knew that he could keep iron control over her by controlling her purse strings, but frustrating her and humiliating her had little appeal to him now. He had made her suffer enough already. Stifling her freedom by using the laws which were in his favor smacked suspiciously of continued revenge, and would be like caging a delicate bird. He did not want to force her to him again. He wanted her to come to him of her own accord, of her own willingness to love him and want him. She was the only woman who had ever humbled him and the only one who had the power to hurt him and make him feel unsure of himself, but she was also the one he really wanted. His impulse to go to Yvette was not what would wound Helena at this point, he rationalized, and he knew in his heart that if Helena would one day give herself to him completely, irrevocably, with no conditions, he could not love another woman in any way again. His attempt at fulfillment with Yvette would only be a pathetic substitute for the real thing—to be loved body and soul by Helena. He was too impatient, however, to wait eternally for her amorous surrender, and the persuasions of his flesh were too fiery to deny.

While Charles read the legal paper before him, Jean Thibédeaux harrumphed indignantly and strode about the room. He managed to warm himself up uncomfortably and had to loosen his tie, which he finally ripped off in frustration on returning to the desk. Charles had signed his name.

"Yes, it's duly signed now," said Thibédeaux. "I'll have this registered in Panama only when you give me the word. In the meantime I'll send the second copy— here, sign it, too—to Paris on the next ship and have my law firm there register it. You know that this is as binding as a marriage contract, and cannot be changed like a will, don't you?"

Charles sighed heavily. "Yes, I know."

"All right, then, you foolish man, I'll do your bidding as soon as possible."

"Fine. I'll see you, Jean. I should be here next week again to hear what you have to say about Helena, but let's vary the day of the week on which we are to meet. You are one person I don't want even my men to know I have anything to do with. If I leave every week or every two weeks on the same day, one of them might get the smart idea of following me. Right now they think that my only tie in the city is Helena, and that is wholly convenient for me."

"That's good, Charles. I do want you to take care of yourself. I know it must be difficult because your type is often so involved in one adventure or another that taking precautions becomes a bore." Then, as if for good measure, he added: "I don't believe you will ever settle down."

"What do you mean? Did you ever know me to go see some puny French consul every week just to find out how my wife was doing?"

Jean Thibédeaux joined in the banter.

"Never! That is true. Them maybe there is some hope for you as a family man." Jean laughed heartily at his own remark, slapping Charles on the back and causing him to choke and cough up a stream of smoke. He finally caught his breath. "Damn it, Jean. You don't have to congratulate me to death. Anyway, I'm not that settled yet, old man."

The two joked in this manner for a minute or two more, but became silent when it was time for Charles to sneak out of the building. Jean went out first, then motioned to his friend to step out, and Charles disappeared into the night.

Arrangements had been made without difficulty. Mr. Terny turned up at the Hotel de las Garzas impeccably dressed, as any Englishman would be, a fitting specimen of the Empire, in a white suit. Only this Englishman was deeply tanned, brown almost, in strong contrast to the immaculate tropical suit he wore.

"Charles! You look wonderful!"

Yvette was standing now in the middle of her sitting room at the hotel, her hair gleaming down to her waist and covering her shoulders like a rich mantle of silk. Her robe was loose enough to reveal the fullness of her breasts that showed white beneath the turquoise color she had chosen to wear.

Charles could not take his eyes off her décolletage until she spoke, and then his gaze was drawn to the inviting curves of her lips and the light he saw in her blue eyes. As if pulled by a magnet he strode decisively toward her. Her immense and eager eyes told him how unconditionally she admired and desired him, and he felt a great flood of satisfaction.

"I can't tell you how beautiful you look to me at this moment, Yvette."

In a rush of feverish passion, without any more preliminaries, Yvette threw herself into his arms, and she quivered when she felt her lover's lips grazing her, his hands loosening her silk robe, stripping her of it, and leaving her exposed to his touch and his desire.

"Oh, Charles! How I have missed you. I just had to see you again. You don't know all I went through to get here to you. I . . ."

But she could not say much more, for he had lifted her in his arms and was covering her mouth with his while he headed for the bedroom. He laid her on the bed, but she sprang up almost immediately to clutch at his pants and pull them down. He discarded his jacket in silence. On her knees now, she cupped his organ, watching it surge impatiently, and he groaned as her lips caressed him. He stood there watching her, taut with the expectation of an ever-climbing joy.

He lifted her to her feet then and kissed her hard, almost cruelly, until his lips opened passionately and softened into a hint of tenderness. His kisses left her breathless, as they had always done. His hands roved over her, clutching her flesh in desperation, for he was now like a hungering wild man. He couldn't seem to get enough of her.

Yvette's arms softened and melted over the male expanse of his shoulders. She teased him with her fingers, entwining them in the fur of his chest, letting them linger, then letting them rove down to his buttocks and to the throbbing maleness of him. Charles was beyond thinking. He crushed her to him feverishly, kissing her, arousing her to the pitch of his own body. Then he pushed her gently so that she lay across the bed and he fell greedily to nibbling and sucking all the crevices of her beautiful curvaceous body. By this time Charles was totally consumed with desire.

Yvette arched her back, hinting without words that he should pierce her sweetly now, for she could not contain her excitement anymore. When he entered her, he thrust deeply, bringing her quickly to a rapturous height that easily matched his own.

They lay quiet for a few minutes, not daring to speak, as if each knew that their only tie was this marvelous physical release.

With great languor Yvette got up and washed herself gently with a monogramed towel by the enamel basin on her commode. She splashed some diluted cologne all over herself so she would feel fresh, desirable to him once again. Then she returned to his side, smiling at the admiring stare.

They lay down together and Charles was kissing her again. His hands had landed on her buttocks and were holding her close to him. Then he turned her over on her stomach, kissed the nape of her neck, slid down to her waist, and finally found her from a strange new angle. He knew he was thrilling her. Her writhing was barely controlled so that he would not lose the pressure of his tongue on her, but it took an effort on her part not to lurch wildly from the excitement of his boldness. When he entered her this time, she almost passed out from the pleasure.

How many times they took each other that night they did not later remember. Charles did not leave until just before the earliest breakfast call was rung.

The hotel clerk looked up in surprise at the Englishman who was leaving the hotel without even eating, so early in the morning. Because of the heat, the Europeans tended to sleep as much as they could before the scorching hours of the day made it impossible to lie in a bed. He had never in fact seen a European leave the premises before eight in the morning.

In the days that followed, however, this clerk as well as all the others who tended to the hotel desk came to recognize the generous tipper that was Mr. Terny, the Englishman.

Then, as soon as Madame Lamère departed for Peru about a week later, Mr. Terny disappeared, and they never saw him again.

Chapter XVIII

Some perversity in Helena's character had made her welcome the obsequious advances and compliments paid to her by Raúl Santana, and this perversity was intimately linked with a growing desire within her for revenge. Her wish to humiliate Charles even in some small way loomed larger every day, side by side with the hope of actually witnessing his reaction, of beholding his face grimacing in shame or frustration. Thus she began to discern in herself a twist of nature which she had never before realized existed in her, but which somehow she must satisfy, or lose rest.

Raúl Santana became merely a tool for her purposes. She did feel isolated moments of regret about using the man, however little respect she held for him. It was obvious to her that Raúl Santana was desperate for money, and desperate people, she was beginning to discover, were easy to manipulate. In any case, she rationalized that his hypocrisy entitled her to use him. She felt only the slightest twinge of guilt. She did not seriously consider the possible adverse repercussions of her actions, for it seemed to her that it would not be difficult or complicated to get rid of Raúl Santana's advances and send him off on his way once she was through with him. In the meantime Raúl was allowed to pay her frequent visits in the afternoon, visits which were chaperoned every moment by Rosario.

"I'm scandalized, Helena," Rosario would venture every once in a while, once they were alone again. "You are now a married woman, even if it is a secret. May I say that it can't remain a secret too long, or no one will believe you when you finally announce that you were married all along. And here you are accepting gentlemen callers!"

"I don't care if anyone believes me or not," pouted Helena. "I have the papers for legal proof. Besides, Raúl Santana is no gentleman," she asserted. Sometimes Rosario was incredibly bossy! "He's only a foolish man born of foolish parents. Everybody knows his story, and furthermore, everyone knows that the man is absolutely desperate to get his hands on my money, hoping to squander it away as fast as he did his own. Well, I'm no fool, Rosario, and with this kind of man, it is better, I am sure, to lead him along just enough to give him the proper setback, and he'll never bother me again. But if I don't give him the chance to get close to me, I have the feeling that he won't ever give up trying. That is, until he discovers some other heiress more apparently willing than I. With the economic situation the way it is in Panama, I'm afraid that great heiresses are scarce!"

Helena was somehow ashamed to have let Rosario in on her real plans for using Raúl as an object to bring out jealousy and rage in Charles de Thierny. Fleeting thoughts, too, of what her dear mama might have thought about all this made Helena question her decision, but she brushed her sense of guilt quickly away. Her present need for satisfaction overrode any qualms she experienced about her plan.

Her stratagem for revenge was bound to succeed, for what man could stand by without feeling pain and know that his wife was cuckolding him? And he help- less to defend his honor, verbally or otherwise, or complain? It was perfect! And Rosario had to under- stand how much the man had hurt her and how she, too, needed a revenge even if it were slight compared to what he had done to her. What did it matter as far as her personal morals were concerned, as long as she actually had no intimacies with Raúl? The important thing was to give Charles the impression from the gos- sip that she planned to stir up that she had taken a lover. What a coup that would be! Especially as she knew how much this "honor" meant to Charles. Hel- ena's eyes narrowed, and lights of excitement and cruelty flared from them.

It frightened Rosario to see her like this, for it seemed to the little seamstress that Helena was bound to hurt only herself with her hates and her passions.

Plans for the December ball continued to be elabo- rated and embellished by Rosario and the household staff.

"I must say, Helena, that at least having a ball in this lovely house should put you and lots of other people in a better mood than you've been in since your so-called wedding."

Only Rosario could get away with such flippancy. Helena had become almost despotic lately, tolerating very few irritations to herself. It seemed almost as if the early spoiled years of her life and the few years before her voyage to France were creeping out of hiding, and reasserting themselves in her personality.

One evening just before the ball, Raúl Santana began serious overtures which led nowhere. Rosario had left the room, busy now more than ever with the many details of the fiesta.

"Helena." Raúl had practically rushed to her side the moment Rosario excused herself. "I have been waiting so long to speak to you alone."

Helena looked terribly uncomfortable.

"You must know by now how I feel about you. You are not only the prettiest girl in Panama, you are also—"

"Please don't say any more, Raúl. I'm too saddened by the death of first my mother at the end of last year and then my poor Uncle Benito and Tía Alejandra. You must know that all of my superficial laughter is only an attempt on my part to forget these very sad events. I fear I shall take much more time getting over them entirely."

"Telling lies with so much truth in them only makes the lie believable," thought Helena almost callously.

Raúl was actually encouraged by her intimate avowal of great suffering and took her confidence as a sign of favoritism in his behalf. It seemed to him that her sweet confession only hinted that he need not give up, for it was all a matter of time before she would accept him. So Raúl stuck fast to his decision to captivate the heart of the stunning, bold, beautiful, and rich Helena Canales.

He had not taken to studying too much about her past, for he had always suspected the truth about his own mother's wanton youth, and he could not afford to be a snob. He still recalled bitterly the insinuations made by his adolescent companions at the priests' school near Santa Ana, and the ironic looks of their parents when they spoke to him. Having a clever mind, he was not impervious to the hints, and if he did not investigate them further, it was because he was afraid that his pride would not be able to take the full truth without breaking. Better keep the past hidden from his heart, and keep his self-respect intact.

But his self-respect had been affected, in spite of his measures and precautions, and Raúl had grown up insecure and bitter. His most positive actions were usually in the direction of self-gratification, even if those fleeting pleasures later caused him pain. Thus he was now coveting the fortune of the young and unprotected Helena.

Long ago he had given up trying to convince his mother that she should provide for all of his expenses, for he had learned too well how impossible it was to budge her from her hoard.

Sometimes he felt like telling his mother, Laurie Lee, exactly what he thought of her and of her cheap taste, manifested in that ludicrous, dried-out tinted red hair of hers. In fact he sometimes longed for the courage to rip away her too colorful clothes and dress her instead in solemn gray.

But Raúl bit his tongue and said nothing, because in her home he had at least the security of food in his belly and a roof over his head. Sometimes he could even get drinks there when he was feeling especially low. Even if she never gave him money, he could not afford to antagonize her to the point of being evicted from her house.

Laurie Lee was old and in many ways senile, but in general she was shrewd. She had led a rough existence early in her life and counted her lucky stars that she had had sense enough not to share her part of Don Agustín's inheritance with her son. She would not pay a single one of his debts. He'd go to jail first.

Raúl knew how serious her threat was. He had always observed her passion for holding on to what was hers and spending recklessly what belonged to others.

Laurie Lee loved her son in her own way, but she loved her money even more. Raúl had no choice, then, but to seek other sources for the support of the lifestyle he preferred. What better source than a beautiful and immensely wealthy young woman like Helena Canales?

At eighteen Helena was the embodiment of a goddess of love. She had a way of looking at men that excited him, a glancing and a sideways sweeping of her eyelashes which apparently she had no idea she practiced. It seemed spontaneous and natural and yet so wicked.

And she had inherited the total estate of Benito

González, an empire of business enterprises—a vast fortune!

His performance at the ball might well earn him the legal rights to that fortune, for Helena had granted him an honor in asking him to wear a specific costume. She had chosen for him that of Henry Morgan, the English pirate who had burned the old city of Panama. The ugly wrinkled hag that chaperoned Helena so assiduously, had even presented him with a ready-made costume of the famous buccaneer. There could only be one explanation for such graciousness. Her mistress Helena, who had certainly arranged the gift, probably needed to recognize him in order to shower her favors upon him. So Raúl Santana was looking forward to the masked ball with relish.

Among the guests invited to Helena's ball were several young engineers who had been making studies and surveys for the proposed canal through the Isthmus of Panama. Having done most of the jungle trekking and surveying that was necessary, Napoleon Bonaparte Wyse, Armand Reclus, and a Latin American colleague, Pedro Sosa, were ready to celebrate, for they were proud to think that their proposed project would be accepted by the great de Lesseps, who would be coming himself to the Isthmus less than a year from now. They were fairly sure that everything would be in order for his arrival, for already the two French engineers had received communications from the French government that agents had been seeking out information that might have bearings on the safety of de Lesseps and on the project itself. If the engineers themselves heard any tidbits of news which might prove useful to the agents, they were to report to the consul. So far the two Frenchmen had heard only lavish praise for their canal builder, and words of encouragement for the commencement of the digging from members of the community of Panama and Colombia.

Their work accomplished, the young engineers were making the most of the many social invitations extended to them by members of Panama's best society, who also wanted to celebrate the forthcoming canal construction.

The French engineers were shocked, therefore, when at a reception in the home of the wealthy and elegant Esquevedo family, Don Manuel Esquevedo himself spoke harshly of one Juan Jiménez, a notorious member of the Liberal party about whom apparently all the Panamanians knew and about whom the Frenchmen had barely heard.

"You know, of course," said the Conservative Don Manuel to his engineer friends from Europe, "that Jiménez is dead set against the coming of de Lesseps to build the canal. He himself has no financial problems, and is afraid, apparently, that once the canal is begun both parties will make up their differences, and the revolutions and the violence will come to a halt. The very idea is terrifying to him, for he needs this sort of disruption to feel important and necessary. He's absolutely crazy.

"I tell you, war and killing and terrorism are in his blood. How he once found time to work on making his fortune, I'll never know, or maybe his mind became warped with a lust for power after he'd tasted it

in the business world. All I know is that he is a very
dangerous man to reckon with. I'm afraid that you
and other engineers from France will not find it easy
to go about your work as long as men like him are in
the area. Sabotage of the canal project is very easy in
a country like this."

Don Manuel's words left Wyse and Reclus in a deep
and thoughtful mood, for they both knew how dangerously vulnerable their proposed project was to the
apparently senseless machinations of such a man as
Jiménez. They had not realized before that the man
was so dangerous and had thought, from their knowledge of politics on the Isthmus, that Jiménez was
merely a fanatic Liberal whose wish was to ensure a
freer system of law, a very progressive constitution for
Panama. Now they suspected painfully that he posed
a real threat to the canal, even before it came into
existence.

As the conversation continued Wyse and Reclus both
learned a great deal more about the power-hungry
Isthmian.

Jiménez was a man who fed his spirit on chaos.
Though the cause for which he fought seemed noble
enough, he was actually, deep inside, an anarchist and
an iconoclast, never content with his status in the
world or with his relatively fortunate social and financial situation. His violent disapproval of members of
the Conservative party went beyond political enmity.
Jiménez, it was whispered surreptitiously, was a
bloodthirsty man who did not want peace with the
Conservatives under any circumstances because if and
when the wars came to an end, his spirit would

starve—or, more to the point, he would, if he continued his terrorist tactics after an armistice, be branded an ordinary criminal rather than honored as a Liberal hero dedicated totally to the principles for which the party stood.

Besides his bodyguards, he had surrounded himself with vicious persons who remained for the most part in the mountains of Panama awaiting his orders to attack and plunder whenever he deemed it convenient to their "cause." He himself mingled freely with all persons of his social level even though his friendship was not coveted. At least in public he deported himself correctly and spouted forth only words of idealism. Besides, nothing had ever been definitely proven about his terrorist activities.

He was perhaps one of the wealthiest men on the Isthmus and certainly the wealthiest Liberal. Other members of his party could not afford to lose the support of a man like Jiménez, so they said nothing to anger him, and kept their distrust to themselves, venturing only a few whispered words in the privacy of their homes.

The Conservatives, however, were bolder, and now that the French were definitely coming to Panama, they were more so than usual. Their opinions of the man were well known by now, but somehow the young engineers had been too concerned with their technical work before this to have been aware of the danger the man posed for their project. They were not sure, but they felt that their consul in Panama probably was not aware, either, of the exact nature of

Jiménez's aims and the extent of trouble he could bring about.

Fortunately Jiménez had gained such notoriety that, even with all his money, he was having trouble purchasing the guns and ammunition he required. Everywhere now the Americans had hired spies to watch his movements, because they were bent on keeping the railroad clear and functioning at all cost. Jiménez and his uncontrollable desires to fight for the thrill of adventure and power was a threat to the safety and smooth management of the railroad.

Though his goal was to disrupt the Isthmus with the hope of freeing it eventually from the dominion of Bogotá, his deep-rooted impulses came from a greed for power which under the present system was difficult to achieve. Jiménez wanted to rule.

Like many of his fellow Isthmians, his immediate ancestors had come to the tiny slender tropical soil to escape the rigidity of an aristocratically oriented society in South America where a man's brains and ambitions had very little to do with his economic opportunities. The great landowners had settled into a rigid hierarchy very soon after the Spanish conquistadores had swarmed over the land and taken its choicest morsels for themselves, and for the Church as well. Only trade and commerce was left for the latecomer, unless by some stroke of luck he managed to marry into the old families. Since the Isthmus was the place for trade, as it had always been—a transient gold mine of flowing goods and services whose intrinsic value wavered up and down according to the amount of

wealth that passed through its jungles—his grandfather had decided to settle there and exploit the
great possibilities for commerce in Panama. Jiménez
himself had increased the family fortune.

Having been made aware of Jiménez's intentions,
Wyse and Reclus gathered more details by talking to
other gentlemen at the gathering in Don Manuel's
home—details that verified and added to what Don
Manuel had told them.

The next day, as early as diplomatic hours would
allow, Napoleon Bonaparte Wyse and Armand Reclus
arrived at the door of the Consulate of France in Panama City, for the importance of the news they bore
could not be made to wait unnecessarily.

The day of the party had finally arrived. The shutters were drawn against the still, oppressive heat of
the noon hours, though the temperatures did not rage
on as they had before because it was the beginning of
the dry season and the humidity had fallen.

Helena slept her siesta with gusto. She reposed exquisitely on the massive bed that some González
ancestor from Spain had had made to order in the
style of his Peninsular folk. Her pregnancy no longer
gave her any nauseous feelings, nor did the thickening
of her waist give her away except to those who were
familiar with the astonishing usual smallness of it. Her
dresses were discreetly cut and decorated to camouflage the changes in her body. Rosario had had to
make new clothes to this end, for Helena's breasts
were enlarged and the taut bodices of her previous
wardrobe were very uncomfortable. Hiding Helena's

growing waistline, however, had truly taxed the imagination of the little seamstress, who discovered with her experimental designs that V-shaped flounces on the bodice which were cut on the bias to fall gracefully to just below the waist were very effective in dissimulating Helena's condition.

Helena had been feeling superb, and reveled in the petty intrigue in which she had embroiled herself. Oh, she had her doubts, for her training had been, as it was wont to be in her day, very rigorous with regard to the moral standing of women within the community. But she had the security of knowing that her marriage to Charles de Thierny was valid; furthermore, she did not plan on having carnal contact with the man whom she was using so wretchedly to tarnish Charles's reputation by destroying her own with a public display of immorality. She wished she had the courage to betray him in actual fact, but some restrictive inner voice would not allow her to do so. Nevertheless, later, when Charles came to claim his husbandly rights as he had insisted on doing the day of their marriage when he'd set *his* terms, he would be laughed at as the biggest cuckold on the Isthmus, whether in actual fact he was or was not.

Helena gloated at the thought that Charles wouldn't dare to show up now to thwart her revenge, and that the whole time he would be aware of what she was doing to his honor that he valued so greatly. Rosario's errand to "tattletale" on her would have taken care of that angle. He would know, he would squirm and he would rage, but he would not dare to appear in public or come to the ball, for it would mean uncovering his identity and his work would be lost. Either way she would be avenged!

Santana would probably not understand the game she was playing, but what did that matter? Somehow, she thought, she could pay him for his puzzlement and troubles with a generous gift of money. That would set her conscience completely at ease, for after all, wasn't money what the man wanted?

So Helena had everything planned. She had reason to sleep soundly; not only was she content about her plot, but she was several months pregnant and often felt sleepy and lazy. Because of her superb physical condition and the fact that this was her first child, so that her taut muscles restrained her expanding waist, she was able to hide the new contours of her body successfully with the clever design of her clothing. Her incipient roundness would not betray her yet. The thought of her revenge made her happy as a child is happy at the thought that a satisfying treat is in store.

Evening descended with its usual astonishing rapidity at about six o'clock. Helena was awake now and relaxing after a nourishing snack, studying the dress she had chosen for her costume: a lavishly embroidered pollera with yards and yards of the finest white linen adorned with handmade laces. The skirt and petticoat had been starched until its layers stood out gracefully and crisply.

The pollera was a more elegant version of the skirts and blouses which the Spanish colonial ladies had designed originally for their personal black or Indian house slaves.

The blouse of the costume had been designed to cling to the shoulders, allowing the smooth roundness of the wearer's upper arm to show. The jealous ladies of the house frequently caught their husbands' eyes lingering on the soft shoulder of a maid or a nanny, and they naturally soon took to wearing the pollera themselves, discarding when entertaining at home, their austere imitations of central Peninsular Spanish dresses.

Helena's idea to wear it to the costume party was original only in that everyone else hoped to take advantage of this unique opportunity to wear a European dress. Surely Marie Antoinette would be much imitated, as well as Queen Isabella. Queens, kings, and other assorted royalty were bound to dominate the scene that night.

About ten o'clock the guests began to arrive, the first wave composed mostly of older folk. The younger girls would come as late as they could so that their entrance would be that much more impressive and admired. If it were left up to some of them, they would not arrive before midnight in hopes of being the last to step into the ball area and thus dazzle a greater sized audience.

"Good evening, Doña Sarita, Don Manuel," greeted Helena, as the Quijanos stepped onto the terrace, unmasked. Though she was disappointed in the fact that most of the older guests did not wear their masks, Helena was actually not too surprised. Society in Panama was dominated by conservative traditions brought from Spain directly or via Bogotá. It was already a victory for modern outlook that the younger people were not ridiculed by their parents for wearing masks and that the young girls were actually encouraged by the older womenfolk to dress in elaborate costumes and were allowed to come to a ball given by a most disruptive young heiress.

The party was already swaying to European music that had been somehow changed by the influence and addition of some instruments of native design. Some of the lilting waltzes which were the latest rage in Europe drifted pleasantly through the heady evening air. Certain tones in the music bespoke of the wailing songs of long-vanished Arabian ancestors from Spain and plaintive lyrics of the Cholos such as she had heard in the mountains of Panama.

A stab of pain at the remembrance of those days when she had been forced to roam in the jungles and the hills of the Isthmus surprised Helena by its unexpectedness. Would she ever forget?

Guest after guest greeted Helena, for the brazen décolletage of her pollera blouse, as well as the unusual gold of her fine hair, gave her away. The tiny jeweled mask she wore hardly concealed the perfection of her features, or the inviting curves of her mouth. It had been a clever costume for her to wear, for the waist was covered by the generously gathered and starched ruffles of the blouse. The colonial ladies had thought of everything when they had decided on the final design of their dress.

"Hello, Helena." It was one of the shy, yet much admired Arosemena girls. She and all her sisters had been tutored well in the academic subjects by their grandfather, Don Mariano, an advocate of female education. The girls' intellectual attainments were legend.

"I'm so glad you came, Marcela. I simply love your costume. It's so lovely. Let me see. Are you perhaps Marie Antoinette?"

"Yes. How did you guess?"

"Ohhh. I don't know. I suppose it's because you look as pretty as she might have been. Here, slip your mask on before the other guests see you."

Marcela Arosemena's happy laugh assured Helena that her guest would probably join the festivities in the proper frame of mind. For one fleeting moment Helena envied the girl's youthful air of innocent delight.

Though she took the time to be friendly to everyone and tried to make them all feel at ease, her eyes kept sweeping the ever-more-crowded floor of the terrace as she sought the pirate costume she had asked Raúl Santana to wear. She was almost relieved every time she missed seeing his figure, for the thought of her plan and the enormity of what she was about to do now frightened her in spite of her determination to go through with it.

After a few dances with the constantly begging younger men, Helena approached one of the several linen-covered tables which had been loaded with delicious tropical foods. Rice with *guandú*, or Congo peas, as the French called them, rice and coconut, bowls of ceviche or lime-marinated corvina fish, soups, cake soaked in rum sauces, egg custards, lentils, corn, coconut bars, tropical fruits cut in slices to garnish the other dishes—in short, as many of the native foods as would not readily spoil during the warm and balmy evening covered the table.

The sky was strewn with stars, and the moon glittered off the waters of the bay, stopping at the edge of the terrace where it seemed its beams could no longer find a placid spot from which to reflect.

The music became gayer and gayer as the musicians were offered more and more to drink, until the native sounds in the tiny orchestra began to take over and overwhelm the more refined strains of the European melodies. Then a bongo broke with European tradition altogether and a daring young man leaped to Helena's side to guide her through the paces of a native dance—the inimitable tamborito with its syncopated beat which literally made all the toes on the terrace twitch with delight.

For a moment the charm of the dance filled Helena and she forgot her quest for Raúl, her unknowing partner in scandal.

Whoops and calls of delight and joy were thrown at the dancing couple as they swayed and turned. Helena held the generously wide skirt of her pollera out about her like a huge upside-down fan, and her shoulders barely moved as her feet kept rapid pace with the bongo. Her partner, as was customary, gyrated about her with less elegance and more body movement, approaching her suggestively, but never touching her. These were the rules of the dance—a flirtation of great beauty put to music. The drumbeat and the flutes reverberated against the wall of the house on the terrace, bouncing out to sea and disappearing over the lapping waves.

Helena was happy, so happy in fact that she forgot momentarily about the ugly revenge which was the original purpose for this party. Oblivious to all but the music, she found herself freed in spirit for the first time in eons; she could not remember when she had felt so carefree.

It came as an unpleasant interruption, therefore, when another man leaped into the circle made by the onlookers and took her away from the young man with whom she had been dancing. Her new partner, she observed wryly, had worn his costume as she had asked. Raúl's dancing, though acceptable, was not as spontaneous and delightful as her previous partner's, but then, Helena reflected, he was a larger man, not expected to be as graceful.

Her former partner asked another girl to dance and soon the terrace was teeming with couples who felt the call in their blood to participate in the wail and beat of their beloved tamborito, usually reserved for family parties in the country and for the popular festivities of the more common people. But tonight was a very different and exciting event, and young and old alike were delighted with themselves for having accepted Helena Canales's invitation.

The gusto fled from Helena as she continued to dance with her pirate partner, and she was relieved when he led her outside the area of whirling dancers as if to take her to the refreshment table.

Helena felt frightened suddenly, more than she had suspected she might feel, by her now apparently ridiculous scheme and futile and puerile attempt at revenge. Perhaps she would just forget about it while she still had time.

She was not able to do so, however, for the masked pirate Morgan began guiding her toward the great hallway and the stairs leading to the upper regions of the house.

"Raúl!" she blurted out. "What in the world are you doing? I want to stay here with the dancers."

Raúl's voice sounded strange, husky and muffled, and suddenly Helena's eyes flared up into his face. She was astonished beyond words by the gaze she met there of a pair of speckled green eyes. A bronzed hand reached up and rubbed his sideburns, a familiar gesture.

Staring in amazement, she let Charles de Thierny continue to guide her toward the entrance area where the curved stairs began. Their eyes were locked, hers in nervous wariness and his bright with desire—and something else which in Helena's experience was tenderness, reluctant as she was to believe it.

Finally Charles broke their silence, still moving along with her. They were at the foot of the stairs, and he had caught her hand in his, holding it tight, yet not with painful pressure. His hands felt extremely warm, thought Helena, especially since her own had turned to ice.

"Helena, Helena," Charles murmured. "What are you doing to yourself? Don't you know that we are one now, that our child will have to suffer for your mistakes as well as for mine? Don't do this foolish thing you are planning."

Helena found her voice, too, at last.

"What are you talking about? Are you insane, coming here? What if you are recognized?"

"At a costume ball?" Charles laughed scoffingly.

"Even at a costume ball. You know how small this community is, and soon the tongues will be wagging about the man whom no one recognizes. You are risking everything you claim is for the good of Panama and France to come and tell me what to do with my life. Haven't you ruined it enough already?"

At this Helena felt a sob welling up inside her, a sob of frustration at her inability to carry out her plans for revenge, at her own fears that remained turbulently confused in her heart, and at the sudden realization that she was absolutely thrilled and excited by the proximity of Charles de Thierny.

"Come, Helena. Let us go where we can be alone for a few minutes."

It crossed Helena's mind that she could resist, and only Charles would be in danger. She had nothing to lose. And yet, something inexplicable told her that this was not what she wanted to do. She surveyed the area with one sweep of her black eyes. All eyes were turned inward to the salon where the music still vibrated to accompany the dancers. Then she slowly climbed the stairs to the balcony.

But she had missed the look casually given in their direction by Juan Jiménez, who, like most of the leading social figures, had been invited to the party. Jiménez smiled knowingly to himself at the audacity of Helena Canales to lead a man upstairs in her house full of guests. He wondered, as any man might, who the lucky devil was. He might be able to find out, for the party was only bursting out into full swing now. It was all very interesting, and he had always found it profitable to know everyone else's business.

In the alcove before the door of her bedroom, Helena stiffened. Her heart was beating thunderously in her breast.

"What did you want to discuss with me other than to give me instructions as to how I should deport myself?"

"I just wanted to see you, Helena. I heard you were giving this ball, and as it was going to be a masked ball, I thought it would be the perfect opportunity. After all, you *are* carrying my child."

He began to slip his arm around her waist, but she twisted away.

"Unfortunately it is your child. You are right!"

The scorn in her voice was unmistakable, though the bewildered look in her eyes gave her away.

Even as the words still lingered on her lips, she was aware that Charles de Thierny had taken possession of them, and very gently, but with a quickening pressure, his kiss began to overwhelm her.

An ache permeated her arms, and soon, as if of themselves, they began to reach upward toward his shoulders. Then he was carrying her toward the bed.

Even while his lips were on hers, he laid her down on the mahogany bed and slipped his hand gently along her leg. His fingers kneaded her thighs very softly with just enough pressure to heat the blood that raced through Helena's veins. A wave of ardor overcame Helena, and her mouth parted and then pressed against Charles's own, where it seemed their very souls mingled and melted into one. Charles moaned with desire, and Helena felt the bulge that pressed against her thigh. She could scarcely contain herself and with determined relish began to strain upward to meet him.

Suddenly and brusquely Charles tore himself away, and, cursing softly as if trying to regain his control, he left her on the bed and composed his rumpled clothes, replaced his mask, and determinedly left the room.

Outside he leaned against the balustrade for a few seconds to catch his breath; then he descended the steps very quickly and quietly and rejoined the general melée below.

Helena did not know exactly when he had gone, for her eyes had remained closed as if to block out the painful reality of her warring emotions. She had shamelessly craved the sweet impalement of her body by Charles's own. She had missed his embraces, his kisses, his caresses, and yes, even his presence alone, and she was his wife, carrying his child.

A stream of shiny tears oozed out from under her long black lashes and trickled down her cheeks into the golden bejeweled mass of her hair on the pillow.

She wanted so desperately to hate Charles.

The confusion in her soul made her feel weak, small, and totally stupid. Was there any point in resisting the attraction she felt toward him? Why not just succumb to his easy promise of love and forget the past? Was it only a false sense of pride that kept her hatred alive? Or was it a righteous indignation toward a cad who might perhaps never change the inner workings of his own savage pride?

No, it was impossible for her to forgive and forget. Totally impossible. Yet she could not deny the presence of a secret hope in her heart that he might love her more than her rational mind acknowledged. His words of love and his offer of marriage in the mountains had not convinced her, for she had reasoned that they had been prompted by his feelings of guilt, perhaps also by gratitude for her condolence over his mother's tragic life.

But Helena had not failed to be moved by the absurd sacrifice Charles had made when he had denied himself the right to consume his obvious desire for her this night. Either he was determined to keep his promise not to force her in any way to accept his love-making or he was taking into consideration the fact that her pregnancy was well advanced and he did not want to cause her harm. Helena was aware by now, for she had made it her business to find out, that opinions were divided as to the wisdom of intercourse during the last few months of pregnancy.

He had once told her that he loved her. Perhaps he had been sincere after all. At the very least Charles's self-denial proved that he had developed a deep consideration for her. She found herself wishing, however, that he had not been so splendidly considerate this time. Her blood was still hot, and she longed for the touch of his hands on her.

She finally got up, realizing that the jewels in her hair were in an incredible tangle. One by one she removed them, brushed her own long hair out, put the braids back up the best way she knew how, and stuck the pretty trembling *templeques* back in her hair. Al-

most an hour had gone by, and she must return to her
guests. She washed herself at the basin that was always filled with fresh water for her and, feeling refreshed again, descended the stairs just in time to
bump into Raúl Santana, who had arrived about half
an hour before.

For a moment Helena's heart jumped. But the eyes
peering through the mask at her were not the fascinating ones that hypnotized her and broke her willpower.
She couldn't help hoping that for his sake he had already escaped without being seen.

"Helena!" exclaimed Raúl Santana. "Where in the
world have you been?" His voice betrayed the fact
that he was more than a little cross. He had been expecting a warmer welcome, and Helena's strange reception and aloofness were very irritating.

"I felt somewhat ill from dancing so much. I had
expected you a bit earlier, and when you didn't come,
I danced with others."

"You didn't lead me to believe I should come early,
Helena."

"There's no use arguing about it, Raúl. Let's go
back into the hall and join the others. Somehow or
another I don't feel too well anymore."

Even through his mask Helena could see the disappointment in Raúl's expression. His miserable attempt
to hide it made her feel almost sorry for him. She was
using him so horribly. Or at least, she had planned
originally to use him. Now, instead, she was determined that he should become aware little by little,
but with utmost certainty, that she did not love or
want him, and that she was carrying another man's

child. For the latter information, however, she would wait until she had no choice.

She slid her arm through his, and with an effort, she smiled at him as they joined the dancers.

With his usual keenness of sight Juan Jiménez noticed the hostess as she approached the crowded dancing area with her partner. He watched as long as he could but could not make out exactly who the masked pirate was, and as the evening wore on and became the early hours of dawn, he still had not had the opportunity to approach him, for Morgan the pirate kept himself busy tagging behind Helena or joining the laughing groups of younger men with whom Juan Jiménez rarely consorted. Thinking he had heard and seen enough to know some of these younger men, he finally approached, unmasked as he had arrived, and asked discreetly who Morgan was, receiving some vague and laughing answers, along with wafts of whiskey on the breath of the men who spoke. In disgust he turned away, almost bumping into Henry Morgan himself.

"Pardon me, señor," replied the pirate.

"That's quite all right, Mr. . . . , uh, what is your name, sir?"

What a stroke of genius and luck. The pirate was bound to fall for it, unless he had something to hide at this precise moment.

"Why, I thought everyone here would recognize me, even through this mask. It is indeed a pleasure that my costume is clever enough to hide my identity from you, Mr. Jiménez."

"Then, you know me, sir?" asked Jiménez, a little

peeved by the fact that because he had not worn a mask, this stranger should have the advantage of him.

"Yes, and you know me, too, I believe. I'm Raúl Santana, at your service, sir."

"Ah! Raúl! You scoundrel, you! So it is you who has won the favor of this beautiful young hostess here tonight! Well, I'll be. . . . I had heard that she was partial to you, but I had no idea things had become so cozy between the two of you. Congratulations, my dear fellow."

The pair of eyes behind the mask twinkled merrily, their myriads of specks glittering gold and green and brown.

"You know, Raúl, you are just the one I would like to talk to. I understand that you have a gambling debt to pay."

"Where did you hear that, Don Juan?" The pirate seemed genuinely disturbed.

"Here and there. You know how it is on the Isthmus, my dear boy, Nothing can be kept a secret for very long."

Was Juan Jiménez threatening to gossip about what he had seen or was this just an impersonal statement? Charles de Thierny did not know, and simply pretended that the last statement had gone over his head.

"There is no use denying it, Don Juan. I'm up to my neck in trouble. My only hope is . . ."

Charles's pretense of being Raúl Santana extended even to the device of leaving his hopes unmentioned. Everyone knew how desperate he was to marry Helena for her money.

It was very lucky indeed that Helena had given this

party, Charles thought. It was even better than if he had planned it this way, for the guest list had not been difficult to get, once he had enlisted the reluctant help of Rosario. They had met secretly on several occasions to maintain some control over the matter of Helena's using the unsuspecting Raúl Santana, perhaps to ruin forever her good name, which would indeed have enough criticism to bear during the next few months and after the child was born.

"Please, Rosario, for Helena's sake?" he had cajoled. "You yourself know how dangerous this game is that she's playing, and I swear, my way will ensure a rapid conclusion to my job here. Then afterward, why, Helena and I would be able to announce our marriage."

The little brown seamstress had stood petulantly before him, pretending that she was not easy to persuade, just in case he was trying to trick her into something that might hurt her Helena. But his assurances that the quicker his work was done, the sooner Helena could assume the role of a decent married woman, had lured her into his benevolent trap.

"All right. I'll help you with anything as long as it is not in direct conflict with Helena's orders."

Rosario had not only given him the guest list, but had secretly added Juan Jiménez's name, then had sewn two very similar pirate costumes and delivered one to Raúl Santana. This last she had been extremely reluctant to do, for she apparently felt extremely repelled by that knave.

For Charles it had been a lucky stroke, too, that the opinions about Juan Jiménez made by many sober men of the Isthmus had reached the ears of French officials, and thus his own. A man like Jiménez could pose a real threat to the French canal and to de Lesseps himself. He had to be kept under control somehow, or quietly destroyed. Without his money outlaw bands of Liberals could not persist in their rebellion. The solid and genuine Liberals were almost as afraid of Juan Jiménez as the Conservatives; the French, no less than the Americans, were not keen at all about the frequent skirmishes along the railroad from Colón to Panama City. According to the Bidlack Treaty the United States was to defend the line, and with the Liberals constantly threatening to disrupt traffic, it was difficult for the Americans to keep the line clear without venturing into the internal affairs of Panama. For the French it was not possible to get even near the internal affairs of Panama, without a legality such as the Bidlack Treaty. Their interference for the protection of their interests had to be done in silence and with great caution. If they were exposed, the Colombian government would not be pleased, even if the greater part of the time the central government treated the Isthmus as if it were just a colony from which to extract the last ounce of wealth and service. The projected plans for the canal had to be protected with cunning and skill.

Once they had found out that Juan Jiménez and his bands of men could indeed pose a real threat to the safety of the canal project, it had not been difficult to spy on him, or to discover that he needed armaments, and was looking around for men who would be disposed to help him get these arms. The list of possibilities had been narrowed down to only a few men who could possibly have the connections required for the job. With the aid of the consul Charles had studied that list, and found that though a few names were already known to him, that of Raúl Santana sounded most familiar. Later, as he thought restlessly about this particular person and tried to place him in his memory, he had leaped up from his hammock to look at the guest list of Helena's party which Rosario had sent to him at his request. He had heard that name before somewhere, or seen it. It was one of the first names on the paper. He was fleetingly puzzled. Why had Helena invited such a shady character to her party?

When it struck him, it hit like lightning! Helena's proposed lover!

Now, in Helena's house, luck had come in even more generous dosages, but it was up to his skill and shrewdness that Juan Jiménez should approach no other than Raúl Santana, or at least the man he felt was Raúl Santana. Once that contact was established, Jiménez was bound to spill at least part of the plans which he had no doubt concocted for making trouble on the Isthmus in the near future.

"Raúl, I have a proposition, my boy." Jiménez's arm patted the pirate's shoulder patronizingly as he led him toward the balustrade that overlooked the sea.

Mist was covering most of the water now, for it was the coolest part of the night, the wee hours of the morning before the rays of the equatorial sun began to reach the Isthmus.

Jiménez appeared not to notice the slight trace of a foreign accent in the pirate's Spanish, perhaps because he was so eager to carry out his plans. In any case, it was he who dominated the conversation with his proposals.

"Raúl, how would you like to participate in a patriotic, though audacious, enterprise and thus gain the eternal gratitude of all the Isthmian people who are valiantly struggling for their freedom?"

"Freedom from knaves like you," thought Henry Morgan, but only answered laconically: "What's in it for me?"

Jiménez laughed vociferously.

"You certainly don't mince words, Raúl. Ha. Ha. Hell! I've got to give you credit for not having hair on your tongue, as we say, and getting down to essentials. Listen, this deal is only the beginning. You'll take ten percent of the value of the merchandise which I'm going to ask you to handle for our cause."

"Money?"

"Yes, money! More money than you could possibly win even in the highest-staked poker game in Gringo Town. And the risks for you, being a friend of the sweet Miss Helena, are very low, practically nonexistent."

"Helena?"

"Certainly! To deliver the merchandise—new armaments for our men who fight so gallantly—it would certainly come in handy to use one of the many small ships of her fleet which are thoroughly unsuspected. For you, my boy, it should not be difficult to acquire the use of one. After all, you are obviously close friends—your visiting her in her chamber and all. . . ."

The pirate had only one objection: "Surely Helena will not agree to this. What should I tell her the guns are for?"

"Don't be silly, my dear fellow, you don't tell her they are guns! My agent already has orders to disguise the arms as digging tools for the canal—a sort of business-speculation deal. All he has to do is get them off his ship far out in the bay and onto one of the González's ships. The González fleet which plies the Caribbean side is made of smaller ships anyway. You might even convince Helena to use two ships. That way there would be less suspicion from each crew because the quantities would be less noticeable. The transfer would be done at two different times."

"What about the American navy? Their ships are up and down the coast constantly."

"Don't worry about them. For one thing, the sales agent is an American himself. He's bringing the arms from the States. The naval officers here will be less disposed to suspect a fellow American. Secondly, I'll help you synchronize the transfer so that there will be little chance that the navy will come upon either vessel—Helena's or my agent's."

The pirate stood pensive for a while, as if thinking over the amazing offer he had just received from Juan Jiménez. At last, he turned from the balustrade to speak directly to the Liberal.

"How can I keep in touch with you without being seen with you?"

"Well, we certainly cannot use any normal notes, can we? Do you have someone you can trust to send me messages in code? Preferably someone who cannot read at all?"

"I think I can find someone."

"Well, then, the code is a simple one. Simple reverse the alphabet. It's just enough to keep the information from being too easily read by a servant or someone like that. The main thing is to keep any contact between us in total secret. Your man and mine will meet in the cathedral during the six o'clock mass every day—near the door. My man, a lifelong servant who owes me many favors, will wear European clothes, including a jacket. No one else who stands near the door of any church here would be wearing such clothes, for as you know, the gentlemen prefer to sit right up in the front."

"Very well," answered Charles. "And my man shall wear a simple *montuno* shirt and short pants. In the city not many people wear that, especially if they are churchgoing folk."

The two men laughed and shook hands, and Don Juan Jiménez left the party in very high spirits, even though he should have been tired from staying awake all night.

Nobody noticed that the appearance of the man in the pirate costume, who could be seen circulating so frequently at the fiesta, had suddenly become scarcer.

Nor did Helena realize that night that two Henry Morgans had remained a very long time—at the same time—at her well received and original party.

❋ ❋ ❋

His mother's house was empty when Raúl arrived to see if she could house him for a few nights. His landlady had sworn he would not sleep in the apartment until he came up with the rent. Not even his assurances that he was soon to wed a very wealthy woman had made the old biddy budge. He had had an unlucky streak and lost all his money, that was all, but soon his luck would turn and he would win big. Then, just for the hell of it, he would throw the rent money in the old witch's teeth and leave that ridiculously unsuitable apartment for good!

Since Tito had probably accompanied his mother out—the old bag didn't dare leave the house alone anymore for fear of being teased and taunted by the ruffians in the streets—he'd make himself at home. Wait! Better still . . . This was one of those rare chances to look for his mother's hiding places. She must keep her money in the house somewhere.

He tore off his jacket and threw it on the first chair he saw, then gingerly climbed the worm-eaten, termite-infested stairs to the bedroom level. He hesitated before cautiously entering his mother's darkened room. The shutters had been closed and the curtains drawn to keep the cooler air of the night in while keeping the daytime heat out. Once his eyes became accustomed to the gloom, he began the search which he had surreptitiously been making for several years.

Where the hell could she be hiding the gold? She must have huge piles of it somewhere, for surely she did not spend very much. He looked in disgust at the state of the bedroom. The bedcover was simply a travesty of lace. Huge holes in it had never even been camouflaged. The curtains had great faded spots, and the hems were in tatters. Truly disgusting.

He began tapping the walls to see if some hollow place might reveal the thin lines of a secret door. Nothing. He looked behind one of the few old paintings of his father's ancestors still left in the house. Some of the better ones had even been sold by the irreverent widow. Well, he didn't really give a damn about his ancestors, but he really should have received part of the money she'd got for those paintings. After all, they were his ancestors, not hers. He'd better hurry, though. Each time he'd looked around for his mother's money, he had been interrupted too soon to make any real headway in his search.

This time was no exception. Just as he had begun to inspect the baseboards, he heard his mother calling out to him from the hall.

"Is that you up there, son?" Her voice was cracking worse every day. The old bat.

He left his mother's room. At the top of the once magnificent stairway, now dangerously eaten by a tropical plague of termites, he pretended casual surprise as he smoothed his hair.

"Yes, Mother. I thought you might still be sleeping."

"At ten o'clock in the morning? You know I get up early now all the time, son. Can't sleep like I used to."

Tito stood behind Raúl's mother, the disdain for his mistress's son obvious on his mulatto features. Raúl sensed that Tito knew very well what he had been up to. But what did he care about a servant's opinion? He wouldn't dare warn his mother against her one and only son, would he?

"Are you staying with me for a while, Raúl?" asked his mother. Raúl, with his usual insensitivity, failed to be grateful for the tactful and considerate remark. It might have embarrassed her son if she had asked him point-blank what he was doing there, for he would have had to answer that he had no other place to sleep. Laurie Lee loved her son. Raúl simply did not appreciate her efforts to show it because they never included financial assistance, and that, to Raúl, would have been the only worthwhile proof of her love.

"How did you know it was me?" Raúl asked as he cautiously descended the treacherous stairway.

"Oh, I saw your coat on that chair as I came in."

Jesus! The old bag didn't miss a thing, even in the ever-darkened house. As old as she was, her eyesight was as sharp as a hawk's.

Raúl stayed two days, at the end of which, still not having recovered his gambling losses, he lengthened his visit. His bad luck at cards had not changed, but he felt at last that his luck was changing one day when, while Tito was taking his mother to the market-place, he received a caller—a Cholo Indian who handed him the note that would change his life, a message and proposal from a man whose vast power and wealth could not help but impress him—Juan Jiménez.

When Laurie Lee returned, her basket filled with the cheapest victuals available for human consumption, her son announced happily that he would be staying with her an indefinite period of time. She was delighted, except for the extra expense this would mean to her, but had no idea that Raúl was busy with a certain dangerous business.

Charles slipped his watch back into the pocket of his faded gray pants as he waited patiently on the street under the wall of the cathedral. He gazed aimlessly about in the gentler shadows of dawn, his eyes hesitating here and there on the insignificant adobe walls of the old and unassuming buildings of the center of Panama City. Finally his hazel eyes glowed with relief, then anticipation, as he spotted Pablo trotting across the cobblestone street from the corner of the plaza to the side door of the cathedral.

Its colonial domes were beginning to reflect the light of the rising sun. The six o'clock mass was about to begin.

Charles felt apprehension and excitement as the Cholo Indian approached him.

"Here I am, Patrón. With a note for you. The same man I went to the other day gave it to me—just like you told me."

It was the most enthusiastic declaration Charles had heard from Pablo since he had first met him, and it demonstrated the increasing self-confidence of his band of Indians, about which Charles was pleased. Training useful personnel was part of his duty.

Charles took the note eagerly and scanned it, his initial smile broadening into a great grin of satisfaction. His plan was working well. Raúl Santana had fallen into the trap and was already immersed in his preparations for business. From now on, Charles knew, each note Santana sent to Jiménez, and vice-versa, would first pass through his own hands.

Handing the folded note back to his man, Charles instructed him to enter the church and deliver the note into the hands of Juan Jiménez's servant, whom he described carefully and whom he had already witnessed entering the cathedral. Pablo, however, looked suddenly dejected.

"What's the matter?" questioned his *patrón*.

"Nothing, Patrón, it's only that I do not . . . well, that I . . . Do I have to go to mass? The whole time?"

Charles laughed.

"No, but Pablo, I don't think it would hurt you to hear a few words of wisdom once in a while. They might help overcome the influence of your friends down at Encarnación's Bar."

"Ah . . . Patrón," answered the Indian in an embarrassed tone. It was difficult to tell when these strange men from across the sea were serious and when they were jesting. And it wasn't that Pablo resented listening to the padre's words, which he never fully understood anyway, but he was reluctant to be pointed out as a country bumpkin. The *patrón* had insisted he wear the short loose pants and shirt of the peasant that he was. Pablo sighed in resignation as he trudged up the sidewalk to the main entrance. He didn't dare disobey. He had long ago decided that the *patrón* was not the sort of man to abide resistance, nor to make long and detailed explanations of his motives.

Chapter XIX

On his next visit to Thibédeaux's office Charles became worried. The consul had not been able to discover exactly how Helena was faring, for she had not left her house, and the only one who visited her was Raúl Santana. Rumors had begun to circulate viciously through the ranks of the wealthy and the powerful about Helena and her scandalous pregnancy. Charles felt a terrible resurgence of guilt and a yearning to console poor Helena, whose pride must be suffering the final blow of having been exposed. She was being criticized severely, without mercy, by the chatterboxes in Panama.

When Jean Thibédeaux questioned him about the Peruvian ambassador, Jean Lamère, Charles was vague except in his assurance that he would not see the alluring wife of the ambassador ever again.

"I told her I was married. She didn't believe me at

389

first, but I assured her it was true. When had she ever heard me lie about anything like that? I'm not frightened enough of *any* woman to have to lie to her."

"Charles, do you think that to a woman like Yvette the fact that you are married will make any difference?"

"Yes, and no. She had special designs on me, you see, and she figured that eventually she would blackmail her husband, or something equally distasteful, and get a divorce on some trumped-up charges. She knows I have no family to worry about, and that I would be free to marry her if I really wanted her— that is, if I were not married to Helena."

"And don't you want her?"

"Of course, but never enough to marry her. But I tell you, she is the best thing for a man who is depressed. I suppose I love her in my own way, but I am not the man for her. She was very upset when she found out I had married. Well, what can I do. . . ."

Changing the conversation, Charles asked the consul: "Has Helena announced our marriage, or has she considered doing so?"

"How should I know? She certainly does not keep *me* informed of her intentions. As far as I have been able to find out, nobody on the Isthmus knows you even exist."

She had not announced her marriage. For her, that would be a solution; though, of course, for *him* it could be disastrous at this point. If Jiménez or even the Americans suspected that Frenchmen, other than the French consul and the few engineers whom everybody knew, were arriving in Panama, everything could be lost. For one thing, the Americans would set out their own spies to keep control of the French and the situation, and men like Jiménez would do so, too. The success of blowing Jiménez's plans to pieces depended wholly on secrecy at this point.

The thought occurred to Charles that the reason why Helena did not announce her marriage—a measure which would protect her—could be because she was ill; perhaps her isolation had nothing to do with her embarrassment at exposing herself, big with child, to the critical eyes of her former "friends."

Charles decided that he would go see Father Rafael. The priest would know if Helena was in good health, if everything was going well with her and with his unborn son.

He had seen Father Rafael a few times, always for the purpose of verifying other accounts of how Helena was feeling, what she was up to. He knew how loyal the priest was to Helena, and cleverly, in order to bind the man to secrecy, Charles had approached him in the confessional, thus exacting silence under the laws of the Church.

The confession booth was open for the men; that is, no screen was placed between the sinner and the priest. Only the women enjoyed the privilege of hiding their embarrassment along with their identity from the father confessor who was to absolve their sins in the name of Christ. Charles felt sure, in his own cynical way of looking at religion, that this was one reason why more women than men bothered to receive the sacrament of penance.

391

Originally Charles had no intention of being sincere during these confessions with Father Rafael, for he was only interested in maintaining a secret tie between himself and Helena through the priest who had married them—a tie that later might help convince Helena that she should love him.

But Padre Rafael was a realist and psychologist of the first order, and Charles had underestimated him. He found himself lured by the priest's uncanny perspicacity to pour out at last the terrible doubts and sins that had burdened his soul and had caused within him a disgust for what he had become—a hard man, unscrupulous in his hatreds, a man who had lost a great measure of his capacity for compassion.

On this occasion, as he had the last time he had seen Father Rafael, Charles found himself suffering the spoken truth of what he had done. This time he spoke of his visit to his former mistress and of his impenitence for having committed this betrayal of his marriage vows.

He had gone to Yvette in search of acceptance, of pleasure, of that intimate avowal of admiration that was the sexual act, even though he loved Helena more than he ever thought he could love another human.

"My son, do not judge yourself too harshly. Helena, too, is guilty, for her sin is also the sin of pride. Pride, too, led you first to harm her. And now pride stands in the way of forgiveness.

"Your physical release with another woman who was more than willing to have you is not nearly as great a sin as pride, Charles. Pride is destruction.

"And pride is the most difficult of our weaknesses to overcome. Even a saint can find himself feeling pride for his goodness, as though it came solely through his efforts and not as a gift of God."

Charles remained pensive at the priest's words, quiet for a while.

The church was almost empty and the shadows of the night had invaded the pews, unable to penetrate completely the vicinity of the altar because many candles lit by devout members provided intense pinpoints of light. A few penitent parishioners were still praying before the altar, perhaps bargaining with God or praying for the soul of some deceased beloved, or merely hoping that the grace of God would pour over them to help them overcome the grief which life persistently meted out.

The two men left the confessional area; Charles had waited to be the last to approach the seated priest.

He had knelt beside Padre Rafael, but the priest had seen no reason why he should force the penitent Charles to remain there long. So he had risen and patted Charles on the shoulder, indicating that they should walk the length of the aisle to the doorway together.

Then the priest offered to tell him how Helena was faring. He toned down his story somewhat where it concerned the inner turmoil and frustration the girl was suffering as the whole of Isthmian society pointed its finger of scorn at her.

"I tried to get her to announce her marriage, but she wouldn't."

"If she did, Father, it might mean the end of my career or worse still, my death," replied Charles.

"Ah! So that is why. She cannot bring herself to hate you irrevocably, Charles, and that should give us hope. As proud as she is, she prefers to suffer this humiliation rather than to cause your destruction."

Charles had not looked at it quite from that angle, and now a surge of gladness coursed through him at Father Rafael's words.

When finally he left the priest, who stared compassionately after him until he had disappeared into the already lonely streets, Charles felt the touch of a song on his lips, a rush of youth and delight in himself and in his personal potential and possibilities that had been exiled from his heart many years before.

Nobody invited Helena out anymore. Suspicious minds had been able to ascertain the nature of her condition. For her part Helena was not interested in having to cope with society when she felt so unhappy. She felt despondent from the heat and depressed by the fact that her movements were now clumsy and her figure so thoroughly transformed that there was, of course, no use pretending not to be expecting.

The baby kicked her mercilessly, and though she had felt a thrill of some primeval expectation when she felt his first flutterings in her womb, she had lost much of her enthusiasm, and resentment had once again crept in to replace it.

Her whole life could have been different if it hadn't been for the unwelcome intrusion within her. She found that the fact that it was the child of Charles de

Thierny no longer mattered as much as the sad limitations put on her ambitions and plans by her pregnancy. Because of her distended belly she was forced to hide as if she were responsible for the shameful deed that had produced this unwanted child. It was difficult, moreover, to think of the fetus as a baby. His faceless, shapeless presence could only be felt, and it brought her no comfort, no joy, for she had never dreamed of having him—not now, not in this way, and certainly not by its father, who had forced her to him with all the physical power and supreme arrogance of which he was capable.

The only one besides Rosario and Father Rafael to persist in his attempts to mollify Helen's apparent and recurrent indifference and depression was Raúl Santana. Raúl was so persistent, in fact, that Helena was becoming desperate; she found his attentions more than ever obnoxious. He brought her no comfort.

It was common knowledge that Raúl was courting the pregnant heiress, and tongues wagged mercilessly over the unusual situation.

"But my dear," whispered the ladies behind their fans at every *tertulia*, "would you believe that she turns a cold shoulder to his entreaties?"

"Perhaps she's waiting for the father of the child to offer his recognition or to marry her now that she's rich, *querida*," answered other voices amid the eternal gossip.

"Well, I heard that the man is probably married. It certainly makes sense. After all, she *is* beautiful, there is no denying that, and with all that money . . ."

And so the tongues wagged over Helena's difficulties. Only Rosario and Helena's confessor, Padre Rafael, knew the truth.

Others, including Padre Rafael's fellow priests, had been kind to her, each for his or her own reasons. Even the Bishop of Panama had come to regard her with affection on the few occasions they had been together for certain inaugural ceremonies to which she had been invited frequently as acknowledgment that she had donated some large quantity of money. Everyone knew of her generosity to good causes—especially educational ones. And in spite of the interest in her financial support, many of the people with whom she came in contact during these affairs came to recognize a certain quality of love about her and to find joy in her friendly smile. Now that her pregnancy was obvious, even these had preferred to forget about her.

Ironically, she was criticized most viciously by the servant class. Her own female servants scorned her present state, for by it she had proved that she was no less vulnerable to the wiles of men than they were, and they talked about their mistress disparagingly, without a shred of compassion for her impossible situation. However, they realized that few employers in Panama paid the generous salaries that Helena paid them, and they kept their remarks discreetly among themselves. Besides, they had no wish to deal with the sure wrath of Rosario, who protected her "ward" as a lioness does her cub.

Earlier Helena had refused even to consider salvaging her reputation by announcing her marriage. But now she had finally decided to summon the French consul to her seaside mansion and ask him point-blank what he thought the repercussions would be if she declared the truth of her marital status to the world. Maybe Charles's life would not in fact be in danger, and if that should be the case, why should she hide and suffer so much humiliation?

Now, waiting nervously for Monsieur Thibédeaux, Helena was almost sorry she had asked him to come. Perhaps he was her enemy. After all, Charles had seen fit to let him in on their secret, and he must therefore trust him a great deal. "He must be his friend and not mine," she thought.

Nervously she began to pace the living room floor, her hands twisted together, her fingers entwining and disentwining themselves, her worried frown a clear indication of her uncertainty and fears. She was wearing a long, flowing gown reminiscent of the one the Indian women had made for her in the mountains of Santa Fe. It was gathered at the lace yoke so that its intense pink batiste fell to the floor just above her short pink pumps. It was a lovely gown, years ahead of its time, which Rosario had designed and sewn for this advanced stage of Helena's pregnancy. Her lustrous golden hair shimmered in the bright daylight, piled in great curls on top of her head. She looked neat and lovely in spite of her agitation.

Rosario entered and crossed the sitting room in her direction.

"Señor Thibédeaux is here, Helena."

397

"Yes . . . Please tell him to come in, Rosario, and please . . . I would like to be left alone with him. But have one of the girls bring some lemonade first, please."

Rosario scurried away to make the arrangements. Helena quickly sat down on the settee in order to appear more composed and dignified, and less pregnant, and arranged the folds of her gown just before the French consul entered the salon.

Monsieur Thibédeaux was a medium-sized man with a comical air of swashbuckling self-assurance that was almost challenging. His voice when he finally spoke was booming and loud, unpleasantly aggressive, and he seemed to be sizing her up with what Helena instantly considered insolence.

"Madame, Jean Thibédeaux, at your service."

He bowed gallantly, but Helena was annoyed by his attempt to make himself important, and by his assumption of superiority. She felt a flush of blood in her cheeks, and knew that in spite of herself sparks of anger were escaping from her eyes. She rose with all the arrogance she could muster in her pregnant state, and gave him a very cold look as she spoke.

"Thank you for doing me the honor of accepting my invitation, Monsieur Thibédeaux."

Thibédeaux's insolently appraising look softened considerably when he heard how perfectly she spoke French. Like most Frenchmen, he loved his native language, and hence was delighted that the woman who had finally trapped Charles into marriage spoke it fluently and graced it with a refined manner, though there seemed to be not a trace of warmth in her voice. He was suddenly relieved and somewhat pleased.

But it was too late. Helena was determined by now to be as disagreeable as possible, to match his pomposity if she could, and her scorn was unmistakable when she spoke.

"I don't want to waste your time or mine, monsieur, so I'll try to be as blunt as I can. You must understand that very little ever gets done when one uses diplomatic language."

"How would she know?" wondered Thibédeaux sarcastically, taken aback though he was by her haughty attitude. His previous assumptions as to what Helena was like quickly reasserted themselves, and the intense distrust and dislike in the air was suddenly electric, bristling.

"Yes, madame; by all means, madame." His answer was spoken as coldly as possible. What an arrogant woman this was. And his friend had turned over all that power to such a minx? Ye gads! She needed to be tamed. How could Charles stand her the way she was—aloof, haughty, selfish?

At that moment the maid came in with a sterling silver tray that some traveler in the family had once brought from Peru. A crystal pitcher full of lemonade and two tall glasses garnished with lemon slices stood on it.

"Shall I pour, madame?" asked the well-trained servant.

"No," responded Helena, who was so agitated by the presence of the consul that she forgot the usual gentilities of please and thank you.

"What an arrogant, self-pampered individual!" thought Thibédeaux. The woman acted as though she owned the world. What she needed was to know how close she had come to not owning a penny!

"Would you care for a glass of lemonade, monsieur le Consul?" Her question was phrased politely enough, but the tone made it obvious that she found his presence distasteful. Why had she summoned him, then? To embarrass him?

"No, madame, thank you. You said that we would not waste time?"

"Yes, I certainly did say that, didn't I? What I would like to know, monsieur, is the following. . . ." Helena waved the maid away, and as soon as the girl closed the door, she continued.

"I want to announce my marriage to Charles de Thierny—*now*."

"*Sacré bleu*, woman," the consul burst out, unable to control his fiery temper any longer. "What do you want? Blood? Isn't it enough that the poor man signed away all his rights to your money and that he pines away because he cannot protect you directly and be with you? Do you wish to destroy him? Is it any wonder, madame, that he must try to forget your blasted superiority by seeking consolation elsewhere?" And on he ranted and raved, while a terrible silence emanated from Helena. She felt herself fall at last like a ripe mango on the couch, staring incredulously at the man who was revealing fact after fact about Charles's actions. It all came to her in such a rush, so suddenly and richly, that she could absorb but a fraction of what the wildly gesticulating man before her was shouting. Suddenly the consul stopped, realizing that Helena had turned white—chalky white. He looked worriedly at her, squinting his eyes to study her better.

"Are you all right, madame?" As he became aware of the enormity of his accusations, he felt his pulse quicken not only with regret but with fear as well. Gads! If he had made her seriously ill, Charles would never forgive him! When would he learn to keep his mouth shut and not fight other people's battles for them? Damn it! She looked so pale sitting there, not saying a word.

He came to her and lifted her hand, which had fallen limply to her side, and bent to look at her squarely. His voice was no longer booming. In fact it was quite gentle as he said:

"I'm sorry, madame. Please, don't look at me so. I . . ."

She was staring at him as if she were a corpse with its eyes open. Finally her lips moved, but her voice cracked to a barely audible level.

"You mean Charles and another woman . . . I mean, the money; Charles did what with my money?" Her question drifted off into a defeated whisper. She was clutching desperately to salvage her pride by pretending that the subject of the money was uppermost in her mind. But the full import of Jean Thibédeaux's words had fallen on her like a blow, and the money part was not what was crucifying her.

Her lips were quivering, and Thibédeaux felt suddenly very much ashamed of his crazy impulse to bring her down a peg or two. What did he know about her after all? Only that Charles had married her, that she was to have his child, and that she was very rich, having inherited much wealth. He knew some rumors, but about her deepest self he had no real knowledge, and after all, if Charles had found her worthy of his love, she must be exceptional. He bit his lips, tormented by the worry that he'd hurt this woman who, suddenly, struck him as very fragile.

"Madame, listen carefully; I didn't mean to upset you. It's just that Charles de Thierny is my friend, and he suffers so much because he loves you. And you do not seem to respond to his tenderness. You have been flaunting your wealth and independence, and I have known the whole time that you were married to my good friend. I lost control—my resentment was so great, that's all."

Tears glistened in Helena's black eyes, and the consul took the hand he still held in his own and brought it tenderly to his lips.

"Forgive me, madame, for being so cruel. I didn't realize that perhaps you were suffering even more than my friend."

"What do you mean, that Charles signed away his rights to my money?"

Thibédeaux was again confused. He had expected love for Charles to pour from her lips, or at least concern that he had slept with another woman. After all, she knew now that he had performed a sacrifice for her. But instead, she seemed more bent on finding out about legalities concerning her money than about the torture in Charles's soul.

"Madame," he ventured gently but firmly, "in the eyes of the law, in Panama as well as France, a married man automatically acquires the rights to his wife's fortune unless the marriage contract states otherwise. Charles felt that you were not aware of this fact, and because, ever since the death of your guardian, there has been no one to advise you of this financial restriction, he felt a duty to sign his rights away, his rights to tell you what to do with the money. He wanted to be sure not to take advantage of your ignorance in these matters and sure, too, that you enjoyed complete financial freedom—legally. The statement in which he gave up his rights is irrevocable; it cannot be taken back or changed as one could perhaps change a final testament."

Helena's eyelids fell, and the long black lashes, still glimmering with unshed tears, made dark shadows on her pale cheeks.

"I see," she murmured, and she stayed quiet for a long time.

"May I have some of that lemonade now, madame?" She looked up at the consul.

"Yes, of course, please . . . could you help yourself?"

Jean Thibédeaux's hands trembled slightly as he poured. He was very upset with himself. He filled the two glasses and insisted that Helena take one as well.

Two hours later, when he left the house with the lovely terraces that reached out into the very bay, Jean Thibédeaux was convinced that Helena Canales was the most exquisite creature he had ever met, and that furthermore, not only Charles, but she also, was tormented by dark and turbulent conflicts. He prayed, as a good friend would, that they would make it safely through the storm.

However, he was also incensed at his good friend Charles, who had audaciously and cruelly betrayed his wife—the sweet lass. It made little difference to Thibédeaux, now that he had met Helena, that Charles's excuse might once have been Helena's aloofness, her reckless flaunting of her attractions at the males of her social circle, or her unnatural and irritating independence. Thibédeaux felt remorse that he had stupidly misjudged Helena and wounded her, that madonnalike creature whose vulnerable blond beauty promised to haunt him uncomfortably. His mistake caused him untold embarrassment and, in order to soothe his humiliated ego, he resorted to blaming Charles de Thierny for the whole thing.

Chapter XX

Laurie Lee Jenkins de Santana de Saavedra was terribly upset. She sat in her salon, which reflected the flamboyance of her taste and the state of decay of her present situation. Great worn spots on the once rich velvet curtains resembled mange on a dog. The carpets which the merciless climate of Panama had abused were more disgusting than decorative. But this was not what bothered Laurie Lee, and in fact, hardly bothered her at all these days, for absolutely no one of importance ever paid her visits anymore. The allure of her vast fortune and of her husband's distinguished family name had vanished, and along with that loss and the advent of her own eccentricities, all her former friends had fled.

The only person who remained was Raúl, the one satisfying result of her marriage to her foolish deceased husband. Raúl was such a handsome boy, and though he had inherited only her natural good looks and not her shrewdness, at least he was not as insipid as her husband had been. Still, she had to admit that Don Agustín had lavished his personal devotion upon them and never denied her or Raúl anything that money could buy, as if in spending so wildly he were compensating for the total loss of his family's respect.

Had it not been for the extravagances of her husband, paid for with hard cash, she would not have had any pleasant memories at all of her marriage to Don Agustín. It had cost her almost a superhuman effort to remain faithful to the scion of the Santana de Saavedra family. Her previous lascivious and lurid life had been too deeply ingrained in her for its allure not to have revivified from time to time during her marriage, especially as she had originally chosen her career of prostitution more from perversity than from need. From the effort of holding back the tide of lust she had experienced great unrest and frustration. She was certain that if her husband had even suspected any betrayal on her part she would have found herself out in the street, for it became evident to her that her husband had turned his back on all that he held important because he considered that only he knew the real Laurie Lee, while the others were totally mistaken in their cynical appraisal of the girl he loved, the mother of his son. For her own sake she had not dared to disillusion him.

Most of the time the sense of independence which she acquired from her money had soothed her rage for living. Other times her passionate and lustful senses had driven her to such a state of frenzy that she'd had to resort to the clumsy lovemaking of her husband, who had no idea that he was the worst lover she had ever known. And she had known too many to count. Besides, as he grew older, the impotence caused by his psychological inhibitions had been compounded by physical problems whose nature finally prevented him from coupling with Laurie Lee at all. It didn't seem to bother him, but Laurie Lee was deeply affected, and even before his death she had begun to focus her energies on grotesque projects like designing her own gypsylike clothing and amassing gold and silver coins which she counted secretly with more and more frequency and relish.

Every day she became more neurotic and eccentric, until she was where she was—in a run-down house, with a son who had few good qualities. She had no friends, no contacts except her one servant, Tito, no faith, no hope, no plans except to live from day to day like a hermit in her cave. She had come to dread her outings, for hoots and whistles of derision reached her and angered her, spoiling her ever rarer excursions into the outside world.

One thread still connected her with the living, however, and that was Raúl. For this consolation she was not consciously grateful, simply because she did not realize that he was that single slender thread between feeling alive and being buried alive. Thus, because she did not know, and even though she loved her son, Laurie Lee had long ago warned him that she would never give him any of her money, neither the money she had hidden year after year, nor the smaller share of the inheritance bequeathed to her by her husband, an inheritance which was pitiful when compared to what once had been a vast and impressive fortune.

Despite denying him her money, however, Laurie Lee was willing to give affection to her grown son, and provide him with a place to stay and to see that he ate well and carried on as the man of the family. This last he was loathe to do, it was apparent, but at least he did stay home often, especially when he owed too much to too many people, as seemed to be the case more and more every day.

Now Laurie Lee was terribly upset, for her servant Tito had just informed her that by coincidence he had discovered that her son had become involved somehow with the notorious Juan Jiménez, wealthy Liberal leader whose passion for guerrilla warfare was already legend, and who could involve her son in serious trouble.

"Tito," she asked for the second time, "are you sure that you followed the right man?"

"Yes, señora," the mulatto answered patiently. "The man I followed was very easy to keep track of, for not many people in the city wear the authentic *montuno* dress. Besides, I did not just follow him once, but twice. The second time I followed this man, the one Don Raúl gave the paper to, all the way to the cathedral, to the six o'clock mass. But halfway to the church another stranger took the paper and looked it over, as if reading whatever was written on it. Then he handed the paper back to the *montuno*, who continued his trip to the church, where he met another man and handed him the paper. This last fellow was one of Don Juan Jiménez's servants, for I have seen

him around many times. But just in case, I verified
with one of the kitchen maids at the Jiménez house. I
have my ways of treating those young girls from the
hills very specially, and anyway, they like to make
themselves important."

The mulatto servant, who acted as handyman and
errand boy for Laurie Lee, chuckled at this observation, but Laurie Lee did not see anything funny about
it, and remained staring at him solemnly, almost as if
he were not there. Consequently Tito wiped the smile
from his face.

Laurie Lee's mind was already racing ahead, trying
to figure out what connection her son could possibly
have with a man as dangerous as she had always
heard Juan Jiménez could be.

"Tito," she finally said, "I want you to keep track of
how often this exchange of notes occurs."

"Ma'am, I think that the Indian in the *montuno*
comes every day and then meets this other fellow
from the Jiménez household at the six o'clock mass at
the cathedral. At least, that is what I suspect from
what I observed for several days before I began following the Indian. You see, when I first noticed it, I
didn't think to tell you about it, but as it kept on hap-
pening, I thought you should be aware."

"Yes, thank you, Tito, it was the right thing to do.
After all, this is my house, and if my son brings trouble to it or to himself, he brings it to me also. Now,
here is what I want you to do."

The old woman and the mulatto servant stayed together for quite a while hashing out plans to get hold
of the information which was being passed between

Raúl and Juan Jiménez. The role of the man who intercepted and read the letter before it reached the cathedral remained a mystery to them, but was not an important link in finding out the contents of the notes. Finally they agreed that Jiménez probably threw the notes in his trash can, and that it should not be hard to convince one of the maids at his house, perhaps the same one with whom Tito had created such good rapport, that she should look through the trash when they brought it downstairs to throw it out into the larger bin. There was the danger, of course, that most of the messages had been discarded already, but perhaps the most recent ones would enable them to find out exactly what was going on. In general it seemed like a good and simple plan. Laurie Lee was determined to know into what straits her son might have gotten himself, and this seemed the only way to do it.

She was angry at him, too, for jeopardizing his apparently good friendship with Helena Canales. Unlike the more active members of the community, Laurie Lee was not aware of Helena's cool reception to her son's advances. Laurie had not heard that Helena Canales was pregnant, or she would seriously have wondered why the girl did not accept her son immediately. She was under the impression that the girl might want to test Raúl a long time before accepting his inevitable proposal of marriage. But her son could be such a fool! If he got into a scandal or real trouble with the government in Bogotá or even in Panama City, his carefully worked rapport with Helena Ca-

nales would have been to no avail. Gradually Laurie
had begun to take a real interest in the possibility of
her son's marriage to the heiress and decided that she
would have to protect Raúl from his own stupidity if
the union was ever to come about.

Soon after Tito's successful efforts to get hold of
those notes written personally by Raúl, and the
search in the house trash bins for the crumpled notes
of his partner, Juan Jiménez, Laurie Lee was able to
piece together almost the entire scheme in which Raúl
had involved himself. From a financial point of view
the plan seemed promising to her and her own love of
money would not permit her to ruin the project by
meddling personally. However, she was afraid his
scheme might backfire, and that perhaps he might be
trapped; her greatest fear was that Raúl would either
be hurt or else captured and jailed, thus ruining the
last vestiges of his good reputation and losing his opportunity to wed Helena Canales.

Meanwhile Helena had been open in her mistreat-
ment of Raúl, but he apparently took no note. Because
he wouldn't speak of his love and acted even shy at
times, it occurred to Helena that perhaps he wanted
something more than her hand in marriage—
something immediate and concrete, something material, in short. She was losing patience with him, and
she asked him one day, quite bluntly, "Raúl, is there
something worrying you? Somehow I have the impression you want to tell or ask me something."

To Raúl the words rang beautifully. "Oh! Bless you,"

he thought. He had been trying to broach the subject of his petition with delicacy, so as not to frighten Helena away and let such a charming source of future fortune slip from him. Seizing the opportunity, he immediately replied,

"Helena! How in the world did you guess? You are certainly attuned to my moods, it seems, and I am extremely flattered. Not only are you the most beautiful woman in Panama, you are the most intelligent."

"And the most pregnant," thought Helena dismally. She was sickened, too, by the mellifluous words from the wretched courtier, but Raúl, in his usual egocentric blindness, did not notice the grimace she made, and continued.

"I was reluctant to ask you, but I desperately need the use of a ship, even if it is the smallest one in your fleet!"

So it was out. Helena was relieved, in a way, that his favor involved her so little in any personal way. She instantly took the view that surely if she granted his request he would no longer need her and would maybe go away more easily, although such a supposition carried no guarantees that he would leave her alone forever. She had certainly gotten herself into the proverbial mess of pickles, and all because she had thought herself so clever and ruthless. She realized that ruthless she could not be, for the very thought of humiliating Raúl, her victim, was now horribly distasteful to her. She knew what humiliation was—only too well. At the same time, she was growing weary of following the cruel impulses that had sprung up in her character during the aftermath of the rape. She did not want to hurt the unhappy Raúl Santana, yet she knew that she would eventually have to be harsh. He didn't take hints, and her enormous belly which, because she was small, seemed to her to take up one third of her body, was even more than a hint. He didn't want to give up trying to get to her money. Nevertheless, if she didn't get rid of him without hurting him too much, she would not be able to live with herself. After all, she had lied and misled him terribly, and even if he was a scoundrel, she had to try somehow to ease for him the pain of her denial and her disdain.

Helena summoned Mr. Suárez, the general manager of her local shipping concerns. A man in his fifties, neatly dressed, his white starched long sleeves held up by two thin black garters at the biceps, his suspenders neatly in place, Señor Suárez was obviously not thrilled to make the acquaintance of Raúl Santana. In fact, he wondered indignantly why he should be subjected to the presence of a man of his dubious reputation. Nevertheless he controlled his contempt and tried to be his usual correct and efficient self. Raúl was under the delusion that he was impressing the little clerk, as he considered Suárez.

"Señor Suárez," began Helena graciously as she welcomed him into the library after the introductions had been made. She was instantly interrupted by the obnoxious Raúl.

"I'm glad you came quickly, Suárez. I don't have all day. Miss Helena has informed me that you would be the one to assign a ship for me on a specified date. I need a small ship, but one with proportionately gener-

413

ous holding capacity. It must not be filled with fishing gear. I'll be transporting certain digging tools to shore from a larger vessel. How long would it take you to get such a ship ready for me?"

Of all the nerve! Helena was suddenly very angry at the way Raúl had taken over, as if he owned the fleet himself. But she bit her tongue, for greater than her wish to make Raúl aware just who the chief was around here, was her desire to ease him away from her. Mr. Suárez's own patronizing condescension toward her was bad enough. Now she was caught between *two* unbearable martinets. Oh! how she was getting tired of inflated male conceit! Again she held back her lashing remarks and simmered while the two men handled this stupid affair in their own petty and rude way.

"Sir," began with false meekness the general manager. "You do not seem to be aware that to dismantle the gear from one simple fishing vessel means days during which that vessel cannot be put out to sea to fish!" By the end of the sentence, Suárez was yelling.

"Helena can afford it!" responded the callous Raúl with equal animosity.

Helena's eyes opened wide in disbelief at the utter ingratitude of her guest. At least Suárez was valuable to her. She could contain herself no longer, and turning to Raúl, her voice wavering from the anger she was trying to control, she said:

"Raúl, I'm afraid that you don't understand certain sad facts. One of them is that my fishing fleet is not the great money-maker you think it is. The second is that if I'm going to lose any profits, I prefer to do so by giving them away to some charitable cause, a description which I don't think applies to you." She paid no attention to the protest Raúl started to make.

"Now, Mr. Suárez here has done a good job for years, has much more experience than either you or I with the equipment end of the business, and he will be the one to decide which ship will be used, and during which period of time you can have use of the vessel. I suggest you give him the approximate dates on which you expect your cargo to arrive, and then he'll be able to handle his end of the arrangement by himself."

Señor Suárez stared in dumbfounded admiration at his petite boss. Each day his approbation of her had been growing greater, mainly because of her clear vision of things and her assurances that she was proud of his work. It was certainly unfortunate that her inferior sex limited her to the lesser duties of breeding. Had she been a man, she might have done great things in the business world!

Helena left in a huff to let the two men work out the details. In spite of his very male attitude Señor Suárez felt secure in the knowledge that whatever he decided, she would support his decision and that her support was becoming increasingly valuable to him. Santana, in the meantime, had had the wind taken out of his sails; the pun caused Señor Suárez to chuckle to himself as the two of them sat at the working table in the beautiful mahogany-paneled library.

* * *

Despite her promise to lease him the ship, however, Raúl Santana continued to hound her with continual calls and visits, begging constantly (Helena sensed it was an excuse to make conversation) for details concerning the vessel. She let him know all she could and in turn asked him very little about his purposes. She only knew what he claimed: he had invested in digging tools which could perhaps make him his fortune when the French arrived to construct the canal, and he wanted to unload the cargo out in the deep part of the Bay of Panama onto one of her much smaller ships. Investing in tools seemed a bit risky financially to Helena, especially at this stage when even the engineers might not know exactly what tools they would need, but he was bent on doing this thing. Anyway, he must have found a few backers, for where else would he have acquired the funds to invest in his crazy scheme?

The day came that Raúl and Juan Jiménez had arranged for the delivery of the weapons. It was a clear and pleasant day, and a little breeze would assist the small sailing vessel of the González fleet to meet the larger steamship on which the American agent would be bringing the shipment of guns and ammunition. It would be anchored for the transfer well within the outer limits of the bay. Because of its size it could not enter the shallower waters of the bay as could Helena's tiny vessel. Neither, however, could the United States naval boats that patrolled the bay so faithfully; they were bigger and clumsier even than the agent's ship. But even if those vessels should spot them, the Americans would have to be very suspicious indeed to lower their emergency longboats, which could come as close to shore as they wished.

Laurie Lee and Tito were wide awake before dawn and heard the movements made by Raúl in his room as he prepared to leave the house and board the sailing ship that would soon be putting out into the bay. He had asked that they pull away at the same time as the other fishing vessels in order to avoid suspicion. As soon as he left the house, Laurie and Tito lay back in their beds, each thinking his own thoughts and hoping that nothing dangerous would befall Raúl or themselves. Tito had never been involved in anything as adventurous as this intrigue, and he was fascinated by it all. In fact, he was amazed at the agility of mind and cleverness that the old woman exhibited, and he had gained new respect for her.

Before the usual breakfast hour, however, they were off, too, the wrinkled and aging mistress in the most unobtrusive clothes of her wildly colored and impoverished wardrobe, and the servant in his usual loose pants and rough linen shirt.

Except for the carriage, they could have blended in with any of the usual buyers at the fish market, where they knew that Raúl planned to land the weapons. Their carriage, fortunately for them, fit in easily with the commercial ones of the González enterprises as well as with the wagons provided by Juan Jiménez which would be waiting for Raúl, his men, and the load of guns camouflaged as digging tools. From the fish market both Laurie Lee and Tito would be able to keep a benevolent eye on Raúl to make sure that all went smoothly up to the very end. If there was to be any trouble for her boy, Laurie Lee and her servant had decided that it would come at or near the closing of the deal with the American agent and not before.

In spite of the possibility of such misfortune, however, in her heart, Laurie Lee did not suspect treachery. She was cautious by nature and had always been cold-eyed about business matters, even in the days when she made her living from entertaining men. She'd known treachery, and had not been sorry that she had once or twice had a hand in disposing of a few very avaricious customers who wanted not only to enjoy free entertainment, but to steal her hard-earned money from her as well. Often she had had to grope for the pistol under her pillow in order to threaten some man or another, and for some mysterious reason they had taken her threats very earnestly indeed and disappeared, feeling lucky to get away intact.

But on this occasion at the fish market, Laurie Lee truly did not expect to find trouble as swiftly as it came.

She did not notice the American ship *Galena* right away, for it was still far out in the bay and behind the little fishing vessel that Helena Canales had lent to her son. What she did not know was that already a longboat from the American ship was heading toward the fishing vessel to inspect it in order to ascertain whether the information received by the Americans from a mysterious source was correct or not. Laurie Lee had eyes only for the longboat heading for shore with her son and a few other men in it. She could not be sure, but she had the feeling that things were going according to plan. No one had heard any shooting. The boats were still a bit far out in the bay for the sounds of shooting to reach the market, but Laurie Lee did not think of this possibility.

She was totally shocked, therefore, when her son landed amid a flurry of excitement and disorganization, and when the silhouette of the large American ship appeared to close in behind the tiny fishing vessel which Helena had rented to Raúl.

Laurie Lee took in the surrounding area in a flash, for she did not panic from her surprise. She drew her pistol from her market bag and signaled to Tito to do the same. With all the commotion, nobody noticed that among the buyers who were relatively close to the point of the final disembarkation of Raúl and his men, stood an old woman and a man dressed in rather typical and colorful tropical attire of the poor, both of whom had fine-looking guns held discreetly by their side.

Just as Laurie Lee was beginning to think she would not be needing her pistol after all—for it seemed that Raúl was not being stopped by anyone on shore—she saw an arm rise, gun in hand, from behind one of the young guava trees that abounded near the open fish market. Even before the man had stepped entirely forward from behind the tree, she pulled the trigger, and heard at the same time another shot which she hoped was Tito's, and not the stranger's bullet surely meant for her son. Observing that her son and his men had continued to run and had disappeared in the clump of trees ahead, she moved away

419

from the smoke which her pistol had left lingering in the air. Hiding the gun very agilely in her generous shopping bag, she pretended to be as curious as the rest of the women and the men who were suddenly jabbering very loudly. The incident had taken no more than a few seconds.

The sudden and ominous shots which rang almost simultaneously from the American longboat, however, paralyzed the people who had already witnessed the scene of the shoot-out. Though some of the vendors and their customers noticed that two Cholos were dragging a white man away and mounting him with some trouble on a horse tethered behind the numerous wagons which had collected on one side of the place, no one moved to interfere one way or the other. Nobody wanted to get involved with the United States Navy.

It had not been easy to convince the manager of her small but admired fleet that Raúl should rent at cost, for it was certainly not good for business just to break even. But Helena's was the final decision, and the manager washed his hands entirely of any eventual responsibility for the results of such a bad decision. The clash with her manager had not been a pleasant encounter, but her determination to be rid of Raúl as gracefully as possible had prompted her to support his project.

She had absolutely no further use for Raúl Santana, not even for revenge against Charles, who had betrayed her again, in another way she had not even thought about earlier. She had known what the French consul meant when he had shouted that Charles felt the need to seek consolation elsewhere. Elsewhere. Where else but in the arms of a woman?

But even the knowledge that Charles had apparently betrayed his marriage vows could not tempt her into using poor Raúl again for revenge.

Helena was a bit embarrassed by a triviality concerning Raúl. Apparently he had not paid his fee for the use of the ship in advance, and she had had to suggest that he do so in order to appease her manager, whom she did not wish to antagonize unnecessarily. Good supervisors were difficult to find, and honest and imaginative ones like Mr. Suárez were almost impossible to hire. Usually, if they were that good, they had their own business. No wonder Uncle Benito had always raved about his wonderful manager.

She reflected that Mr. Suárez was the kind of man that the Isthmus attracted—independent, shrewd, and, above all, an imaginative businessman. Not for them the vast land tracts of the Colombian oligarchy and the tedious pace of sitting on the land while others worked it. No! Action, wheeling, dealing, and handling vast amounts of money, finding new markets, transporting the goods—these were the appealing ways of earning a living and maybe a fortune for the man who found the Isthmus alluring and who was truly enterprising.

Just as she was thinking vaguely about all these things, her fleet manager, Señor Suárez, was announced. Marta, the braided and spotlessly clean girl who had been hired by Rosario to attend to Helena when she herself could not, added also that Mr. Suárez had apparently stormed to the house and was in a tremendous state of agitation. Helena thought the worst. One of her ships must have sunk!

She was thoroughly embarrassed when Mr. Suárez announced that the ship that had been leased to Raúl Santana had been practically confiscated by the American navy!

"What! What in the world would the American navy want with one of our ships?" Helena always talked to Mr. Suárez as if he were part owner of the fleet, a small detail that gave him a sense of power and authority and pride in Helena's enterprises.

"Ma'am, it seems that your friend, Señor Santana, fooled all of us."

Helena's eyebrows went up in an unspoken question which Mr. Suárez answered spontaneously.

"He told us that he was importing digging tools for the French effort, should it materialize, a speculative sort of business, anyway, but the fact is that the tools turned out to be a massive collection of guns and ammunition."

"Guns and ammunition!"

The words took a while to reach her properly, and then Helena asked in a voice that she tried to keep steady and calm, "How was he discovered?"

"Well, ma'am, according to the captain of our ship, an American ship, the *Galena*, appeared from nowhere. When that happened, Raúl Santana and the two helpers he'd brought with him turned on our crew and warned them not to attempt anything, because we would lose at least three of our men if our crew did so."

Helena sat down suddenly from the surprise and the disgust which the tale had inspired in her. Wait till she got her hands on Raúl Santana!

"Our ship was already close to shore and our men made it to the area where small rowboats were awaiting our crews, as usual. As you already know, ma'am, there is no natural harbor deep enough for us to use in Panama City. . . ."

"Yes, yes." Helena waved him on, but was not offended at the usual tone of patronizing condescension that implied she could not possibly be aware of the details of her various business enterprises because she was a woman.

"It seems that Santana and his two men took off with one of our men as a hostage," continued Mr. Suárez, "and that is the last we have seen of him. Apparently the American longboat was approaching from our starboard, and they missed him. By the time they realized he had escaped, he and his men had landed and left their hostage on the shore. There was some firing from the shore, so I suppose the Americans had left men there in case the culprit escaped. But apparently Santana got away scot free."

"What did the Americans want? Were they looking for Raúl or for the weapons? Somehow they must have found out what he was up to. But how? We didn't even suspect and nobody would ever have thought . . . Well, Raúl was clever, wasn't he? He knew we had an impeccable reputation. I wonder how the Americans knew. . . ."

"I can't answer that, ma'am, but the fact is that they did. It was almost as if they knew *exactly* what had been going on. They quoted the Bidlack Treaty to us to justify their boarding our ship but were extremely formal and polite, I must say.

"Their commander was dressed in a very impressive uniform, I heard. He certainly put the fear of the devil into our men.

"Our captain told the Americans that our men knew nothing about the weapons and that the whole thing was just as much a surprise to them as to the owners of the ship when they found out. Fortunately our man had the legal papers showing the ownership of the vessel and the one which leased the boat for the purposes which Santana had originally told us."

"Did the Americans get in touch with you?"

"Did they? Even before our captain did, because the Americans held our ship until they could verify the story with me. I was so shocked that I believe their man could tell I was telling the truth. Anyway, I explained to the Americans that under no circumstances were you to be advised directly of what had happened because of your delicate state. They seemed ready to agree, and apparently they are just very glad that they intercepted that huge shipment of weapons. Whoever paid for them must have spent a veritable fortune."

Helena wondered, too, about the source of Raúl Santana's money, for surely he himself did not possess a single centavo that wasn't borrowed. Nobody in his right mind in Panama would lend him such vast quantities. Could he have stolen it? But no theft of such proportions had been discovered in Panama recently. The whole thing did not make sense.

After Mr. Suárez left, she was rubbed down by Marta, who enjoyed pouring the refreshing lotion on her mistress's back; Marta was the great-granddaughter of Helena's former cook, old Doñita, who had been retired with a generous income and who had returned happily to her native village of Chorrera. Helena had to lie on her side now, for her abdomen had grown considerably. The lotion smelled delicate and clean. Helena finally fell into a relaxed sleep, but not before thinking a little about the outcome of Raúl Santana's wild venture into crime. At least now she would be rid of his constant endearments, for he would obviously wish to remain in hiding from her and from the authorities as long as he could. What a scoundrel! No wonder he had kept on trying to get in her good graces! Even as pregnant as she was.

The scandalous incident caused by Raúl did not affect her as radically as it might perhaps have done earlier in her pregnancy. Since the French consul's visit much of the bitterness she had felt at the beginning of her pregnancy had vanished. A strange calm mood of serenity had started to develop in its place. A newfound sense of balance and serenity had allowed her to see things in a slightly better perspective. Other vague anxieties beset her now, sensibilities which she could not pinpoint, but the furious distortion of previous weeks had passed.

* * *

Two days later the soaring temperatures of the dry season practically prostrated Helena, who with her advanced pregnancy was acutely aware of the merciless climate of Panama. She felt just miserable, though she knew in her heart that it was not all due to her physical discomfort.

She lay in her bed a few minutes longer, shifting positions to find spots where the sheet was not sticky with her body's perspiration. At times like these she felt like crying simply from frustration and anger at her condition, at the heat, at Charles de Thierny, and at the world in general. Even the tenderness and consideration of Rosario no longer filled her, for what she felt was more like some indiscernible longing to be protected and cherished, pampered and loved. Poor Rosario's efforts somehow did not fill these vague and embarrassing needs. And she had, in truth, no real husband to console her. In fact, he had added insult upon insult in his usual detestable way. Helena began heaping blame on Charles in order to relieve her frustrations, although she realized that convincing herself of his faults no longer gave her the satisfaction she longed for.

The door was opened almost insolently, and Helena was so startled that she turned to chide the upstairs maid for frightening her. Instead, she was confronted with the sight of Rosario in a terrible state of agitation.

"Helena," she exclaimed, without preliminaries, "get up immediately. Charles de Thierny has been gravely wounded and two of his men have him downstairs. I think he is dying. For God's sake, come quickly."

Chapter XXI

Helena remained quiet and still, with a look of incredulity on her beautiful face as Rosario's words registered in her mind. Rosario moved toward her and began to help her, her worried expression so dramatic that Helena thought she must be exaggerating. Helena was dragged out of the bed, her negligée of finest pink batiste thrown over her. Soon, fully awake and aware, Helena was clattering down the stairs in her velvet slippers behind Rosario.

Charles de Thierny lay as if dead on a couch in the hall of the side entrance, Pablo and Pedro looking on with anguish written on their usually impassive faces.

"What happened?" cried Helena, feeling a stab of pain in her heart. "What happened to Charles?"

She ran to kneel at his side, hardly noticing her clumsy belly. Pablo noticed, however, and lowered his eyes; her fecundity pained him somehow. Helena took one of Charles's hands that lay so still by his side, and was relieved to feel that it was still warm. Its clamminess did not fool her into thinking him dead, and instead of panicking, Helena was suddenly filled with courage. He was still alive, and it was up to her to see that he had every possible chance to live. At that moment she had no time to question her motives, for her feelings were racing through her with zealous fervor, making her heart pound and bringing incredible strength to her will.

In a quiet, almost dangerous voice she gave out her orders. "Pablo, are you here on horseback?"

"Sí, señora."

"Then ride to the doctor's three blocks from here." She gave him more details about where to find the doctor who had attended the González family and her own mother for as long as she could remember, and then she turned to Rosario.

"Rosario, have the cook boil as much water as she can. The doctor is bound to need it when he arrives. We'll have to help him bathe Charles."

Her eyes turned again, full of compassion, on Charles de Thierny, the man who had ravished her for revenge and then made her desire him and, yes—love him—in spite of her vows to hate him forever.

She finally admitted the words to herself. It was a crystalized moment of truth and the self-revelation stunned Helena.

She loved him!

How could she possibly deny it to herself any longer?

Her eyes, brimming with tears of fear and regrets

and love, were fastened on Charles's pale face. How frail and vulnerable he looked now.

His clothes were terribly soiled, with dried blood everywhere.

"Pedro, I want you to help me take his clothes off as soon as we get some warm water. We'll use it to help get the material off where it has stuck to him."

Helena bent down and tried to lift his shirt, but it stayed as if glued to his skin.

"We can't take a chance of ripping open any smaller wounds. It looks as if he were cut all over at once. What happened?"

"Mistress, the Liberals must have shot him. At first we thought you might have something to do with this, but then Pablo learned that your ship had only been hired out. We have had Don Charles almost three days like this, and only when we realized that we could not hope to cure him ourselves without our proper cures did we dare to take the chance and bring him here. We have removed the two bullets, though."

"Why didn't you bring him here to me at once?" Helena's question shot out bitterly at the Indian, who was consumed with shame and embarrassment.

"Well, you see, mistress, by the time Pablo found out these things, two days had gone by. Don Charles passed out before we knew the whole truth. We did not want to bring him here for fear that you would try to finish him off, and we really had no safe and decent place to take him."

Pedro was embarrassed enough to clarify that he himself had not agreed with his brother's opinion that Helena was capable of cold-blooded murder. Pablo had insisted that Helena was different from the women they knew and that she was quite capable of killing her abductor. It seemed outlandish but somehow Pablo believed this and as he said to the other Indians, would they ever understand the ways of the whites anyway?

Because of the uncertainty caused by divided opinions, the Cholos had been afraid to risk Charles's life. Supposing that Pablo's warning about Helena was the truth?

Fortunately for Charles, Pablo's opinion did not prevail. The other men had simply preferred to believe that Helena, like most of the females of their experience, was too weak emotionally to be capable of physically violent retaliation and that she had, instead, succumbed to the charms of her master.

Helena's first reaction was one of indignation. But the task at hand immediately absorbed all her attention.

She touched Charles's forehead, where fever was burning hotly. At that moment Rosario returned with some cool water and with small towels which she guessed Helena would require. Together the two women began to bathe Charles's face, then his neck and finally his shirt until they were able to pull it off more easily. A swollen wound in his arm made Helena wince. It looked terrible!

She sent Rosario for covers and sheets, and after drying his torso gently, she covered his chest. Then she and Rosario began cleansing his legs. The Indian averted his eyes as if embarrassed at the helplessness of his master, but to the two women Charles's nakedness did not exist, so great was their concentration on their purpose of making him more comfortable. There was another torn part on his thigh, and blood had caked all through the furry hairs that covered his legs. It was dangerous to disturb the area, so they simply patted him dry, and covered him well until the doctor could get there.

It seemed to Helena that she waited an eternity before Dr. Uribe arrived. By then her nerves were raw, and she was in a state near collapse herself. The doctor gave his orders to Rosario, the first of which was that Helena should be sent back to bed with a cup of hot lemongrass tea.

"Don't worry, Miss Helena, we'll have this man up and about in no time at all. Who is he, by the way?"

Before she could think clearly, Helena blurted out, "My husband," and reacted only when the doctor looked up in surprise. But she said no more and left the doctor wondering as to the identity of the suddenly appeared husband of Helena Canales. The rest of the day the doctor was in and out. Having realized the state of nerves in which Helena was struggling, he decided that what she had disclosed, without thinking, about the strange injured man was a secret. Dr. Uribe prided himself on his discretion, in the fact that he kept well hidden the personal problems of his patients, a virtue not practiced by all medical men, as he well knew.

Helena could not sleep at all until late afternoon, but she was invaded by a feeling of illness that had nothing to do with the normal development of her pregnancy, and she was glad to remain in her room. She needed time to think.

Helena had understood, even without a clear explanation from Pedro, the Cholos' mean opinion of her, and at first she had felt no small indignation that they had dared to discuss her and judge her. She was not embarrassed, however, by the fact that their doubts concerning her strength to retaliate with physical cruelty for the damage to her honor had a foundation. Once she had had the opportunity to kill Charles, and she had not done so. No longer ashamed of her inability to destroy him, she was glad instead that she had been too weak to do so. And she was certainly not going to hurt him now. Finish him off, indeed! When she loved him more than she had thought possible? How ironic this all was. Just when she had finally realized how much she wanted him near her, and how much she longed to be in his arms, she was about to lose him. How foolish she had been to allow her pride to overwhelm her.

It was true that Charles had raped her, but she could not find it in her heart to sincerely complain about his actions later on, when he had confessed his love for her and when she knew that he thrilled her as no other man ever could. Furthermore, she had often considered the immense hatred and misunderstanding he was laboring under at the time of his revenge, yet she had refused to let her reason convince her of the validity of that excuse. Then, in spite of his pride, he had begged her forgiveness in so many ways. How could she have kept on forever despising him for the past?

It was she herself who had later led him to that other woman's arms. It was her own sin as well, and she could not hold that against him now. She had prodded him mercilessly until at last he had had to satisfy his natural cravings for love and admiration elsewhere.

Admiration. She had come to admire so many of his qualities and abilities, not the least of which was his ability to make her bend to his will, his ability to make every fiber in her body long for him and every chord of her mind relish his voice and his ideas and his way of speaking, but she had cruelly decided not to voice them, not to let him enjoy the secure knowledge of her admiration and her desire of him.

Perhaps she would have been justified in hating Charles forever, if she had not fallen in love with him. But even before he abducted her, when they had been on the ship together crossing the Atlantic, he had attracted her like a magnet, and she in her total inexperience had been frightened by the strength of her own emotions. She had been a foolish chit worrying about her violent loss of virginity and her honor before this world of men, afraid of her own thoughts, like a frightened doe—and thus, when she had fallen in love, her love had been obscured even from her own heart. How much time she had wasted! She should have married Charles the minute he first asked her.

In the meantime Rosario wholeheartedly supervised the cure which Dr. Uribe had begun on Charles's wounds. The wounds were bathed gently with solutions which he brought himself, and Charles was moved to a more comfortable room near Helena's, a back room with a window that looked out on the bay and which was quiet and peaceful because the clatter of the traffic below the front of the house could not reach it.

When the doctor arrived again in the late afternoon, Helena had awakened from a restless nap. She asked to see him.

"When can I see my husband, Dr. Uribe? Is he going to live?"

"My dear, I can answer the first question with reasonable accuracy, but the second question depends not only on my medicines but on the Good Lord's help. However, the wounds are clean now, and unless he is especially weak, and has lost too much blood, he stands a good chance of making a decent recovery. He may continue to have a limp once he gets well, but the main thing is to save his life. As soon as he is awake, you must see that he is fed some strong beef broth."

"Isn't there anything I can do?" Helena's question was full of anguish and frustration at the certain knowledge that there was very little she could do now.

"Yes, there is. You can take care of yourself. I don't want a premature delivery. Neither you nor the baby is going to benefit by such an accident."

When the doctor left, Helena meditated a little on what he had said. It was true that if she had any problems and they affected her or her baby, she would not be doing Charles a favor either. Nevertheless that night Helena felt a strange low back pain that spread until she felt as if she were in the viselike grip of a huge monster that was trying to tear her apart. She screamed at last, and Rosario rushed upstairs, suspecting the terrible truth, that Helena was having pains a few weeks before the baby was due. She gave orders to one of the sleepy younger maids who had awakened with Helena's shrieks, and the young girl ran off to urge one of the house guards to run and get Dr. Uribe again.

Charles was still unconscious in his room, but accompanied around the clock by a maidservant.

Groans escaped painfully from his mouth as the mist of the past began again its tortuous dance of delirium. He could see the elongated faces of his father and of Francesca, his stepmother, and they were ghosts from the grave coming at him weeping for their own failings and perhaps for his. He squirmed in his unconscious state, and the images became clearer, more like a usual dream now, with a compound of scenes that he interpreted as one does a dream that is still being experienced. If he could just write it all down, it would be so clear, so real and so painful, just as it had been some years ago.

He saw his father's coffin, draped with flowers of every hue and brilliance. He could see himself, just as he had felt then, bowed down in grief and with an indescribable sense of loss. His insides began to dry up and shrink until he felt very small. Perhaps if he drank water he could quench the thirst that was desiccating his soul. Oh! how it hurt near his heart. Then the coffin was lowered, slowly, oh, so slowly until only a tiny speck could be seen in the chasm of the grave; he was only mildly surprised when his father's hand reached out of the grave and handed him a sheaf of papers, neatly bound in blue ribbon, the letters which he had kept because he could not bring himself to destroy them, and Charles immediately forgot the grave and sat down on the grassy lawn to read the mail, the letter from his mother, but its delicate scrolls did not make as much sense as the other letter, the letter that was clear, oh, yes, very clear, his grandfather's warning, stern harsh eyes warning, always warning that his father had better get out, he had better. Bastard! Bastard! Bastard! A voice called to him to taunt him, and Charles knew that the voice came from Panama, where plants began to steam and rub against him, amid the vivacity of shimmering black eyes, eyes filled with tears and compassion for him. He felt the moisture stream down his forehead, into the corners of his lips. He should open his eyes now, but then the brilliance of the black eyes would fade away. The dream was tiring him now, but he could not open his eyes, not yet. Maybe with a small effort. Perhaps with a heaving push he could open them. At that moment Charles's lids fluttered as a wailing piercing cry echoed in his brain, and then disappeared.

So it happened that the very minute that Charles de Thierny opened his eyes for the first time since he had passed out in the company of his men, he heard the wailing cry of his newborn daughter.

Later one of his regrets was to be that because of his accident, he had failed to be near Helena during her labor, to fondle and caress her and perhaps kiss the dreadful pain away. He had wanted so badly to help her carry the burden of birth, since he had inflicted it on her against her will. But nature did not provide a direct outlet of sympathy for the guilty man, and his wounds had further hampered his good intentions of at least suffering mentally with Helena at the moment of giving birth.

Charles surprised himself with his tender longings for his wife, for he had thought himself hard and unyielding, and a woman's pain and heartbreak had once not seemed at all important.

Helena had suffered her pains bravely, but Rosario had been frantic with fear, for the baby should not have arrived for at least two or three weeks. Helena's whimpers and moans during her labor were searing reminders that premature babies and their mothers often fared badly. If these two should be lost to her, Rosario was certain that she, too, would die. So even while scurrying about giving instructions here and everywhere, she had held her rosary beads tightly in her dark bony hands and prayed to the Lord above with more fervor that she had ever managed before in her lifetime.

"Oh, God! Spare these two for me. Dear Lord, please!" This was her constant prayer. And her God had answered her compassionately this time.

As the days passed, strength was restored to both Charles and Helena by the ministrations supervised by Rosario. She did everything, including making arrangements for a wet-nurse for the baby because Helena was too weak to nurse her herself. Gradually the convalescents in the house regained their health.

The day arrived when Helena carried the baby into the room where Charles still lay, unable to walk about. As she entered the room, the light from the window blinded her for a second. Then her eyes adjusted and met those of Charles. So much was reflected in their looks, so much was said wordlessly that it took Helena's breath away and she stood still for a long time, until the baby stirred in her arms.

Then she approached Charles with something of solemnity in her steps and bent down to place the baby by his side. There, with his one good arm, he unwrapped her tenderly and cautiously, peeling away the embroidered sheet that protected the newborn from the draughts that might venture into the house.

His voice was gruff with emotion when he finally spoke.

"She's the most beautiful thing I've ever seen in my life."

Helena's eyes filled with tears, for she was touched by the tenderness Charles showed for his daughter. She began to say something, but Charles interrupted her with words that cried out his shame and his remorse.

"Helena, if I had it to do all over again, how different it would all have been. I didn't mean to hurt you, not you personally. I was too arrogant and assumed I knew exactly what I wanted to do. Poor devil that I am, I realize now that I was only desiring you and wanting to make you mine and yet I knew that if you were truly of the González family, I would never be able to possess you honorably, for my pride and my hate would have been in the way forever. If only I had found out more about you before. Then I would have been free to court you like any decent man."

Helena was too choked to answer. But she thought about what Charles had said. Yes, how different it all could have been. Instead of wasting her time in hate and frustration, in anguish and shame, she could have been loving him as she could never have loved any other man, for now she was sure that destiny had placed them in each other's paths, for better or for worse.

At that moment the baby began to whimper, as if awakening from a hungry dream. She opened her eyes, and Charles saw that they were as black as her mother's, and he was delighted. The baby's features were as perfect and filled out now as if she had been born on schedule, and her tiny hands clutched about her greedily looking for some delightful source of food. Charles could not help but laugh at the enchanting antics of his first offspring.

"Let's name her Lucinda," he said on an impulse.

Helena agreed readily, but added: "And let's give her a middle name to make up for all the sad past. Let's call her Lucinda Benita."

Charles looked up into Helena's eyes that were still shiny with unshed tears, and nodded.

"Yes, let's name her Lucinda Benita."

Charles continued to stare in wonder at his baby daughter. He had never before seen such a tiny creature, and he was therefore unprepared for what happened next. In an amazing transformation, before his very eyes, the whimpering of the wee Lucinda Benita turned into a raging squall of hunger, and her sweet little features were contorted and reddened by her astounding and demanding anger.

Suddenly Charles, staring in disbelief at the incredible metamorphosis, said quickly: "Here, Helena, you'd better take her. I think I did something to her, though for the life of me, I don't know what!"

Helena chuckled as she took the screaming bundle from Charles, and without another comment left the room, calling to Rosario, who was in the nursery very close by.

"Rosario, come get your baby, please!"

A whole month had passed by the time Charles finally told her the story of his accident.

Helena was surprised to learn what a big part she had unwittingly played in the intrigue.

"One thing I don't understand, Charles, is how Raúl finally got involved with Juan Jiménez. After all, Jiménez actually talked to you at the party and not to Raúl Santana."

"Well, you see, I had to think about it for a long time, but it helped that we were not to have personal contact, Jiménez and I, but contact only through his servant and my Pablo.

"I then wrote, in the name of Jiménez, a note to Raúl Santana, which I sent with Pablo. In it I offered him the exact terms which Jiménez had offered to me at the party. Of course, being as desperate as he was, he answered right away. I then wrote him another note and told him the details of the operation, just as Jiménez had done to me. All this I did under Jiménez's name, copying his hand, pointing out in subsequent notes that there was never to be any personal contact about this deal between the two and that our names would no longer be referred to or mentioned in any way in our notes."

The deep baritone voice of Charles fascinated Helena almost as much as his story. Her little face remained upturned to his, and Charles could not resist a sudden urge to kiss her mouth.

"I suppose I shall not hear the rest of the story now, Monsieur de Thierny. You are incorrigible!" Helena made a saucy sort of pout with her lips, and Charles laughed good-naturedly.

"All right! I'll go on with the tale, but stop trying to make it so difficult for me to concentrate on telling it!"

"You know very well that I did nothing to bring on your advances, Charles."

"Darling, perhaps not knowingly, but I assure you that I find you to be easily the greatest distraction of my life!"

They laughed together, and then Charles finally went on.

"Every morning Pablo would arrive at Raúl's mother's house to pick up the messages which Raúl might want to send to Juan Jiménez. Of course, I intercepted them before Pablo turned them over to Juan Jiménez's man at the church."

Helena expressed her astonishment at the deception.

"And Jiménez never suspected?"

"Apparently not, for we did the same with the notes

which were given to Pablo. We read every word, and followed every move they made."

Charles did not mention to Helena that the first time he had gone to spy closely at Raúl Santana and had seen how comely he was, he had felt an unbearable stab of jealousy. And Helena, not comparing the two men in her mind, did not realize how much Charles detested the poor man. She never noticed, either, the lull in his story as he paused with chagrin to remember the intensity of his jealousy.

"But how did it backfire, and how did you get shot?" she asked.

"Actually, it didn't backfire, for the American ship did recover the weapons, even though Santana got away. I am confused about many small details, and Pablo cannot find out from the Americans what actually happened. For one thing, they are not about to openly confess the facts of the matter to just any old Cholo Indian. Our part in the whole affair was done anonymously, and the Americans have no way of knowing that they can trust us."

"Just as your men did not trust me!" accused Helena, a hint of anger in her black eyes.

"I can explain that somewhat, Helena. You see, Santana's note to Jiménez about his plans had been too general, too vague, to either implicate you or clear you. My men panicked when they saw my condition, especially as they are far from their homes and in a strange milieu where even the medication is different and they know no one.

"Thank God that the men decided in time that you had nothing to do with the firing at all. Only then did

442

they risk bringing me here. And besides, by that time they thought I was quite ready to go to my eternal rest!"

"Yes, I know," answered Helena bitterly. "They thought I might just finish the job Raúl had started."

Charles pretended not to notice Helena's unhappiness at the suspicions which his men had conceived. There was no use helping Helena's temper to flare, and he preferred to go on with the comments about the episode in general.

"In the meantime Pablo and Pedro have found out that Raúl has disappeared. However, the Americans now know that it was Juan Jiménez who backed the whole scheme. That much the public has knowledge of, although there is talk that the most important witness against him, our friend Raúl, is missing. But the American agent who brought the weapons from the States was captured. I suspect it was he who told about Jiménez, the man with whom he had originally dealt. I suppose it was either tell the truth and gain leniency in his own country, or protect Jiménez and get a stiff jail sentence."

He paused to let his words be absorbed by Helena who gave him a questioning look.

"I wonder how he will fare, poor devil. . . . I mean Raúl, of course." She did not continue to explain to Charles the feelings of guilt she had experienced concerning Raúl and the immodest way she had planned to use him to create jealousy and suffering in Charles's soul. He did not notice the crimson blush that covered her face at her self-induced embarrassment, for the sun had begun its sudden and typically tropical descent, creating a splendid glow of red that camouflaged it.

"As to what the Colombian government plans to do with Jiménez and with Raúl when they find him, I won't discover anything until I am well and active again. Pedro and Pablo can only gather general information for me, things that everyone in the city is talking about. The inside decisions and problems have to be more discreetly uncovered. I cannot go into the open yet. We'll just have to wait and see, and I have to make sure that my health is exactly as good as it was before this damned business with Jiménez began."

Charles began hesitantly to pace the floor, leaning gingerly on a walking cane made of fine black palm and tipped in silver. It had once belonged to Benito González. His limp was still quite noticeable. Then he sat down abruptly. Helena frowned, suspecting that he was tiring more quickly than he cared to admit.

She listened quietly and attentively as Charles caught his breath again. He had begun his exercises in earnest that very morning, but was supposed to avoid movements that might tear open his healing muscles. The exercises were actually more for the sake of his general health, to stimulate his circulation. The healthful and frequent nourishment he was receiving was also helping him to recover his former vitality completely.

They were in the spacious sitting room that led to the terraces overlooking the bay, and a delightful breeze from the open portals refreshed them.

"The worst part came after Pablo and Pedro and

the other men helped me to get away from the market. I knew that I was losing a lot of blood. By the time I passed out a few hours later, I thought I had seen my last."

"Oh, darling!" cried Helena. "I'm so glad that the men brought you here to me. If you had been left to die . . ."

Helena had approached Charles's chair and suddenly he put his good arm out and scooped her toward him.

"Your arm, Charles! I'll hurt you!"

But Charles did not care, and he simply stopped her cries of concern by putting his lips on hers and pressing down on them passionately.

The days that followed seemed to Helena to be filled with the greatest tenderness she had ever known. Her baby against her bosom made her quiver with love at times. Lucinda Benita's beady eyes stared intensely at her as if scrutinizing her effectiveness as a mother. Helena found her quiet, unmoving gaze very amusing and would swoop down gently to the baby's rosy cheeks and press her dear little face to her own.

Charles watched these moments with a swell of pride and love, and often joined in to caress the females, as he labeled them good-naturedly.

"Females! You just watch how you describe us, sir! We are not just females!"

"Well, the inordinately intelligent, beautiful, and extravagantly delightful females of the family, then!"

"That's *much* better, monsieur!"

His jovial and easygoing manner delighted Helena, and the affectionate coos and caresses Charles showered on their child moved her deeply, especially when she recalled how cold he could be and how controlled.

She was almost afraid to think about that other Charles she knew, the one whose fiery nature and whose embraces could send fire through her own blood. He thus far had only kissed her, but he had the sense to know that any active lovemaking could easily reopen his wounds, and he was determined, it seemed, to abide strictly by the doctor's orders in this regard as well as that concerning the delicate state of Helena after her traumatic delivery. Still, the thought of his making love to her wormed its way into her consciousness, and left her in a state of suspense and anticipation.

For Helena this was a time of contentment, a time of peace and tranquility—the idyllic experience of the warm and gracious home she had once dreamed about before life had betrayed her and made her hard and spiteful.

It came as a complete shock, therefore, when Charles disappeared without a word from the house a few days before he should have been declared completely healed.

Ony a slight stiffness in his thigh as he rode astride faithful Chocolate over the noisy cobblestones reminded Charles that he had narrowly escaped death only a few short weeks before. Now, amid the clatter of hooves, his Indian band was accompanying him to

the home of the one who had inflicted his wounds
upon him—Doña Laurie Lee Jenkins de Santana.

It had been easier for Pablo and Pedro to investigate the truth of the matter than Charles had at first
thought possible, for the naturally humble appearance
of the Indians had enabled them to camouflage from
the witnesses at the market landing their avid interest
in exactly what had happened the day their *patrón*
had been shot. About two weeks after the incident,
just as Pedro and Pablo had begun to suspect that no
one who frequented the fish market had seen any more
than they had already confessed, they began to overhear scraps of conversation in which the shooting was
discussed. No doubt the speakers felt that the danger
of involvement with the United States commander of
the *Galena* had passed and they felt free to gossip and
show off their true knowledge of the dramatic happenings at the market.

"The old lady . . ."

"The second shot . . ."

"I know that fellow. . . ."

"No use getting involved. . . ."

"A white man and two Indians . . ."

"What did they have to gain. . . ."

"Someone else could have been shot. . . ."

"Maybe the bullets were meant for the escaping
men. . . ."

"Apparently the white man got it. . . ."

"She was aiming right at him. . . ."

The Cholos had reported back to Charles, who was
then recovering with amazing rapidity because of the
wonderful care he was receiving in his wife's home.

He encouraged both of his Cholo friends and followers to find out if anyone really knew who the old lady
was, or if they had any idea how she had arrived at
the market. But Charles was still too weak at that time
to think of detailed ideas which might help his men,
who were not trained sleuths as he was. He had sunk
back onto his pillow and stared tiredly after them as
they had left with eagerness to pursue this mission
which they were to carry out on their own. And they
had succeeded beautifully.

Their questions were interpreted at the scene of the
shooting as a desire on their part to know about
the horrible excitement which had descended on the
usually tranquil fish market where arguments normally had to do with the price of fish. Three days of
discreet questioning yielded the information which
they sought. There was no doubt that the servant of
Laurie Lee de Santana had been in the fish market
and that both he and she had fired at their master,
Charles Terny. Obviously they had been planted in
the area for protection in case anything went wrong.
It struck the Indians as depraved of Raúl Santana to
put his own aging mother in such danger, and it never
occurred to them that she had done it all on her own.

"Men, you have done a fine job! You are truly
worth your weight in gold to my government and I
shall see to it that you and your tribe profit from your
devoted and efficient work."

The two Cholos did not say anything besides "Gracias, Patrón," and stood in their usual taciturn and
misleading Indian humility before their employer.
Charles knew better by now than to think that Pedro

and Pablo thought they did not deserve his praise or his promises of help for their people. On the contrary they were expecting such results for their efforts because they were a desperate abandoned tribe who had finally found a true friend—one who bargained with them as equals to lose or to gain from any given venture they undertook together—and they expected justice from Charles, who in their eyes had proved himself a man of honor.

Charles had thought also about how much he should reveal to Helena concerning these plans and problems, then decided that he wanted neither to lie nor involve her, nor to arouse suspicions that she was harboring a stranger in her house who was a secret agent from France and her husband to boot. Already too many people knew about his presence there, and it was bound to get to the wrong ears. No, the best thing would be to leave quietly, get the work done, and return, free at last, to Helena, to the baby, and to his life as a family man.

It was with great reluctance that Charles left Helena and Lucinda Benita, but his years of training had won over his personal desires, and like a shadow, he had slipped out to his waiting Indians.

Now, as he approached the once-elegant, two-story mansion of the Santana widow, Charles was once more aware of the distaste and revulsion he felt toward Raúl, recognizing this time, however, how much of his repugnance was founded on jealousy. There was no doubt that Raúl Santana was very good-looking, but worse, he had been hovering over Helena all during her pregnancy when he himself had not been allowed that privilege. Some anger at Helena's brazen interest in that scoundrel surged within him even now, as he dismounted and strode decisively to pound on the great worm-eaten mahogany door. Three of his men formed a semicircle behind him.

A pair of frightened dark eyes peered out the door. Charles pushed the door wide open, at the same time shoving the poor mulatto servant aside.

"Where is he?" he commanded brusquely.

"Where is who?" stammered Tito.

Tito found himself accosted by looming Indian muscles and menacing looks, and at that he became so frightened that he would have told these ghouls and demons exactly where his own mother lay buried if they had asked him.

"Nobody is here except Doña Laurie. She is upstairs already retired for the night. I'll go get her," he said meekly.

"No, you don't. You just stay here and don't move a muscle. I shall cope with the lady."

Charles was not sure if the servant had told the truth, and gun in hand, he cautiously creaked up the stairs, only to be confronted by the sight of Doña Laurie's profile at her dimly lit bedroom door. The heavy revolver in her hands stared with its evil eye at Charles.

"Ma'am, I only wish to speak a few minutes with you." Charles spoke in English, having found out much earlier that Doña Laurie was American. Not only his use of her mother tongue, but his unexpected British accent startled Laurie Lee so that she lowered the aim of her weapon.

"I only wish to talk to you, ma'am, for your sake as well as for the welfare of your son."

"Who are you, to burst in here like this and confront an old lady with a gun in your hand?"

"Ma'am, if you will notice, the one confronting me is you. I haven't even raised my gun—yet."

"What do you want? Who are you?"

"Well, I'd rather we sat down comfortably somewhere, if you don't mind. There are many things I must first discuss with you. Then, I'm sure you will help me to help your son, for his life is at this moment in grave danger."

Laurie Lee hesitated, made a pained grimace as she realized that she had no choice, glanced down at poor Tito, shaking violently among three stocky Cholo Indians, and with her head signaled Charles that he should follow her into her bedroom. As he followed the old woman, Charles was overcome by a wave of nausea at the stale odor of medications and urine that permeated the decay of the once richly appointed chamber. He swallowed hard, and strode, without asking permission, to the balcony to open one of the shuttered windows. Then he turned abruptly toward her.

"Ma'am, do you know who Juan Jiménez is?"

His sudden question took Laurie by surprise, and she could only answer yes with a nod of her head.

"Juan Jiménez is looking for your son. If he finds him before I do, Raúl will be shot down like a poor beast. If I find him first, however, he will only suffer at most a few short years imprisonment in Bogotá at Panopticón, and probably, if he cooperates with the

American authorities, who exert great influence in these matters with the local governor, he'll only be exiled to some godforsaken province or even be allowed to leave the country. Don't you think it's worth it to tell me where Raúl is hiding?"

"I don't know where he is," was Laurie Lee's quiet answer.

Charles lost his temper, and forgetting the pitiful state of his hostess, strode toward her so menacingly that the old woman cringed.

"Listen, woman, you almost killed me with your meddling a few weeks ago!" he shouted. "That your son could stoop so low as to involve his ancient mother in such danger is bad enough, but that she should be so depraved as to accept is even worse. Now, you tell me where Raúl is because I need him, and I don't need him dead! Jiménez has his men scouring the countryside looking for him right now."

"Yes, I know you're speaking the truth, mister," the old woman said, as tears sprang to her eyes and streamed down her wrinkled cheeks. "Jiménez's men were here already, looking for him, but they took my answer as the truth. They did not know of my part in the raid at the fish market. And please, mister, I did that on my own. My son has no idea I got myself involved. You've got to believe me, and you've got to find him."

Charles had no choice but to believe her and try to enlist her help. "I can't do that unless you give me some idea where he might have gone. I wouldn't know where to begin." Charles's voice registered regret at the earlier force of his manner.

"I can list a few possibilities. I'm sure he would be somewhere that he knows well."

"Fine! Just tell me all you can."

In a considerably more gentlemanly fashion, Charles listened carefully to Laurie Lee's remarks.

Before he left the house, he apologized to the old woman for his misunderstanding, and warned Tito to stay with his mistress, because Juan Jiménez's men just might return—not that he believed that probability, but he didn't want Tito meddling in his search for Raúl Santana.

After studying the list Charles discarded several places automatically, but still, a surprising number of locations on the list could offer Raúl Santana safety from his enemies.

Several days of searching brought no success, and Charles finally decided to spread his men out in order to cover more territory.

Dawn was bursting swiftly as Charles walked stealthily toward the stables some yards away from the groom's hut. The stables were beginning to echo with the restless stomping of the horses in their stalls. Soon the head groom or keeper and the boys who came during the day to help him exercise the animals would be scuffling about the place like so many ants, each one carrying out his assigned duties, feeding the horses, getting them ready for exercise, leading them to pasture. Charles was familiar with the intricacies of running a stable full of purebred horses, for in his youth, riding and hunting had been a passion with him, and he had learned to admire the devotion and the skills required to keep horses healthy and ready for sport. He imagined that in a sapping climate like Panama's, horse breeding and care would be even more complex and demanding, requiring special knowledge of tropical diseases and prevention and medication against parasites and the variety of fungi that flourished in the moist warmth of the Isthmus.

Among the most likely places Charles had chosen from the rest of the list Laurie Lee had given him, were the stables of Mr. Carroll, an American who bred many horses and cared for them for the aristocracy of the capital. This place afforded Raúl Santana several good possibilities for refuge.

Charles had learned early in his career that one hunted a man down just as one would an animal. Man, after all, was an animal, with an animal's needs.

Raúl would need shelter, but he would need nourishment also. In some of the places he had to choose from for a hideout, Raúl would have to forage for his breakfast, a very dangerous activity when the entire American navy in Panama, and who knew what others, were behind him. Raúl must surely have realized the high risks he would run if he did not choose his hiding place with care.

If Raúl had any intelligence at all, he would prefer to hide somewhere where a friend or someone he could trust would get food for him. He would also logically look for a place where he could find suitable transportation if possible, to aid him in fleeing should his enemies close in on him. The stables were the last place on the list not yet investigated which fit Raúl's requirements to perfection. He felt almost sure that his quarry was here. According to Laurie Lee her son often rode horses at this place, and the groom, at least, must be his friend.

Charles strode toward the stables and lifted the wooden plank across the huge door of the main entrance. A shaft of tender morning light entered the gloom of the hay-strewn building, and even as Charles watched, the sunlight seemed to brighten into full-blown day.

Raúl would probably not be in the stable itself; he certainly was not known for his ruggedness.

Several of the horses whinnied, anticipating their breakfast, perhaps.

Charles strode toward a black stallion that was more restless than the others and straining to get out of his stall.

"Extraordinary beast," he mumbled to himself, unaware that this was one of the González horses which Helena did not ride because of her pregnancy. It was totally black; there was not a white spot on him. The eyes and the configuration of its face were dramatically beautiful, and the horse stood tall, arching his neck and pawing the floor of his stall with impatient energy.

"Don't worry, boy," Charles said to the animal. "You'll be getting your exercise soon."

Almost as if the horse understood him, he whinnied again in answer and nudged Charles heavily with his head, pushing him away in his eagerness.

Charles wisely did not attempt to saddle the black

steed alone. He managed to get a bridle on him which he picked from several finely made ones hanging on hooks in the stable.

He brought the stallion out into the sunlight and leaped onto the animal's back.

Now! To flush Raúl Santana out!

Just as he was attempting to control the cavorting of the horse, Charles noticed from the corner of his eye that the groom, a short, swarthy fellow, was coming at him from the hut, aiming a rifle at him.

If Charles knew anything, however, he knew that the man would never risk shooting the valuable animal.

"Mister," Charles yelled as the horse turned friskily about trying to adjust himself to the feel of this man clinging to his back, "if you shoot that rifle, you'll miss; but you'll get it from me!"

The groom was amazed to discover that while handling the turbulent moves of his mount with one hand, Charles was aiming a pistol at him with the other. The revolver seemed to remain pointed directly at him all the while the horse was spinning and snorting. The groom dropped his rifle.

"Señor! Please do not shoot!"

Charles didn't bother answering the man's request. "Where is Raúl Santana? It's him I want to see—not to hurt him but to save his neck!"

Just then Charles heard a bullet whiz past his ear, and he broke decisively into a mad gallop straight for the groom's cabin.

The groom shouted to Raúl Santana as the latter

ran, panic stricken and shooting wildly, out the door of the little hut. "You bastard! You promised you would not shoot at my horses! You stupid donkey! Do you want to ruin me? That's a González horse you're shooting at!"

But his complaints against the man he had foolishly befriended were drowned amid the continued shooting.

By this time three of the stableboys had arrived. All three were hiding around the corner of the main stable, where their boss soon joined them to protect his own hide as well. The boys were slender and black, and the whites of their huge eyes stood out against their dark skin as they stared at the unexpected drama that had interrupted their morning.

When Raúl realized that his gun was out of bullets, he threw it down in frustration and scurried away as fast as his legs could carry him to the building where the saddles were kept. These were not the silver-decorated dress saddles that the hidalgos from the city brought with them for their own pleasure riding, but the small leather saddles which the groom used for exercising the magnificent animals under his care.

Charles watched his prey coldly until he'd disappeared behind the saddle warehouse. The black stallion reared as if to wind himself for the chase that was to come, and then horse and rider thundered across the open space, drawing up where Raúl Santana was cowering and wondering what to do next.

Charles enjoyed a fleeting moment of humor at the absurd situation. He had the impression that he was perhaps using a cannon to shoot a fly.

He dismounted and grabbed Raúl by the collar.

"You stupid fool! Why don't you find out what you're doing before you shoot the wrong man! I came here to help you, you damned coward!"

"What?" stammered Raúl. "I thought you were . . . someone else!"

"Did you think I was perhaps one of Jiménez's men come to shoot you down like a dog?"

"Jiménez! Why would he want to shoot me?"

"Don't be a fool! You know damned well that Jiménez can have no further use for you and that you could complicate things if the Americans or the police authorities catch you. Do you think Jiménez would like it if you squealed to save your neck? It would be much easier for him to get rid of you once and for all before anyone catches up with you and forces you to tell the truth about his involvement in this damned affair!"

"How do you know about Jiménez?" Raúl had found a tiny portion of his courage again once Charles had loosened his grip and finally set him free. Raúl lifted his hand to his neck and rubbed it where Charles had hurt him.

"Who are you, anyway?" he managed to demand, each word more assured than the last.

With the sudden and cruel intention of lording over Raúl his possession of the same woman they both wanted, Charles answered:

"I'm the husband of Helena Canales—the father of her child."

Charles's words had a challenging ring of triumph in

them that piqued and surprised Raúl Santana instantly. In his bewilderment Raúl thought only of saving his pride. He had been crushed both physically and mentally within the span of a few minutes, and in fury he lashed out the best way he could—in calumny of the woman who had befriended him—Helena.

"You mean, you *think* you are the father!"

At that Raúl saw a flashing fist coming at his face, and that was the last he knew until he regained consciousness on the cot he had been using during his weeks of hiding in the head groom's cabin.

Still groaning and holding his broken jaw, Raúl heard the words that this madman who had appeared from nowhere was trying to get him to understand. He did understand at last that every word that came from Helena's husband made sense. It was, also, as if the man had followed his every move for the last few weeks, but Raúl was in too much pain and distress to try to analyze how this could possibly be. Why, he had never seen this stranger before. All he knew was that he must do as the man told him, for if what he said was true, he was in more danger of Jiménez than he was of anyone else. Furthermore, going to jail was one thing—he could manage that—but remaining in perpetual fear of getting killed when he least expected it, like some animal that was being hunted down with hateful calculation, was another.

Charles bound the whimpering Raúl's jaw, then went outside. He ordered the groom and his stableboys to hitch up a cart using two of Helena's sturdier horses.

Raúl withstood the pain of the ride back into town only because he had no choice. Charles had tried to disguise him, but there had actually been little need to do so, for the binding and Raúl's swollen jaw had completely transfigured the poor wretch.

Chapter XXII

As soon as Helena discovered Charles's absence, she was desolate and pained.

Charles had been sharing her great canopied mahogany bed for a few nights, and although his kisses were not meant to arouse her, Helena had been poised breathlessly for the day he could finally make love to her. The doctor had been adamant about Helena's period of healing after the premature birth of her daughter and had also warned Charles that any indiscretions could cause the mending tissues of his wounds to tear and bleed internally. Patience would have to be their byword. Their control had been paying off, however, and the doctor believed that in two or three days Charles would be as good as new.

The morning after Charles secretly left the González house, Helena awakened languorously to touch the empty space beside her on the bed. Her eyes flew open in surprise, and turned to look for Charles elsewhere in the room. She felt an uneasy stirring of suspicion, for the space where Charles had lain held no trace of warmth, and yet it was still relatively early in the morning. Wide awake now, she sat up in bed and called softly, "Charles! Where are you?"

But only the rattling beginnings of the daily traffic outside her window answered her.

She moped about most of the day and avoided Rosario's innocent questions about Charles's health. The baby's cries did not penetrate her pensive mood, and Rosario wondered at Helena's indifference until she discovered that Charles had not been seen all day. She tried to console the obviously worried woman.

"I wouldn't be surprised if he just stepped out to buy you some flowers down at the market, Helena. He'll be back soon, I'm sure."

"He's been gone six hours, Rosario, or maybe more," she said dismally. "The flowers would be wilted by now."

Rosario recognized the deep mood of uncertainty that had come over Helena, and she sighed in dismay.

"It was just an idea. There could be many reasons for his leaving without saying anything. It would not be the first time he has been secretive about his actions and his whereabouts. I think it's too soon to draw any conclusions."

Helena's eyes looked silently at Rosario. She had an uneasy feeling that her own premonitions were more accurate than Rosario's speculations, but she said nothing.

For two days after that Helena wandered about her

lovely mansion, quietly pacing the great tile floors or sitting in the comfortable overstuffed linen-covered chairs, ignoring the workings of the house and the care of her baby. Once or twice Rosario tried to coax her into activity, but she gave up tiredly. Helena was determined to wait exclusively for Charles's return or for a message from him. No message came, however. Charles had surely left. Then anger slowly started to have its way with her, and she ended by feeling a bitterness not unlike the previous one she had held for him. A sort of lethargy overpowered her, leaving her almost indifferent to the thought of having found love and then lost it so humiliatingly. She turned her energies to Lucinda Benita, and lost herself in the daily and relentless routine of raising her baby.

Her faithful Rosario made no more comments concerning Charles's disappearance, thinking that perhaps she had been wrong to help him win her friend and mistress, her daughter. She kept silent so as not to bring up the painful subject of that man again. She, too, concentrated her energies and her love on Lucinda Benita, even to the point that Helena began to worry about her.

"Rosario, did I hear you get up last night for the baby?"

Helena asked the question with a discernible note of disapproval. "You know that Fernandita can do it. I pay her well enough. And you need your rest at night, my dear woman."

"But she's so adorable, Helena, with that hair like the purest gold. And her eyes fascinate me, even when she wakes me up at night. I keep wondering what color they will finally turn. Really, it's what keeps me young, that child."

Helena laughed kindly at that remark, for Rosario looked so old and wrinkled, the poor dear, that it was hard to think of her as young.

"All right, Rosario, but promise me that if you feel tired during the day, you will let the others do the work. I certainly don't want you to come down with something. After all, you stayed awake with Charles, and then with me, so long, that you have weakened your own resistance. It worries me, you know, and you don't want to worry me any more than I am, do you?"

Rosario stared long and knowingly at Helena, and finally answered.

"I don't want to worry you at all. Just save your own strength, honey, because one never knows about these things. Your life has taken so many strange turns already, that only heaven knows what you can expect. I'll promise to take care of myself, if you promise the same about you."

"It's a deal, my friend."

Tenderly, the two embraced and Rosario felt the warmth of Helena's tears as they flowed uncontrollably down her face. And she knew for sure that Helena Canales still suffered.

The days sped by, and Rosario insisted one day on taking Helena with her to the silk-and-thread shops near the Santa Ana park. If anything would lift the young woman's spirit, it would be buying material for a new dress.

"Rosario, I am certainly glad you made me come out in the open carriage. Everyone will see me and know that I do not care what they think. Look! Over there goes one of the Arosemena girls!" Helena waved her handkerchief in greeting, and was suddenly disheartened when she saw her former friend turn her head quickly to pretend she had not seen her. It was then that Helena realized that she did care what they thought, after all. She became so unhappy at her discovery that the rest of the shopping trip went by as if she were a zombie. When she got home, she went straight to her room.

That night Rosario came to her bedroom with a hot toddy.

"I know it's very warm, and that you are going to say you will just get too hot to sleep. But believe me, a little rum never hurt anyone, and you will sleep like a baby."

Helena drank it all, and as a feeling of pleasant peace descended on her, she lay down and soon fell into a deep sleep.

She was dreaming about Charles. His breath was hot and heavy with passion on her neck, on her bosom. He had taken hold of her hands and was kissing them with such intensity that Helena sighed restlessly in her sleep. Then his lips were pressing her down, down into an eddy of pleasure, almost suffocating her with love. Her eyes fluttered open, and by the light of the moon that streamed in so clearly at this time of the year, she made out the figure of Charles.

"Charles! You went away," she said almost petulantly, still half asleep.

"Yes, but not for long, my love. I could never stay away from you for very long."

Then silently, strongly, decisively, he unbuttoned his shirt and pulled off his trousers, and slipped to Helena's side, pushing and tugging at her fragile gown until her breasts were uncovered.

His lips roamed over her with relish and delight, pausing here and there along the curves of her body, lingering provocatively to arouse her to such a pitch of desire that Helena thought her very blood was on fire. Yet the languorous sensuousness of sleep still lingered in her muscles, making her arms move slowly as she reached to run her fingers through Charles's hair.

How he loved this woman! Every time he held her in his arms, it was with a renewal of desire, of wanting desperately to possess her, of yearning to hold within him the essence of what she was, her beauty, her wanton innocence, the mischievous stubbornness of her very soul. He crushed her delicate rosy body to him, stopping the force of his embrace only enough not to hurt her.

But he could stand the delicious yearning no longer and, pressing his advantage, drew her thighs to either side of his loins and entered her. The exhilaration of this intimate touch fanned the fire in his veins even more vigorously. He drew himself over her, and waiting no longer to assuage the sweet ache that sought release, he began in earnest the strokes of lovemaking, feeling all the while the urgency in her own response as she clutched him and paced the swivel of her hips to match his rhythm. It was not long before wave after wave of delight swept over them both. Charles stifled her scream of uncontrolled passion with his own mouth, thus putting his own seal of ardor on their act of love.

Finally they drifted off to sleep, their deep breathing unbroken by any sounds until the early morning hours when a few carts and ponies of the city began their daily routine journeys in the street below.

Helena was awakened not by the noise of the as yet sparse traffic outside, but by the wet feather kiss of Charles. She felt his hands gently probing and exploring the curves of her body. He pulled her to him, very close, scratching her delicate skin with his unshaven chin, but murmuring sweet and exciting secrets that brought to high tension the tumultuousness of her passionate nature. He rolled her over upon his lean and sun-darkened body, and taught her how to love him in a new way that left her slightly dazed with delighted shock but desirous of more.

They rested for a few minutes in each other's arms, Helena wondering at the complete deliciousness of belonging to Charles and he to her. They were surely made for each other, for could another woman possibly feel in his arms the magnetism of his body's message—that he loved her more than anyone else, that only she could possibly bring about the utter ecstasy of this mutual lovemaking? While sensuously pondering these thoughts, Helena began to feel a deep urge to pleasure him, to regale him with passionate caresses of her own making. The deep tenderness then gave way to almost hedonistic pleasure at the generous physical beauty of her husband. She lowered her body until she could caress his manhood with her lips. Ardently she pressed her mouth to him as Charles groaned with unsurpassed pleasure. There was such boldness, and yet such tenderness, in her gesture, such a complete giving of herself, that Charles, too, gave himself up without reservation in a complete surrender of his own.

Then Helena's hair was swinging in golden arcs over his chest as she mounted him in the exciting way he had taught her. He pushed rhythmically upward into her until he felt her body tighten and quiver from the rapture she had reached; then he made his final thrust with all the virility of his passionate love as she collapsed—sated and thrilled—within the hollow of his great enfolding arms.

She spent the entire night learning about love, but by the time both she and Charles came down for breakfast certain reservations had crept into Helena's heart. Charles had given orders before washing up for the day that breakfast was to be served downstairs for his wife and for him, thus informally announcing his marriage to her. Helena wondered about this, not without resentment, for she felt that she could not count on Charles to stay put and behave like a proper husband. He would probably disappear again, leaving her in suspense and anguish.

"Charles," she ventured as they walked to the small dining room where a simple but plentiful breakfast would be served to them, "I have to know my status with you now. I can't go on wondering if you will be here, if we can or cannot announce our marriage, if you are faring well, if, if, if. I can't stand that anymore."

"Don't fret, darling, for everything has been solved and I am free at last. Today we announce our marriage to the world!"

Helena stopped and turned to look up at him in amazed eagerness, for the announcement of her marriage was just what she had been longing for so anxiously.

Charles looked down at her from his towering height, his eyes twinkling with a thousand lights of merriment at the delighted surprise on Helena's face. He grabbed her hand spontaneously and held it tight as they continued into the dining room.

The smell of fresh corn tortillas, eggs, and steak filled their nostrils, and Helena and Charles sat down to the most wonderful and delightful breakfast they had ever enjoyed, so happy were they.

Somewhere upstairs the healthy wail of their baby could be heard, until someone compassionately picked her up in loving arms and fed her. Along with the wet-nurse, Rosario was bound to be there, too.

Later on, as Rosario joined the two who were at last at peace with one another, Charles recounted the tale of his search for Raúl Santana, leaving out certain details he felt might embarrass Helena.

"I was not really interested in venting revenge on his mother. You should see her, the poor old thing. I wouldn't want to add to her miserable state. But I was anxious to find Raúl before Juan Jiménez did. Besides the American agent, Raúl is the only other witness with whom Juan Jiménez was involved. In fact, Raúl is certainly aware that Jiménez instigated the whole thing in order to cause trouble along the railroad and discourage the French from building the canal. If ever stability and prosperity reached the Isthmus, Jiménez and others like him, who have nothing more to gain financially, and who prefer war over peace, would be at a loss as to what to do with their personally unproductive lives.

"Raúl's in the custody of the Colombian government now, and soon Mr. Jiménez will find himself in exile, if not worse. Which means that I am free, for any other threats to the project have long ago been taken care of or reported by our consul to the government. There is nothing there that they cannot handle. And the Americans are so interested in keeping their railroad functioning that even they are helping indirectly by maintaining their brand of order near the places where the engineers will begin their digging."

Rosario was suddenly alarmed at the thought that soon she might be losing her loved ones, and with a noticeable quivering of her voice, she asked: "Does that mean, Don Charles, that you are finished with all of your work here on the Isthmus? Will you be going back to France?"

Charles understood the real question behind Rosario's words, and hoping to put her at ease, explained his plans for the future.

"Rosario, wherever I go with Helena and the baby, I hope you will agree to come, too. But I won't be leaving for a while, because until Ferdinand de Lesseps arrives, I must stay here. Then, while he is here, I am to act as a sort of personal bodyguard and guide. With all the experience I have accumulated in the last year here, I can even be of help with the terrain studies for the canal, since I'm a qualified engineer. Who knows how long I may have to stay? In any case, I might make a trip with just Helena to England to settle my estates there and transfer my funds in an orderly fashion so that they will be more readily available to me. Perhaps I should have some monies in the United States as well as in France and England."

The whole time that Charles was speaking, Helena was mesmerized. How little she knew about this man whom she loved so profoundly in every way that a woman can love a man! Her coal-black eyes glinted with emotion, and as Charles caught sight of her, he laughed lovingly, and brought her head to his shoulder without moving from the settee where they were seated.

Rosario's wizened face brightened when she saw that anything ugly in the past had been forgotten in the discovery of love and that her charges, as she now considered Charles and Helena, could look forward to the fulfillment of that love.

Immediately after Charles had installed himself at Helena's house, the house in which his mother had grown up, he dismissed his Indian partners with generous payments of money and with fine hunting weapons. They were free to go back home and lead their people a little while longer in an effort to survive with dignity. Before they parted, however,

Charles made arrangements with the two men to hire, unseen and relying only on their good judgment, some of the younger men from their tribal village in Santa Fe so that they could come to work as guides and bodyguards for the engineers.

Charles reflected sadly that the simple lives of these Indians were already being churned into lives of involvement and paradox. Their old ways of hunting for food and living off the land were bound to be affected with the advent of more and more settlers, who in the future would colonize there because of the canal. Already, he knew, hundreds of French engineers and skilled workers were making plans to leave their shores in pursuit of glory, success, and wealth. How these great numbers would change directly or indirectly the lives of the Cholos still far away in the mountains, he could not tell for sure, but he knew deep inside that change was bound to come, just as it had always come to the Isthmus of Panama. He only hoped that it would be for the better, and reasoned sadly that he could only do his small part in trying to make it so.

In the months that followed, Charles's life was enriched by his discovery that Helena was indeed the woman he had sought and the woman who was meant for him, who had been meant for him perhaps long before he was even born. He felt awed before such sweeping possibilities, and yet, if some unknown force had bothered to preordain such happenings in his life, perhaps he himself was more important among the cogs and wheels of the universe than he had ever considered. It was curious that at this point in his life, Charles de Thierny, the cynical and vengeful man who had left the shores of France to satisfy his lust for honor, had discovered a love so deep and true and strong that it had set in motion again the wheels of his soul, had restored to him the impetus to search for the source of all existence, and the reasons and justifications of his life. He had the sensation that this search was just the result of a new and better understanding of himself, reluctant though he was to admit that he might never have really understood himself before—understood the passions and complexes that had to some degree warped him. He realized that if it had not been for the childhood of love which his father had made certain he enjoyed he might never have been healed, even with Helena at his side. A great feeling of relief came over Charles, as the years of hate and self-criticism and thoughts of revenge were lifted from his soul. He prayed in his own silent way that these monsters would never return to embitter his life, and hoped fervently, too, that Helena might forget completely the horrible suffering he had imposed on her.

Charles found during these months to what extent he could be a complete man. It was not easy, by any means, for the responsibilities were great, and he had already begun to get set in his ways, in his total independence. To change so rapidly his style of living, and to consider so constantly the other members of the family was something of a feat. But love was easy, and he yearned for his wife's arms, her dark eyes filled with tenderness or passion, her golden hair that reminded him of the goddesses about whom he had read in his youth.

He encouraged Helena to participate outside the home in the establishment of schools. He had long known about her interest in this matter. He did not want to be entirely selfish and keep her by him as he would a gentle and well-trained pet.

It was only after the return of Charles that Helena was able to participate with full confidence in the founding of a normal school in Panama.

Because it was not allowed by the government, Helena could not enlist the help of the nuns in France whom she so admired, and she suspected early in the negotiations for the school that petty strife and economic problems would soon undo it. Nevertheless, it was a beginning, and perhaps she should not be so pessimistic. Later, perhaps, once the French were established on the Isthmus, she would involve herself with a school of a private nature in which a freer policy in the choice of teachers would be assured.

Her activities away from home stimulated Helena but did not detract from her devotion toward her child and her husband. She had suffered too much for their sakes to consider any activities outside her home as more important. Indeed it was for that reason that she involved herself in few trivial causes, and limited her social contacts. That way she could spend any extra time she had doing what she really considered worthwhile, even if it was simply sitting and chatting with Charles, whom she suspected of laughing unkindly at her efforts to negotiate important events.

Nevertheless, though she sometimes wished he would take her work more seriously, she loved him with undiminishing passion.

"Come snuggle up to me, sweetheart," invited Charles downstairs in the sitting room. Great windows looked out on the terrace and, farther away, over the glittering Bay of Panama.

They sat a long time, his great arms around her pulling her toward him tenderly, as if he were relishing every moment of this repose.

At long last, as they were daydreaming together, Charles murmured something in her ear. Helena smiled. Then, very close together, they moved in the direction of their bedroom, his arm still around her waist—which was still incredibly small, considering that she was now a mother.

As he tied his immaculately white cravat in the proper European fashion, a custom that to Charles seemed ludicrous to observe in the sweltering climate of Panama, he thought about how lucky he was that he had found Helena while he could still enjoy the strength of youth. His thoughts had gone also to his idol, the canal builder, Ferdinand de Lesseps, who had also found love and married after so many lonely years fighting for the right and the money to build the Suez Canal. That he had succeeded in spite of the jealous criticism of his enemies was truly wondrous, for with a loving woman by one's side, Charles now felt, a man could accomplish great things. But alone, the bitterness resulting from a man's struggles could become overwhelming, and de Lesseps had main-

tained his sense of dignity, his charm, and his opti-
mism in spite of his loneliness.

Now the great de Lesseps had arrived amid the
cheers of yet another prospective triumph. He had
been greeted at Colón by the dignitaries of the Isthmus and by many others who had come expressly for
the occasion from various parts of Colombia and especially from Bogotá.

Panama City had also awaited, with festive enthusiasm, his arrival by train from Colón, and the great
canal builder had been touched by the total trust and
reverence the people so obviously held for him. During his next few days in the capital of the province, he
only reinforced these impressions.

According to the plans for the celebration on the
first of January, 1880, the distinguished guests were to
go by boat early in the day to a spot three miles along
the coast at the mouth of the Río Grande, where the
Pacific end of the canal was to be and where the ceremony would culminate in the digging of the first
shovelful of damp soil that would signal the beginning
of the Panama Canal effort.

By the time Helena and Charles were also aboard,
about six hundred people had arrived at the dock, all
expecting to get on.

The presence of Cholo and French bodyguards was
arranged in such a manner that no one would notice
them. Only Helena, of the ladies, was aware that their
own attendance at the ceremonies was heavily
watched by waiters, boatmen, and other rugged types
that Charles had hired, and that precautions even for

the security of Ferdinand de Lesseps and his entourage had been thought necessary.

Helena looked stunning in an original gown designed for her by Rosario. Its red, white, and green calico cloth was done into an exquisitely cut dress with a bustle, and her red parasol was the perfect and only decoration it boasted except for a tiny ridge of lace that outlined the major seams of the gown and the daring décolletage.

Charles was wearing formal attire and suffering from the heat, swearing that he would eventually exchange his top hat for a fine Ecuadorian straw with a wide brim or know the reason why! But he was too excited with the significance of the event unfolding before them to pay too much attention to his discomfort.

"My God!" cried Charles. "Did you ever see people wanting so passionately to be near a celebrity?"

Helena's eyes twinkled as she answered with a teasing purr in her voice: "Well, I don't know about other people, but I know one person who wishes passionately to be near you!"

Charles looked at her, responding lovingly with a renewed pressure of the arm he was holding round her waist.

"Yes, there is no denying that you are passionate indeed, my love."

Not caring whether people looked at them in disapproval or not, he swept her toward him and kissed her resoundingly on the mouth.

At the side of the Bishop of Panama a priest stood who was itching unhappily from the sun that beat down mercilessly on the boat and on his long black garb. It was Father Rafael, secretly cursing the terrible delay that had caused the boat to miss the tide.

He had spotted Helena and Charles, who stood out even among the splendid crowd of French engineers and their families and Panama's best society. Then he saw Charles kiss his wife unabashedly.

"I guess those two will just never do anything in their marriage conventionally," thought the priest happily. He couldn't help grinning at the nerve of that beloved sinner, Charles de Thierny, who had been blessed at last with tranquility and happiness. He was luckier than most, the confessor decided.

The future left many signs that day, but they were obscured from mere human minds, and total happiness reigned and inspired every man and woman gathered to witness the first real attempt to build a wonder of the modern world on this tiny isthmus.

No one suspected that in just a few years, in the wake of the scandalous financial misdealings of the French Canal Company, de Lesseps would be a scapegoat, made to shoulder the responsibilities for bankruptcy and corruption. His honor would be smirched, his reputation trodden upon, and indignities heaped without mercy on his aging head.

History would record not only the personal failure of de Lesseps and the formation of a new French canal company, but also the tragic loss of brilliant minds and brawn to yellow fever, malaria, cholera, and other tropical diseases that ravaged the builders of the Canal. For twenty more years the French would struggle in frustration to overcome these mysterious health problems and to appease the giant ditch that devoured the financial and human resources of their country.

The sun bore down upon the heads of the unsuspecting champions of the French canal as their boat pulled away from the city and hugged the dense jungles of the shoreline. A wild exuberance and ambition underlay the great French project, and the engineers were filled with a self-assurance that verged on the blasé, certain of their ability to overcome the obstacles that nature had left behind just, it seemed, to test them.

The French ambition, the dream, would one day fall to the men of the American colossus, but the new heroes from the north would already have behind them the bitter experiences of the French, and their own cheers and whoops would not sound quite so brazen piercing the hostility of that environment.

From all corners of the world men would come here to build, to make Panama a better place to live, even as they improved their own lives or lost it. Many would come to Panama with plans to get rich and return to their permanent homes, but many, like Charles de Thierny and his wife, Helena, would remain and settle there, attracted by the lush beauty of the land they had come to love.

Eloquent words were spoken that day of the opening ceremony, both in French and in Spanish, and the group of French engineers and their wives who had come with de Lesseps clapped enthusiastically at each emotion-ridden phrase. Never again would the Isthmus know such wonderful hope and joy, or champagne and cognac be so generously distributed under a torrid sun, and never again would the ardor of the French on this New Year's Day be equaled here.

The sun shimmered on the waves of the Bay of Panama, its blinding brightness giving way unnoticed to the slanted rays of the afternoon. Sea gulls dipped perpetually, with graceful unconcern, into the sleek, blue waters. In the distance the isle of Taboga seemed to beckon across the luminous air, as alluring as the legendary mermaids of the sea.

As the heat of the day began its imperceptible retreat, an innocent breeze cavorted above the tiny newly formed crests of the sea, then spun away, then dipped close to the azure waters once more. It was gathering force and coolness before it began its evening advances upon the green land.